ALWAYS
A
BRIDE

BOOK YOUR PLACE ON OUR WEBSITE AND MAKE THE READING CONNECTION!

We've created a customized website just for our very special readers, where you can get the inside scoop on everything that's going on with Zebra, Pinnacle and Kensington books.

When you come online, you'll have the exciting opportunity to:

- View covers of upcoming books

- Read sample chapters

- Learn about our future publishing schedule (listed by publication month *and author*)

- Find out when your favorite authors will be visiting a city near you

- Search for and order backlist books from our online catalog

- Check out author bios and background information

- Send e-mail to your favorite authors

- Meet the Kensington staff online

- Join us in weekly chats with authors, readers and other guests

- Get writing guidelines

- AND MUCH MORE!

**Visit our website at
http://www.zebrabooks.com**

ALWAYS A BRIDE

Betty Brooks

Linda Cook

Denise Daniels

Zebra Books
Kensington Publishing Corp.

http://www.zebrabooks.com

ZEBRA BOOKS are published by

Kensington Publishing Corp.
850 Third Avenue
New York, NY 10022

First Printing: June, 1999
10 9 8 7 6 5 4 3 2 1

Printed in the United States of America

CONTENTS

MAIL ORDER LOVE

Betty Brooks

Chapter One

As the covered wagon lurched forward, Abigail Carpenter clutched at the frame, trying to retain her seat beside William Brady.

Although Brady's attention never wavered from the mules that strained to pull their load up the rough mountain, he was, nevertheless, aware of her predicament.

"Mayhap you'd best ride inside the wagon with Sarah, missy. The road don't get no better up ahead an' you got more to hang on to in there." His voice was rough as an old corncob, but there was real concern for her safety in his words.

"Yes, Abby," Sarah urged from her place inside the wagon. "Come inside with me."

"I would rather ride out here." Abby glanced at the older woman inside and offered her a brief smile before she faced forward again. "I'm anxious to see my new home." She squinted against the afternoon sun, then raised slim fingers to shade her eyes.

"You're likely to be disappointed, ma'am," the old-timer

beside her said. "Victor ain't nothin' much. Just a few buildings throwed together to hold supplies and a lotta people. Certainly nothing to be anxious about."

But she *was* anxious. So anxious that her mouth was dry and her stomach coiled into a tight knot. What had she gotten herself into? In her haste to escape her cousin, she had signed a contract that bound her to a stranger for the rest of her life.

The wagon lurched again as the wheels rolled over another large rock and she tightened her grip on the wagon frame until her knuckles showed white.

"Easy there, mules!" William roared, pulling back on the reins to slow the animals that had suddenly picked up their pace.

The reason was obvious as the wagon lurched once more, then topped the rise, allowing Abby her first glimpse of the mining town that was to be her new home.

It was an ugly place, crouched there on the mountainside like some monstrous spider, as though waiting to catch an unwary traveler in its web. And Abby *was* caught. Trapped by her own hand. She wanted to flee, to escape the fate that awaited her, yet knew she could not—in all good conscience—do so. She had signed a contract that bound her to a man named Bush Tanner, and no amount of wanting would undo what had already been done.

Why had she acted so recklessly? If she had waited a few days—a week perhaps—perhaps she would have found another solution. It was too late now. She would have to live with her impulsive decision. She had no other choice, since she owned nothing of value. And even if she had taken the few dollars old Mrs. Johnson had urged her to accept, it wouldn't have lasted more than a few days in a mining town where—according to the wagonmaster— men paid a dollar a night to sleep on a pool table or on the floor in the back of a saloon, where water was in such short supply that it sold for five cents a bucket from a horse-drawn water wagon.

No. There was nothing for her to do except abide by the contract she'd signed.

A sigh shuddered past Abby's lips, but she straightened her back and focused her gaze, and her mind, on the town that was destined to be her new home.

As the wagons drew nearer the town, they passed lean-tos that had been thrown together with hides or canvas as though the men who'd built them had no time for such luxuries as home and hearth.

What kind of men would settle for such a home? Abby wondered. And would she be expected to live in such a place?

Although there appeared to be no pattern to the buildings erected for the men's sleeping quarters, the town's business center had some semblance of order. The flimsy, false-fronted pine buildings faced on dirt streets and board-walks. And as the wagons rolled into town, men poured from those buildings like water through a dam that had suddenly burst.

Abby was suddenly overwhelmed with fear. There were men everywhere—of all shapes and sizes—and not a woman in sight.

The men appeared frozen as they stared at the women perched on the high wagon seats. Their eyes were devouring and hungry, and Abby controlled an inward shudder as she tried hard to ignore them.

Oh, God, what have I done?

The lead wagon, driven by the wagon master, pulled up beside a high platform that had been erected outside the general store. Within moments, it seemed the entire town had gathered around the wagons.

"Wouldja look at that, Abby?" Sarah Larsen's voice came from behind her shoulder. "Just look at all them men, and most of 'em hungry for a woman from the looks of 'em.''

Abby was all too aware of that fact. She saw it in their eyes—the hunger, the wanting.

Oh, God, she silently cried. *Why didn't I take William's advice and ride in the back of the wagon with Sarah?*

But she had not. Instead, she'd insisted on riding out front, perched atop the high seat on display for all who cared to look.

Her mouth was dry and she gripped the canvas of the wagon so tight that her knuckles were white. A hand gripped her shoulder suddenly and she realized that Sarah, who had been so excited during the entire journey, was almost as frightened as she was.

"Are you as skeered as I am?" Sarah's voice quavered.

Abby glanced at the woman, whose brown eyes were huge in her pale face.

"Of course, I'm not afraid," Abigail lied, patting the other woman's hand soothingly. "Neither should you be, Sarah. These men won't hurt us. Why should they? Anyway, our future husbands are among that crowd, and they will see to our well-being." At Sarah's skeptical look, Abby went on. "They paid dearly to bring us out here, Sarah. And Mr. Simon guaranteed they would all be decent, hardworking men. What more could we ask for in a husband?"

"Nothing, I guess," Sarah conceded. "At least not me. But you, Abby . . . You're not like the rest of us. You're young and pretty. In fact, you're about the prettiest thing I ever did see. Looks like you could have found a man without coming all the way out here."

During the long trip west from Chicago, Abigail had never once spoken of why she'd chosen to come here. Nor did she now.

"Looks are not always beneficial, Sarah." In Abby's circumstances—as maid in her great-aunt's home—her looks had been a curse. "Anyway, you are a handsome woman yourself. Any man would he proud to have you for a wife.''

Sarah gave her a quick smile. "I know I'm not much to look at, Abby, but I thank you for saying so anyways.'' Her gaze scoured the crowd of men gathering around the wagons. "These men out here need a strong, hardworking woman and maybe won't mind that I'm no beauty.'' She leaned closer. "Would you look at that lot? They look like they been rolling in mud.''

Sarah was right, Abigail realized. Most of the men were dirty, some of them encrusted in mud, as though they'd just come from the mines.

The crowd of men began pushing closer around the wagons, their necks craning as they stared at the women who were destined to be their brides.

"Let me through!'' a male voice suddenly demanded from within the crowd. "Clear the way.''

As Howard Simon, the wagon master, pushed his way through the crowd that had suddenly converged on the wagon, the men around him became quiet, watchful. Their avid gazes skittered between the wagon master and the women in the wagon.

"You men move back.'' Simon frowned impatiently as he stopped beside Abby's wagon. "Give these ladies some breathing room.''

There was a slight shifting of the men as they moved back slightly while Simon reached up to help Abigail down. When her feet touched the ground, Abby felt as though she had just entered a cage that had walls made of human flesh.

Howard Simon's gaze took in Abby's wan features and he squeezed her hand encouragingly. "Go wait beside the platform with the other women, Abby,'' he said gruffly. Then he turned to help Sarah descend.

Although Abigail turned toward the lead wagon, she was unable to venture forth. The crowd had closed around them again. She shifted restlessly beneath the men's stares as they looked her over quietly. It was all she could do to hold her ground beneath those bold looks. She most certainly could not have cleared a path through them.

When Sarah stood beside her, William, as though just realizing her dilemma, set his jaw at a hard angle and sent an equally hard gaze over the crowd. "Get back, the lot of you, and let these women through." When the crowd was slow to move, he climbed out of the wagon and shoved his way through the crowd, making a path that led the women to the platform beside the lead wagon, where four other women already waited.

As the crowd closed around them again, William mounted the platform and addressed the crowd. "You men move back and give these women room to breathe or else they'll be going back east when these wagons pull out again."

The threat caused a slight shuffling of feet, leaving a cleared space of almost ten feet between the crowd and the women.

Clarabelle, a middle-aged, wiry woman, sent a skittering gaze over the men, then turned to Helen Jackson, who had been her companion on the journey west. "They appear mighty anxious, don't they, Helen?"

"Shhhhh," Helen whispered, her windburned cheeks reddening even more. "It ain't polite to talk about 'em when they might hear."

The two women fell silent then.

Abby tried hard to ignore the men, but their stares made that impossible. Which were the twelve men who'd sent for brides? she wondered. More to the point, which man was her own fiancé, Bush Tanner?

Howard Simon returned with Judith, Mary, Faith, and Lila. And after giving the crowd another warning look, he hurried toward the last wagon for the other two women. When all twelve women stood beside the platform, the wagon master took his place on the scaffold, then motioned to the first woman in line.

"Come on up here, Helen. Your groom is somewhere in this crowd, and he's mighty impatient to wed up with you."

Caleb Montgomery's narrowed gaze moved slowly over the women and his lips curled with disgust. He should have known this would happen. Damn Bush Tanner for a sidewinder. He'd extracted a promise from Caleb that neither man had expected would be put in to effect. But here he was, with that damn promise hanging around his neck like an albatross, faced with a duty that he'd rather dodge, yet could not in all good conscience do so.

In all her imaginings about what their first meeting would be like, it had never been like this. Abby had expected the meeting with Bush Tanner would be quiet, and somehow private, but to be brought before the whole town and made to stand on a raised platform while the groom's name was announced to all and sundry went beyond the pale.

Howard Simon had explained his reasons for doing so—actually seeing the brides brought forth made more miners sign the list for the next batch of brides. Only that made the trips profitable—but understanding the reason didn't lessen her embarrassment.

A stirring in the crowd caught her attention and the crowd parted to allow another miner to claim his bride. And then it was her turn.

Drawing a quick breath of courage, Abigail mounted the platform and stood beside the wagon master. His kindly gray eyes met hers.

"There's still time to change your mind," Simon said

quietly. "You don't have to go through with this. Say the word and I'll make up a name and you can go back east with me."

Back east? There was nothing for her there. Aunt Amelia would not allow her back in the house again, not with Leonard's accusation against her. And there was no way to resolve the matter, for her aunt would never take Abby's side against her own son.

Abby lifted her chin a degree higher. Somewhere in this crowd, there was a man who wanted her for a wife. "No," she replied, forcing her lips to smile. "I'm ready. Announce his name."

Howard Simon turned to face the crowd, which had become silent. "Bush Tanner!" he called out. "Come on up here and get your bride!"

My God, Caleb thought, *surely the woman standing on the platform can't be the one destined for Bush Tanner.*

It was worse than he'd thought it would be. She was tiny—she couldn't have been much more than five feet tall. And even in that heavy maroon skirt and tucked shirt-waist, she couldn't have weighed much more than a feather. How in hell would a woman like that survive on his mountain? The answer was simple. She could not survive.

Caleb turned away. The whole thing was best forgotten. He'd just pretend he hadn't been there that day to see the brides arrive, and by the time Bush returned, she'd be settled in whatever alternative future she decided on. Yeah, that was the best thing to do: just walk away and leave her there.

"Bush Tanner!" the wagon master called again, louder this time.

Caleb halted abruptly, wondering how long it would take for the man to realize Bush wasn't among the crowd. He wondered, as well, just how long the woman would have to stand on that platform with the crowd of men gaping at her.

Feeling more like a slave at an auction than a bride who'd come to wed her groom, Abigail lifted her gaze beyond the crowd and focused on a man who stood on the boardwalk apart from the miners who formed a circle around the platform. He was a tall man with a heavy build, but his face was in shadows beneath the brim of the black slouch hat he wore. His apparel had seen better days but he had an aura of masculine strength about him that automatically drew the eye.

"Bush Tanner!" the wagon master shouted again. "If you want your bride, get your butt on up here and claim her before somebody else does!"

"I'll take her!" shouted a scrawny miner from somewhere in the crowd.

"If she's up for grabs, give her to me!" yelled another man.

Abigail's hands trembled and she clenched them tightly as a flush of embarrassment crept up her neck. She wished her fair skin didn't so readily betray her emotions. She wanted to hang her head in shame, yet she forced herself to lift her chin high and focus her attention on the tall man across the street who stood watching her.

"Dammit!" Caleb cursed. "Bush Tanner deserves to be shot!"

The woman's ivory cheeks were flushed with embarrassment as the crowd continued to harangue the wagon master, offering to take the woman if Bush Tanner didn't want her. And there was no way Caleb could walk off and leave her in that predicament.

"Dammit!" Caleb cursed again. Shooting wouldn't have

been punishment enough for Bush. Caleb would have to beat him to a pulp first.

"Get outta the way," he snarled, pushing aside the men who blocked his path.

The force of his huge body moved the smaller men aside and those who were large enough to withstand his strength took one look at the expression on his face and stepped back to allow him room. As Caleb neared the platform, the wagon master looked relieved and a wide smile split his face.

"Here he is folks," he hollered. "A late arriver coming to claim his bride."

The man said something to the woman, who smiled tentatively at Caleb, then slowly descended the steps toward him.

Finding himself impatient to be away from the crowd, Caleb reached out and lifted her down from the steps. Then, gripping her small hand in his much larger one, he quickly led her away from the platform.

Caleb was aware of the softness of her skin against his callused palm and his heart quickened at the feel of it. She tugged against his hold and he stopped abruptly, meeting her blue eyes with an inquiring gaze.

"We need to get my luggage," she explained. "It's in the second wagon." Her voice was soft as velvet, as he'd expected it would be.

Caleb watched her with a narrowed gaze, taking in her delicate features. Her lips were curved, full and lush, incredibly tempting. And her vivid blue eyes were framed by long sweeping lashes that were slightly darker than the honey-colored hair that was braided and wound around her head in a soft, shiny coronet.

Although he had no intention of fetching the satchels, Caleb needed to find a quiet place where they could talk together without being interrupted. And he supposed the back of the wagons would be as private a place as he would find in this mining town.

He followed her to the second wagon, where she pointed out her luggage. He paid no attention to the contents of the wagon. Instead, he continued to survey her with a sober expression that caused her extreme trepidation.

"Is something wrong?" she asked hesitantly.

"You might say that, ma'am," he said gruffly. "Fact is, I'm not Bush Tanner."

Panicked dismay swept through her, creating a sickening knot in the pit of her stomach. But the only outward sign she gave was a slight widening of her azure eyes. "Then who are you?" she asked. "And why did you come forward when the wagon master called out the name of my fiancé?"

"My name is Caleb Montgomery, ma'am. And if I hadn't come forward, you'd still be waiting on that platform with all them miners gawking at you."

"I see." But Abby didn't. "You obviously know something about my fiancé or you would have no way of knowing he wouldn't claim me."

"He couldn't, ma'am. He's not in town."

"I see," she said again. "Where exactly is Mr. Tanner?"

"He's gone to buy traps over in Colorado City."

"Colorado City?" Abby chewed her lower lip, something she always did when faced with a problem. Then she looked up at Caleb again. "Is that very far from here?"

"Yes, ma'am, it is. It's on the other side of the mountain."

She looked at the mountain, which rose high above them. "Then Mr. Tanner wasn't expecting me to arrive today?"

"No, ma am. He had no idea when you'd be coming. Or if you would. But before he left, he stopped by my place and asked me to check on the wagon train when I rode down to sell my furs."

She looked at the wagon master, wondering if she should

seek his help; then she realized that she could not. His job was done when they reached Victor. It was up to her to solve her own problems now. She looked at the crowd, which still surrounded the platform, even though most of the brides had been claimed.

"It appears that my wedding will be delayed awhile," she said softly.

"Yes, ma'am," Caleb said gruffly. "It surely does."

Suddenly, Abby knew what she must do. She smiled up at Caleb. "It was lucky for me you were here, wasn't it?" she said sweetly. "Now you can show me the way to my fiancé's house."

Caleb's expression became suddenly grim. His lips tightened as he frowned down at her. "No, ma'am. I surely can't do that."

"Why ever not?" she asked, arching a delicate brow.

"Because Bush don't live here," he explained. "His cabin is located on top of the mountain."

Abby smiled with relief. "I am so glad to hear that. Although I wouldn't have told him so, I must admit the thought of living in this town fills me with dismay. I imagine Mr. Tanner's cabin will have a nice view. Those are my things there." She pointed at the satchels again, and when Caleb made no effort to take them out, she put her foot on the wagon frame and climbed inside to get them herself.

"Now, ma'am," Caleb said quickly, "don't do that." He curled his hands around her slender waist and lifted her away from the wagon. "You don't need to be lifting on those things. Anyways, you won't need to take them out. This place is too rough for the likes of you. You'd best go back east with the wagon master."

Abby lifted her small chin to a defiant angle and fixed her eyes on him. "Are you saying Mr. Tanner has changed his mind about marrying me?"

"No, ma'am. I'm not saying nothing like that. But he's not here and there's no place for you to stay. You might have noticed there's no hotel here, nor no boardinghouses neither. Folks around here count themselves lucky to find any place indoors to sleep."

"A hotel would do me no good anyway," Abby said grimly. "I don't have funds to pay for a room. No, the best thing for me to do is to wait at Mr. Tanner's cabin for him to return from his buying trip." She eyed Caleb severely. "And if you won't take me there, then I'll just have to find my way alone."

Caleb realized the woman had more grit than he'd given her credit for. If he didn't take her, she'd either find someone else to do so, or even—she certainly looked stubborn enough—attempt the climb alone. And although he felt certain she would never reach the high mountain valley where he and Bush had built their cabins, if she sought aid from one of the miners, she could find herself in trouble before she was halfway up the slope.

Dammit! Beating Bush to a bloody pulp before shooting him wasn't enough. Caleb would skin the skunk first. Then he'd beat him to a bloody pulp and shoot him.

Muttering curses beneath his breath, Caleb reached for Abby's baggage, tucking one of the satchels beneath his arm before hefting the other two in his hands. Then he strode swiftly toward the stables, where he'd left his pack mules. He would take her to Bush Tanner's cabin and leave her there. And if Bush wasn't back within a week, then he'd find a way to send her home again.

Chapter Two

The stable had been built to withstand the harsh winter storms that plagued the Rocky Mountains, and although the wide doors had been flung open, most of the interior was in shadows.

The bright afternoon sun was harsh, and as Abigail stepped inside the stable, she paused a moment to allow her eyes to adjust to the shadowy interior. In that moment, she was struck by the familiar scent of hay mingled with horseflesh and old leather.

A loud snorting and heavy thud nearby startled her, and she jerked slightly, then hurried after Caleb Montgomery, whose stride had never faltered. He stopped near the back of the building where three pack mules—already loaded with supplies—were busily munching hay.

Depositing the bags beside the largest mule, Caleb began working at the knots holding the supplies on the animal's back. He was aware of Abigail Carpenter's eyes on him and the feeling made his fingers clumsy, the knots harder to undo.

Abigail's voice broke the silence. "Are those your supplies, Mr. Montgomery?"

He paused momentarily, then turned his attention to her. "Yes, ma'am."

"You're not going to leave them behind, are you?"

"No, ma'am. I need 'em to get through the winter."

She looked at the other mules. "Are those animals yours as well?"

"Yes, ma'am." He went back to working on the knots and was immediately rewarded for his efforts. He tossed the sack of flour to the ground, then unlooped the box of canned goods and set it beside the flour.

"I don't think you have room for my things." Her voice was soft, almost timid. "Perhaps we could leave most of them behind in storage. Mr. Tanner and I could pick them up when we return to be married."

Caleb turned to face Abby, his gaze thoughtful. "I suppose we could do that. Jim Savage, over at the general store, might be accommodating enough to store them awhile. But you'd best not leave anything of value there. Things have a way of disappearing." He looked at the luggage stacked at his feet. "Which ones do you want to take?" He pointed at the largest case. "How about this one? What have you got in there?"

"My winter clothing."

"You'd best not leave that one behind. Nights get cold on the mountain." Caleb pointed at a smaller parcel. "What about that one?"

Abby felt warmth flood her cheeks. "My—my n-nightgowns and . . . uh . . . unmentionables are in there."

The thought of Abby wearing nothing but a thin white nightgown caused Caleb's pulse to race and his body to harden. The mule snorted beside him, giving him the opportunity to turn away before she noticed.

"Easy, mule," he said gruffly. "Easy."

Then with his emotions firmly under control again, he

turned back to her. "Daylight's wasting, ma'am. You'd best pick the bags you're wanting to leave behind."

"Well, uh"—she studied her luggage for a long moment, her gaze flickering between each one, then expelled a heavy sigh—"I don't have anything that can easily be replaced."

"Nothing?" Caleb found that hard to believe. "What's in here?" He nudged a bag with his moccasin.

"I can't leave that one." Abby hurried to explain. "That bag contains my grandmother's tea set. I would rather leave my clothing behind than take a chance on it being broken."

"Then we'll take it with us."

"I'm sorry," she apologized. "I don't want to appear unreasonable, but everything I own is packed in those bags."

"Don't worry about it," he said gruffly. "The mules can carry the extra weight."

"Are we riding mules, or do you have horses?"

Caleb's brows drew into a heavy frown. "We won't be riding, ma'am. I thought you knew that."

"Oh."

"Oh, hell!" he exclaimed. "You can't walk up that mountain!"

Her chin lifted slightly. "I can do whatever is needed, Mr. Montgomery."

He grunted, then turned his attention to rearranging the supplies to make room for her luggage. He was securing the last satchel—the sturdy squared-off piece of luggage that contained her grandmother's tea set—when he was suddenly distracted by a man who'd just entered the building.

"Headed back up the mountain tonight, are you?"

As Caleb turned toward the newcomer, the luggage containing the tea set slid sideways out of the loosely wound rope.

Realizing the bag was in danger of falling off the mule, Abby cried out sharply, "Mr. Montgomery! The tea set! It's going to—"

Caleb jerked back, saw the danger, and made a grab for the piece of luggage, managing to snatch it against his chest before it struck the ground. But in doing so, he knocked the slouch hat off, and as he straightened up to secure the bag again, a ray of sunlight that had found its way into the barn illuminated his face, starkly revealing the ridged lines that ran from his cheek to his collar.

Abby sucked in a sharp breath. *Oh, God,* she silently cried. *What happened to him? What made such terrible scars?*

As though becoming aware of her fixed stare, Caleb looked up and caught her horrified eyes. Then, with jerky movements, he turned away, hiding his scarred face from her. His gaze swept the ground until it found his hat nearby. His movements were stiff as he retrieved the hat and jammed it on his head, tugging it low again to hide his scarred cheek.

The silence was absolute for a long moment; then the newcomer spoke again. "It's a mighty long ways up that mountain, Caleb. You sure you don't wanta let the little lady rest here tonight afore you head out?"

Caleb straightened abruptly. "There's no place around here for a lady to stay, Jake. You know that."

"Why I got plenty of room here, Caleb." The hostler's mouth widened, showing uneven brown teeth. "Only cost you a dollar apiece too. I'd throw in a blanket or two so's she would keep warm enough."

Caleb looked at Abby as though the decision was up to her. Dismay swept over her. Sleep in the stable, with no locked door between her and all the miners who occupied that town? She had no desire to do so.

Abby shook her head and offered Caleb a tentative smile. "I would rather go on if you don't mind, Mr. Montgomery. I'm anxious to see my new home."

"There's not enough daylight left to reach the cabin tonight," Caleb said gruffly. "But I reckon it would be safer to sleep on the mountain than to stay in town. We're gonna need some blankets though."

The hostler grinned at them, obviously not displeased with their decision. The reason became clear when he spoke again. "I got plenty of extra blankets. I could sell you two of 'em. Won't cost but a dollar each."

It was an outrageous price. Abby was on the verge of saying so when Caleb tossed the man a coin. "I can get four for that price at the general store."

"This is only a dollar," the hostler complained.

"It's all you're gonna get," Caleb said grimly. "Now go get the blankets, Jake, or I'll take the time to visit the store again."

Grumbling beneath his breath, the hostler went into a back room and returned with two blankets. Then, having obviously decided he'd get no more money from them, he left them alone and began pitching fresh hay to the horses stabled there.

"How's your shoes?" Caleb asked, leaning over the lead mule to fasten the blankets atop the supplies.

"I beg your pardon?"

Caleb pinned Abby with a hard gaze. "The way up that mountain is steep. If you don't have good soles on your shoes, then you're in for trouble."

"My shoes are quite comfortable," Abby replied. "And I have always been partial to a good brisk walk."

Caleb laughed abruptly. "You're game enough. But you may wish you'd chosen to stay here."

Abby's mouth tightened. "Just lead the way, Mr. Montgomery."

He wasted no more time on words. After fastening the mules together with a rope, he gathered up the reins of the lead mule and strode quickly from the stables, the mules—and Abby—trotting along behind him.

The pace Caleb set was a brisk one. Soon the town was left behind and they entered a forest of aspen and pines. They followed a narrow trail that curved and wound through the dense growth of trees, making it impossible to see more than a short distance ahead. But even if it had been night, Caleb would have known his way. He'd followed that trail so many times over the past ten years that he was certain he could find his cabin blindfolded.

Caleb kept a close eye on Abigail, knowing the altitude would make the going rougher for her. She surprised him with her stamina. Most women would have been complaining before now. But he had already discovered, she was not as fragile as she looked.

Abby hadn't appeared to mind his scars; she hadn't even flinched when she'd seen them. But he had no illusions that a woman could live with seeing them on a daily basis.

Hell! Even the boys who'd attended school with him had been repulsed by his scars and the girls had been frightened, as though the scars made him, somehow, less than human. It was the reason he'd sought the mountains. He was comfortable with the complete solitude, with the utter lack of human companionship, except for an occasional visit to town to renew his supplies and the occasional trapper—like Bush Tanner—who stopped by once in a while. But now that solitude had been threatened by a fragile beauty who looked as though a good stiff wind would blow her away.

Abigail was lost in her own thoughts. She was beginning to wonder if she was up to snuff. Although she was used to hard work; the altitude drained her strength, made it hard, at times, to fill her lungs with air. But Caleb Montgomery seemed aware of her difficulty and stopped often, on some pretext or another, to allow her to rest.

He was a kind man, obviously, although he presented a gruff exterior. Perhaps his scars had made him defensive and his gruffness was his way of hiding his vulnerability.

The town of Victor lay far below them when Caleb suddenly called a halt to their journey. "The light fades fast when the sun goes down," he explained. "And we need to gather some wood before dark."

He tied the lead mule's reins around the base of a pine tree and worked at the ropes holding Abby's luggage atop the animal.

"What can I do to help?" Abby asked.

"Nothing." His voice was abrupt. "You're about done in from the climb already."

"I can at least gather firewood."

"Rest yourself first."

Abby didn't have to be told twice. She sank gratefully down on a nearby rock, watching as Caleb opened a pack and removed several items from it. But when he began to dig a firepit, she pushed herself upright and hurried to gather wood for the fire.

Moments later, she tossed an armload of wood beside the pit, then turned to search for more. She moved deeper into the thicket of trees, pausing long enough to relieve herself behind a bush, then continued her search for wood. When her arms were loaded, she returned to the campsite.

Caleb was stooped over the firepit he'd surrounded with stones, blowing on a small flame. It caught quickly, then ate greedily at the kindling he'd piled in the hole. As the branches caught fire, the flames crackled and popped, leaping erratically, as though engaged in some erotic dance.

Abby shivered at that thought. Then she realized the air had turned cold when the sun dropped below the horizon.

Although Caleb had seemed too absorbed in building the fire to notice her shiver, he looked up and frowned at her. "You'd better dig out those winter clothes," he said gruffly.

"You're right," Abby agreed, turning to the pile of luggage nearby. Moments later, she shrugged into her gray wool coat and felt its warmth enclose her.

"I should have remembered you'd need it." Caleb would have, he told himself, if he had been thinking clearly. But he'd been knocked for a loop the moment he laid eyes on her . . . the moment he'd realized this woman—whose fragile beauty could rival that of the angels—was meant for the likes of Bush Tanner.

They ate their meal of canned beans and hardtack in silence. Then they lingered together over coffee, busy with their own thoughts as they watched the flames dance around the logs.

Abby wondered about the man who sat across from her. He was a loner—that much was obvious from the lifestyle he'd chosen. But didn't he ever feel the need for someone to love? Perhaps she read him wrong. Perhaps he had known love before. There might even be a woman waiting for him somewhere.

From beneath a fringe of lashes, Abby watched Caleb, hoping he wouldn't notice her interest. Were the scars on his cheek the reason for his lonely lifestyle? Or had he always preferred his own company to others? He was obviously embarrassed by his scars. He'd made that obvious when his hat had fallen off. Even now he wore the hat, with the brim pulled low as it had been—except for that brief moment in the stable—since she'd first laid eyes on him. How could Abby tell Caleb she didn't mind his scars without embarrassing him even more? She could not, she realized. It was better not to mention it at all.

As though aware he was being watched, Caleb looked inquiringly at Abby. "Something wrong?"

"No," she said huskily.

Abby turned her gaze toward the fire, yet her thoughts were still on the man. How long had he carried his scars? she wondered. If he'd been scarred since childhood, it explained his embarrassment. Children could be cruel to those less fortunate than themselves. She had reason to know, being an orphan, as well as her great aunt's personal slave, since early childhood. No more though. That was behind her. From now on, Abby would be a wife; she would have her own house and be slave to no one. And if her husband-to-be—Bush Tanner—had other ideas, then she'd best know them before they wed. Perhaps she could gain some insight into his personality from the man who sat across from her.

"Is my fiancé a trapper like yourself, Mr. Montgomery?"

"Yeah, I suppose." He threw her a curious glance. "I guess you don't know much about him, do you?"

"No. We were told that most of the men who signed up for brides were miners. I'm thankful Mr. Tanner is not. I don't think I would have enjoyed living in Victor."

"The frontier is hard on women," Caleb said gruffly. "You'd do better to go back home."

"You've given me that advice already," Abby said, her lips turning up in a wry grin. "Several times. But there is nothing for me back there. Had there been, I would not have come here."

"I suspected as much, ma'am," he admitted quietly, "which makes the whole thing even worse."

"What do you mean?"

"Just that you won't have no choice when you realize you're not strong enough for frontier life. In fact, you look downright frail. No bigger'n a minute. And you don't weigh no more than a handful of feathers." Something flickered in the darkness of Caleb's eyes. "A good strong wind would be enough to blow you right off this mountain. And we got plenty of those around here." He sipped at his coffee, watching her over the rim of his cup. "You'd best think hard about where you're headed, Miss Montgomery. And about what your life is gonna be like when you're married to a man like Bush."

A thrill of fear slid over Abby. Had she leapt from the

firing pan into the fire? "Is Bush Tanner such a hard man then?"

"Reckon so."

She shivered as she held Caleb's gaze. "A cruel man?"

Caleb wished he could claim so, but he knew he could not lie, not even to make Abby go back down the mountain. "No, he ain't a man to beat a woman—if that's what you're asking." A good thing too, Caleb told himself, or Bush Tanner would have Caleb to reckon with. "But he is a hard man. Life has made him that way."

"Like you're a hard man?" she asked softly.

Caleb bent over to add more wood to the fire, making it impossible for Abby to see his expression. When he settled back again and met her watching gaze, he realized she was still waiting for his answer. "I forgot the question," he muttered.

"I asked if you considered yourself a hard man, Mr. Montgomery."

"I reckon so," he said gruffly.

"Then I imagine I can put up with Mr. Tanner."

She smiled at Caleb and the expression on her face was dazzling, making him feel as though he was warming by a hot fire while all around him the world was freezing.

Dammit! He'd strangle Bush. Slowly.

"Mr. Montgomery . . ."

"Just call me Caleb."

"Caleb, then." Her expression was earnest. "Caleb, I know you're just trying to help me, but you must understand that I really have no choice in this matter. I can't return east. I left a situation there that had become untenable." Abby was ashamed to say her aunt had thrown her out, even though she knew she had not been at fault. "I have nothing—no one—there. No future except what I make for myself. I am like all those other women who came on that wagon train. A woman searching for a place to call home."

"It won't be an easy life here," he said gruffly. "There's other places to make a home. I have some money set aside. Maybe—"

"Absolutely not!" When Caleb looked offended, Abby said, "Even if I took your money, Caleb, how long do you think it would last? I would need to find a position, some way to make a living. And I have no training, except as a housekeeper."

"Well . . . uh, I guess . . ." He met her gaze with a long look. "Could you maybe teach school?"

"Where, Mr. Montgomery? I saw no school in Victor."

"No, but there would be one in Colorado City."

"And how many men who are capable of teaching school are living there?" she asked quietly. "Even back east they prefer men teachers."

"Uh . . . well . . ." Caleb racked his brain, but he couldn't come up with another suggestion for earning her living. "There must be plenty of men back east who would like to have you for a wife," he blurted out.

"There was one," she replied coldly. "But he was a cruel man. I would rather die than be forced to live as his wife for the rest of my days."

Caleb couldn't stand the thought of Abby married to a man like that. Perhaps she was right. Bush would treasure her. At least he'd better, Caleb thought grimly, or Caleb would damn well know the reason why.

"I reckon you chose the best way to go, ma'am," he said gruffly. "Guess we'd better turn in now."

"Yes," Abby agreed. "I'm tired."

She spread the blankets out, one on each side of the fire, then reached up to unbind her long braids. They fell across her breasts and lay there like thick golden ropes while she rubbed her head where the hairpins had held her hair captive. She would wait until morning to brush her hair since it always seemed to have a mind of its own and would need work to untangle the snarls if left unbraided.

Abigail was unaware of Caleb's gaze on her as she settled down for the night, stretching out on half of the blanket while pulling the other half over her, then spreading her coat atop that.

Then, with a heavy sigh, she closed her eyes and was soon fast asleep.

Dawn was breaking over the farthest mountain when Abigail opened her eyes again. It spread a golden flow over the forest, a breathtaking sight.

Upon pushing herself to a sitting position, Abby found herself alone in the clearing. But the crackling of the fire and the coffeepot that boiled over hot coals that had been raked to the side made it obvious that Caleb had awakened earlier.

She worked quickly at her braids, hoping to have some order about her hair before Caleb came back. She was unaware of the way she looked, the way her arm was curved over her head, holding the hairbrush aloft, when he returned.

Caleb was mesmerized by the woman who sat brushing her hair. He'd never seen a more beautiful sight in all his days of living than the woman who sat beside the fire brushing her hair. It swirled around her head like a golden halo, tumbling in wild abandon around her shoulders and back. He felt as callow as a boy who'd just become aware of women, and the embarrassment he felt made his voice seem harsher than usual when he spoke.

"I made some biscuits and coffee. It should last us until we reach the cabin. Then we can have a proper meal."

Abby jerked slightly at the sound of his voice. Then she turned her head to smile up at him. "Biscuits and coffee are fine. I don't usually eat much in the morning anyway."

Setting aside her brush, she parted her hair and went about the business of braiding the golden strands. Caleb watched quietly for a long moment before going to the firepit and pouring two cups of coffee. When her hair was wound around her head again, Caleb handed her a cup, then sat across from her, sipping the hot liquid from his cup.

Caleb could have sat there all day, he knew, watching her snuggled in her coat, eating biscuits and drinking strong black coffee. She looked so incredibly young, as vulnerable as a child. How could she even consider living in the wilds and marrying a trapper? It was a life that would be hard on any woman. A woman like her wouldn't last more than a few months. But how could Caleb convince Abby to leave when she had said she had no place to go?

He'd have to study on her situation, he decided. There had to be another way out for her rather than to marry a stranger and live a life of deprivation in these mountains.

Chapter Three

They had been traveling several hours when Caleb—who had been alternately cursing, then cajoling the lead mule in his attempt to keep the animal moving—suddenly stopped in the shade of a large boulder. He fastened the reins around a sapling, then retraced his footsteps to help Abby over the rough trail.

She took his hand gratefully, allowing him to steady her as she continued the steep climb. "I know I must be slowing you down and I apologize for doing so." Her words were jerky, coming with each gasping breath she took, and the smile she offered him was wavery, uncertain. "I never . . . never dreamed the way would be so s-steep."

"It's a mountain, Miss Carpenter." Caleb's lips twitched in a slight smile, the first one he'd given her.

She wondered if he ever laughed. "How much farther is the cabin?" she asked, looking toward the peak, where the mules waited patiently.

"We're almost there."

"Thank God."

When they reached the boulder, Abby realized why Caleb had chosen to stop there. They had reached the summit and the view was magnificent. She gasped with surprise and delight.

"Oh, Caleb, it's beautiful."

Spread out before them was a high mountain valley, where a narrow creek sparkled like a thin silvery band as it flowed swiftly, rushing toward some unknown destination. And nestled in the middle of that valley was a log cabin.

Her new home.

With her heart swelling with joy, Abigail turned to Caleb for confirmation. "Is this it?" she whispered. "Is this Mr. Tanner's cabin and my new home?"

Caleb wished he could answer in the affirmative. He didn't want to be responsible for dimming her excitement. But he could not do so. He shook his head. "This is my home," he said gruffly. "Bush built his cabin farther up the valley."

She tried to curb the disappointment that statement brought. Her new home would surely be as nice as Caleb's, but even if it wasn't, she could make it so.

Narrowing her gaze, she sent it farther up the valley and tried to locate the other cabin, but there was no other dwelling to be seen.

As though reading her thoughts, Caleb spoke softly. "You can't see the other cabin from here. Bush went down to the tree line on the other side and built it in the forest. A smart move too, I reckon. The trees afford more shelter from the winter storms than this valley does."

"He appears to be a forward-thinking man."

"Yeah." *Damn forward thinking,* Caleb told himself. Tanner had the foresight to send for a wife; he would have the company of the fairest of women to keep him warm through the long, cold winter ahead.

Damn him anyway!

Abby measured the distance of the valley with her eyes.

It appeared to be a long way to the other end, where a slight rise hid whatever lay beyond.

She smiled at Caleb to hide her anxiety. "How far is it between the cabins?"

"There's only a few miles," he replied gruffly. "Two or three maybe."

Miles. Her spirits plunged sharply. Three miles was a long way to walk in an emergency. But perhaps Mr. Tanner had a horse she could ride. If not, then she would make it her business to learn how to handle a mule. She refused to rely solely on another human being for her safety, even if the man in question would be her husband.

Caleb's voice jerked her out of her thoughts.

"If you're feeling able now, we'd best be going on. You can rest longer at my cabin while I unload the supplies and see to the animals."

"I'm ready whenever you are," she said quietly.

Caleb unfastened the reins of the lead mule and headed out. He felt an eagerness to reach the cabin that had been his home for the past ten years. He'd worked hard to make it comfortable, and he wondered what Abby would think of his efforts. He had made the table and chairs himself, working with the pine found on the mountain. But the brass bed had been ordered from Chicago and hauled up the mountain on his mule, as had the big iron stove. He was proud of his home and eager for Abigail to see it.

When they reached the cabin, Caleb opened the door and stepped aside to allow Abby entry. "Just go on in." He spoke abruptly to hide his eagerness. "I reckon it's past time for a meal. Trail food will do in a pinch, but when there's a choice, I'd prefer a decent meal"—he sent a quick glance her way—"if that suits you."

She was quick to agree. Although she wasn't very hungry, Abby didn't look forward to being left on her own so far away from civilization. "After all, if my—Mr. Tanner—is away from home, it won't matter what time I arrive, will it?''

Caleb frowned. "I can't say for certain he won't be there."

"But . . . you said . . ."

"Yeah. I know. He's only been gone a few days, but if he hurried right back he might've had time enough to get home. Trouble is, he don't usually come right back. Usually stops off for a few drinks and . . . Well, never mind. He prob'ly wouldn't do that now. But something else might've delayed him, or he might have decided to wait until I got back to leave . . . just so's he could be sure you hadn't come yet."

Caleb sincerely hoped that was the case. He hated to think of leaving Abby alone at Tanner's cabin, so far away from help of any kind. If she hurt herself, he would feel responsible. Perhaps he should suggest she stay with him until Bush Tanner returned. As quickly as that thought occurred, he rejected it. Better not to even consider such a thing. To linger longer in her company would have been folly. As it was, his dreams would be filled with her for a long time to come, the way they had been last night. If she even suspected his thoughts, she would run from him, screaming at the top of her lungs.

No. Caleb would not keep her here longer than necessary. He would unload his supplies, feed her, and afterward, they would continue their journey. He would leave her at Bush Tanner's cabin as she had requested. Then he would depart as quickly as he could, before he committed some unforgivable sin that would damn him forever in her eyes.

Abby entered the cabin and stopped short. It was obvious Caleb expended a lot of effort to make the room as comfortable as possible. And he had succeeded. The room was obviously used for both kitchen and living quarters, with a wood stove and long cabinet taking up one entire wall.

A pine table with two ladder-backed chairs stood nearby; on the table rested an oil lamp with pink flowers painted around the base. Placed near the wall farthest from the stove was a rocking chair flanked by a small table, where the mate to the oil lamp on the table took pride of place. The rest of the furnishings consisted of a trunk with a high, curved top and a highboy, which contained a set of china.

China. The dishes were a complete surprise to Abigail. She turned to face Caleb, who was watching her quietly. The interior of the cabin, along with the fragile china that appeared completely unmarred, had given her an insight into the man.

"You have a beautiful home, Caleb," she murmured softly. "I didn't expect to see such furnishings so far from civilization. How did you get them up this mountain?"

"The mules carried the bedroom stuff and the stove," he said gruffly. "I made the rest of the furniture."

"That beautiful table and chairs—and the highboy?"

"Yes," he said quietly.

"But they're wonderful, Caleb." She ran her hand over the highboy, finding it smooth beneath her fingers. "Why are you hiding your talent in these mountains? This furniture is exquisite. You would be much in demand in Chicago."

"I like the mountains," he said gruffly. "I came here to get away from civilization." As though tiring of the conversation, he turned away from her and began laying a fire in the stove. "There're some canned beans in the cabinet, and potatoes are in the storage bin. How does that sound for a meal?"

"Wonderful," Abby enthused. "And if you have the makings for biscuits, I'll whip up a batch of those. If you don't . . ."

"I have the makings. The flour is in the large can on the shelf. And the baking soda is in the tin beside it. You'll find everything you need there or in the cupboard. Just make yourself at home."

While Caleb went outside to unload his supplies, Abby busied herself preparing a meal. Before another hour was done, she and Caleb sat together at the table, shoveling down fried potatoes, canned beans, and hot biscuits washing it all down with hot coffee.

Abby left Caleb's cabin behind with mixed feelings. She was anxious to see her new home, yet knew she would be lonesome left on her own.

Since Caleb had unloaded his supplies, they were able to ride the mules, and they made short work of the miles that separated the two cabins.

Disappointment flowed through Abby when she finally stood inside the cabin that would be her new home. It was obvious that little thought had gone into its construction. The one room was even smaller than Caleb's living quarters and served for both kitchen and bedroom.

The stove occupied one side of the room, while the center was taken up by a rough-hewn table and two benches. At first glances, Abby saw no bed; then she realized the two wide planks fastened on one wall could be let down at night to afford a sleeping space. Her roving gaze fell on the pile of furs stacked in one corner, and she turned curious eyes on Caleb.

"Mr. Tanner didn't take his furs with him?"

"No, they fetch a higher price at Victor. Some of the miners use them for beds," Caleb explained. "But the stores there don't stock traps, so we're forced to fetch them from Colorado City."

"I see."

"I'll unload your luggage while you check the supplies on that shelf." Caleb indicated the long plank nailed on the wall above the stove. "If you don't have enough food-stuffs, I can bring some from my cabin."

"I couldn't take your supplies," Abby protested.

"Tanner will replace them when he comes back." Caleb looked at the planks that were fastened to the wall, imagining Abby lying there with Bush Tanner, their limbs entwined in passion. Then he abruptly pushed the vision away. He didn't want to think about the two of them together.

Abby shifted uneasily. It wouldn't be right for her to accept supplies from Caleb. He'd already gone to a lot of trouble, getting her to this cabin, and she was determined to make it on her own now. "No, please," she insisted. "I feel certain there are enough supplies to last me until he . . . my . . . fiancé returns." Abby offered Caleb a quick smile. "Anyway, I wouldn't dream of taking your supplies, lest you run short yourself."

Caleb's mouth tightened grimly and he tugged the brim of his hat lower to hide his expression. "No sense in arguing over it until we see how you're fixed." He moved over to the shelf nailed to the wall behind the stove, and he pushed a few cans aside to peruse the back row of goods. "Looks like he was running low on most everything when he left. You check what he's got and tell me what you need. And I'll bring it over tomorrow."

"What if he doesn't bring supplies?"

"It don't matter. Soon as he comes back, the two of you will be heading off to Victor anyway. And you can stock up while you're there."

Abby continued to resist. "You can't possibly know when he plans to go to Victor."

"It had better be as soon as he comes back," Caleb said grimly, "or else he'll have me to answer to."

"I don't understand."

"You'll be needing the preacher." The words were

almost gritted out through a tight jaw. Then, without another word, he left her alone in the cabin.

Abigail thought about what Caleb had said while she acquainted herself with the foodstuffs stored on the shelf. He'd been so grim, so tense, as though he were angry, yet why should that be so? Unable to find an answer, she turned her attention to the job at hand.

Several large tins had been left on the shelf. In them were coffee, sugar, flour, and dried beans. But there was only a meager supply of each. If rationed carefully, there might be enough to last her several days.

Caleb entered the room again, loaded with her baggage. Abby felt disappointed that she could not reward him with a hot meal for the effort he'd expended on her behalf.

He'd been so attentive to her needs and now she must appear ungrateful. And she might never see him again! That thought caused a lump in her throat, and she swallowed hard to keep sudden tears at bay. What was wrong with her anyway?

Putting her emotions down to her weary state, Abigail blinked rapidly to dry her eyes, but the slump in her shoulders gave her away when Caleb, who had deposited her luggage near the bedboards, turned to face her.

"Is something wrong?" he asked gently.

His gentleness was almost her undoing. She blinked hard to dry her eyes. "No, nothing," she whispered.

"Abby," he said softly, using her given name for the first time. "I know the cabin has to be a disappointment, but it can be made better. I can help Bush build another room and we—"

"No!" Abby said quickly, feeling horrified that he'd misread her. "I wouldn't be so mean-spirited. I will be proud of whatever accommodations Mr. Tanner wishes to provide."

Caleb squeezed her shoulders gently. "Then what's wrong?"

Abigail realized she would have to tell him, lest he think her an ungrateful wretch. "I was hoping to cook your evening meal, but there's nothing among the supplies to fix that wouldn't take several hours."

"Is that all?" He released her and she felt a keen sense of loss. "Don't worry about it. Anyway, it hasn't been long since we ate. And I wouldn't feel right using up your supplies. There's little enough here to begin with." He looked around the cabin. "Now, what do I need to do to make you more comfortable here?"

"Not a thing." Abigail forced a lightness into her voice that she didn't feel. "I believe I have everything I need."

"Matches?" he asked. "Oil for the lamp?"

She frowned. "I'm afraid I found none of those things."

"Did you check the big wooden box on the floor?"

"No." She bent over the box and lifted the lid, searching through the contents quickly. But the box appeared to contain only a few towels and blankets and assorted clothing.

"I'm almost certain that's where Tanner keeps a tin of matches." Caleb leaned over and slowly emptied the box, taking each item out one by one and piling them on the floor next to him. At the very bottom he unearthed a small tin, which did, indeed, hold matches. "Here we go." He handed them over. "There're some candles here too, in case you run out of oil."

"I didn't find any oil," she reminded him.

Although they searched the cabin thoroughly, not a drop of lamp oil could be found. After replacing everything in the trunk, Caleb lifted the lamp with its soot-darkened shade and shook it gently; then he set it down again. "I think there's enough oil in the lamp for tonight," he said. "And I'll bring you some more tomorrow."

"You don't need to do that," Abby protested quickly. "I'm certain you have more important things that need your time."

"No trouble," Caleb said abruptly. "Anyway, if circumstances were different, and I was the one waiting for my bride, I would expect Tanner to act accordingly." He moved toward the door. "Guess I'd better be leaving now. Bar the door after I'm gone. And close the shutter on that window when you go to bed."

Abby stood in the doorway, watching Caleb ride away. She felt like a child who had been unexpectedly abandoned by a beloved parent. She didn't question her feelings, nor allow herself to dwell on them. Instead, she turned back into the cabin and, remembering Caleb's warning, barred the door, then set to cleaning the cabin and finding a place for her belongings.

She unpacked her grandmother's tea set, checking each piece over carefully before setting it on the rough-hewn table. She needn't have worried about it though, she realized. Caleb had seemed to know how much it meant to her, and he had exerted every care when handling the bag where it had been stored.

Caleb.

She sat back on her heels and looked toward the door. Had he reached his cabin yet? How long had he been gone? She tried to push thoughts of him from her mind, but found that impossible to do. He had gone to a lot of trouble on her behalf and she must think of a way to repay him.

Yes, she must do that.

With that decision made, she realized she now had a legitimate reason for thinking about him. She must, she told herself with a smile, or else how could she decide on a just payment for services rendered.

Best to remember everything that had happened on the journey up the mountain, every moment she'd spent with him. It was the only way she would know how to repay him. She must first remember every detail, every nuance of his voice, every look he'd sent her way, so she could figure out his makeup—if she could ever do so.

Caleb had a habit of hiding his thoughts, as well as his face beneath the brim of his slouch hat, yet at times, she had seen signs of the man inside. And there was one thing that stood out clear. He was a gentleman, one who sympathized with her plight. And he was an educated man, a man of talents, who had been cruelly treated at some time in his past.

Perhaps he needed a friend, she thought. A good friend. A woman like herself to talk with. She could make herself available whenever the need arose and they could . . .

Abigail shook herself abruptly, afraid of where her thoughts had been headed. She was as good as wed and could not be having such thoughts about another man.

No! She couldn't allow that to happen. But for a moment there, she'd been basking in such a warm feeling that it was hard to set thoughts of Caleb aside.

But she would, she thought grimly. She wasn't a woman to betray the man she'd promised to marry. She didn't have much left, but she did have her integrity and she was determined to keep that.

So she'd best stay clear of Caleb.

Chapter Four

Even as he rode away from the cabin, Caleb fought the need to retrace his path, to go back and confront Abigail, to demand that she stay with him, at least until Bush returned home.

But Abby was not his to command. She was *Tanner's* woman, and before the week was out, they would stand together before a preacher and make their vows.

Dammit! It wasn't right. Tanner didn't deserve a woman like her! Abby needed to be cherished, loved, protected.

What in hell did Bush Tanner know about love? Absolutely nothing. A woman like Abby needed to be handled with tenderness. Tanner knew nothing about women like her. How could he when his own mother had abandoned him almost at birth, giving him over to a peddler in exchange for a case of rotgut whiskey?

Caleb had heard the story several times since Tanner was inclined to seek sympathy when he imbibed too much. And Caleb did sympathize with the other man. But not so much that he could easily accept the marriage that would take place when Tanner returned.

The attraction Caleb felt for Abigail was almost overwhelming, but he fought against the feeling. What was there about Abby, he wondered, that made her so special? Granted, she was beautiful, yet he'd known other beautiful women, and he'd had no trouble leaving them behind. But hers was not only an outward beauty. Her reaction to his scars—or perhaps calm acceptance was the correct term—told him there was a rare quality about her, a gentleness that was absent in so many other beautiful women.

Abby would make a wonderful wife—a willing, uncomplaining helpmate. He would have given his soul if she could have been his.

But it was not to be.

Caleb knew his own limitations. He was a loner. His scars had made him so. And even though Abigail had appeared to accept him for what he was, he couldn't expect a woman of such fragile beauty to go through life hidden away in the mountains. Nor could he live any other way.

He sighed deeply. It didn't bear consideration anyway. She was promised to Bush Tanner. But the thought of her living with another man, so close to his own home, was almost more than Caleb could bear.

Perhaps it was time for him to mosey on, to travel westward. He had never even considered moving before. Had always thought he'd made himself a permanent home. But if Tanner stayed on the mountain . . . with Abigail . . .

Dammit! Life had been simple enough before he'd gone down to Victor, before he'd laid eyes on Abigail and realized she was destined to be Tanner's bride.

Would life ever be simple again?

Caleb didn't think so.

* * *

Abby woke early the next morning. Her eyelids flickered open and she stared up at the rough-hewn log ceiling above.

"Where . . . ?" The query was barely uttered when she remembered where she was. Bush Tanner's cabin. Her new home.

Never one to wake slowly, Abby pushed herself upright on the plank bed, and as the blankets fell away, the cold air made itself known.

Hurrying across to the stove, she struck a match to the kindling she'd stacked the night before. Then, while the flames were lapping hungrily at the logs, she replaced the stove lid and went about making coffee.

The moment the coffeepot was on the stove, she slid on her shoes, snatched up her coat, and went outside. Although the sun had not yet topped the mountain, the forest was alive with sound. Birdsong filled the air as birds fluttered from branch to branch. Crickets sounded from beneath the bushes and somewhere nearby a branch snapped loudly.

Realizing something heavier than a bird had made that sound, Abby jerked around, fear slithering through her. "Is someone there?" Her voice sounded husky, frightened, and she tried to make it firmer. "Who's there?"

Suddenly, as though startled by the sound of her voice, a rabbit darted across the path and scrambled beneath the nearest bush on the other side.

Abigail laughed with delight, the fear draining away as though it had never been. "You almost made me jump out of my skin, you horrid little thing." Abigail spoke aloud, even though the rabbit had already disappeared from sight and probably did not hear her.

It was only a matter of moments before she was in the cabin again, setting the room to rights, folding the bedding she'd used, and storing it away again. Then, with the place as neat as she could make it, Abby poured herself a cup of coffee and went outside to enjoy the sunrise.

The sky was spectacular. As the morning sun burst over the horizon, it touched the tops of the pine trees with a bright burst of color. Abby seated herself on a stump nearby. After they were married, she would ask Mr. Tanner to build her a rocking chair so she could enjoy the sunrise in comfort.

That thought brought to mind the man who'd escorted her here. He was a strange man, a quiet, lonely man who had deliberately set himself apart from the rest of the world. Yet he was a good man, she was certain. A kind man. One who would make a good husband if he would only allow a woman to get close enough.

She sighed heavily, thinking of the woman who might, sometime in the future, claim a place in Caleb's heart. He needed someone special, she knew, a compassionate woman who wouldn't mind his scarred face, who would chase away the shadows that lingered within his mind. If only . . .

Abby pushed the thought away. She couldn't allow herself to think that way. She was promised to Bush Tanner. Honor bound to marry him. And she would do exactly that . . . as soon as he returned.

It was midmorning when Abby left to explore her surroundings. She followed the pathway that she'd traversed earlier that morning, enjoying the birdsong as she searched for wildflowers and edible plants. She had gathered several wild roses when she heard the sound of water in the distance.

Was she hearing the creek that flowed near Caleb's cabin? Her pace quickened as she hurried forward, slipping and sliding as the path began a gradual downward slope.

The sound became louder as she neared the creek, and moments later, she discovered the reason. The trail curved when it reached the edge of the water, then turned downward sharply, following beside the creek until the sound became a muted roar.

Soon, Abigail saw the waterfall. The creek appeared to stop at that point, but Abigail knew that was impossible. She traced the lines of the creek with her eyes as the water flowed rapidly toward the huge rocks that lined the edge of a cliff; then the creek seemed to disappear completely.

Abby hurried forward, eager to see where the water had gone. The roaring sound increased as she neared the rocks, and then she was beside the cliff, watching the water plunge sharply downward, where it bubbled and frothed into a wide, pool before it overflowed and wound its way down the mountainside.

Feeling completely entranced, Abby seated herself on a large rock to enjoy the sight. She could find contentment on this mountain, she knew. If her future husband was anything like Caleb, she would be satisfied with the bargain she'd made.

As her gaze traveled over the ferns that grew beside the pool below, she felt a sudden chill shiver across her skin. Goose pimples broke out on her arms and the fine hairs on the back of her neck stood out. A tingle of fear ran down her spine and she searched the forest around her, wondering what had caused such a reaction.

There was nothing to cause her alarm, she silently chided herself. The sun was shining brightly overhead, chasing away the shadows that had lingered beneath the thick shrubs. It was only her imagination.

Dismissing her alarm as imagination working overtime, Abigail rose and made her way back toward the cabin. She had only gone a short way when she saw a cluster of thin green stalks that looked familiar growing near the creek. She bent to examine them closer, realized she'd found a cluster of wild onions, and gathered some.

There were probably other edible plants growing in the

forest, so Abby began a thorough search and, only moments later, found several mushrooms that would go well with the beans she had left simmering on the back of the stove.

More than an hour had passed before she turned her steps toward the cabin again. She had gone only a short way when she heard the snap of branches and stopped short. Then she saw Caleb approaching, a brace of rabbits thrown over one shoulder. As she drank in the sight of him, a sudden warmth surrounded her. It was his presence that caused the feeling, she realized, assuring her of a safe haven should it be needed. She knew the exact moment when he caught sight of her because he came to an abrupt halt.

"Hello, Abby." His voice was calm, steady, giving away nothing of his feelings. "I didn't expect to see you out here."

Abby felt pleased at his lack of formality. "Nor I you." She eyed the rabbits. "I see you've already been hunting."

"Yes." He held the rabbits toward her. "I thought you might enjoy some fresh meat."

She smiled with pleasure. "Why, thank you, Caleb. I would enjoy some. But I couldn't possibly accept them unless you promise to join me for dinner."

Caleb basked in the warmth of her smile. He knew he should decline the invitation, yet the words he needed would not come. Instead, he heard himself agreeing to join her for supper that evening. "Is there anything else you need?" he asked. "Some lard maybe?"

"No," she replied. "I won't need much. I have a recipe for dumplings that will melt in your mouth." Her aunt had been particularly partial to game prepared in that manner, so Abby had made the dish often enough to become quite an expert with it.

"I guess I'd like anything I didn't have to cook myself," Caleb replied gruffly. "I'll just come along with you and dress out the rabbits . . . save you that chore"—he cleared his throat—"if you want me to."

She hesitated, then said, "I don't like to burden you."

"It's no burden. Fact is, I'd enjoy your company. It gets mighty lonesome on this mountain sometimes." Dammit! Now why had he gone and said that? "Of course I'm used to being alone."

"But it's good to have company occasionally," Abby said gently. "And since these mountains are so different from my former home I would appreciate yours . . . although I don't want to cause you any trouble."

"You couldn't if you tried," Caleb replied gallantly.

On the way back to the cabin, Abby asked about the berries and plants they passed that were unknown to her, and Caleb answered each question as though it were of extreme importance.

"Those glossy white berries over there look tasty enough," he explained as he pointed out the bush, "but they aren't. They're deadly poison."

"What about those?" she asked, pointing out a berry-laden bush she'd passed earlier without noticing.

"Those are gooseberries." He left the path to pick a handful, then he handed them to her. "They make excellent jelly or pies."

She tried them and found them delicious. "We're not far from the cabin, are we?"

"No. Why?"

"These are ripe enough to pick now, aren't they?"

"Yes, but don't come here alone."

"Why ever not?"

"Because bears are especially fond of these berries. And they don't like poachers."

"Bears?" Abby looked behind her fearfully. "I wonder if that's what I heard earlier."

He frowned at her. "What do you mean?"

"I went to the waterfall and while I was there I had

the strangest feeling that someone—or something—was watching me." She shivered at the memory; then she met Caleb's eyes again. "Do you think it might have been a bear?"

His frown deepened. "It might have been. But usually they make themselves known when they consider their territory invaded." He scanned the forest with his eyes, then turned to her again. "If you want some of these berries, I'll help you gather them."

"We don't have anything to hold them"—she eyed his hat—"unless you're willing to give up your hat for the sake of your stomach."

"My hat stays on my head," he said sharply, his gaze sliding away from hers.

"Caleb." She curled her fingers around his forearm and felt his muscles tense beneath her fingers. "You don't have to hide yourself from me."

"I don't like exposing myself to ridicule, Abby," he said gruffly.

"I would never ridicule you, Caleb."

"I never take my hat off," he said stubbornly.

"It makes no sense to hike to the cabin when your hat would hold all the berries we need." She smiled up at him. "Please. If we don't gather them now, the bears might beat us to them."

Abby didn't know why she persisted in the face of his resistance, but she did. She was unwilling to allow him to remain locked inside the hard shell he'd built around himself.

Caleb was a stubborn man though, a man determined to hide himself from those around him, a man who had spent years building the wall that she was trying so hard to tear down.

Reaching up, she tilted the brim of his hat upward and placed her palm against his scarred cheek. Although a muscle twitched in his jaw, he allowed her to touch him.

His dark eyes were molten lava as he held her gaze. Her fingers stroked gently against the ridges that marred his face as her other hand pushed the brim higher, then lifted the hat away from his head.

"There!" she exclaimed softly. "Now that wasn't so bad, was it?" As her breath quickened beneath his heated gaze, she felt a warmth flooding the apex of her thighs and her stomach fluttered wildly, as though a thousand butterflies had taken up residence there. She forced her lips to curve into a smile; then she looked at the hat in her hand. "We'd better get this thing filled up before that bear discovers what we're about."

When the hat was full of berries they made short work of the journey to the cabin. It was a silent journey because each of them considered what had gone on before.

Abby was still amazed at her temerity in taking Caleb's hat away. That he had allowed it was the most amazing thing, and she hoped it would lead to a better understanding between them.

All too soon, they reached the cabin, and after she'd dumped the gooseberries in a bowl, Caleb pulled his hat on again and pulled the brim low.

"Look . . . about tonight. I—"

"You promised, Caleb," Abby said sternly.

He nodded abruptly. "Yeah, I guess I did. But—"

"I'll expect you at sundown," she said quickly. "Now go on home so I can prepare these rabbits."

"I was gonna do that for you."

"That's all right. I can do them." Abby needed time to think, time away from the man who made her body come alive with unexpected desires. "You go on now."

Perversely, he seemed inclined to linger. "You seem in an almighty hurry to get rid of me, Abby. You got something stuck in your craw?"

She laughed and lifted her gaze to his. "Stuck in my

craw?" she questioned. "What in the world does that mean, Caleb?"

"Just that ... down by the creek ... Well, you didn't seem so anxious for me to be gone then."

"I know." Abby looked away from him; then, deciding honesty was the best policy, she met his eyes again. "There's something about you, Caleb, that attracts me. And sometimes that attraction is so strong that I forget I'm soon to be wed. I think we must both be on our guard against that happening."

As though his hand belonged to someone else, it reached toward her. "Abby ..."

"No! You'd best go now, and we're going to forget this conversation ever happened." She lowered her lashes quickly to hide her expression. "Please help me, Caleb. I'm afraid I cannot do this alone."

"If that's what you want," he said gruffly.

"Thank you, Caleb. And good-bye, for now."

Without another word, Caleb left her alone.

That night, Abby dressed carefully. She wore a blue gown with a full skirt that was scooped low at the neckline to reveal the swelling of her breasts. Over the garment, she wore a long white apron.

When Caleb entered the cabin, one look at Abigail told him he'd made a grave mistake in coming. It had been the height of folly to accept her dinner invitation, he realized. The soft light from the oil lamp seemed to enhance Abby's beauty. He couldn't take his eyes off her. She could have been the model for the painting he'd once seen of an angel, with her blond curls piled high on her head and the blue of her gown exactly matching her eyes and the flush on her cheeks highlighting her magnolia skin.

God! What a fool he'd been to place himself in such a situation. If he had any sense at all, he would turn around and walk right out the door. He would run from the cabin and never look back.

But how could he leave when everything within him urged him to stay? Caleb knew he should keep his distance from her until Bush returned and bound her securely in marriage. But, hell, his feet refused to move. And his damned legs felt as though they would buckle beneath him if he didn't sit down somewhere. And yet he could not. No gentleman would seat himself while a lady remained standing.

Caleb cleared his throat, feeling suddenly as callow as a youth in the throes of a first love. Hell! He'd never had a love, not a first one nor any other. Until that moment, no woman had had the power to touch his heart. And it had to be a woman who was betrothed to another man!

"Good evening, Caleb," Abby said softly.

Only then did Caleb realize he was standing in the doorway of the cabin, staring at her as though he'd never seen a woman.

You haven't, his heart cried. *Not like this one!*

"Evening, Abby," he replied, his gaze devouring her.

Why couldn't she have been an ordinary woman with ordinary looks? he wondered. If she had, he might have been tempted to throw out his scruples, to court her, to try to win her away from Bush Tanner. But nothing about her could be called ordinary. And he would not be so presumptuous as to think she might be courted and won by someone with a scarred face and body. Even if she had admitted to being attracted to him, she hadn't seen the worst. Nor would she ever.

Granted, Bush Tanner was not the handsomest of men, yet his face and body were normal enough that he didn't have to worry about frightening little children.

"Come in, Caleb," Abby said, stepping aside to allow him entry.

"I hope I'm not late," he said gruffly.

"No, your timing is perfect. The meal is ready to go on the table. Please take a chair."

"I'll wait until you're ready," he said awkwardly. He wasn't sure what to do in a case like this. He only knew that he shouldn't seat himself before she was seated. Since she was busy putting the meal on the table, he had no choice but to stand.

"Go on," she said with a smile. "This won't take me long."

Reluctantly, Caleb seated himself and watched her move around the room, placing food upon the table. A bowl of greens joined the platter of biscuits and the large bowl of rabbit dumplings. Then a tray holding watercress and scallions was added to the selection and hot coffee poured into the cups that Abby had placed beside the plates.

"I'm afraid I used all the sugar in the apple dumplings," Abby said quietly. "I forgot you might need some in your coffee."

"No, I don't use sugar." Then, realizing what she'd said, he gulped. "Apple dumplings? You made apple dumplings?" At her nod, he asked, "Where did you find apples?"

"There was some dried fruit in one of the tins in back of the stove. I hope Mr. Tanner won't mind that I've used it."

"He won't mind," Caleb said gruffly. Tanner had better not, he told himself. Not after what he had put Caleb through.

Although the rabbit was so tender it required little chewing and the dumplings almost melted in his mouth, Caleb hardly tasted the meal. His mind was occupied with the vision who sat across from him and occasionally threw shy glances his way.

When Abby served the apple dumplings, he was astonished that anything as ordinary as dried apples could be made to taste like ambrosia. But then, he reminded himself, he shouldn't have been surprised since an angel from heaven had made them.

The evening passed swiftly, and all too soon, the last dish was washed, carefully dried, and stored away on the shelf. The china looked completely out of place in the crude surroundings, as did Abigail. Caleb hated the thought of Bush Tanner returning, of the man having the right to put his hands on her, to touch her in the ways of marriage.

As Caleb hung the dishtowel on the nail provided for that purpose, he turned awkwardly to face Abby. "Well, ma'am, I guess I'd better be going. But I want to thank you for the meal. I never tasted the likes of it before."

"Ma'am?" she questioned, smiling teasingly up at him. "Are we being formal again? I refuse to go back to calling you Mr. Montgomery, Caleb. So I insist that you continue to call me Abigail . . . or Abby, whichever you prefer."

He struggled inwardly, wanting desperately to snatch her against him and somehow finding the strength to keep his distance. "All right . . . Abby."

Her smile dazzled him. "Will you join me for dinner again, Caleb?"

He wanted to say yes, but how could he put himself through this torture again and remain sane?

"I'm not so sure that's a good idea," he said gruffly.

"Why?" Her eyes were round with surprise . . . and something else. Was she hurt by his refusal?

He knew he owed her an explanation, yet how could he find the words without revealing that he was falling in love with her?

"Well, seeing as how you're almost married to another man, I thought it might be best if—"

"You think Mr. Tanner might object to you having dinner with me? Is he really so unkind as to want me to stay alone in this cabin without any other human contact?"

How was he supposed to answer that? Caleb wondered.

If she had been his fiancé, he would definitely object to her keeping company with another man. And yet, if he told her so, she would not feel able to call on him in case of an emergency. And she had to feel comfortable in doing so, because they were alone in this wilderness. Any number of things could happen where she would need help . . . or protection.

"Of course he wouldn't be so mean minded as that," Caleb said, answering in the only way he could.

Abby smiled at him and the world became as brilliant as though it were the brightest day. "That's settled then. And I will expect you to dinner around the same time tomorrow. But I'm afraid the fare will not be so fancy as tonight, since I used all of the sugar and most of the flour and lard on the dumplings."

Caleb sighed inwardly. He had a good supply of food-stuffs, and felt obliged to offer her some. Yet it would mean a trip to the cabin tomorrow morning as well as tomorrow night so she had the goods in time to prepare the evening meal. Although he relished the times he would be able to see her, he knew he was flirting with danger. Not a physical danger, perhaps—rather the danger of losing his heart so thoroughly that he might forget what was right and give way to his feelings.

If he did, how would she react? If he followed his heart and took her in his arms and kissed her would she run screaming in fear or would she welcome his embrace?

Dammit! He had to get out of there! Had to put some distance between himself and her.

With an abrupt good night that bordered on rudeness, Caleb turned and almost ran from the cabin.

Chapter Five

As the first light of dawn chased away the deeper shadows, a sound—sharp, clanging, as though metal had scraped against metal—woke Abby with a start. Her eyelids flew open and she jerked upright, trying to identify the sound that had awakened her. Then she flung back the covers and slid from the bed, grimacing as her bare feet found the cold planks of the cabin floor. After hurrying across the room to the window, she peered outside.

Abby saw no movement in her line of vision, nothing there to cause her alarm. And yet, the sound she'd heard had been real enough. It had seemed to come from the overhang beside the door.

Deciding to err on the side of caution, Abby waited several moments for the sound to be repeated, but except for her own breathing, and the heavy thud of her rapidly beating heart, there was only silence.

Slowly, she eased back the bar that locked the door and opened the door just wide enough to peer outside. She could see the washbasin that rested on a crude table outside the door, but the pan that usually covered the bucket at night lay on the ground. Abby frowned, feeling a shiver of alarm. Something—or someone—had been at her door.

Abby's first instinct was to slam the door shut again, to bar it as quickly as she could and cower fearfully inside the cabin until Caleb came back. But she knew that a quick reaction on her part might alarm the person—or beast— enough to react before she could lock the door, so she began to ease it quietly shut again. When there was only a small crack left, something flickered across her line of vision and she heard a chittering sound.

Too curious to remain frightened, Abby opened the door wider and saw a furry black creature with a masked face stop momentarily to stare at her before spinning around to scamper into the forest. She laughed, feeling her tension ease away as though it had never been. The noisemaker was only a raccoon, obviously seeking water and too lazy to go the extra distance to the creek.

Becoming aware of the cold morning air, Abby closed the door and hurried to light a fire. When the wood was blazing, she dressed quickly, then flung the door wide and went outside to wash.

Moments later, she was humming softly while she ground a few coffee beans to add to the coffeepot. She'd been quick to adopt the method of making coffee that Caleb used. Things were done differently in the mountains, he'd told her. Every effort was made to conserve food since a long journey was required to replenish supplies. Because of that, it was Caleb's custom to keep the old coffee grounds in the pot and add water and newly ground coffeebeans to the old. The result was a potful of strong coffee that she thoroughly enjoyed.

Abby didn't waste time preparing breakfast. While the coffee was boiling, she busied herself by cleaning the cabin. It didn't take long. A quick sweep with the broom she'd fashioned from some rushes growing near the creek

cleared the floor of any debris that might have accumu-
lated the day before. She poured herself a cup of coffee
and took one of the biscuits she'd saved from the tin and
sat down to enjoy her repast.

Abby thought about Caleb while she ate. Her visits with
him were becoming an important part of her day. Too
important for her peace of mind. Was she becoming too
attached to him? she wondered. If only he had, as she'd
first thought, been the man who'd sent for her.

But then, wishing was for fools, and Abby was no fool.
These mountains had been a rebirth for her, a time of
healing.

Perhaps she did allow her thoughts to dwell overlong
on Caleb, but was that so surprising? He was patient with
her, unfailingly gentle and kind. And from the time she'd
gone to live with her aunt at an early age, she'd had only
harshness directed at her. During all her years with Aunt
Amelia, Abby had never received one thank-you for her
services. Perhaps that was the reason she'd felt nothing
but a sense of duty toward the woman who'd given her a
home when she had no other place to go.

How Aunt Amelia had railed at Abby, accused her of
the most horrible things, when she'd done none of them.
It was her cousin who had acted improperly, not Abby. Yet
she'd known she would never convince her aunt of that
fact. Not even after her cousin had told his mother that,
since he'd compromised Abby because of her forwardness,
he would do the honorable thing and make her his wife.

All lies, she thought, her mouth tightening grimly. Every
word he'd uttered had been a lie. But she hadn't given in
to him, had continued to refuse to marry him, and as a
result, her aunt had thrown her out of the house, had
barely given her time to pack her belongings.

"At least I was able to take Grandmother's china with
me," Abby muttered grimly. But that was only because
Aunt Amelia had no idea she'd packed it away with her

clothing. If Aunt Amelia had known, she would have stopped Abby from removing the china from the house. Not that Aunt Amelia needed it. She had her own china, yet she would have claimed it just to keep Abigail from having anything that had belonged to their family.

Suddenly realizing that she was allowing memories from the past to spoil her day, Abby mentally shrugged them aside and rose to wash her cup and saucer. Then, picking up the basket that she'd woven yesterday, she hung it over her arm and left the cabin, closing the door behind her, lest the raccoon return and do some damage in the cabin.

Her errand was a simple one. She was going back to the gooseberry bush to gather more berries before the bears arrived to lay claim to them. Although Caleb had warned her against going there alone, Abby was afraid to wait, lest the bears find the bushes and strip them of berries. She felt certain there would be no danger. Hadn't she already been there and seen nothing that might do her harm?

Following the trail she had traversed before, Abby hurried through the forest. It didn't take her long to reach the bushes and before an hour had passed her basket was almost full.

When she discovered that she was having to reach farther into the bush for berries, and getting pricked with the thorns for doing so, Abby searched for—and found— another berry-laden bush a short distance away. She was reaching out for a handful of berries when a crackling sound behind her caught her attention.

The bear! Abby's heart skipped a beat as she whirled around to face the beast. But instead of the monster she'd expected, she saw a large man dressed in buckskin.

"Oh, you gave me a fright!" she exclaimed breathlessly. "I had no idea there was anyone nearby."

A grin spread across his unshaven face. "I been watching you for some time, girlie. But I figgered it'd be best to keep out o' sight till I was ready to make my move."

"I . . . I don't understand," Abby said shakily, feeling her alarm deepen at the look on his face. "Why have you been watching me?"

"Now I'd be plumb crazy if'n I didn't like watchin' something as pretty as the likes of you." He laughed harshly and his gaze slid downward, seeming to pause a moment on her rounded breasts, on her shapely hips, before sliding upward to meet her eyes again. "And I dang sure ain't crazy. Not yet anyways. Can't say as I wouldn't've been afore long if I had to keep on watching you like I been doing." His gaze slid downward again, stopped on her breasts, and stayed there. "You shore do look purty dressed in nothing but that white thing you sleep in at night."

"You saw me dressed for bed?"

"Shore did. More'n once too."

Abigail's fingers tightened around the handle of her basket. The stranger was a definite threat—more so, probably, than a bear would have been. And they were completely alone in the forest.

What could Abby do? There was no one about to hear her scream, even if she tried. And to do so would surely only enrage the man, yet she couldn't stand there and submit to whatever he had in mind for her.

"What do you want?" she whispered, trying to keep the fear from her voice.

"What do you think, girlie?" he growled, not even trying to disguise the lust gleaming in his dark eyes. "I been waitin' on you ever since I saw you standing on that platform in Victor. And when Caleb Montgomery walked up and claimed you, 'stead of Bush Tanner, I figgered old Bush was off somewheres and Montgomery is so honorable he'd not be messin' with somebody else's woman. Now me, well, I don't have that problem."

Abby's fear increased, but she dared not show it. She tightened her lips and lifted her chin, her blue eyes hard as stone. "Let me pass," she demanded.

The stranger grinned at her, but there was no humor in his expression. Only an intense satisfaction.

"I wouldn't try anything if I were you," she said coldly. "Caleb Montgomery should be here momentarily."

"Is that a fact?"

"Yes," she lied. "We made the arrangements last night."

"Then he ain't keeping none of those arrangements, girlie. I saw him at first light—afore I went to Tanner's cabin to spy on you—an' Montgomery was busy working some hides. He'll be scraping on 'em and salting 'em down for most of the morning. Plenty of time for me to finish with you."

His eyes gleamed with satisfaction as he reached out for Abby, but she dodged quickly away, barely managing to elude his grasp. Laughing harshly, he reached out again, making another grab for her. Again, Abby dodged away. But he'd expected her reaction and made a lunge for her, his powerful hands reaching out to grip her forearms tightly.

Abigail dropped the basket and the berries spilled out and rolled away, unseen by either of them. She opened her mouth to scream, even while she felt that the effort would do no good, yet he was too quick for her. Before she could utter a sound, his hand covered her mouth to muffle her cries.

Kicking out wildly, she connected with the man's shin and he grunted in pain, yet he did not loosen his grip. He dragged her hard against him then, his muscled body so solid that it rendered her struggles ineffectual.

Abby found herself barely able to breathe with his large hand covering her mouth; nevertheless, she opened her mouth enough to sink her sharp teeth into his hand, feeling immense satisfaction when he grunted in pain and tried to shake her loose.

Abigail hung on grimly, refusing to let go, tasting the warm copper flavor of blood in her mouth.

With a loud oath, the stranger released her suddenly, flinging her to the ground. The world spun dizzily around her as she pushed herself to all fours, realizing she must flee before her attacker recovered. Before she could do so though, he struck a sharp blow against the side of her face and she felt the ground smack her cheek again.

Fighting hard against the dizziness that assailed her, Abby tried to crawl away. The stranger kicked her legs and sent her sprawling again. She had little time to consider the pain before he kicked her again, landing a hard blow against her side that sent what breath she'd managed to hold whooshing out of her mouth.

Groaning softly, Abby curled into a ball, trying to protect her stomach and vital parts from the blows he rained down on her until finally, as though becoming impatient with her, he landed one last blow against her hip. Then he reached down and pulled her upright.

Although Abby tried to stand, her legs refused to hold her. Her attacker cursed angrily, then threw her across one shoulder and held her there with a big, meaty hand. Unable to bear the pain, she closed her swollen eyes and succumbed to the darkness.

It was early afternoon when Caleb arrived at Tanner's cabin. He'd busied himself most of the morning, curing hides that he intended to sew together to make a rug. It was his intention to give the rug to Abigail for a wedding present.

The cabin door was closed and the place had a loneliness about it that told him she was nowhere about. Perhaps she'd gone to the spring to fetch water, he told himself. A quick glance at the waterbucket told him he was wrong. He knew Tanner had only one bucket, and it had been left behind.

Where could she be?

Caleb knelt to study the ground, easily picking up the tracks of her shoes. He followed her trail to the gooseberry bush and found the basket on the ground, the green berries crushed underfoot.

Thoroughly alarmed, he quickly found the larger footprints that told him someone else had been there. A large man too, judging by the footprints, and since Abby's footprints had ended there, she'd obviously been carried away.

Who in hell had taken her? Very few people came to that mountain since no gold had been found there. But someone had come that day.

Caleb sprang to his feet and began to follow the trail Abby's abductor had taken.

Chapter Six

Abby regained consciousness slowly. She was aware of the sound of heavy thumps, of a sharp clanging sound. Then the pain hit her. Pain everywhere, on every part of her body.

Memory returned, and she opened her eyes to a mere slit and studied the man who stood several feet away. He was unaware of her wakeful state, busy with whatever he was doing, which seemed to consist of moving several heavy sacks to one side of whatever sheltered them from the sun.

The shelter was a lean-to, she realized, upon discovering three sides of the dwelling were open. It appeared to be made of several poles that had been set into the ground so they would stand upright and hold the canvas that was stretched tautly across the top.

It was a crude shelter, but cleverly constructed. The sides had been rolled up and fastened with leather straps, but could easily be let down if it started to rain.

Her tormentor lifted another large sack and tossed it beside the others. Then he paused and turned in her direction. Abby reacted instantly, closing her eyes and slowing her breath to make him believe she was still sleeping. She could feel his eyes on her and wanted to scream out her fear and anger, yet she could not.

Pine needles dug into her bruised flesh. She could smell their fragrance, mingled with the musty odor of dried hay. Was the lean-to where he kept his animals? It was entirely possible.

Oh, why didn't he stop staring at her?

Abby tried to devise a plan for escape, but she could not. In her condition, the large man would catch her before she could regain her feet, much less outrun him. And as before, he would only be enraged at her efforts to escape him and would beat her senseless again.

Had he raped her while she was lost to the world? That thought caused a new surge of horror.

God, please don't let it be so!

Her ribs appeared to be damaged the most—at least they were more painful than her other parts. Had he broken them when he kicked her? She had to escape from him before he did more damage!

Even though her mind screamed for her to escape, Abigail forced herself to lie quietly, to keep her breath even to simulate a deep sleep. Yet still she could feel his eyes on her.

A sharp nudge against her ribs jerked her eyes open. She stared up at her abductor with hate-filled eyes.

"Awake, are ye?"

His voice was harsh, grating, and she felt terror rush through her, like spiders tiptoeing across her flesh.

Abigail's blood pounded heavily in her ears above the sound of her madly beating heart as the stranger stood over her a moment, gazing in satisfaction at her frail body. Then, with a grunt, he reached down; grabbed her wrist, and jerked her up so hard that her teeth snapped together. Twisting her arm behind her back, he thrust her against his hard body. Shuddering with horror, Abigail turned her head aside, trying to avoid his foul breath and lustful gaze.

"I waited long enough for you to wake up," the man snarled, poking his face a few inches from her own. His eyes were cold and hard. "Now I'm gonna give you something that you won't be forgettin' very soon. And if you satisfy me enough, I might decide to keep you alive, so's I can enjoy you whenever the notion strikes me."

The words chilled her and Abigail swallowed hard, trying to control her terror. She'd rather die than be kept alive for his purposes.

"You can't get away with this," she gritted. "Caleb will find you and he'll see you dead."

"Montgomery won't know a thing," he said, grinning down at her. His eyes held a cunning look. "By the time he knows you're gone and thinks to look for you, we'll be so far away from here that he'll never find you."

Abby's tormentor ran his hand down her back and over her buttocks; she cringed, her flesh shuddering at his touch. She felt helpless against his strength, totally at his mercy, and she knew somehow that he was a man without an ounce of pity.

She had to keep him talking, she realized. Had to keep his mind occupied with answering questions instead of doing what he had every intention of doing.

"What do you mean?" she asked sharply.

"Just that I changed my mind about trapping this mountain. When I'm done with you, we'll be heading west. The traps will catch just as many varmints there as they will here." His smile was evil. "Now shut your mouth! I got better things to do than to talk."

His rough hand moved between them and he squeezed her breast with cruel fingers. Gasping with pain, Abby twisted frantically, trying to free herself, but her efforts only served to make her arms ache more. He continued to squeeze her breast with one hand while the other reached to pull her skirts higher.

No! her mind cried. *Don't let this happen? Oh, God, help me!*

When the stranger's hand slid beneath her skirt and covered the soft mound between her legs, Abby felt a terrible anger surge over her. With a strength born of that anger, she turned her head back to him and fixed her eyes on his ear. Then, quick as a wink she fastened her teeth on that organ and bit down hard.

Howling with pain, her attacker gripped her head with both hands, trying to dislodge her from his ear. Abby tasted blood as she hung on. He struck her sharply and her ears rang; then she turned loose and rolled quickly away. The stranger covered his bleeding ear with his hand and shook his head, spattering blood on the ground where she had lain only moments before.

Abby crawled away quickly, pushing herself to her knees, then to her feet. Swaying unsteadily, she gripped a support pole to hold herself upright. Then, knowing she had only a few moments before the man recovered his wits, she threw one desperate look at her attacker and found him still kneeling, head down, moaning with pain.

Fearing she would never have another chance to escape, Abby whirled toward the forest, running as fast as she could, determined to get out of sight before her tormentor took up pursuit.

She ran mindlessly, as branches tore at her face and arms. Her chest was on fire and blood, mixed with mud and thorns and sweat, flowed from small cuts on her face and hands. Yet still she ran, too terrified to pause for a rest, hearing nothing but the heavy pounding of her heart.

Abby didn't know how far she ran; she only knew the desperate need to escape, to flee from the man who would surely have killed her if he found her. She was aware only of her thundering heartbeat, of her throbbing temples, of the sharp pains that pierced her side with each step she took. Her breath came in stabbing gasps as she raced head-long through the forest, yet she did not stop, did not dare pause for a moment lest the stranger catch her.

But finally, she could go no farther. She sank to her knees, breathless. She could not find the strength to move even when she heard the crackling of branches underfoot and knew that her attacker was nearing. He would surely catch her again, and this time, she would be lucky to come out of the assault alive.

Suddenly the forest was still around her. Not a sound could be heard save for her own breathing. She raised her head and forced herself to face her attacker . . . and her eyes widened.

"Caleb?" Abby's voice was a mere croak as she stared at the man, who must have been an apparition that she'd summoned up from her own mind. "Is . . . is it really you?"

Caleb dropped to his knees beside her and touched her bruised face gently. When he spoke, his voice was harsh. "Abby, what has he done to you?"

She didn't stop to wonder how Caleb knew what had happened to her. His husky voice served to release the tears she had been holding at bay. With a desperate sob, she wound her arms around his neck and buried her head in his shoulder.

"Oh, God, Abby. Please don't cry." His voice was a husky rasp, harsh with feeling. "I'll kill him for this. I swear it. I'll track him down like the animal he is and I'll make him pay for what he's done." Then his voice softened. "Don't cry, honey," he pleaded. "It's all over now. It's over. You're safe here with me." His lips touched her cheek and he stroked her back gently, trying to stop her sobbing. "Please, Abby. Don't cry this way. You'll only make yourself sick."

Suddenly, Caleb pulled her away and gazed down at her bruised face. "What did he do, Abby? What did that animal do to you?"

"He beat me," she said fiercely. "And he intended to . . ." She squeezed her eyes shut tight. "You know," she finally whispered. "He intended to r-ruin me."

"He only hit you?" Caleb had to know. It was a need that gnawed at him. If that animal had ravished her . . .

"No."

Dread settled over him. A muscle flickered in his jaw as he fought for control. "Tell me what he did, Abby."

"He kicked me . . . hard."

Caleb tilted her face up and made her look at him. "Abby, I have to know . . . Did he . . . ?" Caleb knew there was no delicate way to ask the question, but he found it hard to say the words. "Abby . . . tell me . . . Did he do anything else?"

Her eyes widened. "Wasn't that enough?" she asked angrily. "He hurt me. I think he broke my ribs."

"Dammit! I'll kill him!" His face was grim as he gazed at her. "Abby, I have to know. Did he take you?"

"Yes!" she raged. "He took me to his camp and meant to ravish me but when he j-jerked my s-skirt up and t-touched me th-there . . . Well, I was so angry that I bit his ear!" Her blue eyes flashed with rage. "I got loose then and I ran away."

Caleb went limp with relief. Her attacker hadn't raped her. He'd done other damage, but that would heal.

"Thank God," he muttered, smoothing back her hair. "Thank the Lord, he didn't accomplish what he started out to do."

Abby didn't have to ask what he meant. Her eyes were misty as she looked up at him. "I'm so glad you came, Caleb. I was so frightened."

His lips came down to smooth against her forehead. "I'm only sorry I didn't come sooner."

A tear trickled from the corner of her eye and he kissed it away. Her eyes seemed even larger than usual, and there was blood at the corner of her mouth. Was it hers or her attacker's?

Carefully, Caleb wiped the blood away and found a split at the edge of her lips, where she'd been struck. He felt enraged again, but curbed his anger. She didn't need to experience his rage. She had already been through enough.

Caleb studied the curve of her lip. There was a slight puffiness there—a slight darkening that told him she would have a bruise tomorrow. His hand traveled over her side and she winced with pain.

"We'd better get you back to the cabin so I can check you over," he said gently.

Abby lay back in his arms and closed her eyes. He watched her steadily, feeling a need to make her feel safe again. Then, before he could stop himself, he bent his head and brushed a velvet kiss across her mouth.

Abby sucked in a sharp breath. The touch of his mouth was heady, making her senses swim. Needing his strength, she slid her arms around his neck to steady herself. The feel of his mouth, so hot and firm, combined with the warmth of his body, sent a quiver of sensation through her.

Caleb had only meant to console her, had already begun to pull away when he felt her response. The tight control he'd been exercising broke and he crushed her against him. Her lips parted on a gasp and his tongue slid within.

Abby trembled as moist heat spread to her core. As his hands covered her breast and he spoke reverently, she came to her senses and uttered a cry of horror.

What was she doing? She was engaged to another man!

"Don't," she cried. "We mustn't!"

Caleb released her immediately. He met her horrified gaze. What in hell was he doing?

"I'm sorry." He raked a hand across his face, trying to chase away the memory of her lips, responding to his kiss.

"I didn't mean to do that, Abby. I don't know what got into me."

"I was equally at fault," she said. "But it must never happen again."

"That goes without saying," he muttered. "We'd better get you home now." Caleb twisted his lips into a smile. "Need to patch you up."

And he needed to distance himself from her. The best way to do that was take up the trail of that scoundrel who had so misused her.

But first, he would make sure she was locked into the cabin, where she would be safe. Then he would go after her abductor and make him regret the day he had been born.

Chapter Seven

Binding Abby's ribs proved to be a painful task, not only for Abigail, but for Caleb as well. Although he stood behind her while he wrapped her torso with linen, he was all too aware of her immodestly clothed body, and if his thumbs brushed against the underside of her breasts more than was absolutely necessary, he convinced himself it was completely accidental.

Tension stretched tautly between them, and he fought the urge to spread kisses across the soft skin of her shoulder as he put the finishing touches to the bindings and tucked the ends beneath the folds of fabric.

"There," he said gruffly, feeling a need to clear his throat. "It's finished. Now, as soon as you put your shirt-waist on again, I'll see to those scrapes and cuts on your face and arms."

Her cheeks were a bright rosy hue when she finished buttoning her blouse and turned to face him. She kept her eyes lowered, peering at him through a fringe of thick lashes.

"My ribs were the worst," she said softly. "I think I can manage the rest for myself."

"Damn him," he muttered, tilting her chin upward and stroking her swollen lip with the tip of his thumb. "It will take a while for this to heal." His gaze flickered upward, studying the skin around her eye that was turning a bluish-purple color. He touched the bruise gently. "Your eye is going to be a nice shade of purple. More'n likely it'll be swollen shut come morning."

Abby heard the anger in his voice and attempted a feeble smile, which made the blood well up in the cut again. "Oh," she muttered. "I'm going to start bleeding again."

"Let's get this cleaned up so's I can put some salve on it. And then I'll be leaving you for a while."

Panic swept over her and she clutched at Caleb desperately, her blue eyes wide with fear. "No, please. Don't leave me alone here."

"I have to," he replied. "But only for a little while. I can't just let him go, Abby. He might decide to come after you again."

"But what if he comes while you're gone?"

Caleb had already thought about that. He pulled his revolver from its holster and held it toward her. "I'm gonna leave this with you," he said gruffly. "Do you know how to use it?"

Abby shrank away from the weapon, a look of shock on her face. "No, I never had occasion to learn," she said, shaking her head as though needing more than a verbal denial to make him understand.

Taking her hand roughly, Caleb forced her fingers to close around the grip. "You're about to get a quick lesson then," he said gruffly.

He explained the workings of the weapon, making certain she understood how deadly it could be. Then, he said, "Use the barrel of the gun like a finger and point at your target. And if he's coming at you, don't hesitate to shoot."

"I don't know if I can," she said with a quavering voice.

"You can." His eyes were hard, cold. "You showed the stuff you were made of when you escaped from him. But you shouldn't have to use the weapon if you keep the door barred."

"What about you, Caleb?" she asked fearfully. "He's dangerous. And if you leave me your weapon, how will you protect yourself?"

"Don't worry about me, Abby." A muscle twitched in his jaw and his stance was menacing. "I'll be stopping by my cabin to pick up my rifle. And, Abby, when I come back, you'll be leaving here."

Caleb still wanted her to leave? That thought caused a stab of pain. But she wouldn't be driven away.

"We've been over that already, Caleb." She swallowed back her tears. "I have nowhere else to go. I have to stay here. I cannot go back east."

He cupped her chin in one large hand, tilting her face upward to make her look at him. "I wasn't suggesting you leave the mountain," he said softly. "Just this cabin, Abby. From now on you'll be staying with me."

Sudden joy swept over her before reality broke through. "But ... that would be inappropriate," she protested. "What would Mr. Tanner think of such an arrangement?"

Bush Tanner. Dammit, Caleb would have liked to forget the other man ever existed. "He'd like it better than coming home to find you dead," he said grimly. "Pack what you need and be ready to leave when I get back."

"But what if that man ..."

He laid the weapon aside and put a finger across her lips. "Nothing is going to happen to you," he said gruffly. "I won't let it. I'll find him before he finds you." He studied her thoughtfully for a long moment, then said, "I give you my word."

"Promise?"

"I promise."

Unable to stop himself, Caleb bent his head and placed a soft kiss on Abby's lips. It was only meant to seal his promise, yet the moment his mouth covered hers, passion flared between them.

Summoning every ounce of strength he possessed, Caleb set her aside, afraid of the emotion that overwhelmed him. He would be unable to leave her if he didn't go quickly.

"Don't forget," he rasped harshly. "Bar the door behind me."

She nodded, unable to speak after the moment they had shared. She was completely shaken by the kiss ... unnerved. She had responded wholeheartedly to his embrace and she realized she should have shown some restraint.

"Abby!" His voice was sharp as he stood outside the open door.

"What?"

"Bar the damn door!"

Caleb waited until he heard the bar drop into place, securely shutting her away from the rest of the world. Then he turned quickly and strode away into the forest.

Abigail's emotions were a mass of jumbled confusion. She wanted to go home with Caleb more than she'd ever wanted anything else, yet she was afraid to do so. Already she felt too much for him, and since he'd kissed her, she didn't know how she could bear for another man to touch her.

Oh, God, she silently cried, *I'm in love with him!*

She felt stunned by that revelation. When had it happened? She'd only known him a short while, yet she felt as though she'd known him forever. Why couldn't it have been Caleb who'd sent for her? Why couldn't Caleb have been the one who wanted a bride?

Abigail knew she would have found heaven in his arms. He would have made a wonderful husband. He was so generous, so kind, so considerate of her welfare. And not just because he felt honor bound to be, she was certain. He really cared about her. It showed in everything he did.

Oh, if only Mr. Tanner would never return. Suppose, she thought, that she just refused to marry Tanner. Would it be so wrong to back out now, to tell him that she'd fallen in love with another man? But how could she confess her feelings when Caleb had not spoken his aloud? And was she misreading his actions, were they only those of a caring man?

He had never spoken a word of love, had never indicated, except by action, that he cared more than he should. But every deed, every look that he bestowed upon her was gentle, almost worshipful. He had to care for her, at least a little.

But was his caring of a familial kind? Did he think of her as an older brother might? Her heart told her no. His kiss had not seemed like a brotherly kiss, yet she had nothing to compare it with. His kisses were the only ones she'd ever received.

Realizing she was still standing with her hand on the bar, she turned away, determined to be ready when he returned.

If he returned at all.

Caleb stopped by his cabin only long enough to fetch the rifle he'd left hanging on the wall of his bedroom. Then he loped across the valley, taking a shortcut to the place where he'd found Abby.

It took only a short time before he'd retraced her path to the lean-to, where he found the trapper stowing his belongings on two pack mules while a horse stood nearby.

When the stranger became aware that he was no longer alone, his movements stilled. The rope he'd been using to tie the packs in place went slack.

Caleb's narrowed gaze went to the man's ear, which was covered with some kind of poultice. His mouth tightened grimly and the look he turned on the trapper would have melted steel.

The other man's stance was tense, his attitude belligerent. But as Caleb watched him steadily, his mood changed. He appeared almost jovial. "Didn't expect to see nobody else on this mountain."

"Looks like you weren't planning to stay yourself," Caleb said grimly.

"Matter of fact, I was just on the point of pulling out when you showed up." The man turned back to his work, but his fingers were clumsy as they tried to knot the rope around a sack. "I was just tying these packs on my mule; then I'll be moving along."

"By yourself, I presume."

The trapper froze. Then he turned slowly, his stance becoming defensive as he saw the expression on Caleb's face. The trapper's eyes narrowed slightly, and when he spoke, his voice was belligerent. "I don't reckon there's nobody here but me."

"Not now." Menace laced Caleb's voice. It was in the stance of his body, the set of his wide shoulders as he fought for control.

"What are you gettin' at, Montgomery?"

"So you know me."

"I seen you a few times in Victor."

"Just like you saw Abby?" Caleb asked softly.

"I don't know what you mean."

"You know." Caleb's hands clenched again, his knuckles whitening as they itched to strike out. But Caleb fought the urge. The time wasn't right. Not yet.

"I don't go in much for playing games," the trapper said.

"Not with anybody that's up to your weight anyway." Caleb's lip curled contemptuously. "You look for somebody smaller, weaker than yourself. You like to play games with women, don't you?''

"I don't know what you're talking about." The stranger's eyes slid away from Caleb's.

"Oh, I think you understand me completely."

The trapper seemed to shrug his massive shoulders; then he lowered his head slightly. "You seem to think you got some kind of beef with me."

"I do. I don't like the games you played with Abby."

"That little wench? Is that what this is all about? Why, I didn't do nothing she didn't ask for." He touched the ear that he had covered with a poultice of healing leaves. "You shoulda seen how this looked afore I put this poultice on. I woulda bled to death if'n I hadn't found a way to stop it. That little bitch near bit my ear off." His lips peeled back in scorn. "But it ain't over yet! She ain't seen the last of me."

Unwise words, he realized too late. With a roar of rage, Caleb lunged. He struck the trapper with enough force to send them both to the ground. Then he struck the man a hard blow on the nose, feeling gristle crunch beneath his fist. The trapper's eyes watered with pain, and before he could recover, Caleb twisted the coarse black hair in one hand and hit the trapper in the face again.

The blow landed with a heavy thump, and for a moment, the trapper lay stunned. Then, giving a bellow of rage, he rolled away and quickly regained his feet. Before Caleb could guess his intention, the stranger swept up a knife that he'd left nearby. Then he turned toward Caleb again.

"You're gonna regret the day you ever come here," the trapper snarled, making a swipe at Caleb with the knife.

Caleb quickly dodged the knife and kicked the trapper in the belly, watching with intense satisfaction as the man pitched forward, bent double in agony.

Watching the other man closely, Caleb stood over him, grim and silent. When the trapper regained his feet, Caleb closed in again, kicking out quickly as he tried to knock the knife from the trapper's hands. But the trapper managed to keep his hold on the weapon.

The stranger growled with anger as he circled Caleb, his eyes narrowed with hatred. Then he struck out with the knife, slicing into Caleb's flesh and drawing blood. But when he lashed out again, he found nothing but air, because Caleb leapt quickly away, then spun around to kick the trapper again. His foot caught the other man in the ribs, knocking him aside and sending him staggering against the mule's rump. The mule kicked out, and the trapper yelped with pain as the blow caught him on the knee. His leg buckled and he fell forward with a heavy grunt.

Caleb stood over the trapper, waiting for him to regain his feet and renew the attack. Caleb could have finished the fight while the trapper was down, but he was not ready to stop. The man had not felt enough pain, had not paid enough for the injury he'd caused Abigail.

No, he would feel even worse before this fight was over. And when Caleb had finished with the trapper, he'd never dare return to this mountain again.

Caleb waited, but the trapper remained still, obviously playing possum to catch his opponent off guard. But Caleb was ready for him. Ready and waiting. And his opponent had not yet moved.

A frown crossed Caleb's face. Was the man really playing possum, or was he hurt so badly that he was unconscious?

Cautiously, Caleb bent over, gripping the trapper on the shoulder. No reaction.

"Get up," Caleb ordered coldly.

When there was still no reaction to the order, Caleb gave

the trapper a sharp kick. But the man remained motionless, unmoving.

Caleb bent closer, gripped the trapper's shoulder, and rolled him over on his back. Then he flinched away. His gaze narrowed on the blood that spread in a widening circle around the knife embedded in his chest.

Chapter Eight

Abigail had been living with Caleb for three weeks when Bush Tanner made his appearance. It was a bright, sunny day and Caleb had been chopping wood for several hours. He paused to wipe sweat from his brow, then eyed the woodpile, which was already heaped high with split logs. It would be enough to last awhile, but with winter coming on, they would need plenty of wood to keep the cabin warm.

They. His lips curled in a grin. He liked the word that linked the two of them together.

He raised his ax again, bringing it down against the log with a loud whack. The sound of the wood splitting with a sharp crack covered approaching footsteps.

Suddenly, the fine hairs at Caleb's nape stood on end. He turned quickly to see the man he'd hoped never to see again standing a mere ten feet away.

A cold fist formed in the pit of his stomach, moving up to his chest and settling there. Caleb stared at Bush Tanner, hoping the man was merely a figment of his imagination, yet knowing he was not.

With a huge grin, Tanner crossed the distance between them. "Damn, if I ever thought I'd see you again!" he exclaimed, reaching out to grasp Caleb's hand and give it a hearty shake.

Caleb felt numb. He licked lips that had suddenly gone dry. "You been gone a long while for a man who only went to buy traps," he said gruffly. "Thought maybe something happened to you, maybe you wasn't coming back at all."

Tanner's grin spread wider. "You shoulda known better than that, Caleb. I couldn't just not come back." His expression changed, becoming serious. "I had some unfinished business here. Remember? And as to that . . ."

"Caleb!" Abby appeared in the doorway. "Are you about finished? The meal is—" She broke off as she saw he wasn't alone. "Oh, I'm sorry," she apologized, stepping from the house and starting toward the two men. "I didn't know you had company."

A frown crossed Bush Tanner's face as he looked at her; then his smile returned. "Well, I'll be damned, Caleb! Did you go and get yourself hitched while I was gone?" His gaze flickered between the two of them, then returned to Abby. "Damned fine woman you got too. Can't really say as I blame you." He bent closer to Caleb. "If she can cook as good as she looks, you're probably in hog heaven."

Abby stopped beside them, her puzzled gaze flickering back and forth between the two men. When Caleb failed to introduce them, she wondered if she'd interrupted a private conversation. "I'm sorry," she said hesitantly. "I didn't mean to interrupt." She looked at the newcomer, then turned her attention to Caleb again. "I'll just go back inside, Caleb, but if your friend is hungry there's plenty of food."

"Now that's the best idea I've heard all day," the newcomer said. His narrowed gaze met Caleb's. "Aren't you gonna introduce me to the lady, Caleb?"

"Abigail, meet Bush Tanner."

Abigail could feel the blood draining from her face. It couldn't be! Not now! Not when she'd just begun to think he would never return! But it was. Bush Tanner. The man she'd promised to marry.

Gathering her courage around her like a mantle, Abby held out her hand. "I'm pleased to meet you, Mr. Tanner."

He smiled widely, taking her hand and bringing it to his lips. "The pleasure's all mine, ma'am."

"I was beginning to think you had forgotten about me, Mr. Tanner." She flicked a quick glance at Caleb's rigid features. "We both had."

"Forgotten about you?" Tanner's gaze was puzzled. "I'm afraid I don't understand."

"Caleb told me why you had to leave."

"So he's been talking about me, has he? Now, that is a surprise. What has he told you?"

"Nothing much. I know very little about you, except that you are my fiancé."

Tanner's mouth dropped open. "Your what?"

"Fiancé," Caleb said flatly, trying to control the murderous rage that consumed him. "You told me to watch out for her. Remember? Or maybe you already forgot about her."

"No! I didn't forget about her. She's the reason I came back." He narrowed his eyes on Caleb. "But what in hell is she doing here?"

"Watch your language!" Caleb snapped. "And she's here because you told me to look out for her."

"I didn't say to bring her to your cabin."

"No," Caleb said roughly. "You just said find out when she was coming. But she was there when I got to town."

Tanner's gaze moved between them and something

flickered in his brown eyes. "So you thought you'd make use of her until I got back, did you?"

"Mr. Tanner!" Abby gasped. "How dare you suggest such a thing!"

She'd barely uttered the protest when Caleb's fist shot out, striking Tanner a hard blow that sent him crashing to the ground. Caleb stood over him then, breathing hard, ready to deck him again.

"Now, hold on, Caleb," Tanner said, rubbing his chin where he'd been struck. "Wasn't no need of doing that."

"You deserved it," Caleb said darkly. "And you'll get more of the same if you don't watch your mouth."

Tanner crawled to his feet. "Seems like you're mighty protective of my woman."

"Somebody has to be. And if it ain't gonna be you, then I reckon I'll be taking it on."

"I can take care of my own," Tanner said, glaring at Caleb. Then he turned his attention to Abby. "Get any stuff you got stored here and we'll be heading out to my cabin," he ordered.

Every fiber of Abby's being wanted to protest, to scream out against leaving Caleb, yet he stood there, glaring at Bush Tanner, his hands clenching and unclenching in his anger.

She drew herself up straight. "You may leave if you like, Mr. Tanner, but I am not going yet."

"The hell you say!"

Caleb felt relief flow through him. Was Abby going to refuse to leave him? He hoped it was true!

"I do say so. I, for one am hungry, even if you are not. And since I have spent the better part of the morning preparing this meal, I intend to eat it." She stared at the two men. "You two can do whatever pleases you most. Now, if you will both excuse me . . ." She turned away and stalked across the clearing into the house.

The two men stared at one another for a long moment;

then, suddenly a sheepish look crossed Bush Tanner's face. "Guess I went a little haywire there for a minute," he said. "But you know my temper."

"Yes, I do. And you'll not be taking it out on Abby or you'll be answering to me."

Bush rubbed his chin. "Guess I already found that out," he chuckled. "You kinda like the little lady, don't you?"

"If you're suggesting anything improper took place around here, you got ahold of the wrong end of the stick, Tanner. Abigail is a lady. She would never be part of anything that was the least bit improper, nor would I expect it of her."

"I wasn't suggesting anything of the sort," Bush said gruffly. "Fact is, old boy, reckon I got myself a little trouble here. I didn't expect her to be here yet."

"I reckon you didn't or you would have been here sooner."

"As to that, there's a reason why I didn't come back. A damned good reason too."

Caleb forced himself to relax. "No matter. You're here now."

"Yeah. I'm here now."

"We'd best go eat before Abby gets any madder. She can be a bear if the meal's cold before I get to—" Caleb broke off, realizing Abby would not be cooking for him again. Ever.

Tanner clapped him on the shoulder. "We'd better go eat then. But we have to talk, Caleb. I got a mess of trouble here that I don't know how to deal with."

"You'll get used to her," Caleb said. "Abby's a fine woman and any man would be proud to wed her."

"I expect so," Tanner said gruffly.

Over the meal Bush Tanner told them why he was so late returning. "Had the bad luck to get between two hombres that were bent on shooting it out," he said. "I wound up with a bullet hole in my leg. The bullet had to be dug out and fever set in. I wasn't sure I'd live to see the next day." His smile was almost a grimace as he studied Abby's bent head. "If I'd've known you was already here, I'd've tried to send word, Miss Carpenter."

She looked up at him. "I'm sure you would have, Mr. Tanner. But you couldn't know, could you? Anyway, Caleb . . . Mr. Montgomery has looked after me very well."

"Yeah," Tanner agreed. He turned his attention to his food. "Mighty tasty meal you cooked up, Miss Carpenter. Mighty tasty. Ain't had many meals that tasted quite as good."

"You never had even one," Caleb said grimly. "And see that you remember to thank Abby properly when you're done." He shoved a spoonful of mashed potatoes into his mouth, but the food could have been ashes for all the flavor it had. Then he met Tanner's gaze with a level stare. "You'll be needing to take Abby's luggage back with you. Reckon you can take my mules to carry it, seeing as how you didn't bring your own. And you'll need the mule when you go down to find the preacher."

Bush swallowed hard and found himself tongue-tied. He merely nodded his head.

"When you aimin' to make the trip?" Caleb asked.

"Well, as to that, I got some things that need doing before I go back down the mountain."

"See you do them quick then. She's already waited long enough to be married."

"She stayed with you," Bush snapped.

Caleb glared at him. "That was necessary."

"She coulda stayed at the cabin."

"I did at first," Abby explained. Then she went on to tell him about the trapper who had abused her. "Caleb brought me here to keep me safe . . . since there was nobody else to protect me."

"Then I suppose I owe you one," Tanner said. He looked at Abigail. "I'm sorry for what happened, ma'am. A lady like you ought not have to be near scum like that." He pushed back his chair and stood up. "Reckon we need to talk, Caleb."

Caleb glared at him. Did Tanner think the trapper had sullied her? Well, he'd be damned if he'd discuss the matter with Tanner. "Whatever you want to say, you can say in front of the woman you're gonna marry," he said angrily. He bent his head and shoveled another spoonful of mashed potatoes into his mouth.

"Dammit, Caleb—" Remembering there was a lady present, Bush broke off abruptly. "Hell! What's the use?" he growled. He turned to Abigail. "Are you ready to leave now?"

"It will take a while to gather up my belongings," she said, pushing away from the table.

Bush Tanner looked at Caleb, whose attention appeared to be focused on the plate. He shrugged. "I can help you, Miss Montgomery. It will be quicker that way and I'd like to get back home."

An hour later they were on their way.

The minute the cabin door closed behind them, the starch went out of Caleb. His shoulders slumped and he bent his head allowing the pain he'd been fighting to wash over him. He had been a fool to hope, to believe that Tanner might never return.

Damn the man to hell!

Caleb left the cabin, stalked to the woodpile, and took up the ax again. He spent the rest of the day there, and by the time darkness fell and he dropped exhausted into his bed, the pile had grown to massive proportions.

Chapter Nine

Abigail felt numb in both body and mind as, without a backward glance, she rode away from the cabin she'd shared with Caleb for the last three weeks. She dared not look back, lest she find Caleb watching them leave.

Why hadn't her fiancé come before she had lost her heart to Caleb? But Tanner had not, so she must hide her feelings. Must keep him from learning how she felt.

She rode on, feeling as though her heart would break, hoping that in time she would get over the man she had come to love.

She must get over him. She had made a promise, had signed a marriage contract, and now, no matter how much she wished it were not so, she must honor that contract, must keep her word to marry a man she did not love.

That night Bush bedded down in the lean-to with his mule, allowing her to have the cabin alone. She was grateful for that fact, unable to face intimacy with him when her heart belonged to another.

Although she expected Tanner to announce their departure for the valley, and the preacher who would bind them together for the rest of their lives, he remained curiously silent on the subject. Perhaps, she decided, he intended to allow her time to get to know him before they entered into the intimacy of marriage. She was grateful for that fact, yet she knew he would not delay long, since winter was only a short time away.

But as time passed—two days becoming three days, then three becoming four, and still Bush Tanner did not mention leaving the mountain—Abby began to wonder. She would not broach the subject herself, however, because she hoped the delay would allow her to get over her feelings for Caleb, or at least allow her to deal with them before she entered into marriage with another man.

Caleb paced his cabin. He was angry. And each day that passed fueled that anger, causing it to burn brighter and brighter until he realized he must do something to put out the fire before it consumed him completely.

He was jealous, he knew, jealous of a man he'd once called friend. And that jealousy was eating him alive. But it wasn't the real cause of his anger.

No. He was angry because Bush Tanner had not descended the mountain with Abigail, something he must do before he could marry her.

Not that Caleb wanted the wedding to take place. No. To see her belong to another man was the last thing he wanted. Yet he would not have her reputation sullied either.

There was no excuse for what Tanner was doing. Not even one.

Every day since Tanner had taken Abby away, Caleb had made the journey across the mountain to the cabin where Abby now lived. And each day he'd expected to see the cabin empty and the mules gone—a sign that they had left the mountain to wed. But each day, the mules were in place and Bush Tanner was working around the cabin.

A week had passed in that manner, and Caleb's temper had worsened each day until he was finally unwilling to wait a moment longer.

His hands clenched into fists when he set out for the cabin early one morning. He was determined to get some answers to his questions.

Why in hell hadn't Tanner gone to find the preacher yet? Was he taking advantage of Abby? Was he forcing intimacies on her without the benefit of wedlock?

Just the thought enraged Caleb. No way in hell was he going to allow Bush Tanner to take advantage of Abby's innocence. She needed a husband, deserved to be a wife, and if Tanner wasn't willing to marry her, then Caleb would damn well do it himself!

The sun was setting when Caleb reached Tanner's cabin. The door was open and he could see Abigail moving around the room as she prepared the evening meal.

In a chair at the table lounged Bush Tanner, his expression curiously puzzled as he watched her pull a pan of biscuits from the oven.

As though becoming aware of another presence, Bush looked up and met Caleb's eyes. Something that looked amazingly like relief showed in his gaze.

"Caleb," Bush said, pushing back his chair and coming toward Caleb with his hand outstretched. "Come on in and set yourself down. Supper's about ready to go on the table."

Abby swirled around in a flurry of skirts, her heart pounding with excitement at the sight of Caleb. He looked tired and worn, as though he hadn't been sleeping very well.

"Hello, Caleb," she said softly. "It was good of you to call on us."

Us. Dammit! Caleb silently cursed. There shouldn't be

any *us* between them. It was a word that had belonged to Abby and him until Tanner had returned.

Damn the man to hell! He had the gall to stand there and smile, as though he hadn't been taking advantage of Abby.

Caleb's fists clenched in anger, but he forced himself to remain unmoving. And when he spoke, his voice was calm. "Hello, Abby. How have you been?"

She smiled sweetly at him. "Very well, thank you. And you?"

"Not so well."

She looked at the dark circles beneath his eyes. "You look tired, Caleb. Aren't you getting enough sleep?"

"No." His jaw clenched. How in hell was he supposed to sleep when he couldn't stop thinking about the two of them together?

"Perhaps a good hot meal is just what you need. I made fried rabbit and I know how you like it."

Caleb fought the urge to snatch her into his arms, forced his voice to remain calm. "I didn't come here to eat, Abby." His gaze narrowed on the man watching him. "We got some unfinished business between us, Tanner. Something that needs taking care of right now." He jerked his head toward the door, ignoring the other man's outstretched hand. "Outside!"

Abby's expression dimmed and something flickered deep in her azure eyes before she dropped her lashes to hide her gaze. "I see," she murmured, turning back to the stove. "I'll just get supper on the table. Then I'll leave the two of you alone."

Bush Tanner stiffened and his gaze narrowed as he dropped his hand to his side. "You got something stuck in your craw, Caleb?" he asked belligerently.

"There's plenty stuck there, Tanner," Caleb replied grimly. "But it's between the two of us. And I'd like to keep it that way."

Tanner's quick temper lashed out. "Then you'll damn

well wait until supper's over, Montgomery! Abby spent a lot of time cooking this meal and I aim to eat while it's hot."

Caleb's stance became suddenly threatening. "Seems to me like you're putting a lot of things off that need taking care of these days!" he snarled.

"Now what in hell does that mean?"

"Outside," Caleb said grimly.

"No, dammit! I already told you I'm gonna eat the supper that Abigail cooked up for me. Whatever's stuck in your craw can wait until I'm done."

Abby watched the two men, wondering if they'd both suddenly gone mad. They appeared completely unaware of her presence.

"Maybe I don't like waiting for some things to happen?" Caleb said stubbornly.

"What in hell is that supposed to mean?" Bush asked grimly.

"Just that when a man makes a promise, he'd damn well better be ready to keep it . . . or else he'll find himself spitting out his teeth!"

"Is that a threat?" Bush asked.

"It's more than that, Tanner. It's a promise."

"Maybe there'll be more than one set of teeth missing afore the thing is over!" Bush snapped. "Now you gonna say what's eating at you?"

Caleb considered dragging the other man outside, then just as quickly discarded the idea. There appeared no way to keep Abby out of it. He threw her a quick glance. "Since this concerns you, Abby, I guess you might as well hear what I got to say."

Bush look suddenly discomfited. "It concerns Abby?"

Caleb gave an abrupt nod.

"What you want to talk about?" Bush asked.

"About you and Abby. And why you haven't taken her down the mountain yet."

Bush's expression became suddenly sheepish. "Well . . ." He scratched his head. "Fact is, Caleb, I got all these things that need doing first. They . . . kind of stacked up while I was away and—"

"Hogwash!" Caleb snapped. "There's nothing more important than getting the two of you married right away. It's not right for Abby to live with a man who's not her husband."

"She was living with you when I come home," Tanner said. "Had been, by your own account, for more'n three weeks."

"You've been told why," Caleb said grimly. "There was no other way, not if she stayed on this mountain, which she was determined to do. Anyway, if you'd come home when you were supposed to, it wouldn't have been necessary."

"I told you why I didn't come back," Tanner growled. "No man could've traveled when he was all shot up the way I was."

"Be that as it may, you're here now and you're gonna do right by Abigail or you'll be answering to me. You're going down the mountain come morning, Tanner. And you're gonna hunt up the preacher and do what you should have done the minute you got home."

Bush's face reddened, and he looked at Abby with something like an apology before returning his attention to the man facing him. "I can't rightly do that, Caleb," he said gruffly.

"Why in hell not?"

"Because I already got me a wife."

For a moment, there was total silence in the room. Suddenly, Abby's hand went numb and the skillet she'd been holding dropped from her nerveless fingers and struck the stove with a loud, metallic clang. Pieces of fried rabbit scattered everywhere, along with hot grease, which sizzled and smoked as it struck the stove.

She grabbed a towel and snatched up the rabbit pieces, tossing them toward the skillet. Then she spun around to face Bush Tanner, the man she'd come west to wed. "Did I hear you right?" she asked sharply. "You're already married?"

His head lowered and he gazed at the floor as though he couldn't meet her gaze. "Yeah," he mumbled in a low voice. "I guess I am."

Caleb glared at him. "What in hell are you trying to say, Tanner?" he asked. His hands curled into fists, but he controlled the urge to strike out. "You're not married. Leastways you told me you weren't enough times in the past."

"I wasn't married then." Bush met Caleb's look with a sheepish expression. "But things have sorta changed since I went to Colorado City."

Caleb stared at him in disbelief. "Are you saying you got married in Colorado City?"

Bush met his gaze with a sober look. "Yep," he replied. "Reckon I'm saying exactly that."

Caleb was stunned by the other man's words. "Why you lousy son of a—"

"Caleb, stop!" Abby stepped between the two men, hoping to prevent a fight. "It's all right. Really, it is."

Her words only served to fuel Caleb's anger. She was so gentle, yet she'd been so badly treated by a man who had promised to wed her, a man in whom she'd placed her trust. The anger that he'd fought so hard to control suddenly boiled over, and before Bush could say another word, Caleb lunged at him, landed a solid punch on his jaw, and knocked Bush Tanner flat on his backside.

Chapter Ten

"Caleb!" Abby screamed. "Stop it!"

Caleb paid her no heed. Abby might as well have been talking to the wind. Bush had barely regained his feet from the blow Caleb had dealt him when he found himself on the ground again, his jaw feeling as though he'd been struck with a sledgehammer.

As Caleb pulled back his arm to deliver another blow to the downed man, Abby clutched at his forearm. "For God's sake, Caleb. Stop!"

Caleb tried to shake her loose, yet she clung fast to his arm. "Let me go, Abby," he snarled. "He deserves everything he gets."

Bush stumbled to his feet just as Caleb shook Abby loose. Before she could stop Caleb, he struck Tanner another hard blow.

"Dammit!" Tanner roared, shaking his head as though trying to clear it. "You ain't got no call to do nothing like that! What in hell's got into you anyways?" Bush wiped his nose, then stared at the blood on his sleeve. "Dammit, Caleb!" he grumbled. "Look what you done."

"Not half what you've done," Caleb snarled. His stance was threatening. "You made a promise to Abby, Tanner, when you signed that contract and had her shipped out here. You broke that promise when you married another woman."

"Maybe I did, and I'm right sorry about breaking my promise. It wasn't mannerly of me, I'll admit that much." He squinted at Abby from a swelling eye and pulled his split lip into a smile. "Hell, ma'am, I am sorry. You're the kind of wife any man would be proud to have. But the fact is, I went and fell for the widow lady who tended me when I was laid up."

"That's quite all right, Mr. Tanner," Abby said gently. "I know matters of the heart sometimes get in the way of good sense."

"That still don't make it right," Caleb snarled. Abby was being entirely too reasonable about the whole thing. Bush had broken his contract and, in doing so, had sullied her good name. "And you got a beating coming for what you done."

"You leave Mr. Tanner alone!" Abby snapped, glaring at Caleb. "He can't help the way he feels. Neither can I." She looked at her ex-fiancé and smiled. "Don't feel bad, Mr. Tanner," she said. "I really don't mind. I signed on that wagon train not because I wanted a husband, but because I had no other choice."

"I feel real bad about that, ma'am. But you're welcome to stay here if you've a mind to."

"Not with you," Caleb growled.

"I'm afraid I'm not going to be here any longer than it takes me to pack anyway," Tanner apologized. "My widow lady is waiting for me . . . probably wondering why I ain't come back yet." He scratched his head. "I'll prob'ly have a lot of explaining to do about why I stayed away so long as it is.''

"Then that makes it easy, doesn't it?" Abby asked. "I'll just stay here . . . with your permission of course.''

"No," Caleb said immediately. "You can't stay here alone, Abby. You know what happened before. It's too dangerous.''

She lowered her lashes. "Yes, but there seems to be no other solution. After all, as you have already said, it isn't seemly to stay with a man I'm not married to.''

Caleb was silent for a long moment. Then he said, "We could fix that, I guess.''

"How?" Abby asked softly.

Tanner grinned and took himself off. Neither of them noticed he was leaving, but then, they would probably not have noticed if the house caught fire, so engrossed in each other as they were.

"Well," Caleb said carefully, "you came out here to get married to a man you didn't even know. Would it make a difference if you married somebody else?''

"Do you have someone in mind?''

"Yeah, I guess I do." He swallowed hard. "Fact is, Abby, I was thinking of me. You don't seem to mind about my scars and . . .''

"Go on," she said softly.

"Well, I guess I wouldn't mind having a wife. And I'm kinda used to you." Caleb was making a mess of things. He could see it in her eyes, read it in her expression. "We suit each other well enough, Abby." His chest felt tight, and he could hardly breathe. "At least, you suit me well enough. And since you don't love nobody—''

"Oh, but I do," she said huskily.

"You do?''

"Yes. I love you, Caleb.''

He felt as though he'd been struck by a sledgehammer.

Reaching out, he snatched her against him. "Oh, God," he groaned. "You love me? You really love me?"

"You didn't know?"

"How in hell could I?"

His mouth claimed hers in a kiss so intense that her knees threatened to buckle beneath her. And when it was over, he looked down at her with blazing eyes.

"You little idiot. I've been dying of love for you. I thought I was losing you. I had begun to hope before Tanner came back that you cared a little. But you went off with him and never said a word."

"What else could I have done?" she asked. "You let me go without a word."

"Oh, Abby. I've been such a fool. I love you so much. Will you marry me?"

"Oh, yes, Caleb. I will."

His hand closed over hers. "Then let's go home, darling."

That night, Caleb was making his pallet on the floor of the kitchen when the bedroom door opened.

Caleb's eyes widened as Abby moved slowly toward him. Her hair curled around her shoulders in golden splendor, and the gown she wore clung to her curves so lovingly that his body hardened instantly.

"Abby," he muttered thickly, slowly rising to his feet. "What are you doing here?"

"I've come to take you to bed," she murmured, looking at him through a thick fringe of gold-tipped lashes.

Caleb swallowed hard around the lump that had suddenly formed in his throat. He knew he was a fool to ask questions, yet he wanted to give her no cause for regret.

"Are you sure about this, Abby?" His hands came to rest on her shoulders. "You don't want to wait until we're married?"

She licked lips that had suddenly gone dry. "Do you?" she asked breathlessly.

"Hell no," he growled. He combed his fingers through her glorious mane of hair, his eyes dark, slumberous with pent-up desire.

Abby slid her arms around his neck and threaded her fingers through his dark hair. Then she raised her face to his, her gaze beseeching.

As though unable to wait another second, he closed his mouth over hers in total possession, denying her even the smallest breath. He seemed unaware of his strength as he ravaged her lips with the hunger of a starving man.

But Abby welcomed the intensity of his kiss. Her heart beat wildly as she opened her mouth to him, offering the sweet moistness within, withholding nothing of herself. Her arms tightened around him and she could feel the tension in his body, the pure male strength of him pressing against her belly.

Abby gloried in her love for him. Caleb was her other half, the man who made her feel complete. She would follow him to the ends of the earth if he would only allow it.

With a husky groan, he lifted her and carried her to the bed, stretching her out on the feather mattress. When he reached for the hem of her nightgown, she covered his hand with her own.

"Wait," she said huskily.

He drew back, watching her through narrowed eyes. "Have you changed your mind, Abby?"

"No, Caleb. But I want to see you . . ." She blushed wildly, unable to go on.

"To see me what?" he demanded softly.

"Without your clothes."

A grin spread across his face and the look in his dark eyes thrilled her. He jerked the front of his shirt and the buttons went flying. A moment later his breeches joined the shirt, somewhere beyond her peripheral vision. "All of them?" he asked huskily, and she nodded her head.

He peeled the long johns down his hips slowly, as though he were bent on doing a striptease, and all the while he watched her watch him.

"Oh, my," she said, as his underwear joined the rest of his clothes. A blush swept up her cheeks as her eyes traveled the length of him, then lifted to meet his gaze. "I never knew it would be like that."

Her heart picked up speed as she watched Caleb move closer, his stride measured, his intense dark eyes never wavering from hers. His fingers closed around the hem of her nightgown, then he slowly, sensually, inched it higher.

Suddenly, as though he could stand it no longer, Caleb whipped the gown over her head and tossed it toward his breeches.

Abigail fought her shyness as Caleb feasted his eyes on her lush body. "Oh, my, my, my," he murmured. "And I never realized what was under that gown."

Laughing, she buried her fiery cheeks against his chest. But he was having none of that. He lifted her chin and covered her mouth with a hard kiss. Then his lips moved downward, planting moist kisses across her jaw, her neck, and her shoulders. He moved lower still and captured one taut nipple between his lips.

She uttered a moan and arched her body, trying to get closer to him. As he suckled at her breast, Abby clutched his head, pressing him closer, uttering soft moans as she urged him on.

She was almost mindless, nothing but a mass of raw, quivering feelings, when his hand covered the soft mound between her thighs. As she felt his touch, Abby sucked in a sharp breath.

"Easy," Caleb soothed. "I won't hurt you."

He returned his attention to her breast while his fingers worked magic between her thighs. Soon she was mindless

with desire, whimpering with the pleasure he was giving
her. She was unaware of the hard, probing warmth until
she felt the sharp pain, followed by an incredible fullness.
And then he was moving within her, slowly at first, then
faster and faster, lighting a fire that only he could quench.

Her hair dampened with perspiration as she moved with
him mindlessly, desperately seeking, yearning for physical
release.

She felt herself rising, climbing a distant peak, higher
and higher, until finally, with a last blinding thrust, her
body tightened and she soared over the edge into oblivion.

They lay together in the aftermath of their loving, and
when their breathing slowed so they could speak, she
looked up to find him watching her.

"Any regrets?" he asked softly.

"Not a single one," she replied.

"Still want to marry me?"

"More than ever."

He reached for her then and she buried her face on his
neck. It was a beautiful world they shared. And they had
the rest of their lives to enjoy it.

THE WIDOW THIEF

Linda Cook

For Lura Lincoln Cook
and Alan Lincoln Cook

Chapter One

They reached the river by late morning, and halted on the banks high above the ford at Cagarun. The new pack mule, gaudy white beneath crimson trappings, had proved ill-tempered—a last bad bargain among many proposed by the surly monks at the abbey of Saint Mevennus.

If the Bretons intended an ambush, they would be waiting across the water, in the trees beyond the ford. The dense black green of the forest might conceal a number of armed men, and the small footbridge beside the shallows would prevent the pack beasts from straying downstream during the fighting.

Guyon frowned into the morning sun. It did not help that the abbey bell was ringing, sounding in slow but unmistakable alarm, informing all who heard it that something was amiss at Saint Mevennus' settlement. Respect, the abbot had called it. Respect and celebration that Saint

Petroc's bones, brought to Brittany through mischance by a thieving monk of Breton descent, were on their way home to Cornwall. In the face of the abbot's bland malice, Guyon had swallowed a soldier's curse and taken his party out the monastery gates to ride with all due ceremony to the seacoast, to the small bay where Henry Plantagenet's own ship would meet the packtrain and take Saint Petroc's relics back to England.

The slow tolling of the bell had brought the local folk to gape at the procession bearing the saint home. To the small miracles which Saint Petroc had inspired during his sojourn in Brittany was added the greatest boon of all: There had been no armed men among the muttering folk who had gathered at the edge of the abbey fields to watch Guyon and his men ride past. None of the hard-eyed farmers had attempted to oppose the Norman soldiers taking Saint Petroc to the sea, and thence back to Cornwall.

And none of the Breton folk had noticed a smaller group of pilgrims, clad in sober merchants' robes, who had left by the orchard gate of the monastery while Guyon's splendid procession was making its way east to the river road.

Guyon de Burgh brought his archers forward and rode with them down to the gentle bank above the river's edge. Behind them marched twenty foot soldiers and six mounted men in priests' garb, the last of them leading the unwilling pack mule.

At Guyon's gesture, the column halted.

The first priest urged his horse through the line and draped his cloak to cover the short sword lashed to his saddle. He leaned forward and frowned. "I see only two of them."

"Decoys," Guyon said. "There might be others waiting in the trees." He turned in his saddle and looked up the river. "If there are brigands waiting, they will show themselves soon. Bring the pack mule up here where they will mark it, and have the archers ready."

On the opposite bank, two riders nudged their mounts from the darkness of the trees and began to splash through the ford, close beside the narrow footbridge. Halfway across, they saw Guyon's men and halted.

"By Saint Radegunde's holy tits," came the voice beside Guyon, "there's a prize worth stealing."

"Quiet."

"Look at her, Guyon. Just look at her."

"If you cannot hold your tongue until we reach the coast, your horse and robes will go to young Hugo and you will walk with the others. Remember—you're a priest."

"And you are not."

"I warned you, Algar—"

"They cannot hear me. Look at the woman, Guyon. A treasure like that with only one ragged man-at-arms to escort her—" Algar's arm swept toward the strangers in unpriestly abandon. "These Bretons are mortal careless with their women."

Guyon gestured to the archers to leave their bows at their sides and turned back to watch the forest behind the figures crossing the shallows. "One more word, Algar, and you'll walk behind that mule."

The woman was, of course, hesitant to ride past an armed party, but she seemed determined not to turn back. At the moment Guyon's archers had lowered their weapons, she had turned to place a calming hand upon the arm of the old warrior and had begun to speak to him, as if persuading him to continue.

The old man pointed down the river and the woman shook her head. The river deepened and darkened beyond the safe crossing place, and the steep banks offered no place above or below the ford where a horse might reach the abbey road in safety. The lady's choices were clear to Guyon: She could ride past his armed men to reach the abbey road or turn back and lose herself in the dense Breton woods before the Normans could follow.

"Come across," Guyon called. "We will make way."

The lady pushed back the hood of her mantle to raise a face whose beauty was crowned by a coil of shining plaits and marred only by a frown. Guyon's next words fled from his mind at the sight of that long white neck, unadorned save for the pale mist thrown skyward by the shallow rapids of Cagarun. *A pearl*, thought Guyon. She should have a pearl at the base of that delicate neck, resting light upon the pulse below, to adorn the exquisite rose ivory of her throat.

Algar was right. The Bretons were mortal careless, bloodless men to let such beauty travel unattended. A woman half as fair would have the men of Henry Plantagenet's court at each others' throats to walk with her the few feet from Westminster Hall to the banks of the Thames. Yet here, in Brittany's remote woodlands, beauty rode unprotected but for a slouching, unkempt soldier who had seen a score of years since his prime.

The lady's escort was a stringy ancient wearing a hauberk puckered by clumsy repairs, with a dull sheen of rust blooming upon the mail. He had been riding stiffly, his gaze upon the tangled mane of his horse, until the woman saw Guyon's band and halted. Now, listening to the lady's soft words, the fellow did not place himself between her and the army above, but sent his foul hauberk rippling in a careless shrug and waved her on before him.

After a last hard glance at Guyon's priests, the woman gathered her reins and continued across the river; the old man followed, keeping well behind the lady's mare.

If she had not seen the line of priests placed at the fore of Guyon's small army, the woman might have turned and bolted back into the woods.

And if he had not been responsible for thirty armed soldiers, a clutch of complaining men in priests' robes, and Henry Plantagenet's charge upon him, Guyon might have followed her.

"Have no fear," Guyon called again. "We mean no harm."

The woman turned away and spoke over her shoulder to her escort. The old man shook his head and began to mutter.

Guyon frowned. "You have my oath as Henry Plantagenet's man," he bellowed.

"And mine as a priest," muttered Algar. "Guyon, ask her who she is and where she goes. There's no harm—"

"One word more," growled Guyon, "and you'll row yourself back to England in a privy pot."

The shallows flowed silver past the gray fetlocks of the woman's mare as she rode through the ford. The sunlight, filtered green through the canopy of oak and beech, touched richly hued braids interlaced with ribbons of dark silk. Beneath the lady's small booted feet, tasseled trappings winked and rippled, catching dew from the river mist. Her gloved hands reined the mare to a slow walk and guided the mount between the dark pools of deep water that lay at either side of the fording place. Only when she reached the shore and nudged her horse up the riverbank did she turn her face once again to gaze upon Guyon and his small army.

Upon the western shore, the white rush of the river did not mask the sound of the bell. The slow tolling caused the woman to glance up to the high clouds scudding toward the abbey, then back to the richly draped packframe upon the mule. Upon that fine white throat, a deeper flush of rose betrayed the lady's dismay.

The deep silver eyes darkened in curiosity as their gaze reached the oddly peaked form of the sumpter pack and revealed to Guyon that the lady understood what he was about. For a long, exquisite moment, he thought she might speak to him. But she turned away, and raised a slender white hand to pull the hood of her mantle to cover hair of sunlit gold and features that would haunt Guyon's dreams.

She was beautiful. But by all the saints who watched over the besotted, the woman must have been yet another of the ladies who had nearly ruined Guyon's expedition. Three noble Breton ladies, patronesses of the abbey, had tried to dissuade him from leaving and had demanded that he turn the white mule back to Saint Mevennus' chapel to leave Saint Petroc in his new place upon a Breton altar. The women had gathered in the morning shadows of the cloisters to greet the removal of the saint's bones with laments; outside the gates, a score of peasant women had followed the train halfway through the fields, protesting that Guyon bore away with him their only hope for the cure of a number of ailments, including barrenness. Only Guyon's quiet but mortal threat had kept Algar from answering that last plea with an unpriestly suggestion.

Saint Petroc, it seemed, had gained hundreds of followers in Brittany during the few months his purloined bones had rested in Saint Mevennus' abbey. Only the intercession of Henry Plantagenet and his seneschal at Dinan had persuaded the reluctant Breton abbot to surrender Cornwall's stolen saint; every day that Guyon tarried in recovering the relics was one more day for the local Bretons to raise an army of their own to stop him.

If the lady with silver eyes had been with the other women at the abbey to stop Saint Petroc's removal, Guyon might have delayed to hear the arguments. Indeed, he craved the sound of her voice, and envied the unkempt man who rode beside her.

Too soon, the woman turned her mount to ascend the path from the river. Behind her, the old soldier passed close to the pack mule and gave a long, baleful look to the sumpter trappings; he muttered a fulsome curse and spurred his horse to keep up with the mare.

Guyon released the breath he had been holding and

smiled at Algar's smothered snort. The deception was working. The expensive, well-curried mule—with its prominent, richly draped but empty chest tied high upon the sumpter frame—would accomplish all that the cross-eyed beast had been purchased to do. Already the pack mule had proved its value as a decoy in Guyon's scheme.

With regret, Guyon watched the last flutter of the lady's rich skirts disappear at the turning to the abbey road, and he gave thanks to the saint whose bones he protected that his men-at-arms had kept silent as the lady passed.

Guyon turned back to the river and saw that there was no further movement from the far bank. He ordered his men to dismount to water their horses and fill the water skins; he rode alone into the shallows to search the dense face of the forest for signs of movement or a flicker of sunlight upon steel.

Algar soon followed and turned in his saddle to look back at the abbey road. "Spies, maybe. From Dinan."

Guyon shook his head. "The old man is no part of Dinan's garrison. His mail alone would earn him a flogging."

"And the woman?"

"Needs more than a toothless old dog to keep the wolves at bay. No, she's a patroness of the abbey, I'll vow. On her way to tell the abbot that his ill-gotten booty is on its way home."

Algar grinned. "Maybe she'll follow us to get it back."

Guyon frowned. "If she does, and if you so much as look upon her, I'll have you back marching with the archers. And I meant what I said about the privy pot."

The smile disappeared. "Guyon, by the Rood—"

"You are a priest, Algar, until we leave Brittany. Keep your words priestly clean until then."

"—I lost the top of my hair to a tonsure, Guyon. At my age, it might not grow back. And my foot is lame, as you know—"

"Then stop looking at the Breton women as if you'd devour them. If you cannot keep your wits about you, you'll walk—"

"The woman didn't hear my words."

"—from here to the coast." Guyon sighed. "And you will speak no more of tits, holy or—"

"The lady's?"

"—divine."

The abbey bell had been ringing since Constance of Lanmartin passed the men at the ford, feeding the sharp fear that had taken root when she saw the packframe upon the white mule in the Norman knight's train—a burden that resembled, in shape and size, the coffer she had come to recover.

Though he had spoken only a few words, Constance had known the knight at the ford was Norman. No Breton Celt would ride beneath Henry Plantagenet's banner with armed men through Brittany's forests. No Breton knight would give precedence to six stony-faced priests to lead their showy pack mule before the men-at-arms, advising their leader while the archers stood idly by. And no man in these lands had eyes of darkest midnight blue within a strong, sun-darkened face softened only by the hint of a smile.

The temptation to speak to the knight had been overwhelming. If she had asked him—simply asked him what the mule had carried—would he have answered? Would he have ordered back the men-at-arms, thrown back the sumpter trappings, and revealed the coffer to her? And hearing that the reliquary was hers, would he have given it to her?

Constance heard the abbot clear his throat; the vision of the knight at the fording place vanished, and the walls of the abbey were once again about her. It was too late to regret her timidity at Cagarun, and she had only the abbot's garbled tale to lead her to the coffer—and to the knight who had stolen it.

Constance tried to keep her voice steady. "Say it again," she demanded of the abbot. "Say it again, from beginning to end. Slowly."

"Lady Constance, there was nothing to be done. Nothing to say. The soldiers came, with the blessing of the lord regent at Dinan, to take back the bones of their Saint Petroc of blessed memory. We were lucky, my lady, that they did not raise the altar stone and search further. As it was—"

"They stole your relics?"

The abbot's face darkened in embarrassment. "No, my lady. They but recovered what had been—transported— from Bodmin to this place. The relics of Saint Petroc, brought here in mysterious and miraculous ways, through the actions of one Roger of—"

"I heard. The monk Roger stole the bones from the abbey at Bodmin and brought them here and now the English are angry and the Plantagenet sent his men to recover their saint. But tell me, please, of my reliquary— my ivory coffer. It was not yours to give, yet you say you allowed the Normans to take it away with their Saint Petroc. I must have it back or—"

"I asked them, Lady Constance, to leave it behind. But the leader—no courtesy there, my lady—said that for all he knew we had stolen the coffer as well as the bones. And as they fit so well within the coffer he believed—"

"Within my coffer? You were keeping their Saint Petroc within my coffer? I gave it to you—and paid you two silver pennies—to keep it safe in this place. You were to keep it in the crypt, well hidden."

The abbot stepped back. "There were pilgrims, Lady Constance. Hundreds of pilgrims come to pray before the sacred relics. Was I to keep the bones in the woolen sack in which they came to us?''

Why not? Constance closed her eyes and did not speak the words; the coffer was gone, and she would do no good by adding to the abbot's obvious misery.

At her side, old Lanson buckled his sword belt across his patched hauberk and sighed. "Come, my lady. That's an end to it. We'll return to my lord Maner and tell him it is gone."

Huon de Lezay would be at Bulat, making ready to take his place at Lanmartin and in Constance's bed. Angry that Constance had tried to avoid the marriage by bribing Lord Maner, Huon had followed her with a cold gaze yesterday when she set forth with old Lanson. And when she returned, he would have the right—

"No," said Constance. "It is not yet gone. Not until the Plantagenet's thieves take ship."

Old Lanson's sigh deepened into a growl. "What can we do? I can do nothing against so many Normans. We will return to my lord Maner and tell him what has happened here. He will know what to do. He told me—Lady, come back. My lady—"

Half a day past Cagarun, the roads were quiet once again, and Guyon de Burgh gave leave to the men-at-arms to slow their pace. They passed two villages, simple places that seemed to have no news of Saint Petroc's stolen relics and no idea why a small army of Normans was crossing their lands. The folk at the small manor where Guyon had bought ale and bread for his men, seeing the archers with their weapons at the ready, had asked whether the rebellions had started again.

At the sight of six priests leading a burden draped in rich broderie, some villagers had knelt in respect, and some had asked, in all innocence, which holy relic the white mule had borne past them. Algar had been ready with answers, claiming in one hamlet that it was a vial of Thomas à Becket's holy blood, and telling the next group of farmers that it was a hand of Saint Cuthbert. With difficulty, Guyon kept the villagers from milling too close to the pack mule, and had forced a red-faced Algar to scatter among the poorest folk the pennies that the more prosperous faithful had pressed upon him.

A toothless ancient had been cured of an aching head as they passed and had called glory and gratitude upon the Blessed Virgin, bringing the local priest to ask a dumbstruck Algar to allow a special blessing from the relics. Guyon had drawn his sword and cut a good bit of the tasseled trappings from the sumpter pack to give to the village priest, and he had ordered his men to step up the pace until the mule and its hollow burden were well clear of the excitement.

For the rest of that day, Guyon rode slowly, ensuring that his decoy procession would not reach the sea before the smaller group of Henry Plantagenet's emissaries could reach the second encampment far to the west, in a small harbor down the coast. The other party, five priests and nine soldiers, all disguised as merchant travelers, carried with them the true relics of the Cornish Saint Petroc, keeping the bones in their new reliquary well hidden within a clothing chest within a sumpter basket, trusting that Guyon's men would draw the attention of any pursuing Bretons away from the small, fast-moving party.

By late afternoon, the fields they passed were deserted, and the serfs were resting in the wide shade of Breton oaks, sheltered from the hot June sun. In these quiet hours, Guyon's thoughts returned to the ford at Cagarun and the woman he had encountered there. There had been a quickness to act, a quiet courage about the woman that was rare for ladies of her obviously high station. How had she come to be riding on a remote Breton road with only the old man to protect her? And how, when faced with Guyon's small army, had the old man allowed her to make the decision to ride past? There had been no blushes, no posturing or shyness in the lady's demeanor. Only when she saw the pack mule's burden had the lady shown any sign of emotion, a brief moment of confusion in which Guyon had seen the color of a young rose rising upon that exquisite throat.

It was unthinkable—impossible to accept that he would never see the lady again.

Once he had seen the saint's relics safely aboard Henry Plantagenet's great ship *Esnecca*, then to the port at Hantune, and when he had brought them to await the king at Winchester, Guyon would buy passage back to Brittany to seek the fine lady who had passed him at the ford. He would find, no doubt, that she was wed to another, with the children of another man to bring her joy. But he would know her name, and with luck, he would look upon her face once again.

Guyon sighed. With more luck, he might find that the woman had followed him this day, and that the two horses he had sighted at a distance, far behind them upon the coastal road, carried the woman and her man-at-arms. He cast a superstitious glance at the mule's sumpter pack and the place where he had cut the fine cloth to leave a scrap of it with the village priest. If the Cornish Saint Petroc granted miracles to the faithful who had attended his relics at the abbey of Saint Mevennus, what boon might he grant to a sinful knight leading the decoy procession to protect those relics? One look, just one more look at the woman from Cagarun would be miracle enough.

When they reached their camp upon the beach, there would be days of waiting for the long ship that would bring Guyon and his men back to England—time enough for the two riders following the procession to discover the camp. Would it be the lady from Cagarun and her frail escort, and would they wish to treat with him, to ask for one last attempt at a miracle from the relics? Would the lady approach him, or would she send the old man to bring her kinsmen, and wait far from the camp while others negotiated for a look at the relics? However she managed her plea, there might be a chance to see the lady with the silver eyes once again.

Guyon pulled his hand from its gauntlet and touched the hard stubble upon his jaw. The cold Breton sea would cleanse the dust of this journey from his body, and in his small tent at the beach encampment, he would find clothing more pleasing to a lady.

Constance and the lord Maner's man Lanson had followed the Normans to the coast and beyond, to a small bay beside a fishing village where the soldiers and priests had established a well-defended camp upon the beach. This was no fine harbor with close anchorage for merchant ships, but a launching place for small craft. Far out to sea, beyond the pale water of the sandbanks and shallows, Constance imagined she had seen the dark form of a long vessel upon the horizon, sailing west with great speed. Old Lanson had looked as well, but had seen nothing.

The village's single inn—a dilapidated wooden house with shutters banging in the rising sea wind—offered small comfort and even less privacy to the men who came to the coast each year to find work when the pilchards were running near shore. The innkeeper had been surprised to find lodgers at his door so early in the season, before the shoals of fish had begun to come into the bay, and suspicious to see a fine lady propose to spend the night in his best chamber.

The lady Constance took the only decent bedchamber and paid the innkeeper to leave the small room for her alone. The lord Maner's man Lanson bedded down without complaint in the stable loft, choosing that place because it commanded a view of both the camp and the single door of the inn. No doubt he was keeping in mind that the lady Constance, if unsuccessful in recovering the coffer, might choose to return to Lanmartin without him.

Old Lanson would stop her if she tried to leave alone. He had made a great show of tethering both horses—his own brown gelding and Constance's mare—to the post beside which he had spread his bedroll. No one, he had said with pointed words, would get past him to steal either horse in the night.

Constance had returned to the bedchamber to spread her own cloak upon the straw tick and sit upon the narrow pallet. She had been so close to gaining her freedom. During the past difficult weeks, the lord Maner of Bulat had refused to agree to Constance's first proposal of gold for her freedom, but had led her to hope, as he weighed her increasing offers, that he might consider leaving her unwed for the five years she had requested. At last, Constance had offered to add to the bribe her late husband's precious coffer with its soft ivory panels painted in all the colors of the Holy Lands, and the lord Maner had agreed to consider granting Constance's petition. Before his priest at Bulat, he had sworn that he would not give the lady Constance's hand to any man for the next five years, in return for ten marks in gold and the coffer brought from the Holy Lands by the lady's late husband.

It had been a public oath, sworn before the priest and witnessed by Constance's Lanmartin steward, made only days after the lord Maner of Bulat had appeared at Lanmartin without warning to look about the keep and the chapel, obviously displeased that the coffer had been nowhere in sight.

By keeping the coffer hidden within the chapel crypt, the abbey had helped Constance deal with the lord Bulat, who preferred to rob rather than bargain with his vassals.

How could the abbot have known that a larcenous monk from Bodmin—the saints curse him—would steal Cornwall's Saint Petroc, bring the bones to the chapel of Saint Mevennus, and set in motion a dispute which would bring Henry Plantagenet's thieving Normans to the abbey?

Constance threw her saddlebag into the corner. She longed to strangle the robber monk who had brought trouble upon them all. And strangling was too good for the thieving Normans who had followed, too improvident or too parsimonious to bring their own reliquary to carry the bones back to England.

Constance opened the shutters and looked at the far camp. Even if she had time to summon her own small garrison, they would never prevail upon that army of well-armed Normans. No, her only hope would be to approach the camp and appeal to the priests and, if necessary, to trade the last of her gold for the coffer.

Old Lanson was too nervous of the Normans to visit the encampment on her behalf. Constance herself must negotiate with the thieves. On neutral ground, in the presence of the priests, the Normans would not dare to deal unfairly with her, or insult her in more desperate ways. And in the presence of those holy men, the Norman knight who led them must treat her with respect and conceal the desire she had seen in his eyes.

It had been difficult to persuade the six men to keep priests' robes over their small armor and to refrain from bawdiness while Guyon's camp waited for word from the second party and the crew of the *Esnecca*. The fishing village was small, and its folk nervous to have a large, armed encampment with a royal messenger's banner upon the western beaches; it would be days, perhaps weeks, before the inhabitants found the courage to question the army's presence. To keep the peace, and to slow rumors of his position from reaching Henry Plantagenet's enemies, Guyon had forbidden his men to approach the village, nor would he permit them to find women in the surrounding countryside.

There had been two or three Breton youths, barely out of childhood, who had walked along the dunes to spy upon them. A shouted question and a snarl from the sentries had sent them scurrying back to the safety of their huts. The sergeant who had remained with a few men to guard the camp during Guyon's expedition to the abbey had reported no further trouble from the village: It had been days since the fisher folk had given them so much as a cross look.

At noon on the day of their return to the coast, Guyon's sentries had spied the lady from Cagarun ford and her shabby escort upon the road past the dunes into the village. The men who had been sent to buy food from the villagers had returned to report that the lady and her man had taken lodging at the boatwright's small inn. In the late afternoon, the lady had left her mare in the care of the old man, had retired to her chamber, and had not been seen again.

The rising sea wind had become a near gale, blowing straight out of the north, sending great rolling swells beneath the keel of the merchant vessel that had come near the bay. The master had rowed ashore to speak with Guyon upon his return. He counseled caution in the face of the coming summer winds; he was content to lie at anchor and count the gold the Normans had given him. Guyon had paid well to keep the ship ready for use during these four weeks of June, and it mattered not whether the master had his gold for safe passage or for safe anchorage.

Nevertheless, the man was not stupid, and if Guyon did not give the order to sail when the gale had blown by, the Breton crew would become restless and begin to ask questions—questions Guyon would answer only when the *Esnecca* appeared. Only then, with the royal ship standing off the coast, with every last priest and relic aboard, would the Breton sailors learn that they were to escort Henry Plantagenet's own warship across the sea to England—and find the last installment of their gold awaiting them in Hantune.

As night fell, Guyon walked to the sentry post upon the eastern bounds of his camp. The village was quiet save for the sound of gaming and drinking in the inn. Above the common room, there was the soft glow of a taper in a bedchamber window, and a small shadow danced before the flame.

If the lady from Cagarun did not come down to him, or send her man with a message by morning, Guyon would go into the village to speak with her. To see, once again, that long, elegant face and those wide silver eyes. To hear, for the first time, the voice of that vision.

He turned from the flickering, distant light, which even now might cast its warmth upon the lady's fair body as she slept.

The sea wind was not cold enough to keep the fever from his blood. Guyon pulled his tunic over his head and threw it upon the sands. Then he walked into the dark waters of the bay.

Chapter Two

The priests were sleeping. Constance watched their unmoving forms and heard, with dismay, a prolonged, growling snore loud enough to reach her hiding place— loud enough to wake the lot of them, had they not been so soundly asleep.

She had waited too long. Old Lanson had tarried at the innkeeper's table long after the evening meal had ended, and he had insisted upon seeing Constance to her bed-chamber to hear her bar the door against the night before he returned to his bedroll in the stable. Then there had been footsteps below the chamber stair, the sounds of many who would see her if she left the inn, of a few who might try to stop her.

When the inn had subsided into silence, Constance had opened the narrow shutters of her chamber window and had seen the campfires burning high upon the beach and the shadows of men moving among the tents. She had wrapped herself in her dark traveling cloak and slipped from the sleeping house to walk across the dunes to the Norman camp.

This was her chance—her only chance to treat with the English priests without Lanson present. If, as she feared, the Normans would not give her the coffer, she would use her gold to buy a horse from them. Then she would set out upon the coastal road alone, leaving Lanson ignorant of her direction, unable to tell Maner of Bulat and his man Huon where to find her.

Constance watched the sentries long enough to know which of them was the least dutiful. She moved past his slouched form into the encampment of well-stayed tents snapping in the rising breeze.

A short distance away, a small, wind-flattened fire burned upwind of the largest tent, casting its light upon the priests. From her hiding place between the dunes and a pile of fresh-hewed firewood, Constance saw a tun of wine broached and lightened beside the fire and drinking bowls resting empty upon the sands. Unless awakened by mischance, the clerics would spend this short summer night under the stars.

There were soldiers as well, gathered about a larger fire down the beach. Like the priests, the men were huddled upwind of their campfires and settled for the night. Their voices were indistinct, carried away from Constance by the sound of the rising sea.

They would be angry if disturbed, and outraged that a woman had come past the sentries. When she stepped from the darkness to wake the priests, there would be trouble, but the clerics, however loyal to the Norman soldiers, and no matter how drunk, would not allow the others to put unmannerly hands upon her. Not within the camp that guarded the relics of their Cornish saint.

The leader of the soldiers—the Norman knight who had looked upon her with such intensity at the ford—was nowhere to be seen. He might already be asleep within the large tent where the priests had gathered. Constance put the image of his dark eyes from her mind and prayed that, when it came time to negotiate with the priests, the knight would not be present. She would need her wits about her, and that warm azure gaze might leave her speechless once again.

Constance moved closer to the sleeping priests. Beyond them, the great red tent was dark, and no sound rose above the writhing and snapping of its cloth.

A large hand closed upon the folds of her cloak and pulled her back from the tent. Constance stifled a scream and turned to her assailant, a broad-faced man in light mail squinting the sleep from his eyes.

Constance shook off his hand. "I have business with these—"

A low laugh came from the darkness. The sentry recaptured her arm and shook his head. "With these fine fellows? They are priests, woman. Do you not see?"

One of the clerics awoke and grinned at her.

The sentry dragged her closer to the fire, near to the priests. And she saw what had not been obvious from a distance: These were unlikely clerics. Their tonsures were uneven and newly shaven—stark white, even in the firelight. And below the wind-tossed hems of the Benedictine robes, Constance saw boots too sturdy and too costly to be anything but soldiers' garb.

A voice emerged from the darkness beyond the fire. "A sea-maid come to seduce the priests? Do they raise them so irreverent in these waters?"

It was the knight from the ford, emerging from the hissing shallows of the sea, from the far side of the fire. Smiling as if welcoming an expected guest. Gleaming with wetness and salt. Naked as the day he was born.

Constance turned away from the sight of firelight upon long, well-formed limbs. The sentry tightened his grip and muttered a caution.

The knight heaved aside the stone that had anchored his cloak upon the sand, and he began to wrap the cloth about his body. "Let her go, Martin. The lady is here to see me."

The waking priest muttered something that could only have been an oath. Then he giggled.

The half-naked man held out his hand. "Come, lady," he said. "You are late. I had almost begun to despair."

Around the fire, the muttering devolved into laughter. There would be no help for her from these drunken brigands dressed as priests.

The Norman smiled. "Come now. I have wine to warm you." He made a small gesture; the sentry stepped away.

Constance did not hesitate. One man, however large, however naked, was less of a threat than the score of false priests and sniggering sentries surrounding her. He was the leader of this band of soldiers and drunken, oddly garbed priests. He could return the coffer to her, if it pleased him.

Constance crossed her arms over her billowing cloak and walked toward the Norman. There was no malice in his strong, firelit features. If the man's actions belied his appearance, Constance would not hesitate to defend herself; one naked, unarmed brute would be no match for the long dagger she carried beneath her hem, sheathed in her boot.

He led her west from the firelight, past the larger tent with the armed men, keeping to the hard-packed sand at the high waterline. Ahead were darkness and a small red glow.

When she pulled her hand from his and hitched up her skirts to keep them from the damp, he did not renew his touch upon her. Constance held back and let the distance between them lengthen. Just ahead, where the dunes gave way to solid ground, lay the narrow track to the village.

"You could go back to the inn," came the voice ahead.

The Norman was walking steadily, speaking as if to the night sky, letting the wind carry his words to her. "I will not stop you. If you stay, do not expect to persuade me to give you the relics; nor will I deliver them to you in payment for a quick night's tumble. Take the mule—"

"I am no thief. And I am no bawd."

He turned to her, his hands upon his barely covered hips. "If you go, do not sneak back to try to steal from the priests' tent. I will not fetch you away from the sentries a second time."

Ahead, in the darkness, glowed the faint red of a charcoal brazier set within the entrance to a small tent. His tent.

Constance stepped back. "I do not want the relics. They are yours—Bodmin's. The abbot at Saint Mevennus told me. I have no wish to take them."

There was a brief bark of laughter from the Norman.

Constance flushed. "Once our abbot knew they were stolen, he gave them to you right enough."

The Norman nodded. And waited. "And you, lady?" he asked at last. "What do you want? The chance to touch them, to pray beside them for some miracle of your own?"

"The coffer," Constance blurted. "The reliquary. It was mine—it is mine—and I had given it into the safekeeping of the abbot."

The Norman shrugged. "The priest said as such. But we found the relics fitting so well within the casket that it might have been made to hold them. So I brought it along."

"You must give it to me. I need it."

He laughed. "Not for many years, I trust." His gaze lingered upon the wind-wrapped lines of her body. "Lady, you would be wasted as a saint."

Constance raised her voice. "I need it now. Before the end of a fortnight. Or your theft of it will cause me great trouble."

"A Breton monk's theft of a Cornish saint caused the

trouble, my lady. I did nothing but recover Bodmin's property by the decree of Henry Plantagenet.''

"Your king does not want my coffer.''

"He's your king as well, my lady, and you should call him such. And he might want your coffer. It's a rare piece, worthy of a saint.''

"Surely your King Henry would not want to keep the relics in a stolen chest. And it is not a proper reliquary, not for a Christian saint. It's a Saracen thing, made by heathens in Palestine.''

The Norman shrugged. "I found it before the altar of the abbey. It is not so heathen it cannot hold a saint. Ask your abbot of Saint Mevennus—it was he who put the bones within.''

Constance averted her eyes from the slow descent of the cloak wrapped about the Norman's nether parts. If he shrugged again, the last shred of decorum would fly away in the rising wind. "Heathen or not, it's mine. Mine, do you hear? I put it in the abbey for safekeeping. It was not the abbot's to give to you.''

"If that is so, then where is the reliquary stolen with the saint?''

Constance sighed. "The monk brought them in an old woolen sack. It was wrong of him, and—''

"Come, lady. Would a monk—even that thieving clerk—carry the bones across the sea in a woolen sack?'' The Norman shrugged and tightened the knot of fabric at his waist. "The wind is rising again. We will speak in the tent.''

"I think not.''

"It is warmer within. Believe me, lady, I will not give you the reliquary if you keep me out here in the night wind.''

"And will you give it if I come with you?''

He took her hand and led her to the tent. "I will give you nothing, lady, save my promise that no harm will come to you. When you have finished plaguing me with your demands, you will go back to the village, no worse for my company."

Constance cast a look behind her. The lights of the camp were smaller now, and the village but a few yellow points of fire, dimmer than the stars above.

"I mean to speak with you, lady. Beyond words, you must decide."

A guilty flush warmed Constance's face. Had this Norman looked into her mind, seen her foolish thoughts?

He opened the tent. "You were bold enough to walk into a camp full of men in their cups. Will you not speak with me?"

"I came to speak with the priests. Such as they are."

The Norman drew a long breath. "What do you mean?"

Something in his tone warned her not to speak of the untidy, crude tonsures on the pates of the leering priests. They might not be priests at all, but scoundrels garbed to deceive. Constance pulled back. "Your priests were drunk, sir. You tell me you need a fine ivory coffer to take the relics back to England, yet you have brought careless, ill-spoken priests to care for them."

There was a long silence, a dark stillness in which Constance became aware that they were far from the others, too far to cry for help. She stepped away from the tent. "You do Henry Plantagenet no honor, taking what you will from the abbey, stealing the property of a defenseless widow—"

"You agree then," the Norman began at last, "that we must speak. You seem fearful of a stranger's tent. I will tell you my name, if you are of a mind to hear it."

Constance fell silent. The Norman seemed to have forgotten her words about the priests. The hint of danger had passed, and she must not blunder again.

"I wish to hear it," she said. In the faint red glow of the brazier, Constance saw the Norman's dark gaze upon her;

she sought to keep her voice from betraying the tremor in her throat. "Your name, sir?"

"Guyon de Burgh. Emissary of Henry Plantagenet."

"I am Constance of Lanmartin. Vassal to Maner of Bulat."

His gaze flicked lower, then returned to look into her eyes. "I know something of the lord of Bulat."

"It is his coffer you have stolen."

"You said it was yours."

His voice was low, roughened with an emotion Constance feared to discover, breathing provocation into simple words that should not have sent her heart pounding. Constance drew a long breath and turned her gaze to the dark sea. "I promised it to him."

"Tell him you will recover it when the relics reach Bodmin, if the Cornish priests are willing to give it up."

"Bulat is not a patient man."

The Norman called Guyon frowned. "So I have heard."

"Then you see that you must give the coffer back to me now, before you sail."

He shook his head. "I cannot."

Constance cried out in rage. "Why not? By the time you travel to Bodmin, it will be too late. I have only a fortnight to keep my promise."

"Or?"

"Or I will be wed to Huon de Lezay, a man no better than a beast."

Another long silence. Once again, the Norman held open the tent. "Come within," he said.

"Not with an unclothed man."

"I was bathing in the sea when you came into my camp— uninvited. I intend no insult."

Constance stood silently. Through the opening of the Norman's tent, the brazier cast a narrow spear of crimson upon the sand.

Guyon shrugged and entered the tent. "Wait, then, until I am robed."

The wind snapped the cloth back to cover the Norman's broad shadow.

Constance turned back to the camp and took a few steps toward the distant fires; the Norman called Guyon did not emerge from his tent to stop her. She saw that the men in priests' robes were fully awake and back in their cups.

The oldest priest, the one with the bandaged foot, started at the sight of her and muttered a bloodcurdling oath. He looked again and began to smile. "Back for a visit, sweetling?"

Their laughter followed her back to the Norman's tent. Constance considered retreating to the village track running above the dunes. "If you go, do not return," the knight had said. "I will not protect you a second time."

Constance set her teeth. Her choice was clear: one night in the tent of a half-naked, intransigent Norman scoundrel who might, if she could change his mind, give her the means to purchase freedom from Bulat's plans; or a lifetime, however short, with the brutish Huon de Lezay.

The Norman called Guyon stepped from his tent, dressed in dark chausses and tunic. Without a word, Constance swept past him into shelter.

Within the hard-stretched walls of cloth and leather, the wind's pulse was a muffled, snapping presence that made the brazier coals flare red at its beat. A heavy length of wool lay pegged beside the bedroll, and beside the fine saddle pack was a tumbled heap of clothing.

With a gesture of courtesy, Guyon motioned Constance to the bedroll and moved to the opposite wall to settle himself upon the saddlebag. "Wine?" he asked.

Not for the world would Constance stretch her arm to take the wineskin from the Norman's hand.

"Had I expected a fine lady, I would have brought a drinking cup."

Constance shook her head. "I need no wine. I need my coffer. I'll buy you another in the village."

The Norman's brows went up in surprise. "Come, lady. Do you think I will bring the saint's bones back to Henry Plantagenet in a planked box smelling of fish and ale?"

The cold dread within Constance's chest began to loosen its hold. "I would find a clean, decent—"

"Tell me—if you have such need of that cursed box, why did you leave it at the abbey?"

Constance met his gaze. "For safekeeping."

The Norman's mouth curled into a deep smile.

She bristled. "The abbot is an honest man. I did not expect Henry Plantagenet to send an army to steal the coffer from him."

He ignored her tone. "And why did you promise it to the lord Maner of Bulat?"

His smooth, reasoning voice sent a wave of anger through Constance's spine. "To seal a contract," she said. "It is mine to do with—"

"—as you will." The Norman took a small stick and began to poke the coals into life. "So you have said. Many times." The hint of a smile returned and sounded in his voice. "And why did the lord of Bulat not appear at the abbey to collect his new property? Or follow me here to ask for it himself?"

Constance pulled the damp hem of her mantle from her boots. She shifted impatiently upon the bedroll.

"You are not comfortable?"

Constance ignored the question—and the message in the Norman's eyes. "Bulat did not know until yesterday that I had left the coffer at the abbey."

Guyon laughed. "I see you trust the lord of Bulat as well as most do. So," he said at last, "you had hidden the chest at the abbey against the day you would use it to seal your contract—not a marriage contract, as you said."

She looked up and saw, in his face, unspoken desire as strong as her own. "Not that," she said. "The antidote."

"An antidote to marriage?" He smothered a smile. "My lady, you'll have no need of gold in this life. Hundreds will pay you well for your secret."

Constance frowned. "Do you speak so before your lady wife?"

He raised his gaze to her face and said slowly, "I have no wife."

"You said—"

"An antidote to wedlock might have saved me two bags of gold and a piece of fine meadowland to dower my sister when she was set to wed the costly young lord she had chosen." He shrugged. "We were speaking of your bargain. You say you needed to bribe Lord Maner from giving you in marriage."

"To a landed woman, such agreements do not come cheap. I have given Bulat all he asked but the coffer. I need it now. Right now."

"What else did you offer?"

Constance sighed. The man's questions were becoming bolder, as if he meant to have from her, in this short summer night, the history of her life. Would the tale move him to relent and give her back the coffer? "I had the lord of Bulat's word that if I delivered to him the Saracen chest, two silver trenchers, and ten gold coins, he would leave me unwed for five years."

The Norman laughed and drank again from the wine-skin. "And you believed him?"

Constance's breath left her in a horrified rush. "Of course I did. He gave his word before a priest."

"You were foolish, Constance of Lanmartin. You would have lost your precious coffer to Bulat and found yourself wed the next day."

"He swore—"

"Bulat—any man—would be mad to let you keep land

undefended by a strong lord for five years, all for the sake
of a few gold pieces and a painted ivory chest. He would
have taken your treasure—"

"The lord Maner gave his word—"

"He would have taken your treasure, I said, and wed
you to the first lord who offered a decent bride price. Or
given you to another as ward. A noble virgin—"

"Widow."

He raised his brows. "A noble widow with lands must
be protected. Bulat's word to you would have been as
nothing to his vows to his own lord, and beyond that to
King Henry. He has a sworn duty to defend his vassals'
lands—all of them. If his promise to a marriage-shy widow
would leave her lands undefended, then it would be his
greater duty to place a man upon her lands."

"But not within her bed."

The Norman shrugged. "How better to tempt a man to
keep your lands safe? Are your lands so rich that a man
would wed just to have the rents, or are they wilderness,
as so much of this country is, and useful only to defend
Bulat's fields?

Constance closed her eyes. "If, as you say, I'm unable
to hire a garrison and to know when to use them, then
why speak to me of duty and defense and vows? I think
you are kin to Bulat."

Guyon ignored the insult. "If your garrison is armed as
poorly as the man-at-arms you ride with, then Bulat has
good reason to refuse to leave you in charge."

"He's not my man."

"Then whose man is he? Have you none of your own
to protect you?"

"I came here to recover my property, Norman. Not to
receive your insults. The old man Lanson is from the lord
Maner's garrison, and he will take the coffer back to Bulat."

The Norman's mouth twitched briefly. "And he will also
take care that you do not bolt into a convent or into the

forest to avoid your lord's orders." His gaze passed over
Constance in lazy appreciation. "Lord Maner is a fool. I
would have sent ten men to keep you from widow thieves
looking for lands to wed." The twitch deepened into a
smile. "And another twenty, lady, to keep you from the
hands of lusting suitors, who would want you even if you
were landless." He paused. "He must have sent a greater
escort for you. How did you evade them?"

The Norman was a warlock who could see her thoughts,
or he had spies abroad to tell him of Lanmartin's troubles.

"You tell me," Constance said.

"I believe you left Bulat's escort upon your lands, to
strengthen your own garrison, with some false tale of invad-
ers spotted off the coast. Then you left with the oldest
and weakest of them to fetch the coffer, half intending to
remain at the abbey and send the old man back to Bulat
with the relic box."

It was impossible to stop the crimson suffusing her face.
"You seem well informed, Norman. How long have your
spies roamed these lands?"

Guyon's smile disappeared. "No spies. I know how these
things are done. I can guess how you would go about
ridding yourself of your lord's control."

"And how do your women deal with you?"

"Who?"

"The women who have used such ploys to evade you."

The Norman's features darkened. "I have never tried
to give my women kin in marriage without their consent.
And no woman has had cause to evade me. I do not go
where I am not desired, my lady."

Constance edged toward the opening in the tent. "Then
I bid you good night, my lord."

"Stay. I will take you back to the village."

Panic coursed through Constance's spine. "That is not
necessary."

"Nevertheless, I shall."

"No—thank you."

His hand closed easily about her arm. "You disappoint me. You have given up your coffer so easily, after riding in pursuit of it over a long, difficult road."

Constance stiffened. "I recognize the impossible. I am not stupid, my lord."

"Guyon. I have told you I am Guyon."

"Guyon."

"And I would wager that you will never reach the inn."

"It is not far—"

"No, the inn is near enough. And you have a dagger in your boot to protect you from my sentries, if you do not cut your leg to ribbons fetching it forth. No, my lady Constance, you have no thought of returning to the inn, where Bulat's man awaits you. You are running away."

Constance pulled her arm from his grip. "Are you a crony of Lord Maner to accuse me thus? This is no care of yours."

He grimaced. "It is, my lady. If you disappear, however briefly, after spending one night within sight of my camp, I will be blamed."

"Are you such a whoremonger that all would suspect you of abducting a widow and debauching her within the same camp that protects the relics of your saint?"

He sighed. "Put up, my lady. I am no whoremonger, nor do I steal rich widows to wife. Quite the opposite."

It was impossible not to ask. "Why, then, would they suspect you?"

"It would not be the first time I helped a widow lady to avoid a marriage she loathed."

Constance smiled and drew breath.

"No." The Norman turned his face from her. "Tell me no sad tales of cruel marriages and escape. I have done with such matters."

"Just give me—"

"By Saint Magnus' great toe, I will give you nothing. I

will bring all I took from the abbey back to Henry Plantagenet and hope—''

"Hope what? That none will hear that you robbed—''

"I did not rob—''

"—and left a defenseless woman—''

"Cease." His roar sent the wind-bellied fabric of the
tent back out to meet the breeze.

"Hope what?" Constance shouted back.

The Norman's face darkened. "Hope that Henry Plantagenet will leave with me the lands he had given me before
the trouble. Before I listened to a woman's tales of widow-
hood and cruel lords and disgusting marriages."

"Then you were once a widow's champion."

"I was once a great fool, madam. For the woman was
no widow, and her lord no monster. I was cozened into
taking a lady from Salisbury to Saint Cross at Winchester.
She wished to seek refuge there, she told me."

"And you were punished? Is Henry Plantagenet so
cruel?"

"Henry Plantagenet is a fair lord and king, but not such
a fool as I was."

Constance raised her brow.

"The lady was no widow, and her lord husband far from
dead. She cozened me with tales of a forced wedding, and
she sent word to her lover to meet her at Saint Cross. And
I—the great fool I was—took her two days across country
to meet her leman and betray her husband."

"You did no crime. The fault was with the lady."

"The lady's brother saw me bring his sister into Saint
Cross. And brought the wrath of his order and King Henry
upon me."

"The lady's brother was a monk?"

"A priest. And King Henry's chief scribe."

Constance sighed. "Worse luck."

Guyon made a small gesture of hopelessness. "Since the
trouble with Thomas à Becket, the king cannot risk the

Pope's disfavor. He could not ignore this matter of relic theft, nor could he overlook the debauching of a priest's sister."

"Debauching?"

He signed. "You may stop your shrinking, lady. I did not debauch her. She showed no interest in anything but reaching Saint Cross—and her cursed lover, as it turned out. No, there are women enough in the world without turning to sisters of priests—"

"How many?" What woman, however lovely, however well wed, could look upon this man with the face of an angel and Satan's own dark eyes and pass him by?

The Norman looked up, as if seeing her for the first time. He moved back from her, as if to see her more completely, head to toe. He shook his head, as if to dispel a vision.

Constance moved again toward the opening in the tent. "It grows late."

He rose and stepped before her. "As I said, I will see you safely back to the village. I will not let it be said that I stole a woman in this land."

"With your stolen saint's bones within sight."

"You have the right of it."

Constance sighed. There might be time, after he left her at the inn, to slip away again and start back to the abbey. There would be no use in further appeals to this man. He was resolved to keep the coffer, and he had enough trouble behind him in Winchester to keep him to the word of his duty and more.

A bold thought intruded into Constance's mind and would not be quelled. She drew a long breath. "There is no chance . . ."

The Norman raised one brow and waited.

"There is no chance you would allow me on your ship, to go with you, to appeal to your King Henry to return my coffer?"

"No," he said. "Bring your cloak and follow me."

Constance bit back her next words. She would be compliant and give this man no further reason to suspect her intentions. Compliance would discourage the Norman from seeing her inside the inn, would keep him from watching her shut and bar the bedchamber door, would lull him into returning to his camp before dawn. And when he left, she would slip from the inn a second time, leaving old Lanson behind.

"Yes," Constance said. "I am ready."

He hesitated.

"I will follow close, my lord."

Together they crossed the windy beach. They were nearly past the large crimson tent when the flap erupted to expel two staggering figures. The bulkier of the pair swung a beefy arm at the other, missed, and collapsed into the sand.

"Damn you for a whoreson pirate. You and your cursed dice are the devil's own work—and what will I tell my sweet Nan when I come back without my silver pennies? She'll let me nowhere near her sweet—"

The other figure wove its way carefully toward the first. "Come, Algar. Your whining will wake our lord and his new doxy, and he'll—"

"Thing. God's bones," the first figure lamented. "I hate to come near the woman without silver, for her lust for coin outstrips her need for my—"

"Silence." Guyon's word sliced through the brawling complaint.

Constance edged away, only to feel de Burgh's hand close upon her shoulder.

"My lord," began the more sober of the two. "We were but debating—"

"The virtues of chastity," added his spread-eagled companion.

"Silence," repeated Guyon. "When I return, I'll see you both silent and abed or I'll—"

"You threaten these priests?" Constance said. "When Henry Plantagenet's men last threatened a priest, it ended in murder, did it not?" She turned to Guyon. "It is beyond my understanding that you refuse to take your fine Saint Petroc's bones from his stolen coffer—my coffer—for fear of disturbing them, and yet you offer the saint a much greater insult by leaving his relics in the keeping of these drunken, dicing, whoring—"

Guyon seized her arm. "Walk on."

She shook free. "—poor excuses for priests. If your King Henry—"

"He's—"

"—and my King Henry," Constance added with malice, "wants to avoid offending the Cornish abbot, why did he neglect to send proper clergy? These men are no more priests than I am—"

"Be silent, woman."

"—that brigand's sweet Nan." She shook free again. "Give me my coffer, Lord Guyon, and I will forget I ever saw how poorly escorted your Saint Petroc left this land for his own."

A heavy shadow heaved itself up from the sands and groaned. "Your pardon, lord. I make a sorry priest. If it had not been for my swollen ankle, I'd not have asked to try it—" He hiccoughed and turned his gaze to Constance. "Sorry."

Constance turned away and made for the sentry line. She had suspected the six drunkards were not priests, and they had now abandoned their poor attempt at disguise. The camp had become a more dangerous place.

Beside her, his long strides easily keeping pace with her panicked scramble, the Norman was speaking. A sentry moved into Constance's path.

"Tell your man to move aside," Constance demanded.

"I'll go alone from here. When you reach England, tell your King Henry—our King Henry—that—"

"Tell him yourself," the Norman said. "You, my lady, have seen too much in my camp. I will have to bring you with me."

"I saw nothing." Constance picked up her skirts and saw that the track to the village was but a short distance beyond the sentry. "Nothing. And I will speak to no one."

The Norman laughed. His hand was upon her arm, ending her hope of escape. "I have known you but one brief hour, Constance of Lanmartin. But I have heard enough to learn that you speak too much—and without care. By tomorrow, half the county will be in arms, ready to take back the relics from a band of brigands robed as priests."

Constance stood as still as her trembling legs would hold her. "Then you are brigands," she said.

"No, not brigands. Henry Plantagenet's men. But there is not, as you have guessed, a priest among us."

"That—that is no sin. I will not speak—"

"They are men-at-arms, damned fine archers," he said. "They acted their parts because Winchester had no more priests to spare."

"None to spare? For this? The abbot told me there were five priests with you."

He stared at her for a long moment. "He was wrong," he said at last, "and I will not have you stirring up the local lords to discredit us and get your damned reliquary back in the confusion. With your careless words, you would have Brittany at war with us before we reach England."

Constance had heard tales of Henry Plantagenet's cruelties, rumors of men who had crossed him and disappeared into Norman dungeons. "What will you do?" she asked.

"Keep you silent—"

"You would not!"

"—until Winchester," the Norman said. "And if you

would keep your tongue, then keep your dagger in your boot until I'm rid of you in Henry Plantagenet's court. You may tell him your tales of Maner of Bulat."

Behind Constance, the windblown surf pounded in the night. "You intend to take me with you to Winchester?"

"I do. Moments past, you were pestering me to take you across the sea."

"Not with those animals in priests' robes. You said you wanted no trouble."

The Norman sighed. "Go easy on them, Lady Constance, and there will be no trouble. I have every hope that they will survive the voyage very well indeed."

Chapter Three

At dawn, a rider came pounding down the packed, damp sand above the tide line and brought his mount to a skittering halt before Guyon's tent, shaking Constance from the uneasy, waking trance in which she had spent the early hours of the morning.

Thin sunlight pierced the gloom as the rider wrenched open the door flap and heaved heavy shoulders within. "Guyon, you lazy cur, abed at dawn? You'll—" The bloodshot eyes closed once and then opened to stare at Constance's pale face above de Burgh's bedroll. "Christ Jesus, my lord wastes no time. And where did he find you, pretty thing?"

Constance reached for her boots to find the dagger sheathed between the layers of leather. They were gone. The Norman had taken them from her side, leaving her without a weapon in this camp of strangers.

Over the sound of the intruder's laughter, Guyon's voice rose in lazy authority. "Find her? No, she found me. Come out here, William, and leave the woman be."

The flap dropped again. Constance scrambled from beneath the blanket and dragged her mantle over her shoulders. Her boots were in plain sight beside the small brazier, set on their sides to dry. The dagger was untouched.

"A fisher maid, Guyon? A prize so fine from that miserable village? Fine or not, she'd best not be married, this one." Constance heard the sound of a fist pounding solid flesh. "Eh, Guyon? I'd think you'd be finished with the married ones for a time."

"Be silent. She's no fisher maid. She's—"

Panic raced down Constance's spine. If the Norman lord told her name to his man, word would spread through the whole county that the widowed lady Constance of Lanmartin had spent the night in a Norman army encampment in the tent of a Norman lord.

She dropped the boots and darted out into the sunlight. "Yes, I am—a fisher maid." She glared at Guyon. "And my lord here is taking me to Winchester with him."

A low whistle came from William's lips. "And a fine-spoken fisher maid with a fine lady's mantle upon her. Who is she, Guyon?"

"Nan," Constance said. "I'm Nan. Guyon's sweet Nan, and I'm not wed, and I will cause your lord no trouble. Not here, nor abroad." She looked into the man's astonished face. "And the mantle is mine. Not stolen."

William smiled. "Algar once knew a maid called Nan—"

Constance stepped back. "I'm not that one."

"Sweet Nan, he called her, for she had the best—"

Guyon stepped between them. "You have a message?"

William coughed and turned to de Burgh's stony face. "Ah, yes. The priests send word that all is well, and you're free to sail."

"The priests? Where are those priests?" asked Constance.

"You're free of speech for a fisher maid," Guyon snarled. "If you cannot learn silence, girl, I'll leave you here on the beach."

Constance smiled. "Will you, my lord?"

He kept his gaze upon her as he spoke to William, giving her silent warning not to speak again. "What more, William?"

"They put to sea just before dawn when the wind calmed, a few miles down the coast. They will come for you by midday and anchor outside this bay, as agreed, and wait for the fishing cogs to bring you out. If the weather turns bad again, have your merchantman pick you up and sail for Guernsey when it clears, and find the *Esnecca* in the lee of the islands. She won't sail for Hantune without your merchant ship as escort."

Guyon nodded. "Go see Algar in the red tent there, and tell him to light the beacon fire. And find yourself bread and ale." He turned to Constance. "And as for you—Nan—if you're coming with me, see to the bedroll and drag the brazier out onto the sand."

Being sweet Nan rather than Constance of Lanmartin had its drawbacks. Constance smiled again, over set teeth, and began to assemble the Norman Guyon's possessions. He was not untidy for a soldier on the road, but the tent's brazier was unwieldy and the soot unavoidable.

Guyon had left her to these tasks alone. He walked, leaving his fine gelding upon the picket line with the other mounts, down the sandy track to the village. He returned to find Constance watching a green-faced, belching soldier take down the tent.

"Your escort was as careless as he was ragged," he said. "The old man was gone before dawn, the innkeeper said."

"He's looking for me." Constance heard the tremor of remorse in her voice and steeled herself against its return.

Guyon shook his head. "My sentries saw no one approach this camp after you. The old man went south from here and took your horse and saddlebags with him. He asked no questions in the village, and he spoke to no one but the innkeeper, who stopped him for his ale money." He raised his brows. "They demanded a silver coin from me for your own lodging, my lady."

"I paid that brigand when I took the chamber—"

"So I thought. But my silver and a few words of caution will keep the innkeeper and his wife from raising the alarm."

Constance turned from Guyon to watch his bundled tent dragged away to the pack mules. The army was moving. It would take her with them whether she wished it or not.

She should be frightened. No one, not even the penny-hungry innkeeper, would tell of her departure. Only the old archer Lanson, reporting to Bulat, would give a hint of her whereabouts. And after noon today, when the ship came down the coast to fetch them all, no one in the village would be able to tell Lord Maner where she had gone. She should be frightened to cross the sea with these strangers, but she feared only that the ship would be late and that Maner of Bulat would find her.

Constance looked to sea, to the small merchant ship wallowing in the long swells. Beyond, the sea was covered in a dense white mist. Across that sea, she might find salvation for herself and for her people of Lanmartin. "I will tell your Henry Plantagenet—"

"Your King Henry—"

"I will tell Henry Plantagenet that you had no part in my decision to sail with you. And I may tell him that you—and your men—treated me with circumspect care. If indeed you keep your promises."

She looked down the beach to the black ring of ashes upon the sand. The great tent was down, and its contents already carried from the place. "The coffer is delicate. It needs to be packed within wool with a wooden frame to keep it from harm."

Guyon's jaw tensed. "There is a wooden box built about it."

"Lined with wool? I will look at what you have done—"

"No." His face became hard. "It will arrive safely. You will go nowhere near the thing, my lady, until we reach Winchester."

Guyon walked to the remaining campfire and returned to set bread, cheese, and a wooden bowl of pottage upon a sea-scoured log. He offered Constance the bowl. "You must eat. The boats are nearly here, ready to take us out to the long ship."

Above the camp, a tall stack of driftwood had blazed into life, a high beacon fire bright enough to spread crimson warmth into the banks of morning fog. A horn's blast came across the water, borne upon the sea wind. The painted face of a demon emerged, grew a serpent's neck, and lengthened into a great galley. The ship came out of the mist with oars raised and dripping in the thin daylight; it anchored in the bay, well beyond the line of low surf.

From the village, three boats made their way down the long surge off the beach; near the place where Guyon and Constance waited, they turned to ground their scarred stems into the sand.

Six imperfectly sobered men robed as priests carried the crimson-shrouded sumpter frame to the first small vessel and settled their burden with some care upon the bows. Algar, burlier and more lopsided in tonsure in the morning light, took charge of the loading. "Look smart there," he growled. "This is no sack of barley we've got. It's a saint— damn your black hearts—and yonder, that's Henry Plantagenet's ship. *Esnecca* she's called, and too fine for the likes of you to scrape with your oars. Put a scratch in her tar and I'll put a dent in your miserable pates."

High above the beach, seven men-at-arms were mounted upon the horses that had carried their lord and the priests. Behind them, the remaining beasts stood laden with the tents and sumpter bags. The white pack mule, seeming naked without its broderie trappings, was among them.

Guyon, who seemed to have forgotten Constance in the confusion of loading the small boats, was the only one of Henry Plantagenet's men she could trust. She had never crossed the sea, never even touched a boat.

To show weakness was always a mistake. Constance squared her shoulders and walked to the water's edge. "You promised me the pack mule," she said.

Guyon looked up from the frame that held the sumpter pack. "And you will have it, or another as fine, when the relics are home again. For now, the beasts go back to Dinan. The lord lent us the pack animals, and he agreed to care for our own mounts and that white mule until the merchant ship returns in better weather to fetch them."

"The lord of Dinan? Why did he not go with you? It would have been much safer for all, and easier to understand, if you had—"

Guyon shrugged. "He gave us all we asked, for King Henry's sake. Denied us nothing. He is an intelligent man and a loyal vassal to Henry Plantagenet. He would not have begrudged us a fancy box to carry back the stolen saint. He knows what is proper, and he is not too greedy to give it."

The men binding the sumpter pack to the small boat looked away: Algar, the lover of sweet Nan, emitted what in a smaller man would have been a giggle.

Guyon drew Constance's cloak across to cover her neck and lifted her into the boat. Too soon, the boatmen pushed the carrack from the sand into the shallows and clambered over the side. They scrambled to take their oars in hand and pulled into the deeper water, turning the crude prow toward the great ship that waited offshore. Constance gripped the side of the hull as it turned into the slow-running swells beyond the shore.

The ale-sickened priest had spoken the truth. The ship

riding at anchor beyond the last line of surf was a fine vessel, her smoothly tarred strakes embellished with carving upon the stem, each long plank faired smooth as a lord's drinking horn. The *Esnecca* was a fine ship—a great sturdy ship with a mast higher by half than the spar of the humble merchant vessel that lay anchored close by.

With relief, Constance saw Guyon arrive in the second fishing boat. She watched him swing aboard from the short ladder hanging over the portside planks and heard his brief order for the men at the bows to draw up the anchor. A short time later, the deckmen had pulled up a sodden mass of line and the great pierced stone that had held the *Esnecca* safely in the deeper waters of the bay. Within minutes, the oarsmen were pulling strong and steady against the swells, bringing King Henry's ship from the bay into the wide sea beyond.

The north wind was against them, driving the deep swells to the *Esnecca's* fine bow, sending white foam flying to her deck and green water to surge against the rails. Guyon appeared at Constance's side. He pointed to the wood and awning shelter at the stern. "Go back there, out of the wind."

The makeshift priests had hunkered down in the lee of the bow rails to watch the deckmen cast dice upon the heaving planks of the mast step. Below them, heavy-shouldered men in boiled leather jerkins leaned to the oars.

"Why have your mockery priests thrown aside their robes?"

Guyon's gaze flickered from Constance to the far horizon and back to rest upon her face. "Lady Constance," he said, "you are foolish to speak so boldly among strangers."

Constance ignored his words and pointed to a large timber shelter beyond the mast. The shelter was larger than the framed leather tent upon the stern. "And the other priests—the ones I saw at the bow—are they as false as your own?"

Guyon seized her hand and brought it to rest against his chest, upon the fine dense wool of his tunic. "You will know all at Winchester. Can you not keep your questions until then?"

She snatched her hand away. "Who are the other priests? And why did they not travel with you?"

"Does it matter?"

Constance turned away to the rail.

Guyon's hand smoothed her mantle across her shoulders. "Silent at last, my lady?"

Constance shrugged in a false show of indifference. "What is the use of questions? There might not be a single true priest among your men. None will believe that I came with you in all honor."

"Your good name, lady, was in danger the moment you came alone to my camp and your escort saw that you would not return. You knew that. Priests or no priests, that was the deed of a foolish woman. Whether you bring the coffer back to Maner of Bulat or give it to the Bodmin priests, there may be a shadow upon your name—"

"You need not speak so lightly of it."

"—but not upon your honor. I will speak with the bishop at Winchester to curb the rumors that may have begun."

Constance raised her face. "And I will ask him to return my—" Her gaze turned to the men leaning upon the shrouded crate, then back to Guyon. "If your priests were false, was your whole party no more than a procession of liars and sights for the foolish to believe? Where was my coffer in all this mummery?"

Guyon sighed. "It is safe aboard this ship. My party was but a poor copy of the other, from the clergy to the burdens we carried. My men were all soldiers, skilled archers and men-at-arms, ready to meet any Bretons who wished to stop the return of the relics. All the rest—a few guards, the priests, and the relics—and your coffer—were in the other party, disguised as merchants and their wares."

She stepped away and clutched the rail for support. "I was a fool. A stupid fool. And you let me believe—"

"I brought you to the coffer. I never lied to you." He moved to stand beside her. "Constance, have a care. If you throw yourself into the sea, I may let you cure in the brine. I'll have none of your temper."

"I followed the wrong men. I should have turned back when I saw there were no priests. I"—the hint of a sob came with her words—"I chased your army to the coast, and all the while—" She pointed to the mast, where the peaked crate was lashed to the deck and covered with a tanned cowhide against the salt spray. "I will have my coffer back if I have to beg at your King Henry's feet or steal it from the Bodmin monks. I'll have it back before the end of this fortnight or—"

"Or you will curdle my blood with your threats and send me deaf with your insults." Guyon seized her pointing hand and led her astern, past the chanting oarsmen, to the timber-and-leather shelter. "You will stay here, and you will not berate the helmsman or the oarsmen and turn them from their work. The wind is against us, and we need a swift passage, lady. For your sake and mine."

Chapter Four

At sea, the widow of Lanmartin was less trouble than Guyon had expected, though he worried that she had not eaten since they had sailed. Fine lady she might be, but not so rich that she should turn her nose up at the salt meat and solid bread he had brought to her shelter in the stern at the day's end.

If she were rich enough to have known only manchet bread, she would have sent a pack of hired mercenaries to fetch her damned coffer and waited for them, as a fine lady should, beside her hearth, safe from abduction and dishonor.

Guyon rested his hands upon the rail. Guernsey Isle was ahead, its steep hills showing dark against the far line of surf. Behind the *Esnecca*, the plain sail of the small merchant cog shone rosy in the lowering light.

The lady Constance emerged from the stern shelter and came to Guyon's side. "Why do they follow so close?" she asked.

Guyon smiled. "I paid the master to sail with us as far

as Hantune Water with an empty hold, ready to help in case of storms or pirates. You see, Constance, I put you in no danger by bringing you to sea.''

She narrowed her eyes and watched the *Esnecca's* helmsman turn the long ship closer to the wind to slow it. "Do you expect trouble?"

The cog drew closer, near enough for the master to hail the *Esnecca's* crew. Guyon moved back astern to speak with the seaman at the steering post. As he had expected, the lady Constance gave a sharp cry and followed him, demanding an answer to her question. By God's own bones, the woman never kept her thoughts to herself, never sought an answer in silence before troubling the nearest soul, be he her ancient escort or a knight twice her size at the head of Henry Plantagenet's handpicked army.

"Guyon, do they carry the relics? Is that why you keep them so close?"

"Later. We will speak later."

Constance closed her mouth with an audible snap, but Guyon's relief was short-lived. She was off to the mast, shooing the deckhands from the covered frame, sweeping aside their fallen dice with nary a care for their growls of protest. With the dagger she had so ineffectively hidden in her boot, Constance of Lanmartin attacked the lines binding the crate to the deck. She tore the hide cover from the broderie finery it protected. With relentless speed, she sliced through the corner seam, heedless of Algar's protests of the cost of the cloth. She was hard at work prying the first plank from the crate with the flat of her knife when Guyon took it from her. "You'll cut yourself," he said.

She snatched it back. "Might as well slit my throat in the bargain, for all the help I'll get from your cursed promises," she said.

Guyon seized her arm and removed the dagger from her fingers. "Stop it," he said. "I'll open it for you."

"Now?"

"Now."

When they reached the crude wooden chest within the crate, and Constance had opened it in a last hopeless gesture of completion, she bowed her head for a long moment. "This was what you promised me, sir? An empty plank box beneath a gaudy cloth gold stitched by imbeciles—"

"It was the finest in the market at Dinan," broke in Algar. "And it cost—"

"—and one white pack mule. That is what you promised me."

Guyon thrust her dagger into his belt and spread his hands in open apology and secret readiness to catch the woman should she fling herself to the rail in desperation.

"You lying, despicable varlet. You dishonorable thief. You mockery of a knight. You and your priest-murdering king may—"

"Hold." Guyon seized the woman by one flailing arm and dragged her with him to the stern. "Revile me as you wish, but never, in the hearing of Henry Plantagenet's men, speak ill of our king."

Constance turned from him and brushed the salt spray from her cheeks. "My coffer? It is aboard the other ship?"

"Keep your questions for Winchester. I have told you—"

"You have promised me nothing but a hank of cloth and a mule. Will your King Henry return my coffer to me?"

"I will ask him to. It was not mine to promise you, nor did I speak you false, Constance. Nor did I treat you ill, bringing you aboard this ship. Together, we will sail as far as Hantune and ride from there to Winchester, where King Henry waits. You may petition him, and I will support you."

Constance stood in silence, her face averted from Guyon. When she spoke at last, her voice was hoarse. "Even now, at sea, with your hired ship nearby and Henry Plantagenet's crew about you, you still will not tell me where you have stowed the coffer?"

"Constance, I cannot have you going through the cargo with your damned knife." He placed careful hands upon the lady's shoulders and turned her to face him. "Can you not trust me a little longer?"

"I should never have trusted you."

Guyon seized her hand and brought it down to rest upon his chest. "If I give my word—to a man or a woman—I keep it. I will never lie to you, Constance."

For a brief moment, he imagined she might leave her hand upon him. But she turned and marched into the shelter, then dragged the hanging leather curtain behind her.

The leather flap jerked once, then flew open once again. "Since you are a man of such careful honor, you will not lie to your King Henry, will you? When we reach Winchester, and I beg your King Henry to return my stolen coffer, you will have to explain to your king how you managed to acquire yet another renegade widow while in exile for dishonoring the priest's sister."

"Constance."

"Yes?"

"You will leave Winchester with your good name and honor. I have promised you that much, and I will not fail you."

"How can you—"

"I will. And I will do what I can about your blasted reliquary."

"Then tell me where it is."

"In Winchester—not before."

His need to touch her again was overwhelming. He forced himself to turn away and walk the short distance to the portside rail.

God's truth, she was too ready with her words and faster still when she had complaints of him. But for all her stinging talk, she was a fine woman and had not stooped to tears and whining. And she had not offered her sweet body to bribe Guyon to restore her property.

If she had—by all the saints in England—he would have given her the coffer, and his own lands, and Henry Plantagenet's treasury, had she but asked it. And he would have died a happy traitor.

By nightfall, the wind came around behind them; the boatmen shipped the oars and sprawled along their benches with the bread, ale, and salt meat that the Lady Constance so disdained. Above them, Henry Plantagenet's fine crimson sail spread against the darkening sky, filling hard in the freshening wind. At the stern, beyond the shelter, a small torch blazed to match the brazier fire of the merchant cog sailing behind them.

Guyon made his way aft to the helmsman, a burly fellow with short, powerful legs braced against the kick of the steering oar. Beneath them, the stern rose, yawed, and fell with each hissing wave that passed beneath the *Esnecca's* strong planks. Satisfied that the fellow had taken bearings before the fall of night, and seeing two lookouts posted at the bow to watch for the beacon fires upon the great, wide island protecting Hantune's waters, Guyon began to pace from one rail to the other and tried to keep his gaze from the stern shelter.

From the Lady Constance, there had been no word. The priests had taken refuge below the forward deck, with the wood-crated coffer carrying their saint placed among them, out of the salt spray. Guyon had eaten with them, ignoring references to the fine stern shelter to which he had not welcomed the clerics. Having stayed long enough for courtesy, and fearing that the passage of another hour might bring the questions he dreaded, Guyon left the shelter of the bow and made his way aft.

Had she slipped from the tent and thrown herself over the rail, the lady Constance could not have been more silent. Guyon put from his mind the thought of Lady Constance committing desperate acts. A woman who scoured the consciences of strangers with as little hesitation as Constance of Lanmartin would have no wish to bring herself into eternal silence. Nevertheless, it would not be amiss to ask the woman once again if she wished to eat or drink. If there would be anything worse than arriving in Hantune with an exiled lady, it would be to arrive with her starved corpse.

She did not answer his call. Beginning to fear, he pushed the hanging barrier aside and found the woman asleep upon the small pallet, her face stark pale in the flickering light of the stern torch.

The sea wind was from the west, from the cold, unbounded waters of the sea that touched Ireland and then disappeared into the unknown. Guyon shivered and saw that the oarsmen were pulling their cloaks about them and seeking their rest, and the priests in the bow shelter had closed themselves within the painted wooden walls. There would be no harm in sitting near the lady for a time with the curtain flap open upon the night, showing any curious eyes that he merely sat within the shelter and did not seek to be private with Constance of Lanmartin.

Guyon settled upon the thick rush mat beside the pallet and sat back against his saddle pack, his arms crossed upon his knees. For the first time since he had left England in quest of Bodmin's errant saint, Guyon had nothing to plan, nothing to dread. The pilot was competent, and the *Esnecca's* crew quite capable of bringing the ship and her sacred burden safely home.

There was time, now, to think. And to regret. A few days ago, it had been within Guyon's unwitting power to give this sleeping lady the means to bargain with her lord.

When the bishops had first seen the exquisite reliquary

at Saint Mevennus' altar, and the priests had begun to crate the ivory chest for the journey home, Guyon had heard the abbot's protests that the reliquary was not the abbey's to give. Had he questioned the English priests more carefully and closed his ears to their prattle of the significance of the size of the coffer—God's hand, they said, had fashioned the coffer to fit the bones with precision—if he had done what his instincts had first demanded, the lady Constance would have kept her coffer and would have continued to bargain with her lord.

Instead, Guyon had seen the Breton pilgrims gathering at the abbey gates and heard the protests of the Breton ladies, who had seen God's hand in the arrival of Saint Petroc's relics in Brittany and the devil's hand at work in their return to Cornwall. He had given swift orders to carry the chest and the relics out of the church, and he had turned his attention to the execution of the scheme he had devised to draw attention away from the small party taking the sacred treasure to the coast.

To the propriety of taking the ivory chest, Guyon had not given serious thought. The priests, Guyon had reasoned, were better prepared than he to decide what was just and what was not.

If the lady Constance had arrived but a day earlier—had she been early enough to appeal to him . . .

But she had not.

He looked across to the lady. She was sleeping soundly, as if she had been overcome by exhaustion after her days of anger and pursuit. Still, for a woman with an excess of words for any event, the lady Constance had not complained overmuch on this journey.

Guyon had known worse. The lady Amice, sister of Henry Plantagenet's cleric scribe, had whined in constant complaint during her flight from Salisbury to Winchester, where her lover had been waiting. Guyon's dawning horror, when he had discovered the lady's husband yet lived and was in hot pursuit of his foolish wife, was nothing to his irritation at the lady Amice's lamentations on the muddy tracks and bad weather that had ruined her fine traveling cloak.

"If you must indulge your ill temper, pray do it else-where."

Guyon started and saw, in chagrin, that his hands were fisted upon his knees, and he felt the tight mask of a scowl upon his face. The lady Constance was awake and staring wide-eyed in the torchlight.

"I am not angry with you," he said.

"Nor should you be," she answered. "I am the one with the right to anger."

"And you may show it however you wish, once we reach King Henry's court. But for now, upon the ship with nigh seventy ears tuned to hear our speech, we'll keep our peace, my lady."

She smiled and made a small gesture with her hands. "And have I offered you anything but peace?"

Guyon lowered his head upon his arms. "Christ knows your thoughts. I do not. You have brought me hard words and trouble, Constance."

She placed a light hand upon his shoulder. "And you, sir, have not brought me half the trouble you might have. When this voyage is ended, and I have my coffer back, I will thank you for your courtesy, Guyon de Burgh."

He raised his head. "It was easier to deal with you when you were carping and snooping about my camp. Now, I can do nothing but offer you my regrets that the priests took your coffer. Will Bulat accept nothing but that reli-quary? Would he accept gold in its stead? If gold would help, I have plenty to offer him, and I would willingly—"

Constance sighed. "He wants the coffer. You saw it, Guyon. There is none like it in all of Brittany, nor in all of King Henry's empire, I vow. My husband brought it with him from the great crusade to Acre. He won it from a great knight of Blois in a game of chance; Lord Maner believed that had he stayed in the game, and taken just one more roll of the dice, the coffer would have gone to Bulat, not Lanmartin."

"Bulat is a stubborn man, and a harsh one."

She sat up with cautious grace. "Sir, do you know the lord Maner? Are you a friend—"

"No. I saw him but once, at young Geoffrey Plantagenet's betrothal to your old duke's daughter. Bulat is not a man to leave a vassal in peace if he believes he has the right."

Constance shrugged. "He made no move to take the reliquary from my husband while he lived, but I knew he would try to take it when my husband died. I took it to the abbey for safekeeping, and when it was hidden, I began to treat with the lord Maner for my freedom."

"Your freedom?" Guyon sat up. "You are a free woman, are you not?"

"As free as any widow below the rank of queen," she said. "A landed and childless widow must wed, sir, or lose her estates. I have demanded five years' freedom from marriage."

"And then? After the five years have passed?"

"Lord Bulat's choice of husband, his garrison sergeant Huon de Lezay, will not wait five years for my small estates. He will wed elsewhere, and I will have a chance—"

"A chance for what?"

"To wed better. That is all."

Silence grew between them. Guyon drew a long breath to end it. "You wished to live alone on your lands, with only your servants to help you defend it?"

Constance nodded.

"And you believed that some painted ivory and brass from the Holy Lands would keep Maner of Bulat from sending a strong man to keep his rivals from your lands? He would have no such thought, my lady. He would have

taken your coffer, ordered a few of his garrison without
their livery to attack your serfs at harvest time, sent many
more under his own banner to chase the first away, and
then claimed his right to set a strong man in place to
defend you. And you, looking at the burned huts and
ruined wheat and slaughtered cattle, would have agreed,
for the sake of your people."

"You seem certain—"

"It is what I would have done, given a stubborn widow
as a vassal."

"You would not. You are not so black-hearted."

Guyon shrugged. "I would have done some such thing.
Not as bloody, mayhap."

"And you would not have taken my coffer."

He sighed. "I would have been so sick of the damned
thing I would have given it to you as a wedding gift and
wished your new husband courage in dealing with you."

"You may do the last, I think, should Huon de Lezay
be waiting in Winchester."

"God's blood, lady Constance. If you have a husband
living—if you have already wed the man Huon—if you
have lied to me, if it has happened again—"

Constance sat up. "Happened again?"

"God's truth, lady. The last widow I helped in her journey proved to be wedded still, a trull seeking her lover at
the end of the road." Guyon set his fist to the shelter post.
"Tell me now, lady Constance, and speak the truth: Are
you a true widow with no husband to reproach me?"

She sat in silence, her head bowed into her hands.

"Here, none of that. You know you should have no fear.
If I had wanted to be rid of you, I would have left you on
the beach or cast you into the sea before now. Say the
truth, lady Constance. I'll not harm you for it."

Faint words came from her covered face. "I am a widow.
There is no man waiting for me. Only Huon, a two-legged

beast who has asked the lord Maner for my hand. I am a widow, sir. There is no doubt of it."

She was silent for a moment, then made a small muffled sound. By Saint Agnes' teeth, the lady was weeping.

Panic shot through Guyon's frame. This was how it always began. He could not bear to hear a woman's weeping. Short of treason, anything Guyon might offer that would stop a lady's tears was hers for the asking, if she would promise to stop her weeping. He glanced out to the deck, then to the heaving sea beyond. He should leave her. He should leave her alone and close the leather curtain upon the sound of her soft, buried sounds of sorrow.

He was never right in the mind when a woman wept, and this night was no different. So he did not leave, but stayed with her and placed his hand gently upon her bowed head. And felt the prickle of tears come to his own eyes.

"Will you cease that noise," he said. "Do you want the priests coming back here to hear your confession? Or mine? Do you want the pilot to leave his post to see what ails you?"

Beneath his hand, the silk of her hair shook in brief denial. Constance drew a long, unsteady breath and held it. "I am not weeping," she said at last.

"No? That's as well, then." With reluctance, Guyon took his hand from the softness of her hair and sat back. "You must be hungry, though."

"No."

"You'll sicken, and all will blame me." Guyon pulled open his saddle pack and drew forth a half loaf. "Here. Good bread, not too strong for a sea-troubled gullet."

"My gullet is not troubled."

"Aye, but something ails you. Not the sea, I think."

"Not the sea. It makes me sleep, as I never have since—"

"Since your husband died?"

"Since Lord Maner sent word that he had a new lord for Lanmartin. And for me."

Then Guyon understood. The intensity within the woman's eyes, her constant speech. Her near-foolish decisions. Her unthinking courage. The shadows deepening beneath her fine gray eyes. Constance of Lanmartin had been well on her way to fretting into an early grave when she had appeared at the ford of Cagarun. She had not slept since leaving Lanmartin to deal with Lord Maner.

"Sleep now," he said. "And for once—just once—do not chatter at me. Just sleep. And when you waken, I will open the flask of good wine in my saddlebags, and we will eat the bread and cheese. Trust me, Lady Constance. The world will take a turn for the better when we reach Henry Plantagenet's court."

She did not answer. Exhausted, but safe at last, the lady had fallen back to sleep.

Guyon slipped from the tent and found the night-watch pilot at the helm. The young man grinned in the torchlight. "All's fair and good, my lord. The wind still follows on the port quarter, and the beacon fire grows ever brighter. That's the Saint Catherine light ahead, my lord. The Breton master agrees."

Seeing the distant blaze, Guyon felt none of the elation he had anticipated, though the expedition had been more successful than he had hoped. He was bringing back the relics stolen from Henry Plantagenet's vassal, and he had lost not one life among the men who made up the two parties he had commanded: the great decoy procession and the smaller group that had carried Saint Petroc's bones in secrecy from the abbey. Nor had he shed Breton blood in the retaking of the relics, nor had he damaged King Henry's fine ship.

If Guyon had managed, somehow, to come nigh the lord Maner of Bulat in Brittany, he would have put an end to the knave's schemes to wed Constance to the vile Huon de Lezay. Bulat was known, on both sides of the English sea, for his ruthless greed. It would have been an easy matter to provoke a fight and kill the blackguard, all in the name of King Henry's expedition.

Guyon curled his fist above the *Esnecca's* smooth rail. If the scoundrel Bulat showed his face in Hantune, or at Winchester, he would not live long enough to regret his poor treatment of Constance.

Far out to sea, the beacon fire blinked once and disappeared. It shone again, steady as before, but lost, from one wave to the next, its ragged corona on the eastern side. A dark shape was moving before the light.

Guyon looked behind, to where the merchant cog labored well astern of the *Esnecca.* There was a third ship at sea this night, heading dead steady for the sheltered waters off Hantune.

The pilot grunted and gave the helm to his mate. "We're coming upon another ship. We'll catch it before dawn, beyond the great island."

"Do not."

"Sir?"

"Do not catch it. Slow us, if you can."

The man's next grunt was more pronounced. He reached out to jostle the closest sleeping form and spoke to him. The deckhand rose and reached for a coil of mooring rope; in the light of the stern torch, he began to knot the line into thick, ungainly tangles. With one last knot, the pilot fixed the line to the stern post and cast the heavy confusion of knots into the water. "That will do," he said. "More than that, we'd pull the stern off."

Guyon nodded. "Let me know if we begin to close upon the other ship."

The pilot snorted. "With that witch's skirt dragging astern? We'll be lucky to raise land by midmorning. Why, my lord, must we—"

"It is best you not know."

"Are we in for a fight?"

Guyon smiled. "No, not at sea. If that's a warship, and if she hasn't seen us, we'll not risk a fight so close to home. Let her get ahead, and make harbor before us."

"And the lady's husband?"

The smile disappeared. "What husband?"

"Word has it you've found a lady fleeing her lands. A lady none too eager to have her name known. With an angry lord looking for her."

"She is not like . . . the last one. And she has no husband seeking her. I'll not ask you to fight for her sake. If her lord finds us, I will meet him, man to man, ashore. You'll have no blood on your decks, pilot."

With a small rustle, the lady Constance appeared at his side. "Pirates?"

"You should be sleeping."

"And wake with a dagger in my throat?"

"There is no danger. We have slowed lest we overtake that far vessel before dawn."

"Would pirates dare attack Henry Plantagenet's own ship?"

"No," Guyon lied. "Go to sleep, Constance. You will be safe."

"Could it be Bulat?"

"Does Bulat own a seagoing ship?"

"No, but there was a ship loading timber in the cove when I left him to fetch the coffer."

"The lord Maner may have taken it, then." Guyon gestured to the shelter. "Sleep again, Constance. We will both need our wits tomorrow."

By morning, they had reached the small settlement, where a second beacon fire had guided them into the wide mouth of Hantune Water; they found no messengers, no bailiff's man awaiting them with demands of justice for the wronged lord of Bulat. A timber merchant, half loaded with oak and her decks burdened with armed men, had passed the quays at dawn; it had continued up the coast to Hantune. A pilot had rowed out to the vessel and gone aboard, his small boat trailing behind the swift-oared ship. And from the deck, carried away without bargaining in the merchant ship's haste, the pilot's young apprentice had called out to his leman ashore that they were bound for Hantune port with all speed.

The woman who took Guyon's silver and told him the tale shrugged and giggled. "I called back to him and said, 'Rolf, it looks more a warship than a merchant with all the soldiers aboard.' And Rolf—he shouts to me they're bound for the king's court with the Devil's own speed. And God be merciful if they look crosswise to our good Henry, for they'll need shriving before they raise a sword, says Rolf." She looked at Guyon with a critical eye. "Are you bound to follow them to the king's court?"

"I'm for Winchester."

"In the king's own boat."

"On the king's own business."

The woman shrugged again. "If the Breton devils don't keep their swords in their belts, and if you see Rolf, the pilot's boy, you send him back down the river, sir."

"I'll send them all back down the river if they bring trouble."

"As well you might, a great lord like you, sir."

Guyon ignored the silent invitation in the woman's eyes. After a time, she moved down the pier and engaged the *Esnecca's* pilot in earnest talk. Guyon found a small cart sitting unhitched against the seawall and sat upon it, looking far across the water to where the Plantagenet ship rode at anchor, her painted sail half spread across the deck to be sewn where the strong winds had left damage. If Guyon decided to spend the night in port, he would have the master move the ship closer to the quays, nearer the sheltered waters and greater protection of the shore.

What would Bulat do when he realized that he had passed the *Esnecca* during the night? He was a stubborn, harsh man, but by report, he lacked a subtle mind. It would be his likely move, upon reaching Hantune, to quick march his men to Winchester and arrive by noon, bearing his complaints and bringing a show of strength to impress Henry Plantagenet. God have mercy upon him. The pilot's leman had been right: Any man attempting to bully a Plantagenet would not live to repeat the act.

In the distance, Guyon saw that two men had climbed the mast to the top of the *Esnecca's* shrouds, looking for further weakness. It would not be unreasonable to spend a full day in the safety of this place to make the many small repairs the *Esnecca's* crew must complete. The last part of the voyage, up the tideway to Hantune, would be more sheltered than the open sea, but an ill-repaired *Esnecca* in any waters would displease King Henry and might endanger her sacred cargo.

The lady Constance had agreed—with fewer words than she might, to Guyon's mind—to wait concealed in her stern deck shelter while Guyon made his first trip ashore. He rose and with a broad gesture summoned a boatman to ferry him back out to the *Esnecca*. For the first time in his life—and mayhap the last—he would consult a woman before making a decision of strategy. And likely receive a torrent of words from the lady in reply. They would be true words, though, and useful.

He smiled as the boatmen pulled the small craft to the *Esnecca's* stern rail. The lady Constance, true to her promise, had not left the stern shelter, but she had drawn the hide from the aftermost post and was watching his approach. Was it concern for their plans that had kept her there, watching to see whether he returned safely? Or was it regard for him that had kept her at watch?

Guyon's smile broadened. If the lady agreed, as he hoped she would, that Guyon should send an advance party to report back upon the lord Bulat's whereabouts, then she could hardly blame him if they must pass the night in port.

He would propose to send Algar ashore with enough silver to buy a good horse and bid him ride with all speed to tell Henry Plantagenet that Saint Petroc's relics would reach the port at Hantune within two days. If King Henry wished to make much of the event and impress his bishops, his stewards would have time to arrange a splendid home-coming for the saint, celebrating his progress from the harbor and all along the Winchester road, finishing off with a jubilant mob in place at the city gates. And Algar, after delivering the message, might look about Winchester for news of Maner of Bulat. If the man was there, it would not be hard to discover him.

Constance stepped from the stern cabin and stood waiting, her shining braid blowing in the gentle shore breeze.

Guyon took a long, frowning look at the men atop the mast and counted the knots in the climbing lines, giving his body time to quell the sudden desire that had come upon him.

"Is there trouble?"

"No, not trouble. An opportunity. Maner of Bulat passed us in the night and continued up the shore, thinking we were before him." He reached to steady Constance upon the rocking deck. "If we stay here for a day and a night, while the crew makes repairs to the *Esnecca*, I'll send two men to Winchester to discover how the king receives Bulat."

Constance had turned as pale as the clouds blowing in from the sea. "He will be waiting for us with the king to support him."

"Henry Plantagenet has no patience for brutes and braggarts—unless they have something he wants. Your lord of Bulat has nothing to offer the king but complaints."

"You have not seen his anger. His temper—"

"His temper can be nothing compared to King Henry's will. Your lord of Bulat has made a mistake if he came angry to Winchester; we will give him a full day to show Henry Plantagenet his true colors. What say you, Constance?"

She looked up with surprise plain in her gaze. "You are asking me?"

He shrugged. "Bulat is your enemy. You know the man. You decide."

The lady Constance smiled at him as if he had given her a jewel of great worth. "Then we will stay here," she said. "I have decided." And she smiled again.

The oarsmen, eager to reach the alehouses and brothels ashore, made short work of moving the long ship toward shore, to anchor close beside the quays.

Chapter Five

The strong winds had taken their toll on the *Esnecca*; her master was relieved that Guyon would not continue up the tideway to Winchester's port at Hantune with a split and hastily repaired sail and three oars showing signs of damage. In the day at anchor within reach of shipwrights, the crew would have the ship fit for Henry Plantagenet's critical eye.

For the first time in over a fortnight, the small army aboard the *Esnecca* would sleep on dry land without fear of Breton rebels coming by night to steal back the relics of Cornwall's great saint. The only Breton within a trebuchet's range was the lady Constance; and her weapons, devastating as they were, would be for Guyon de Burgh alone.

It had been a strange thing to be in the company of a woman of blood-stopping beauty—a woman who had asked more than Guyon could possibly consider in the matter of the stolen coffer—and pass two days of earnest negotiations without a hint from the lady of favors to be won. That first night, in the camp on the Breton beach, Guyon had seen the woman's beauty and had steeled his heart and mind from the blandishments that certainly would follow. But the lady Constance had kept to her relentless argument, spending more words in her effort than some women would speak in a fortnight of shared beds and rumpled bolsters.

The questions of bribes, taxes, knights' fees, and boons she had discussed with clarity and little emotion. Only in her pleas for Guyon's help to obtain her freedom had the lady shown her spirits. But never had she spoken of the sweeter impulses of the heart to which Guyon's defenses might have yielded within a heartbeat of her offer.

It was as well that the lady did not look upon him with unreasoning desire. For this time, Guyon could not afford to look beyond his own interests to bring solace to a lady's distress. This time, he must look to his lands and King Henry's good opinion. One more scandal, one more restless woman eager to execute a scheme with Guyon's sword to clear the way, would mean the end of Guyon's hopes of keeping his lands in England or ever holding estates elsewhere in Henry Plantagenet's wide empire.

In this night to come, in this night away from the *Esnecca's* watchful crew and round-eyed priests, Guyon would find the lady Constance a sleeping chamber both well guarded and far from his own bedroll.

When the *Esnecca's* crew had brought her close upon the quay and unfurled her silken banners, a swarm of lighter craft had left the pier to bring the inevitable number of curious merchants alongside. Guyon had summoned the first to arrive and had passed the oarsmen three copper pieces to take him ashore once again.

Guyon scanned the small settlement with a soldier's critical eye. Near the quay he found two inns; the lodging would be comfortable but the lady Constance's location too easy to discover. He had walked from the pier through the first streets of the port and reached the smaller streets above; he roamed the narrow lanes until he found a place both easy to defend and too lowly for Maner of Bulat to seek Constance within its walls. The silversmith who opened the door, surprised to see a fine lord seek lodging in his small house, took three silver pennies in return for his two loft chambers and room beside the hearth for five men-at-arms. He would be glad, he said, to have armed men in the house this Midsummer's Eve to discourage drunken revelers breaking the shutters and stealing his wares.

Guyon had forgotten that the summer solstice was upon them. Midsummer's Eve had come too soon, and he would be far from his lands, from the fine feasting, dancing, and sly lovemaking that made this night the most joyous of the year. His steward would, in his absence, have made the preparations, bought cloth to be given as midsummer gifts to the women, and bid the kitchen folk to slaughter, use, and bake what they needed to give Guyon's people a feast to remember.

Far from his lands, Guyon would sleep through this Midsummer Eve with five smirking soldiers within earshot . . . and an achingly lovely woman not far from his bedroll—a woman whom he must not, on pain of his riches and her peace of mind, bring to his bed for this short summer night.

He had hauled his saddlebags to the foot of the loft stair and returned to the *Esnecca* to bring the lady Constance ashore.

She had been reluctant, at first, to leave the ship. Determined to keep the doors of the forward cabin within sight, and mistrusting the Bodmin priests to remain aboard with the coffer, Constance had refused to budge from her vantage point on the stern deck. At last, Guyon had taken her forward to speak with the priests and to receive their assurances directly.

"They are a good lot," she had said. "Better, I think, than the first clutch of blackguards and drunkards you had tricked out in brown robes to deceive me."

"And you have their oath that they will not take the coffer away."

"They might have allowed me to see it."

"Yours are not the only eyes that would have seen it. Do not blame the priests for their caution."

Constance had turned from the forecabin and looked to a cluster of fishing boats on their moorings. "I could stay here on the ship. I slept well in the stern shelter."

"And if Maner of Bulat comes back down the coast this night to take you, you'll be sitting right where he would first look. If he doesn't find you here, there will be no fighting."

"I'll have no brawling on my account." Constance sighed and took her salt-stained mantle from the shelter. She climbed down the boarding ladder without further comment and placed her hands upon Guyon's shoulders as he swung her into the small boat that would row them ashore. Her fingers had rested a moment longer than necessary upon the broad muscles of his chest, then flew as if scalded to the depths of her mantle. For the rest of the short journey, Constance had sat rigidly upon the bow bench, watching the steersman weave his way through the confusion of port traffic.

Constance and Guyon walked through the small market at leisure, as if they sought only a meal ashore before returning to the ship. At the last moment, after buying Constance a kirtle from a merchant's wife and a fine green mantle from a mercer's stall, they turned into the narrow

Take A Trip Into A Timeless World of Passion and Adventure with Zebra Historical Romances!
—Absolutely FREE!

Let your spirits fly away and enjoy the passion and adventure of another time. With Zebra Historical Romances you'll be transported to a world where proud men and spirited women share the mysteries of love and let the power of passion catapult them into adventures that take place in distant lands of another age. Zebra Historical Romances are the finest novels of their kind, written by today's bestselling romance authors.

Take 4 FREE Books!

Zebra created its convenient Home Subscription Service so you'll be sure to get the hottest new romances delivered each month right to your doorstep — usually before they are available in book stores. Just to show you how convenient Zebra Home Subscription Service is, we would like to send you 4 Zebra Historical Romances as a FREE gift. You receive a gift worth up to $24.96 — absolutely FREE. There's no extra charge for shipping and handling. There's no obligation to buy anything - ever!

Save Even More with Free Home Delivery!

Accept your FREE gift and each month we'll deliver 4 brand new titles as soon as they are published. They'll be yours to examine FREE for 10 days. Then if you decide to keep the books, you'll pay the preferred subscriber's price of just $4.20 per title. That's $16.80 for all 4 books for a savings of up to 32% off the publisher's price! What's more…$16.80 is your total price…there is no additional charge for the convenience of home delivery. Remember, you are under no obligation to buy any of these books at any time! If you are not delighted with them, simply return them and owe nothing. But if you enjoy Zebra Historical Romances as much as we think you will, pay the special preferred subscriber rate of only $16.80 each month and save over $8.00 off the bookstore price!

track leading up the estuary banks to the few prosperous houses beyond.

No one followed them. Five men-at-arms had watched their lord's progress through the market and had seen no sign of brigands or Bulat soldiers. Indeed, the folk who had crowded close beside the lord Guyon and the Breton woman had no purpose but to gawk at the mind-stopping beauty of Constance of Lanmartin.

When Guyon turned from the market to seek the silver-smith's house, Constance stopped to look back upon the *Esnecca* riding safe at anchor in the river with well-armed guards upon the deck to discourage the fishing cogs from drawing too close.

"Lady, if you continue to stare so, many will begin to believe there's treasure aboard, and some may dare to seek it."

"Do you expect trouble this night?"

"No."

"And you will not sail without me in the morning?"

"My lady, do you believe I would have brought you all this way only to abandon you here?"

Constance shrugged. "You have done a good many things, sir. Not all of them honest, I think."

"I have done nothing to harm you, and I have kept my word."

"In a manner of speaking. 'You may have the pack mule and all it carries,' you said. You lured me across the sea with a promise that may prove as empty as that crate upon the mule."

"Trust me, Constance."

"You have not given me your word, Guyon. You will not leave me here when you sail tomorrow?"

He shook his head. "I had never considered it."

Constance turned a skeptical gaze upon him.

Guyon shrugged. "Well, I thought of it. Any man would have." He laughed, then, and took her hand. "I swear I will not abandon you. Now you must trust me and stop looking over your shoulder at the harbor with every step. If I had not been here at your side, you would have fallen in the road or been prey to cutpurses. I bought you a fine new mantle, my lady, and you scarcely marked it."

Her gaze fell to the soft bundle of wool he carried beneath his arm, then returned to his eyes. "It was kindly done, Guyon, and I will give you the silver it cost as soon as I—"

"Will you not accept a gift from my hand?"

"You will have no silver left after paying for our lodging and buying the mantle."

"Constance, I have told you I am a rich man."

"A rich man who has yet to regain his king's goodwill. Lands and gold have been lost over smaller matters than your scandal with the priest's sister."

"It was not my fault."

"Of course not. But until Henry Plantagenet agrees, you might as well set your gold upon the side of the road and ask the king's men to come and take it."

"King Henry is a fair man, and no thief."

"His lords will do a thief's task if he asks it." Constance took a last look at the harbor. "I deal well with thieves, sir. They may steal what is mine, but I find them and get it back. Ask any of the Lanmartin folk. They will tell you."

Guyon frowned. Did the lady hope to spend the night standing in the road, watching the decks of *Esnecca*? He sought to distract her. "Tell me of Lanmartin," he asked. "Your lands must be richer than you realize, for Bulat spent a great sum in gold to use the half-loaded merchant ship to come here and to pay the armed men who came with him."

"Maner of Bulat will have paid for what he could not take outright from the merchant and threatened the man to give him all else. His men will billet where they will, and only the fiercest resistance will keep the louts from taking what they wish from the country folk and riding away without payment."

"Bulat will not dare let them pillage so near Henry Plantagenet's court. If he deals unjustly with King Henry's subjects, or tries to swagger his way into the king's good graces, he will leave this land without his men, his ship, or his life." Guyon frowned. "The man is not stupid. Why has he risked offending Henry Plantagenet?"

Constance shrugged. "He was ever a stubborn man."

"He has crossed the sea, leaving his lands undefended. He must wish to keep Lanmartin well under control or to take it from you entirely. What does he hope to gain?"

She sighed. "Not riches. The land gives enough to live well, if one is careful. My late husband was such a man. He never spent a coin nor hired an extra soldier for his garrison without careful thought. The lord Maner does not understand this. He imagines that the next lord of Lanmartin will bring him greater taxes."

Guyon frowned. "Maner risks much to wed you where he wills, yet he has chosen a landless man, his own creature, whose loyalty he must have gained before this. What does he hope to win by giving you in marriage to a landless man of his own garrison?"

"To keep Lanmartin safe and the road clear of brigands. I have hired a sergeant at arms to oversee the garrison, but the lord Maner is not content."

"Your choice of sergeant did not please him?"

Constance shrugged. "He did not notice the man. The troubles go deeper, Guyon. Maner of Bulat and my husband had many a quarrel before death parted them. I do not understand his actions, but I must deal with him as best I can. And I was doing so, before I lost the only thing that the lord Maner would accept to close the bargain."

"Lady, I have told you—"

Her hand stopped his words. "I know. I do not blame you. And though you took my bargaining pawn, you gave me another more direct way to my freedom. And if Henry Plantagenet fails me, I have one more game to play."

"Do not try a desperate move. If King Henry fails you, come to me."

Constance smiled. "The next game is not so desperate. The lord Maner may wish to claim that my virtue vanished when I left Brittany with you, leaving me unfit for marriage. Though I will lose my lands in that game, I would have my freedom."

Guyon shook his head. "Never wed? Was that your wish? Somehow, my lady, I cannot see you happily settled in a convent. The vows of obedience, lady, would weigh heavily on you. And as for vows of silence—"

A small smile curled the edge of her mouth. "I have enough gold left, Guyon, to dower myself in a comfortable abbey. I will find a place with no vows of silence. Obedience, once this dilemma is past, will be no trial. And chastity—"

Guyon saw the promise of a smile vanish from her face. "And chastity?" he asked.

"—should be no trial."

They had reached the turning place, where the narrow road would take them from sight of the harbor. Following twenty discreet paces behind them, the men-at-arms had not heard their words. Constance took Guyon's proffered hand and made her way past the wagon ruts in the road.

"Tell me what happened when you arrived with the priest's sister in Winchester," she said.

The lady must not be indifferent to him, for she had returned many times to the subject of his indiscretions, real and imagined. "Her brother named me a lecher to Henry Plantagenet," Guyon said, "and I near lost my lands."

"Your King Henry understood that the lady deceived you?"

"He knew."

"And still he took his favor from you?"

"He blamed me for acting as a fool. For allowing the lady, noble as she was, to come near to ruining me with her lies."

Constance arched a brow. "And when you appear, with Maner of Bulat waiting in fury, with yet another sad widow in tow, your Henry Plantagenet will take your lands this time or tax you into penury."

Guyon sighed. "You may have the right of it."

The color upon Constance's cheeks flushed deeper. She turned away and looked past a pair of merchant carts to a long house with trestle tables set beneath the summer sky. "Is that the place? I have some gold, Guyon, and will pay the innkeeper."

"No, we will sleep beyond, at the top of this road, in a silversmith's loft, well away from other travelers."

Constance nodded. "Show me."

They made their way to the end of the track. At the silversmith's door, Constance tarried with the maid as Guyon and the smith haggled over the price of a meal. The men-at-arms brightened at the talk of food and drew lots to decide which two of them would watch the road while the others ate.

Constance returned to Guyon's side. "Do you expect trouble this far from the harbor?"

"We should be well hidden here, and my men will not be obvious sentries. But if your liege lord finds you in our company, lady, before we reach Henry Plantagenet's court, it may come to fighting. How could it not?"

That bright color about the lady's cheeks vanished. "Before it comes to fighting, I will go with him."

At this rate, Constance might decide to go in search of Bulat to avoid bloodshed. "Come, lady," Guyon said.

"Have I not found a place where Bulat will not find us? If he sent men to search every house along the coast, it would be long past dawn before they thought to look for us here."

The smith's kitchenmaid drew near to Guyon and pointed to the men-at-arms eating at her hearth. "Where did you send the others, my lord? My master said they would all watch the house this midsummer night and keep thieves from his silver."

Guyon sighed. "Tell your master to put his silver in the loft, and I'll sleep upon it."

Constance frowned. "You have thieves at midsummer in England?"

The maid bristled. "This near the coast, with the Bretons crossing the sea, we must be careful." She saw the affront in Constance's expression, and the anger in Guyon's, and backed away. "We have brigands of our own, as well. They may be out in the fields this night."

Constance turned back to Guyon. "Might there be trouble near the harbor?"

"The priests will not stir from the ship, and I have warned the *Esnecca's* master to keep a watch for drunken boatmen when the moon rises."

Constance's next words were lost when Guyon drew her away from the door upon the return of the silversmith, a sallow young man with large round eyes made wider at the sight of Constance. A long, searching look ended only when Guyon stepped between the smith and the lady.

"One night?" the smith asked.

Guyon frowned. "I have told you. One night."

"You sail at morning? How early?"

"At dawn." Guyon fixed the man with a hard stare. "I will stay and guard this place, as agreed. And pay for the loft chambers and pallet beds here in the hall. Five men from the ship, good men-at-arms, will watch your doors. You will remain?"

The smith shifted from one foot to the other. "Yes. I'm not one to go in search of midsummer brides and leave my shop to others."

"Midsummer bride? Is this the day when the English wed?"

Guyon was the next to color. "No. The man speaks of women one finds—that he finds in the dancing on Midsummer Night."

"Ah. A bride with no wedding."

"A fortnight from now, when the blood has cooled and the families have spoken, there will be some marriages."

"And for the others?"

"Nothing but memories, and sometimes a child, born early in the spring."

Constance nodded. "Just as in Brittany."

The smith looked from the lady Constance to Guyon, then to the floor. "I'll be here. I'll not go to the fields."

Constance inspected the fall of her new mantle across her arm. "Show me the chamber, then. It had best be clean. And the latch sound."

The smith paled again. "My lady, you will be as safe—"

"As safe as a woman at her own hearth, minding her own lands," Guyon said.

"With no need to follow thieves across the water to regain what is rightfully her own," Constance said.

"Thieves?" The smith's voice lowered. "What thieves?"

Guyon smiled. "Widow thieves. Men of poor wits who steal fair widows."

At nightfall, three burly men from the ship arrived, bearing short swords, pikes, and news from the *Esnecca:* The lord Maner of Bulat, thinking to inform himself of Lord Guyon's plans, had sent five of his own men back to port in the pilot's small boat. A mere hour after Guyon had left the ship with the lady Constance, the Bulat men had asked to come aboard to question the sailing master concerning a valuable coffer taken from Bulat lands by a greedy widow lady. Both the treasure and the lady were missing, they said, and might be found aboard King Henry's great warship.

The lord of Bulat had sent his apologies to the lord Guyon de Burgh and had left the five men behind to assist the *Esnecca's* crew in finding and confining the lady thief.

"You kept them from boarding." Guyon's voice was flat with authority.

"Yes, lord. As you had warned us. When we refused, the pilot boat left, but the Bulat men still may watch the *Esnecca* from the quay. Three of them went to drink at the inn upon the waterfront."

"You were not followed?"

Constance broke in. "I have said I want no bloodshed on my account. I'll give myself up—"

"It's too late for that. If they take you, I will have to kill them to get you back. There is no other way."

The messenger raised his head. "There were only five of them."

"There must be more. Bulat would send more."

"My lord, we will bring more men from the ship."

"No. It's King Henry's warship, and the relics upon it are under the king's protection. Your place is there. If I send for more men, Bulat's spies may follow them here. No," Guyon said, "we are safe here. Go back now. Walk on to the fields and behind the town before you turn back to the harbor."

Constance touched his arm. "The houses will be deserted this Midsummer Eve. If they come, few will mark them."

"They will not come. As long as these folk keep their mouths shut and don't begin to speak of us when they're halfway through an ale tub—"

"My lord, I have said I will not go out to the fields."

He had forgotten the silversmith, who had listened to all they had said. Guyon considered him with a cold gaze. "If any man asks you why your kitchenmaids have been busy, tell them your kinfolk have arrived from some far place and have asked for shelter for the night. And remember this: If the lady's enemies should find us here, before the fighting begins, I'll empty your silver into the street."

Chapter Six

Midsummer Eve upon the seacoast was cold—cold as Eastertide in Brittany's deep inland forests. Constance pushed the casement shutter open upon the narrow track beneath the silversmith's bedchamber loft and watched the youths and maids walking up from the harbor to the fields beyond the settlement. The bonfires had burned since nightfall, casting a faint rosy light far into the lanes that ran into the town, sending the smell of hardwood and aromatic smoke to sweeten the night.

A cold wind blew from the south to meet the heat of the fires, but the youths and maids who walked down the silversmith's lane were lightly clad, their blood hot with the promise of Midsummer Night. As she watched their light, laughing progress, Constance felt a hot blush rise to her cheeks.

It had been difficult to keep her gaze from Guyon de Burgh during the quiet meal they had shared before the silversmith's hearth. He had placed her at his side, with three of his men crowded across the board, and had spoken of the journey to Hantune awaiting them. They had spoken of the splendors of Henry Plantagenet's Winchester, laughing as Guyon described the relief of the king's exhausted courtiers when their travel-hungry lord had settled in Winchester to await Guyon's return.

"We will find well-fed, well-rested courtiers and a restless king in great need of the open road," Guyon had said. "Henry Plantagenet craves a journey as some men need wine. He would have counted it a great affront had we kept him waiting all these days and not brought the saint home." Guyon had raised his mug of brown ale and gave thanks that he and his men would not disappoint Henry Plantagenet.

Constance had heard how much had depended upon Guyon's success and had understood why he had taken the trouble to create a decoy procession. The talk turned to the past; she had listened in awe to the tales of Henry Plantagenet's Winchester and of the ruined splendors of his banished wife's court in Poitiers. Yet she could listen with only half a mind; deep within her thoughts, she turned again and again to that moment upon the *Esnecca's* deck when Guyon had placed her hand upon his breast and looked upon her with unconcealed desire.

And now, in the darkening solitude of her chamber, as remote from the midsummer revels as the cold sea from the summer fires, Constance permitted her mind to wander beyond her present dilemma. She leaned upon the casement sill and followed, with her gaze, the progress of hand-holding lads and girls and watched groups of young women passing solitary youths with sidelong glances of promise and silent beckoning.

What path would her own days have taken if she had followed the track that led from the small manor house at Lanmartin up to the bonfire hill and had once, just once, slipped into the laughing circle and felt the freedom that even the lowliest dairy maid might enjoy during a lovers' meeting on Midsummer Night?

Scandal, remorse, childbed in the cold refuge of a convent and solitude for the rest of the days of her life.

Constance wrenched the shutters closed upon the night wind and barred it to the sight of revelers. Her solitary, borrowed pallet, freshened by linen bought with Guyon de Burgh's silver, waited in the deepening shadows of the chamber.

A soft sound upon the loft stair sent her blood singing once again. She was waiting at the low door when he called to her.

"It was the shutters," she said. "I dropped the bar."

"Will you sleep?"

She pulled the door open. "No, the chamber is cold."

He was standing on the low-ceilinged landing, an arm's length from the threshold. "It's as well, then, that we left the ship. The wind up the estuary brings the cold from the sea." He moved away from the loom of the taper in her hand. "I'll bring my cloak for your bed."

She waited at the threshold. A fortnight hence, she might be landless, cast out by the ill will of Maner de Bulat and by the scandal of her flight to England with Henry Plantagenet's man. She had wagered all she had possessed to gain five summers of freedom from Maner's man, and she might lose more than her land. From Henry Plantagenet, she could expect no more than a bloodless end to her vassal's vows to Bulat and a royal scribe's letter to take her to an honest nunnery. And then would follow the endless season of solitary nights in which she would regret all that she might have done, had she dared. Never again would she have this time of passage, of freedom from the eyes of those who owed her duty, to whom she owed protection.

What she had not dared to do in Brittany, what she could not do within the bounds of her lands at Lanmartin, she could do here, in the darkness of an English Midsummer Night, with the man whose dark, heart-stopping eyes had answered the desire within her own.

Sweet Virgin Mother, if Guyon de Burgh had come to Brittany last summer, before Fortin's death, the man might have tempted her from her marriage bed, might have brought her to dishonor while her husband yet lived.

A night with Guyon would be the end of chastity, and of honor, the beginning and the end of love's joy. This night would be all she might have of love's sweet play for the rest of the days of her life.

With shaking hands, Constance held the taper's flame to her lips and extinguished the light. And left her shift upon the low bench at the foot of the bed. And slid, in the hot glow of anticipation, between the cold, clover-scented sheets of linen.

If he had brought a taper with him, if he had left his cloak upon the threshold and turned away, Constance would not have called to him. But he knew her mind and came without speaking into the darkness of the chamber; there was a long silence, then the fall of the bar into the latch hook.

She made room for him and waited in the still night.

"Is this your wish, my lady?"

"I—"

He waited for a space, then placed his cloak upon the coverlet. "Only one word, Constance? You, who have so many words?"

He was upon the pallet, sitting beside her, waiting.

"No words."

A warm hand closed upon her fingers and took them from the coverlet. "Tell me," he said.

When his lips brushed her hand and moved to the surging pulse of her wrist, she drew away, then placed her fingers upon his mouth. "No words," she whispered again. "Please. Nothing to mar this night."

His lips curled beneath her fingertips, then moved again

to kiss the sweet pulsing above her forearm. And again, to find and warm first one breast, then the other.

And then, only then, did his lips find her mouth and take into him the sounds of her need and move beyond words.

From the barred shutters came the faint sounds of footsteps upon the hard-packed road, and songs—songs made ragged by drunken voices or by the ebb and surge of pulses made unsteady with desire. In the unrelieved blackness of the chamber, Guyon's silent wooing made of the night a seamless, giddy voyage with no landmarks save valleys of yearning and peaks of splendor.

During the troubled, sleepless night upon the *Esnecca*, she had held the memory of his touch and had imagined his body so well that the dense muscle and hard planes beneath her hands held no surprise for Constance. From his gaze, and from the brief touch of his hands upon her own, she had known that he would be skilled. But there had been no hint, no way to know that his touch would at once inflame and madden her, would bring her to the point of oblivion and in the same moment require her to wait, to lengthen the sweet moments of pleasure that he drew from her mind as well as her body.

Once joined, they did not part; by subtle touch and deep caresses, they greeted each moment of ecstasy as merely a harbinger of the next.

Because this was to be the only night, Constance spent the hours in wakefulness, resisting the languor that came each time her lover brought her to the completion of her desires, asking in wordless pleas for that which he gave her willingly again and again.

Only once, when footsteps came fast and heavy beneath the silversmith's walls, did Guyon move from Constance to slip the shutters open and listen for the sounds of his men warning away a party of drunken youths.

"Harmless folk," he said as he pulled the cloak over Constance's bare shoulders.

"We are safe, I think, until dawn. Sweet lady, it is time for words."

She sat up and nestled into the shelter of his arms. "We have the shortest night of the summer, Guyon. Will we waste it in speaking?"

Rich laughter filled the darkness. "If this night were any longer, you would find me cold beside you at dawn—the most fortunate death I could—" He stopped and drew her closer. "Your pardon, my lady. I had forgotten."

She shook her head. "It does not matter."

"How did he die?"

Constance felt an impossible smile move one corner of her mouth. "Not from a night such as this."

His arm tightened around her. "That's as well. How, then?"

"It was winter. He fell from his horse and walked through the rain and sleet. He— There was a fever." She lightened her voice and touched his face. "A tale too sad for this night."

He smoothed her hair from her brow. "We will have many more nights. We will count them as the sands of the sea. And we will waste none of them, my lady." His lips traced the curve of her cheek and brushed her mouth with teasing softness. "In all the years to come, each night will bring us joy."

Guyon waited in silence, his heartbeat slow and steady beneath her hand, for Constance to speak. "That was not an unmannerly bid to make you my leman," he said at last. "It was my clumsy plea to have you to wife, Constance."

"You—"

He kissed her again, as if seeking to draw from her the words she could not speak. "No other," he said. "Guyon de Burgh, bachelor knight with lands in Kent held for ten knights' fees from Henry Plantagenet. I am rich enough," he continued, "to pay a good bride-price to Maner of Bulat. He cannot take you back, Constance. Not unless you want to go."

"You have trouble enough," she said, "without taking a wife who might lose her lands and bring nothing to you."

He covered her belly with his hand. "You will bring me sons. You might already carry my child, Constance."

She covered his hand. "If I fail to keep my bargain with Bulat, and he will not consent—"

Guyon shook his head. "He will consent if he values his life."

"Kill Maner of Bulat and you will lose Henry Plantagenet's favor for all time. Algar told me—"

"Algar talks too much."

"—that your King Henry was angry about the priest's sister, and you had only this chance to regain his favor. Will you present yourself at Winchester with yet another woman who laid her troubles upon you, with yet another scandal to offend the king, then make matters worse by striking down Bulat?"

Guyon stood and began to pace the small chamber. "Henry Plantagenet wants peace in Brittany. He will give your lord of Bulat some trifle to keep him content."

"My lands? They are no trifle, and I will lose them if we—"

"What are you saying, Constance? Are your lands so rich that you would keep them rather than wed me?"

"They are not rich, but—"

"I will ask Henry Plantagenet to bid your lord keep you as his vassal, and I will swear to keep your lands protected. I will find a young knight to be castellan. Or we might pass a season or two, each year upon your lands. Will that keep you content?"

"It is not the lands alone—"

"Ah." He drew a long breath. "You do not want to wed me."

"How can you say that?"

He sighed. "One small mercy in a battle of words I cannot understand. My lady, you are not a woman who takes a man lightly to her bed. Did you believe we would part at Winchester after such a night?"

Constance shrugged. "It is your custom in the Plantagenet's court. I have heard the tales."

"And you wish to become as faithless as those women of the court? You will not succeed, Constance. Not you." With gentle hands, he drew her from the pallet to stand before him. "Now cease your talk of leaving me. I want you, Constance. For all the days of my life. Say you like me not, say that this night was but a game to you, and I will leave you at Winchester. Say you love me not, and I will trouble you no more."

She placed her cheek against his chest and sighed. "I am not free, Guyon. If I had been free to wed or not to wed, just as I pleased, I would not have followed your army from Cagarun to reclaim the only thing I possess that might turn my fate from marriage to Huon."

"I have said you will be free of Bulat and his man, and—"

"If you were in your king's good graces, there might be a chance that he would take me from the lord Maner's wardship and give me to you. But your King Henry will see you return to him with yet another woman after the dozen in your past—another woman with troubles setting you against her lawful lord. Henry Plantagenet will banish you forever."

"Constance, if that were true, would I have come to your bed? I will wed you, if you are willing, and Henry Plantagenet will not stand in my way. The other matter— the matter of the cleric's sister—was a stupid blunder that angered Henry Plantagenet, but did not turn him against me. Believe me, I know his mind. And he would not anger my family without good cause—better cause than taking my lover from me to give her to the cruelties of Maner of Bulat." He drew her closer, warming her against the long, hard length of his body. "Wed me, Constance."

"After Winchester."

"King Henry will give you to me."

"And if he refuses and gives me back to Bulat, will you swear to me that you will not fight him?"

He sighed. "I swear I will not seek his life. Will you wed me then, Constance?"

She nodded and lay quietly in his arms as he carried her back to the pallet.

Before dawn, Guyon slept at last, and Constance lay awake, listening to the sweet sound of his breathing.

The strongest men, the bravest knights, did not recognize true danger when it came outside a battlefield. Fortin had brushed aside her fears as he rode out on that icy day upon a skittish horse, and he had lost his life.

Guyon de Burgh was a man of the Plantagenet court, but he was as heedless of deceit as had been the country-bred Fortin. Guyon did not know, could not know, how dangerous was the temper of Maner of Bulat. Only the vassals and serfs of the lord Maner's lands could begin to imagine the man's stubborn malice.

If Henry Plantagenet forced Bulat to a marriage between Constance and a man not of Bulat's choice, disaster would follow. Her new husband's life would end, by ambush or open attack, before the first harvest.

Without Constance, the roots of Bulat's anger and revenge would wither. She would leave Winchester a nameless woman with enough gold to buy herself a nameless future at an English convent, leaving Guyon de Burgh without scandal, free to wed a woman who would not bring him into the king's displeasure and Bulat's vengeance. Free to live.

Guyon stirred and drew her closer. "You frown?"

In the pale light of dawn, his eyes were as dark as the night sea. Constance kissed them shut and nestled within his arms. "Dawn has come, and I have not slept, as you well know. Of course I'll frown."

"The river will be calm today, all the way to Southampton. You will have the stern shelter to sleep all day. Smile for me, Constance."

They had known each other only three days. He would not know that the smile she gave him was as painful to her as the growing light of dawn.

Chapter Seven

With few words and an impressive threat, Guyon compelled his men to keep their gaze from Constance of Lanmartin that morning. The five sleep-starved men did not look twice at the sight of Constance of Lanmartin descending the narrow loft stair after dawn, the color of passion—and shyness in the presence of those who had stood watch last night—still upon her cheeks. They had the good grace—and good sense—to keep their broad smiles hidden.

Constance had dismissed Guyon after he had washed and brought a fresh jug of hearth-warmed water to the loft; timid of his gaze in the morning light, she had wedged the door shut and banished him to break his fast alone. She emerged a short time later, looking for all the world like a new bride wed in hasty joy after midsummer quickening.

Together they walked from the silversmith's house, with two men before them and three to guard their backs. At the turning place, where the narrow track joined the wider quayside road past the inn and the merchants' houses, Constance stopped and looked back over her shoulder to the smith's high loft window, her smile so sad yet sweet that the man-at-arms behind her stumbled upon the gutter stones and nearly fell at her feet.

To join Guyon's heart, humbled in gratitude that this lady might smile at the memory of their first night.

As he caught the man's fall and heaved him back upon his feet, Guyon smiled. "I'd better practice," he said. "I'll have to do much of that, catching besmitten men from tripping over themselves, if you smile thus each morning."

His lady's smile deepened. "These smiles, my lord, are on your account. How much will you pity the besmitten? Enough to change your ways?"

"Not at all." He took her arm as they continued to the quay. "We will continue our nights, lady, and your smiles. I'll buy my men new helms and let them stumble as often as they will."

The *Esnecca* lay proudly in the seaway, backing from her anchor as if eager to sail for Hantune. The men from the merchant cog had come aboard her. They lined the rail with helms and shields blazing in the low morning sun. Upon the bow stood the brown-mantled priests, gathered close about the crimson-edged drapings of Saint Petroc's sea crate. A small crowd had come to watch from the quay, and word went among them that Guyon de Burgh, the knight who had restored Saint Petroc to England, had summoned a boat to take him out to King Henry's warship.

A wool merchant waved away the boatmen and offered Guyon his own boat and the men of his household at the oars to take the small party to the *Esnecca*. As they neared the ship, they heard the sound of prayers across the water and saw the more daring harbor folk guide their small craft to the *Esnecca's* sides to touch the ship bearing Saint Petroc's rescued bones.

"Do you see, Constance? When the king hears of his

people's good cheer, how could he deny us our own happiness?"

"Guyon, promise me that if the king objects, you will not—"

Her words were lost in the confusion of an altercation within the port fleet, and Guyon's own bellowed orders for the merchant's oarsmen to stay clear of a vessel filled with onlookers, the small hull so overloaded that it rose barely a handbreadth above the gray water.

She held her hand above her eyes and braced against Guyon's side as the rowers negotiated the swarm of small boats encircling the *Esnecca*, then brought them near the boarding ladder.

"There will be precious little quiet aboard this ship," she said.

Guyon smiled. "They won't follow us far. Beyond here, the water will be flat, and you may sleep a bit." He took her hand upon his knee. "We did well, Constance, to have our night when we could."

An odd ache in her throat kept Constance from speaking. *Yes, my dear lord, we did well. We had our night, and none will take that from us.*

The crew ran the great oars through the locks and brought the *Esnecca* forward to where her anchor lay in the river mud. With much heaving and cursing, the deck crew pulled the great stone from the water and rolled it to rest upon the weedy mass of its coiled line. With a practiced grace that brought a smile to Guyon's lips, the larboard oarsmen pulled three mighty strokes, bringing the great ship around to face the north, heading for Hantune. The smaller craft hired by the pious to accompany the *Esnecca* soon fell astern, as the long, swift length of her proved faster than the harbor fleet.

Guyon took his lady's arm and brought her aft as the

crew sweated up the great sail. In the morning wind, the painted expanse shook twice, then filled into a well-curved belly that greatly eased the oarsmen's task. Soon, the smaller boats had been left behind; Hantune Water stretched wide before the *Esnecca's* fine gilded prow.

Small groups of townsfolk were clustered upon the shores, waving kerchiefs, then kneeling to receive the priests' blessings, given in the shadow of the *Esnecca's* long pagan neck.

Once underway in the broad, clear June morning, the priests had carried the reliquary forth from its shelter and placed the wooden crate and its fine pall upon the deck, where all could see. The wind freshened, and the oarsmen ceased their toil. Aboard the great ship, there was thanksgiving and celebration.

From her vantage point upon the stern, Constance watched the priests form a small circle around the splendidly draped relics. She turned to Guyon. "Will you tell me now? Is that my coffer within the priests' sea crate, or is that yet another of your decoys?"

"It is there, my love. Even now, Algar is bidding King Henry to give the news to all Winchester."

Guyon placed Constance's hand upon his arm and stood with her beside the helmsman, watching the jubilation aboard and ashore. "Will this do," he asked, "as a wedding procession? I would wed you soon, Constance. As soon as we reach Winchester."

She smiled. "Even a king's trusted man must wait for his banns to be read." Her smile deepened. "Or have you sent one of your false priests ahead to arrange it? Will I find myself, tomorrow morn, not quite wed and remember only then that the priest who spoke words over us had a lopsided tonsure?"

Guyon laughed. "My lady, I will find us a proper priest. Algar will be disappointed. Even now, he is in Winchester with the best of them, setting his tonsure to rights."

Constance looked past his shoulder. "My lord, if that is the best Algar could do in Winchester, your King Henry keeps a poor court."

"My love, you must learn that he's our king." Guyon turned to follow Constance's gaze. "Turn into the wind," he shouted to the helmsman. "Run out the oars and back them. Pick up that man."

That man was Algar, disheveled and red-faced, rowing with little efficiency across the choppy water, pausing to shout over his shoulder to the *Esnecca* with each splashing stroke. On the riverbank had gathered a small crowd of fishing folk; their shouts across the gray water had no kind words for Algar or the ship he sought.

The men on deck raised their shields and called encouragement to Algar and threats to the lame boatman who staggered along the shore, brandishing a long bow—a great warped weapon that must have had its provenance from William Rufus' time.

"By the Rood, if the old man tries to use that twisted bow he'll strangle himself." Guyon stepped to the rail and began to bellow words to calm the fellow upon the river road and, in return, had a rude gesture from the ancient— a gesture for which the twisted yew was well shaped.

"I believe Algar has borrowed that boat," Constance said.

"I believe Algar will return that boat, or I'll see his tonsure trimmed with my sword," Guyon muttered.

The helmsman had turned the *Esnecca* sharply into the wind; a moment later, he shouted for the larboard oarsmen to bring her back before the sea breeze with a sputtering Algar on board. The abandoned boat was floating free, pushed toward shore with two of Guyon's silver coins resting upon its bench, soon to be recovered by a second craft filled to bursting with offended fishing folk.

Guyon fixed Algar with a stern gaze. "I asked you to inform King Henry that we would arrive in Hantune this day and to discover what you could at Winchester," he said. "Be subtle, I told you. Now I find you on the run from angry villagers with a stolen boat. I will not ask you what you did with the horse you were to buy with my silver."

The oarsmen on the windward side of the *Esnecca* set their backs to pulling the great ship back to her course, straight before the sea wind to carry her up the estuary. When the oars were shipped once again and the clamor had died, Algar pushed himself away from the rail and slowed his gasping breath. "Trouble," he said. "It's trouble again for you. Word is out that King Henry will not forgive you this one."

"Forgive what?"

Algar nodded to Constance. "This one," he said. "Maner of Bulat was at Winchester, and word was that he petitioned the king to restore what you had stolen."

"The coffer?" Guyon placed his arm across Constance's shoulders. "Shall we give the coffer to Bulat? Now that we will be wed, you need not bribe him."

"No." Algar's hands were in his hair, his fingers clenched as if to tug his tonsure straight. "No, my lord. He wants the coffer, right enough. But he wants the lady back. Says he's promised her in marriage and needs the thing done to pay his taxes and tithes."

"King Henry will give the lady to no one but me. Constance is not rich. And her bride-price, if reckoned in land and gold, would be small. I will pay twice the bride-price to the lord of Bulat." He smiled down at her. "If reckoned in truth, her price would be more than any king's treasury."

Algar shook his head. "It's not the bride-price. That's not what the lord of Bulat told the king. Something about tolls and needing a strong man in place to bring them to Bulat."

Constance gasped.

Guyon turned her face to meet his gaze. "Lanmartin collects tolls? Large tolls?"

"Never. Never a single copper piece. My husband would not do it. I did not imagine that Bulat would—"

Guyon's voice was low and dangerous. "Tell me. Tell me all of it."

Constance paled. "Lanmartin is not a rich place, but it overlooks the south road to the abbey. Last year, when King Henry raised the tithes in Brittany, the lord of Bulat demanded that my husband take tolls from those who passed Lanmartin on the abbey road. They're pilgrims, most of them, not merchants. My husband refused, and he got the abbot to speak with the bishop, who asked the lord Maner to leave the road free."

"Bulat yielded to the bishop?"

"He did, but he said that the abbey's revenues should be shared with Bulat, because without the road the pilgrims could not bring their silver to Saint Mevennus."

"And now your husband is gone, and if Bulat puts in place a man who will take tolls, all the clergy in Brittany could not stop him." Guyon groaned. "By Saint Magnus' front teeth, these are bad tidings."

"The bishop would stop Bulat again. He would never allow the tolls."

"The bishop has no garrison to support him."

Algar collapsed against the stern post and began to shake his head. "Guyon. My lord. Is this wise?" He looked at Constance and sighed. "This is trouble beyond what I imagined."

Constance bowed her head. "Guyon, he is right. If it is the matter of the tolls that drives the lord Maner to give me to Huon, there is no hope."

Guyon placed a hand upon the hilt of his sword. "But by Saint Petroc's holy bones, I swear I will not give you up. The lord of Bulat will give you to me to wed, or he will find himself without tolls and without an unbroken arm to reach for the gold. I will ride that road and haunt the lord Maner until he beggars himself buying mercenaries to defend the place."

Algar paled. "Now my lord Guyon, remember why we sailed to Brittany. Remember the trouble. What will King Henry decide for you—or the lady—if you arrive with a stolen widow with an angry liege lord, demand her hand in marriage, and disembowel the lord Maner? A sad end to your task for King Henry."

The first bank of oarsmen, resting idly beneath the well-secured sail, raised their heads. "Kill the lord of Bulat? Aye, there's a thing worth doing. You'll have us at your back, my lord. Say the word."

Guyon's face darkened. "There will be no fighting. No killing. If the lord of Bulat's beard needs trimming, I will do it. No one else."

Constance stepped away. "Your king—"

"Our king," muttered Guyon.

"King Henry was angry with you when he sent you to Brittany. You must not anger him further. You will lose your lands—"

"His life, more likely," Algar said.

"Algar!" Guyon warned.

"Stop!" Guyon, Algar, and the oarsmen turned at Constance's unwomanly shout. "There will be no fighting. No killing." She lowered her arm and looked into Guyon's face. "And no wedding."

"Constance, calm yourself."

"No wedding."

Guyon gave the oarsmen a black look that sent them back to their bench. With a small shrug, Algar followed.

Constance remained in place, her jaw quivering with anger, her eyes desolate. "There will be no wedding, my lord. Not if it will offend your king."

Guyon shook his head. "He will give you to me."

"And you will return with me to Lanmartin and find an

arrow through your throat one morning while riding your lands. And I will need to make yet another bargain with the lord of Bulat for freedom from wedding his man Huon."

Guyon shook his head again. "If that happens, my lady, you will have the gold to make your case and bribe Bulat. I will see you safe, Constance."

"Bulat will see you dead. And I will not be the cause of it. Last night—"

She hesitated, unable to hide the pain in her voice. "Last night was Midsummer Eve, Guyon. A time for unwedded love. I was your leman, but I will never be your wife."

"You gave me your vow, Constance."

"And you would hold me to a promise made in a rutting heat? A marriage negotiated in a midsummer mating is no true sacrament. I—I fear I mistook the truth of it in my weakness."

"Constance—"

She turned away and spoke to the river. "I will pass the rest of this voyage with the priests if they will allow it."

He caught her arm and brought her back to face him. "Rest where you wish. I will not stop you. But at Winchester, lady, we will wed. Leave the lord of Bulat to me."

"And wait and number the days of our marriage, hoping we will have at least a fortnight before an assassin's knife finds you? Hoping that your King Henry will not take Bulat's part and send you to do some dangerous task that will leave you dead and this scandal complete?" She shook his hand from her wrist and turned to Algar. "Speak to your lord and tell him I have the truth of it. Tell him I have no wish to be widowed again."

Chapter Eight

There was no time, no opportunity to speak again with Constance. The broad settlement of Hantune loomed before the *Esnecca* by midafternoon, and the crew, seeing the travelers streaming north along the estuary as if for a festival day, looked to the ship's decks and trimmed the great sail with more care than they had done in the long ocean passage. Guyon's men, seeing his black mood, looked to their weapons and readied themselves for the trouble that might await them all upon the quays.

Only Algar dared approach Guyon where he stood in the thin shadow of the stern post, his eyes upon the fore-cabin, his jaw set in a hard, stubborn line.

"The lady has the right of it," Algar ventured.

"The lady heard too many of your foolish words."

"My words were true. Would you have kept the truth from the lady? She has a good mind, for a woman, and the boldness to act upon her thoughts."

"She'll not act upon these," Guyon said. "And you will see that she does not."

"I do not think—"

"When we go ashore, watch over her."

"Aye, I'll keep her from harm."

"And keep her from leaving the Winchester road. She may have a mind to disappear from sight to save me the trouble that she imagines—through listening to your mindless babble—to save me trouble from Bulat and from the king."

"As I said, my lord, she is a sensible woman. Have you considered that she might be right?"

"Between the two of you and your unreasonable fears, you'll lose me my promised wife and send Constance back to face Bulat alone. I'll have no mistakes on the road to Winchester. If she tries to leave the road, stop her."

There was a movement at the forecabin; the wooden hatch crooked open and a wedge of dark fabric appeared. Guyon smiled. "She already regrets her lack of faith. She comes."

The fabric was the brown cloth of a priest's mantle; its wearer rummaged through the priests' sea chest and darted back into the shelter.

Algar moved to the rail and began to study the low choppy waves of the river.

"By Saint Magnus' teeth, what is the woman doing up there, traveling with a pack of seasick clerics when she could be out in the fine weather?"

Algar shrugged, but did not take his eyes from the water. "Confessing?"

Guyon ground his teeth. "The lady and I are betrothed. We pledged ourselves one to the other. We will wed in Winchester. The lady has nothing to confess."

Algar shrugged again.

With difficulty, Guyon did not send Algar over the side to drown in the water he seemed to find so fascinating. He pushed himself from the stern post and strode forward, the idle oarsmen scampering aside to avoid his determined stride, and began to hammer upon the forecabin hatch.

Constance herself opened it and slipped from the shade of the cabin into the sunlight.

"Have you finished your dealings with these priests?"

She faltered, then drew a long breath and smiled. "Yes, Guyon."

"And will you give me your promise that you will come with me to Winchester? You will not slip away upon the road and lose yourself in some plan to save me from the king's displeasure?"

Her eyes widened. "Why would I not continue to Winchester?"

His eyes narrowed. "Promise me. Promise you will be there at Winchester and appear before King Henry with me."

"I promise. I will give you my oath upon Saint Petroc's—"

"And leave Saint Petroc from your speech."

"Yes, Guyon."

He sighed. "Why, Constance? Why are you so docile of a sudden?"

She shrugged. "You are still eager to wed?"

"Of course I am. I love you Constance. Have I not said I love you?"

Constance paused, then smiled. "No."

"Well, I love you. I want you. And no other shall be my wife."

She fixed him with her pale silver gaze. "You told me you are rich. How rich, Guyon?"

His gaze narrowed in curiosity. "I have silver enough to pay Bulat for your hand. Do you doubt it?"

"No. But you will be glad to have the rents from Lanmartin?"

"Of course. They will but make us more prosperous." He took her hand and placed it upon his arm. "It does not matter if the rents are small. Nothing matters, Constance, but your promise that you will trust me to make all right with King Henry and your promise that we will wed."

The first of the Hantune pilot boats appeared before them with a banner held high at its bow to announce the presence of Henry Plantagenet's emissary.

Together, Constance and Guyon moved to the rail and heard the greetings and the king's order to bring the churchmen and their recovered relics with all possible speed to Winchester from the port. Horses, pack mules, and an escort of King Henry's knights awaited them upon the quay to receive the relics from the hands of the priests and place them upon a fine litter to be borne along the Winchester road by six monks of Saint Cross.

With a flourish of well-timed oars, the pilot boat turned to precede the *Esnecca* to the quays. "Six monks of Saint Cross," Constance mused. "An improvement over your white pack mule."

Guyon smiled. "And will you be content with the mule, or must I bring you the six monks in its place, my lady?"

She smiled back. "No, the mule would be happier and easier to feed."

Together they watched the quays loom larger in their sight and heard Hantune's bells ring their welcome.

In the splendor and confusion of the *Esnecca's* arrival in port, Guyon did not think it odd that Constance had not spoken of her promise to wed him. And Constance, standing silently at his side, did not remind him.

The march to Winchester went more smoothly than Guyon had hoped. The sacred relics, and the procession of clergy and knights that bore them, had passed clusters of simple folk along the way, farmers at the edges of their fields, and charcoal burners come in haste to the road from their hovels deep within the king's forest.

As in the small villages of Brittany, many who came to watch the procession did not know which holy burden was passing upon the road. Those who lived in the shadow of Winchester's court knew that two bishop escorts traveling in their robes of state upon Henry Plantagenet's finest mounts, their gazes never wavering from the shrouded burden upon the fine litter, must have been bringing an object of extraordinary importance to the Plantagenet king. So they knelt, as had the Bretons only days before, at the sight of the shrouded coffer carried high enough for the faithful to see it as it passed.

The roadside folk called to the priests and trotted beside the laboring monks to hear the history of Saint Petroc's journey beyond the sea and his restoration to England; many times, the escort halted so that the clergy might give blessings to the crowds.

Some of the more worldly folk beside the Winchester road had heard the rumors of the Breton monk's theft and King Henry's mission of justice to bring Bodmin's saint home across the sea; over the heads of the pious, they called out words of praise in recognition of Guyon's army. A few bold souls added words of praise for the lady Constance's beauty to the clamor, only to find Guyon's dark gaze forbidding further presumption.

A short mile outside Winchester, a large party of well-mounted soldiers waited before the square gatehouse of the abbey of Saint Cross, their weapons shining bright in the sun. Four of the riders broke from the ranks and spurred towards the procession; Guyon signaled to Algar to draw closer to Constance in case there should be fighting.

As the first of the riders drew near, Guyon waved his archers back and rode forward with Constance to greet Henry Plantagenet, come to ride through the great gate of Winchester with the holy prize recovered from Brittany.

Though the day had turned warm, the royal shoulders
were draped in two mantles of richly bordered cloth with
red gold thick among the threads. Upon the royal brow,
a circlet of gold and precious stones rested in perfect
symmetry, undisturbed by the spirited gait of the king's
fine mount. Above the broderie collars, Constance saw the
leonine face of Henry Plantagenet, florid in the midday
heat and subtle in its inspection of the party behind Guyon.

With a small gesture, the king bade Constance and
Guyon ride ahead with him, preceding the litter. The sweating monks who had carried the relics afoot from Hantune
port tried to speed their pace to follow the king more
closely, but soon slowed, keeping the men-at-arms and
archers far behind Henry Plantagenet and those he had
favored with his attention.

"Well done, Guyon de Burgh," said Henry Plantagenet.
He turned a broad, questioning smile upon Constance
and moved the royal gaze back to Guyon.

"Your grace, this lady is Constance of Lanmartin."

"You are a Breton?" asked the king.

"Yes, your grace."

Guyon smiled. He had never heard Constance so brief.
The Plantagenet's gaze moved back to Guyon. "She
returned with you?"

"I brought her with me upon the *Esnecca*, your grace."

"And have you, at last, returned from your travels with
a lady who is neither wed nor promised nor like to bring
trouble from any other cause?"

The silence grew. Henry Plantagenet sighed. "Of course
not. There is a tale to tell, and I have heard the half of it
from this lady's liege lord. But we will not speak of troubles
here and spoil this fine homecoming." He looked ahead
and saw at the crossroads another gathering of cheering
folk. He nudged Guyon with a none-too-gentle arm. "I've
done it, de Burgh. I've restored Bodmin's saint to England
without bloodshed, leaving my English bishops pleased

and my Breton bishops no cause for complaint. They will not go running to Rome to whine of me over this matter. Well done, Guyon. Well done.''

Over the sound of Winchester's bells came the brilliance of royal trumpeters upon the city walls, the brass notes shining through the bronze tolling, declaring to all below that their king had addressed the wrongs done to Bodmin's Augustinian abbey, adding to his glory both on earth and above, where Saint Petroc doubtless watched his restoration with a kind eye to Henry Plantagenet.

As they passed through the gates, King Henry spurred his mount forward to ride before them all, heedless of his escort's frantic rush to overtake him and shield him from the crowds.

Guyon reined back and reached for Constance's hand. "You see? The king is pleased. All will be well for us, Constance. Trust me?"

She smiled back, then turned her attention to calming her mount, a small palfrey who was, like Constance herself, unused to the bright banners and trumpets of Henry Plantagenet's Winchester.

"And why did you cross the sea to put this matter before me?" Henry Plantagenet shifted restlessly upon his throne and cast an impatient eye upon the distant sight of serving folk carrying platters down the far corridors, hurrying to have them in readiness for the royal feast of celebration for the deliverance of Bodmin's saint.

Upon a linen-covered trestle beside the throne, illuminated by twelve beeswax tapers and under the constant regard of the master Walter of Coutances, rested the reliquary with its brilliantly painted ivory, its polished brass fittings, and its sacred burden, the bones of Cornwall's Saint Petroc.

Maner of Bulat's features had darkened to a dangerously

deep scarlet. "I would not have presumed to stop your men from their tasks in Brittany, your grace. Instead, I followed them here to ask for your justice."

A bejeweled hand brushed across the royal mouth and returned to support the royal chin and hide the beginnings of a royal smile. "And if you had come upon them at sea, in my ship the *Esnecca*, would you have made your complaints to my emissaries?"

The lord of Bulat recognized the trap and dipped his head still lower. At his temples, the rapid throbbing of prominent veins gave warning of his ill-contained anger. "No, your grace. I meant only to bring this matter before you. No other. I never came close to the *Esnecca* at sea."

The king raised his face to contemplate the finely carved rafters above his throne, and he seemed to forget the lord of Bulat's presence. At last, when that discomfited noble had begun to fidget with his surcoat, the Plantagenet's gaze lowered again to stare at the heavy rings upon Bulat's fingers. "And the lord Roland of Dinan," began the soft, barely civil voice. "The lord of Dinan, seneschal of Brittany—your liege lord—did you not wish to inform him first?"

"Your grace, I—" Bulat's mouth snapped shut as he struggled to reason his way past this accusation. Then it opened again with trembling lips. "I did not wish to trouble him."

"I see. You thought to trouble me in his place."

"No, your grace."

"Indeed." Henry Plantagenet resumed his inspection of the rafters. "Continue, Bulat. Tell me of the offenses committed by my man Guyon."

"Not by your man, your grace," Bulat said, "but by my own vassal, the widow Constance of Lanmartin."

Henry Plantagenet pointed a warning hand to Guyon. "I will have silence here, de Burgh. The lady will have her chance to speak in turn. Continue, Bulat."

Lord Maner cast a black look at the place where Guyon and Constance stood together. "The widow Constance of Lanmartin has refused to wed my man Huon de Lezay, a strong and faithful man who would protect her lands. Having refused to take a husband, the lady offered me bribes to keep her lands without a man to defend them. Gold, she offered—and the return of the painted ivory coffer her late husband had stolen from my baggage train on the way home from Palestine, where I fought the infidels for the greater glory of our Lord God."

Three pairs of eyes looked to the lady Constance, and three brows rose in surprise that she stood silent and unconcerned at the accusation.

Henry Plantagenet smiled. "Continue, Bulat. What has this to do with your king?"

"The widow was careless of the treasures she promised."

"You had agreed to take the bribes?"

Bulat's face progressed past crimson to purple. "I agreed to treat with her. But while the woman offered the bribes, she traveled about the countryside, hiding her treasure in diverse places. The worst of it was that she gave the coffer— the coffer her late lord had stolen from me—to your man Guyon de Burgh and bade him take it from my lands as a reliquary for the bones of Saint Petroc."

"And how would this improve her state since she had promised it to you?"

"She used it as a bribe, to persuade de Burgh to take her abroad, to leave my man Huon without a bride and her lands without a protector."

The king leaned forward. "So you have banished her from her lands and given them elsewhere?"

Another trap. Bulat paused to consider. "I might. But I have not yet."

"If you did, there would be no need for the lady to give you the treasure she promised since she would have lost all she had, save her personal wealth."

"She took the coffer. It's mine. And she owes me loyalty. She belongs to my man Huon."

King Henry turned to Guyon. "De Burgh, cease your black looks and growling or I will have you taken where your temper may cool."

"Your grace." Guyon unclenched his fists and sought to keep his voice level. "I have said nothing."

Constance stepped forward. "May I speak?"

Henry Plantagenet nodded. "Be brief, if you would. Our feast will cool in the kitchens."

"Your grace, the coffer was my late husband's prize from the Holy Lands, won in a game of chance in which my lord Maner lost. In all the years of my husband's life, the lord of Bulat never dared claim the coffer was his. I offered the piece and a sum of gold to Lord Maner of Bulat to leave me free of marriage for five years. Lord Maner treated with me in bad faith, as you have heard, for he had already promised me to his man Huon de Lezay. Now I owe him nothing."

"You owe me fealty, witch."

Guyon raised a large fist in Bulat's direction. "I will not have you speak so to the lady Constance."

The lord Maner smiled at Guyon's words, then turned once again to face the king. "She is a witch, as you can see. She has moved this fine knight de Burgh to disobey his anointed king before his throne."

Henry Plantagenet resumed his inspection of the rafters far above the throne. "De Burgh needs no witchery to inspire him to disobedience."

"If she is not a witch, then why did she persuade your emissaries to place the relics within a heathen coffer—a thing of Saracen craft that is painted with designs no Christian would use?"

The king turned his gaze to the reliquary, to the rich colors and gold chasing upon the delicate panels of ivory. He shrugged. "Birds and trees. Unlikely to offend a good

Cornish saint." He beckoned Constance to approach. "What say you, Constance of Lanmartin?"

"King Henry, your priests have accepted the coffer as my gift to the abbey at Bodmin and will place it upon the altar in their chapel to hold—"

Bulat's cry of rage cut off her words. "Given it? You had no right. I am your liege lord, and I order you to take it back or by God I will take your lands from you. Believe it, Constance of Lanmartin."

"My lord of Bulat, my lands were lost to me when my good husband died. You have promised your man Huon my hand in marriage and the governance of my lands. Had I given you the coffer, and all the gold I possessed, would you have sent away Huon de Lezay?"

"I would. I might still if you come back and cease your rebellion."

Constance shook her head. She drew a long breath and smiled briefly at Guyon. "I will not go back to Lanmartin. I deeded it this day to the abbey at Saint Mevennus, as a bequest in honor of my late husband Fortin. Your new vassals are the abbot and his flock. They will do homage to you and pay you tithes and taxes. And to honor my dead husband's wishes, they will not charge tolls to pilgrims and other travelers who cross the lands of Lanmartin."

"She is mad!"

"Master Walter has heard this already from the priests I sent to Brittany, and those priests have made their marks upon the deed. I am landless," Constance said. "And I have no liege lord."

King Henry broke the long silence that had followed Constance's words. "Well, Bulat, are you content? You have lost the widow but gained an abbey as your vassal. She has lost her lands to the abbey, and you have lost nothing."

"My coffer—"

"You wish to take it from the Bodmin monks?"

Bulat raised his head. He had heard the steel in the

Plantagenet's voice. "They may keep it, and a pox upon—"

Henry Plantagenet's eyes flashed.

"—any who would take it from them," finished Bulat in confusion.

Guyon's great shout of laughter filled the hall. He took Constance into his arms and kissed her full on the lips. "I like this, my lady. I like it well. You have rid yourself of land and lord, and no one may deny me your hand. We will be wed this night, and—"

Henry Plantagenet cleared his throat.

Guyon turned his gaze to the king and drew a long breath. "If your grace agrees, we would be wed this night."

Bulat lowered his head. "Your man Guyon has brought a witch slut to your court, King Henry. The woman is the devil's handmaiden."

Guyon's hand went to the hilt of his sword and addressed the king in a cold, lethal voice. "My lord, will you allow this brute to speak so? Give me leave to kill him."

"No, de Burgh. You may not kill him. If you wish to remain at your lady's side, there will be no more talk of killing my Breton guest." Henry Plantagenet sighed. "I am hungry, and the feast in my hall is growing cold. Is there more to your denunciation of your lady vassal, Bulat, or have you brought foul words and few facts before this throne?"

"Your grace, there is more. This woman attacked Saint Petroc's sacred relics upon the very decks of your ship the *Esnecca*. Took her knife to the pall and sought to pry open the sea crate. I had the truth of it from your own priests, who saw her do these things. Who but a witch would steal aboard your grace's own ship to scatter the relics of an English saint into the ocean?"

"I'll scatter your guts to the four winds, you lying cur!"

A long shadow came over Guyon and his prey. Walter of Coutances rose from his place beside the relics of Saint

Petroc. Then he moved to stand between Maner of Bulat and the man who would kill him.

Master Walter cast a baleful look at Bulat, Guyon, and Constance in turn. He turned away from the silenced faces and began to speak to his king. "Neither of these men has lied, your grace. The lady Constance of Lanmartin did indeed give her lands to the abbey of Saint Mevennus and the coffer to the monks at Bodmin. My scribe wrote the deeds and made his mark upon each, for he and the other priests were witness this day aboard the *Esnecca* before they reached port."

He signed and made a small gesture toward Bulat. "This man has also spoken truly, for the priests reported that the lady Constance drew her dagger and cut away the pall sewn to cover the sea crate about the reliquary. And she did then try to cut through the wood to get to the coffer. She had been heard to say that she wished to cast the bones of Saint Petroc from the reliquary and had come aboard the *Esnecca* to do so. Whether she would have thrown them into the sea, I do not know. The lord Guyon stopped her before she reached the relics."

Henry Plantagenet uttered a round curse and rose from the throne. "This is ill news, fit to bring the headache upon me. De Burgh, attend me this night and make no marriage vows until the lady has atoned for her actions and explained what she was about. I cannot have my landed lords wed witches, however fair they might be. The Pope's legates would take up residence in Westminster and never leave."

From Bulat's throat came a satisfied grunt. "I will take her back to Lanmartin and let the abbot at Saint Mevennus convene an inquiry."

"Enough." Guyon's low voice filled the hall with danger. "I have had enough. The lady Constance will go nowhere without me. And we will wed this night. As of this hour, I am no longer a landed lord whose wife may cast suspicion

upon Henry Plantagenet's court and bring Rome's legates
to England. I relinquish my lands and all that I hold upon
them and give them back to my sovereign lord Henry
Plantagenet.''

"Guyon, do not—"

"I keep only my sword, my armor, my horse—and my
lady Constance, who will be my wife. All else I give back
to you, King Henry.''

Constance had retreated from the throne and stood
alone and dry eyed in the gathering dusk. The faint light
of the midsummer evening streamed through the tall
embrasures in Henry Plantagenet's great hall, illuminating
with pale fire the braided glory upon Constance's shoulder.
Interest flared and died in Henry Plantagenet's eyes, and
he shifted again in the throne. He cast a swift glance at
Guyon, then beckoned Constance forward.

"And you, lady? Now that your lands are gone and your
coffer given to the Bodmin monks, do you wish to wed my
man de Burgh, who is as landless as you?"

Maner of Bulat muttered something low and growling
in the language of the Breton country folk.

Constance faltered.

Guyon turned to Bulat, his hand upon the hilt of his
sword.

The Plantagenet's smile narrowed. "Will you have him,
lady Constance? Or will you leave this place unwed?"

She moved to Guyon's side and drew his gaze from
Bulat's chill stare. "I will wed you, Guyon de Burgh.''

There was a long sigh from the throne. "Master Walter,
find a priest, and have him wed de Burgh to this lady. No
banns. You will see that all agree? And see that they are
wed this night.''

Walter of Coutances raised his head. "And if the woman
is a sister to demons?"

"I will take that chance," said Guyon. "Bring the priest.''

Still the cleric did not move. "Your grace?"

Henry Plantagenet beckoned Maner of Bulat to draw closer to the throne. "I have a task for you, Bulat. A gift to be taken to your new vassal, the abbot at Saint Mevennus. And you will tell him, as well, that I will keep the lady Constance at court with her husband de Burgh. If I or my priests suspect that she consorts with demons, or has brought her husband to treat with devils, I will send her back to Brittany to be questioned. Until then, she will be under my eyes." He turned his gaze to Guyon. "De Burgh—"

"Your grace."

"I have need of your strong arm in my household. Now you are landless, you may serve me in my guard. You and the lady Constance will eat at my board and have lodgings wherever I bring my court. Go with Master Walter, find scribes to list the lands you have surrendered, and sign the deeds. And wed your lady before the sun rises."

Chapter Nine

For Constance and Guyon, there was no feast. Walter of Coutances had sent for his youngest clerk, and he had set the lad to writing a list of Guyon's former properties. Halfway through Guyon's recollection of the meadows, small manors, and two sturdy keeps that he had held through Henry Plantagenet's good favor, Master Walter returned to bid Constance and Guyon follow him to a small church near the city walls.

There, upon the steps of the chapel, with a thin new moon shining above Winchester's roofs, and only Algar, Master Walter, two bodyguards, and the homeless beggars of Winchester's streets to witness their vows, Guyon de Burgh, newly impoverished knight of Henry Plantagenet, wed the lady Constance, no more of Lanmartin.

The priest did not bid them into the chapel for a wedding Mass, but he said he feared to open the narrow doors upon the night. Seeing the torchlight strike nervous sweat upon the cleric's face, Constance guessed that word of Bulat's accusations had traveled to the ears of the priest;

she thanked him in few words and turned aside, hoping that he would not dream of her in demon's guise.

When the brief vows had been said, Walter of Coutances and his escort took the priest with them back to the fortified palace in which the bishop of Winchester had disdained to wed Guyon de Burgh to the Breton widow. The beggars stayed long enough to collect the small coins Algar cast to them, and when they found the last of the deniers winking in the loom of his torch, they vanished once again into the shadows in which they lived.

Guyon waited for the sound of the clerics' footsteps to disappear; then he called Algar to his side and drew Constance with them to walk through the dark streets toward the north gate of Winchester.

At last, Algar stumbled against a rough timber wall. "Have you forgotten I am lame?" he said. "My lord Guyon, I cannot continue at this pace."

"Then make your way back to the stables at the king's hall," Guyon said. "Bring our horses to the north gate at dawn."

"Where will you be?"

Guyon looked past Algar to watch for pursuit. In the light of the small torch, Constance saw her husband's mouth curve in a smile. "Hours ago, before I traded my lands for greater riches, I found lodgings—too fine for the landless knight I am now, but well placed for a fugitive—the house of the gatekeeper, hard by the north gate." He gave the torch to Algar and clasped him on the shoulder. "Bulat will not think to look for us there. Go back to the king's hall, Algar, and put the word about that we asked for refuge at the bishop's palace and will sleep there. At dawn, bring the horses, and if any should question you, tell them that you are selling the beasts."

Algar shook his head. "Guyon, I should stay before your door. You cannot mean to spend this night without protection."

Guyon's soft laughter met the rising night wind. "If my wife—my Constance—my pretty witch—should frighten me, I will face the danger alone."

"In truth, my lord—"

"Go now, Algar. And know that I will bring Constance safely to the gates at dawn."

The gatekeeper had bred four strong sons in the narrow house beside the walls of Winchester, and he was pleased to lend two of them, for a price, to watch the twisting stair below the chamber taken by the fine knight and his lady.

"They are so young," Constance said.

Guyon touched her cheek. "They will not fight, but they will warn us if Bulat finds us and comes seeking revenge."

The gatekeeper abandoned his wide, soft bed to his lodgers, and he promised to awaken them well before he walked the short distance to the walls of Winchester to open the north gate at dawn. Constance watched Guyon take silver from his diminishing purse and give nearly half of his remaining wealth for the chamber and the sentries.

"I have gold," she said. "Four gold pieces in the dagger sheath of my boot."

"By all the saints, Constance, what else do you keep in your boot? And how do you remain so light of foot with gold and dagger on one side and only a boot upon the other?"

"A long week's practice. I am in earnest, Guyon. Take the gold."

For a brief moment, his smile faltered. "Keep it safe. I will pay."

"What will we do? Will you join Henry Plantagenet's guard?"

"If Bulat leaves for Brittany, I'll sell my sword to the king, as he has asked. If Bulat stays, looking for revenge, we must lose ourselves, for a time, far from the court. Your gold might be useful then." He lay down across the wide bed and pulled Constance to rest beside him.

A single taper cast its golden light upon the pallet, leaving the crude walls of the chamber in darkness. "I had meant to give you all that my lands and coin might buy," Guyon whispered. "But now you have a new husband, poorer than your first, and it may be years before he gets his lands back."

"You will miss them."

Guyon began to kiss the line of her jaw. "I think not."

"If not today, then tomorrow. It was much to give up."

"I had no wish to see my lands again if I could not bring you with me, Constance."

"Is it so easy for you to imagine that you will never see them again? You were born upon them. You are their lord."

His lips descended to the place where he had imagined a pearl should rest that first morning at Cagarun. "There is a song," he whispered. "A song that the queen's trouveres brought from her court at Poitiers. 'A rose cannot bloom upon the stones of a keep, nor can a man who carries a burden of gold be swift enough to follow his lady love.'" He laughed softly. "It is the song of a landless poet written to win the favor of a lady who might give him a welcome burden in gold for his words."

"Guyon, when dawn comes you will look at your sacrifice in the light of day and—"

His lips stopped her words. "I have been rich," he said at last, "in gold and lands. I have been rich all the days of my life until this night. I know what I have given to win you, and I count it as nothing beside the sight of you here beside me in my bed."

"The gatekeeper's bed."

He raised his head and looked into her eyes. "And you, Constance? You surrendered your own lands to give them peace. How will you greet the morning, my newly landless wife?''

"Lanmartin was not mine to keep. Had my brother lived, it would have been his. It remained mine only as long as I was wed to a man tolerated by my liege lord and subject to his will. Now I feel nothing but freedom. I am free, Guyon—free to love you.''

His hands, which had made short work of the laces of her kirtle, moved to spread her hair upon the bolster, then came to rest at his own side upon the coarse coverlet. Constance's eyes opened in surprise.

"Show me," he said, "what you would do with your new freedom. Love me as you wish. Do as you wish and tell me your desires.''

"All of them?''

He settled back and smiled. "All.''

She laughed then and began to draw his tunic from his broad shoulders. "I haven't enough gold, Guyon, to buy a year's lodging in this place.''

He caught her hands and kissed each palm before surrendering them. "You like it so well?''

"If we stay until I have told you all my desires, our gold will be gone long before I finish.''

Guyon pulled his tunic free and sent it into the shadows beyond the pallet. "Then make a beginning, my lady. And we will attend to the first dozen before dawn.''

The sons of the gatekeeper did not warn them, for they recognized the livery of Henry Plantagenet's men-at-arms and did not dare give warning to their lodgers. Nor did the king's men intrude upon Guyon and his bride, but waited, armed and silent, at the foot of the twisted stair until the narrow door opened at dawn.

De Burgh thrust his wife back into the chamber and faced them, his hand upon the hilt of his sword, his shoulders bracing shut the door, which hid Constance from their view. Through the panels came her cries and the small blows of her fists upon the wood.

"Bar the door," he shouted. "Stay clear."

"Do not—"

He was already down the stairs, blocking with his body the narrow opening past which they must come to reach Constance. The hilt of his sword was hot beneath his hand, itching to sweep aside the men who stood between his wife and freedom—the freedom to ride through the north gate to safe obscurity.

Above him, the chamber door opened; Constance's light footstep sounded upon the stair. Guyon kept his gaze upon the silent men he faced and pitched his voice low to calm his wife. "Go back," he said. "Wait for Algar. He will come for you."

She did not answer, but came closer still. Constance was halfway down the crude stair when she spoke. "I cannot," she said. "I would not know ... Algar would not know where they take you."

From the wall of soldiers came a voice. "King Henry wants you. Wants you both."

Guyon found the speaker and stared into his eyes. "I will give you my sword and come in peace. My wife will remain here. The king's ... words ... are for me."

Behind him, Constance drew still nearer and touched the strained, burning muscles of his sword arm. "I shall come with you," she said. And lower, in a whisper only he could hear, she spoke again. "It is my desire," she said. "My freedom."

Guyon looked beyond the men-at-arms to the narrow city gate and saw that Algar was not there. The horses were not there. There was no choice but to go.

He lowered his sword. "Then come," he said and took his lady's hand. Once again, he faced Henry Plantagenet's men. "If you harm my wife, or if you confine her, you will die. All of you. By my own hand or by the blood vengeance of my kin."

Henry Plantagenet had taken his morning meal of cold meat and hot bread within his presence chamber, hearing the last of his subjects' petitions as he ate. The men who brought Guyon and Constance took them into the great chamber and left them, unguarded and quite alone, at the back of the room. Before the king's plain chair and the small table that held his meal, a small line of petitioners stood rigid in awe and patient in hope that Henry Plantagenet would look upon their pleas and show them favor before he left Winchester that fine June morning.

The king looked up once to see that Guyon and Constance were present. Then he returned to his consideration of a woman whose kin had barred her claim to dower lands after her husband's death. "Ah, widows," he said. "My court at Winchester has become infested with widows and their detractors." He had turned his gaze back to the petitioner and directed his scribe to take the matter to the bishop of Winchester, with orders to take testimony and write his findings.

At last, the great chamber began to empty. King Henry dismissed his clerk and drank the last of his ale before summoning Guyon and Constance before him.

The long silent gaze held no animosity for Constance, but she found that her knees, once they had begun to tremble, would not still. Guyon moved closer and drew her to him, giving her strength to stand silent and wait.

"Madam," King Henry said at last, "you are very likely a witch, a demon, or some such creature. You have robbed

Guyon de Burgh of his senses and brought a pox among my subjects. You," he said to Guyon, "will remain silent as I speak or find that you have lost more than your lands."

He turned again to Constance. "You surrendered your lands to cease your obligations to Maner of Bulat. This I can understand, and I count you a reasonable woman for acting to forestall him. But now Guyon de Burgh, a man of some influence in my court, has done the same for your sake."

Henry Plantagenet rose and began to pace across the audience chamber. "Tell me, madam. Will I find more of my lords divesting themselves of their lands, casting estates aside as if they were tunics in the hands of lads on their way to swim in the river? Is this a plague you have brought to England?"

"My lord, I—"

"Be silent. I will tell you, madam, when I wish you to speak." A large, jeweled hand snatched a vellum roll from the table and brandished it before Guyon. "Do you mean to sign this, my lord de Burgh?"

"If it is my list of lands to be given back to you, then yes, I will sign it."

The royal hand pulled back the roll before Guyon's outstretched hand could grasp it. "If you had kept an eye upon this hall, as would befit a member of my guard, you would have seen Maner of Bulat departing this day. He is on the road back to Hantune, with my escort to watch his men, to take his ship back to Brittany. He carries my thanks and my gifts to the abbot at Saint Mevennus. He will not," said Henry Plantagenet, "soon visit these shores again."

"He may."

Henry Plantagenet's fist descended upon the throne. "Bulat is not stupid. He understands that he must not return unbidden."

King Henry settled back and raised the vellum once again. "Prove to me," he said, "that there is a cure for the plague your lady has brought to my kingdom. Take back your lands, de Burgh, and your obligations to me, and resume your vigilance upon your borders.''

"Your grace, I have wed the lady Constance, and will not give her up."

"And why should you if she is willing to show herself a decent wife and give the priests no cause to censure her?"

Constance raised her gaze to the throne. "Bulat's accusations—"

"Mean nothing. A torn cloth, a scratched crate, and an angry woman will not bring the papal legates to my shores." Henry Plantagenet shrugged. "The lord of Bulat left my court before I could tell him my true views of his complaints. Unfortunate, but unavoidable. If you should see Bulat," he said, "you may tell him yourself."

The king unrolled the vellum scroll and frowned at the writing upon it. "You have a good many manors, de Burgh. Too many. I would count it a fine gift to have your manor in Devon and the meadowlands you hold south of here, up the Hamble."

"You have them, your grace. And I thank you."

Once again, the vellum scroll rose before the royal gaze. "And your mills in Kent," he said.

Guyon set his mouth in a determined smile. "Of course."

"You are still a rich man, de Burgh."

"Your grace, I thank you."

"And capable, no doubt, of giving me four knights' fees for the land in Kent rather than the pittance you formerly owed."

Guyon's smile did not weaken. "Done, your grace." He drew Constance's hand into his own and saw Henry Plantagenet turn once again to the impressive list of Guyon's former lands.

* * *

Algar, ashen faced and sweating, was waiting upon the road outside the king's great hall, holding the reins of three mounts. "My lord and lady," he said, "the king's men followed me and bade me stay clear and give you no warning, for your sake. I could do nothing."

Guyon placed a hand upon Algar's shoulder. "You were right. Against the king's men, in the streets of Winchester, you could have done nothing."

"You are free?"

"We are free." Guyon drew Constance close and smiled upon Algar's relief. "And we are no longer landless."

Algar slapped his knee and grinned. "The king returned your estates?"

"Most of them. Some of them." Guyon shrugged. "The king's wealth has grown by two manors, two mills, and half my meadowlands. My lady," he said, "lost all."

Constance smiled. "Your lady is content." She looked beyond Guyon to the confusion of royal servants, pack mules, and men-at-arms assembling before the stables. "Are we to travel with the king?"

"No. And we had best leave before he appears. I might lose two more manors between here and the city walls." Guyon lifted Constance upon her mount and grabbed the reins of his own. "If we ride east," he continued, "within two days, we will reach the nearest of our remaining lands. What say you to the thought of two nights, or two hundred, in the safety of our own castle?"

"A rose cannot grow in the walls of a keep." Constance smiled and reached to touch his face. "Or have you forgotten the poet's words, now that you have your lands back?"

Guyon smiled back, his eyes shining lighter beneath the noonday sky. "The poet was a fool. Had he known my lady wife, he would have added a verse and sung of a Sussex castle soon to be burdened with roses. Hundreds of them."

Algar sighed. "It will be a slow journey, my lord, if we have but one pair of eyes to watch the road and keep us from—"

He cried out and scrambled into his saddle. It was to be a fast journey, after all, and he would need to stay close behind his lord and lady, lest they forget him.

WEDLOCKED

Denise Daniels

Chapter One

"Here come the brides," Luke muttered as the stage coach approached Dalton's Mercantile. It was just his luck that the damnable stage would be almost exactly on time. He'd been hoping for a reprieve. He'd been hoping he could go back home to his dying mother and say, "No, Mama, they aren't here yet." He'd been hoping he could enjoy a little more freedom before he hitched himself to some big-city gal who would make him miserable for the rest of his days.

His brother Cody paced on the small platform, wiping his palms against his pant legs. "Do you think we'll recognize them? Do you think Tessa will be as pretty as she was when she was a little girl?" He stopped abruptly, a panicky look on his face. "I remember her being pretty. She was pretty, Luke, wasn't she? What if—"

"Relax, Cody. Tessa was pretty then. I'm sure she's even

prettier now," Luke said as he leaned back against the clapboard building and settled his black Stetson even lower over his eyes.

Cody looked at Luke for a few seconds, then nodded. "You're probably right. This just all happened so fast. It's like something out of a dream."

"Or a nightmare."

"Cut it out, Luke," Cody said. "Out here, men marry up with women they've never before seen. Women they don't know from Adam. Hell, we've known Fancie and Tessa all our lives. We just haven't seen them in a while."

Luke sighed. "A while? Christ, Cody, you make it sound like they were over for dinner last week! We haven't seen them in eight years!"

"But still, you *know* Fancie."

"Yeah," Luke said with a grunt. "I know Fancie, all right."

"Well, there you go," Cody said, as though he had found the solution to all of life's problems. "Just give her a chance."

"She had a chance!" Luke shouted, glaring at his brother. "She walked away from it and never looked back."

Cody shook his head and turned away, leaving Luke to sulk alone. At seventeen, Cody was barely more than a child himself. A lot would be changing for him, and yet there he stood, trying to make the best of the situation. Luke couldn't find it within himself to do the same.

Trailing a cloud of dust, the horses pulled up close to the platform, and the stage coach clattered to a stop. "Whoa, there." The driver was a big man; he stood slowly, unfolding his long limbs one by one.

"Howdy, fellas," he said, nodding in the direction of Luke and Cody. He jumped down onto the wooden stoop. "I'd imagine yer waitin' on the delightful Parlay sisters."

"Yes, sir," Cody said, stepping forward. "They make it okay?"

"'Course they did, son!" the driver said, obviously insulted that anyone could have thought otherwise. "When Marty Higgins does a job, he does it right! I agreed to see these two ladies safely delivered to their grooms, an' that's just what I done. Here they are, gentlemen," he said, as he whipped the stage door open with a flourish, "and none the worse for wear, I might add." He held up his hand like a footman waiting on royalty.

A pretty young woman with softly curling blond hair peeking out from beneath her bonnet stepped carefully down.

"Thank you, Mr. Higgins," she said, her voice soft and sweet.

"Tessa?" Cody whispered.

She looked up with big blue eyes. "Cody?"

They stood staring at each other while the seconds ticked by. Finally, Cody smiled and walked toward her. He held out his arms, and Tessa stepped into them, resting her head against his shoulder as though it was the most natural thing in the world.

"It's so good to see you again," he said, holding her close.

"You too."

"How was the trip?"

"Not as bad as I thought it would be."

They stood holding hands, their gazes drinking in the many changes wrought by the passing of time.

Thump!

Luke turned his head in time to see a canvas bag, tossed from inside the coach, come skidding to a stop at his feet. He looked up just as Fancie stuck her head out the door. She ignored Marty's outstretched hand and stepped down onto the platform without anyone's assistance.

"Well," she said as she brushed at her skirt, "I wish I could say it's been a pleasure, Mr. Higgins. However, I'm not one prone to lying."

Marty Higgins burst out laughing. "You done real good, Miss Parlay. Ain't easy travelin' on a coach for days on end."

Fancie smiled and raised one perfectly arched eyebrow. "You're a master of understatement, Mr. Higgins."

Marty turned and began hauling trunks onto the platform, still smiling and chuckling to himself. Fancie had obviously been putting her charm to good use. Stage drivers were notoriously short-tempered with women—understandably so, since most women whined incessantly about the less than ideal traveling conditions.

Fancie wouldn't have done that. Not Fancie, with her strong opinion that women could endure anything men could endure and then some. Not Fancie, who'd been so eager to experience city life that she'd practically gone running out of that cowpoke town.

Luke didn't even bother trying to keep the hostility out of his voice. "Hello, Francine."

She turned toward him, and his traitorous heart tripped over itself at the sight of her. If Tessa was pretty, Fancie Parlay could only be described as breathtaking.

"Hello, Luke." She straightened herself to her full height and her eyes made a swift pass from the top of Luke's head to the tips of his best boots, as though she was assessing the enemy.

He didn't even blink. "It's been a long time," he said quietly, not moving so much as one inch toward her. Just looking at her broke his heart all over again.

She stared at him, her chin lifted upward in a defiant tilt, and Luke thought he'd never seen a woman so beautiful in his life. Like her sister, she had big eyes, but where Tessa's were ordinary old blue, Fancie's were rich amber brown. Nothing ordinary about them. And even from ten feet away, Luke could see the sinfully long lashes that framed them. He uncrossed his feet and pushed himself away from the side of the building where he'd been leaning. The sound of his boots against the wooden platform sounded like thunder in his ears as he slowly walked toward her.

When he was so close that she had to look up to see his face, he stopped. "What's in the bag?" he asked in a voice that sounded as if he might be asking what she was wearing beneath her dress.

"M-my books." Fancie glanced away, obviously irritated that he'd been able to fluster her. Luke hadn't been so straightforward at sixteen, and it was clear that he'd caught her off guard.

He nodded, as though he was agreeing with her, as though he had known the answer all along. "Don't I get a hug?" he asked, looking toward Cody and Tessa, who were holding hands and catching up and gushing all over each other. The two of them looked as if they had forgotten anyone else in the world existed.

Fancie followed his gaze. Her eyes widened, and she opened her mouth. "I-I . . ." She looked away and stepped back, putting distance between them.

Luke smiled and shook his head. "Some things never change, do they, Fancie?" He turned away from her. "That's all right. We've got plenty of time to get reacquainted." He reached down and hefted the bag, which was jam-packed with books. When he stood, he looked into those unforgettable eyes once more. "We've got every day for the rest of our wretched lives."

He turned and clomped down the steps toward the buggy hitched off to the side, leaving his soon-to-be bride staring after him.

How *dared* he dismiss her that way! Fancie sat beside Luke trying her darnedest not to let her shoulder touch his. The way he was driving the horses over the uneven ground, it was a wonder she managed to remain in the buggy at all. She got the feeling Luke was intentionally *trying* to toss her over the side.

Well, it wasn't her fault! It hadn't been her idea to come back to that godforsaken no-man's-land! If he wanted to blame anyone, he could blame his mama. After all, she was the one who had come up with this harebrained idea. Marry Luke? It was insane! She hadn't seen the man in well over eight years.

Fancie would have absolutely, positively refused to go along with the idea if it weren't for that fiasco at that disgusting house of flesh. If she had been able to get out of the building before the police had come, things would have been different.

But she hadn't gotten out. And now her parents had shipped her and Tessa off to Montana to marry men they barely knew. Men who would know nothing of the scandal Fancie had left behind. It was to be a fresh start for Tessa, who had done nothing wrong, but whose name had been tainted because of her sister.

Fancie took a chance and glanced at the man sitting beside her. Luke had grown up. He was a good eight inches taller than she was, maybe more, and he had a stubbly beard, which hadn't been much more than peach fuzz when last she'd seen him. There was a solid, sturdy bulk to him that she didn't remember. He hardly looked like the same person at all.

Still, he was right. Some things never changed. He still had that slow, steady way of moving, as though his every motion was carefully calculated. He still had the deepest, darkest brown eyes and the thickest, most gorgeous hair she'd ever seen on a man.

And he still hated her.

That knowledge settled down around her, and the

weight of it was no less now than it had been eight years earlier.

After tomorrow morning, she'd be bound to Luke for life. It was her dearest dream.

And her biggest fear.

Chapter Two

"Look at the two of you!" Marjorie Winston said, opening her arms wide. "You're all grown-up."

Fancie smiled and stepped toward the bed. "Mrs. Winston, it's so good to see you again." She bent over and wrapped her arms around the frail woman, who had once been strong as an ox. A woman who'd had the strength and determination and sheer grit to stay on the land her husband had worked hard to call his own.

"I'm so glad you came. I've missed you girls so much." Marjorie looked around Fancie. "Tessa, sweetheart, come over here."

Tessa walked toward the bed slowly. She leaned forward hesitantly and put her arms around the woman on the bed. "How are you, Mrs. Winston?"

"I'm dying, dear."

Tessa pulled back. "Oh . . . I-I'm sorry. I-I mean, I know but—"

"Tessa, dear, it's all right. I've accepted it, and so have the boys. We don't talk around it in this house." Mrs.

Winston leaned her head back against the pillows propped behind her. "In a way, I think I'm more fortunate than some. At least I'm prepared. At least I can make arrangements. My poor Billy never had the chance to do that. Those steer knocked the life out of him before he even knew what happened."

She stopped talking and sat very still, looking at both girls as though she was considering something very important.

"Maybe we'd better let you rest," Fancie said.

"In a minute . . . in a minute," Marjorie said, waving her hand, brushing off their pity. "We have some things to talk about first. Fancie, please shut the door."

Fancie opened her mouth to protest, but closed it without saying a word. What could she say that would not come out sounding cruel? How did a person go about refusing a last dying wish? Marjorie Winston would have good days, and she'd have bad days, Fancie's mother had told her before she and Tessa had left for the territory. But the end result wouldn't be altered. Mrs. Winston's tired, weak heart would one day soon simply cease beating. Fancie reached out and pushed the door until it clicked into place. She felt as though she were sealing her own tomb.

"Now," Mrs. Winston began, straightening herself up as best she could, "I know this has all been somewhat sudden. But when the doctor gave me the diagnosis, I began to think right away about my boys. It's not right for a man to live up here in this wide-open space alone. It's a hard life, and a man needs the comfort of a wife to get through the days."

"Mrs. Winston, I don't think—"

"Just hear me out, Fancie," she said, holding up her hands. "Your mother and I have been the closest friends since childhood. Why, we made it through the long trip out here with our husbands all those years ago. We had our babies together. We struggled together. It nearly broke my heart when your papa decided to go back to Chicago."

"Mama missed you a lot," Tessa said.

"We were quite a pair." Marjorie smiled at the memories. "As close as sisters. And so, naturally, when I faced the biggest crisis of my life, I turned to your mother. My biggest concern is not that I'm going to die. That would have happened sooner or later, anyway. I just don't want my boys to be left alone."

Fancie could contain herself no longer. "But, Mrs. Winston, they're not boys anymore! They're full-grown men used to making their own decisions. Do you really think that you can just present them with two women they barely know and expect them to be happy about it?"

"Barely know? Why, Luke and Cody have known the two of you your entire lives!"

"But we've changed a lot, all of us! This is *not* a good idea!"

The older woman stared at Fancie for a few seconds. They were stubborn, both of them. Someone would have to give in.

"You gonna stand there and tell me you don't feel anything at all for Luke?"

Fancie was taken aback. "Well . . . I-I . . ." She blew out a tiny puff of air and stood there, speechless. She hadn't been expecting anything that direct.

"All right. There you have it. I may be sick, but I'm not blind, Fancie. You and Luke always had something between you. You've been back less than an hour, and I can see that it's still there, strong as ever."

How could Fancie deny it? They'd had something, all right. And it hadn't take Fancie long to realize that whatever it was, it was still simmering just beneath the surface.

"And, Tessa, honey, your mother has told me so much about you. You're so much like Cody. The two of you have the same gentle hearts, the same loving ways. How much more could you ask for in a marriage?"

Tessa blushed. "I feel like I was never away from him. It's like coming home to my best friend."

"You're happy about marrying him?"

Tessa nodded. "Very happy," she said with a small smile.

Mrs. Winston considered this for a moment, looking Tessa up and down, as though examining her stability. "Your mama told you . . . about your wedding night . . . what to expect when—"

"She told us!" Fancie burst out. She nodded her head too fast. "She told us," she repeated in a calmer tone of voice. Lord, she couldn't bear to stand here and talk about *that* with the mother of the man she would be marrying!

Mrs. Winston nodded. "Okay, then. The wedding will be tomorrow. You brought your dresses?" Both girls nodded. "Good. There's nothing more beautiful than a June bride. Your mother was married in June, you know."

Fancie nodded. "Yes, I know."

"Well, of course you do," Marjorie said, waving her hands again. "I'm sure mothers and daughters talk about those sorts of things all the time. With sons, it's a different matter altogether. With sons . . ." She let her words trail off and sat shaking her head. She seemed to be lost in long-ago memories when she suddenly snapped back into the present. "My roses are in full bloom. Tomorrow morning you can both go out and cut as many as you want for your bouquets."

"Thank you," Tessa said softly.

"No. Thank you, child." The woman looked up at Fancie and said, "I want you to be happy. I want all of you to be happy."

Fancie tried to smile reassuringly, but found she couldn't quite do it. The following day, she'd marry Luke, the man she'd loved forever. The man she'd left behind. And she knew that he must have been feeling a lot of things right now.

But no matter how hard she tried to twist her imagination, there was no way she could pretend that his feelings toward his approaching nuptials were anything that even vaguely resembled happiness.

Luke sat out on the front porch steps, watching the fading sun streak the evening sky orange and purple. His elbows were braced against his knees, and his hands cradled a cup of coffee, which had long ago grown cold. Sounds of Cody's voice and Tessa's laughter drifted around from the side of the house.

Lord, he didn't want that day to end. Because when the sky brightened with the approach of another day, he'd be facing down the devil, and he knew it.

How could he stand before God and promise to love, honor, and cherish the very woman who had ripped his heart out?

But how could he not? How did a son deny his mother her last dying wish? Marjorie was one of the most determined women Luke had ever met, and when she got hold of an idea, she didn't let go. There was no changing her mind. The only thing he could do was to simply refuse her last wish.

And there was no way he could do that.

He stood up and flung the dregs at the bottom of his coffee cup into the grass. The following day, he would marry Francine Parlay, undoubtedly the most beautiful, desirable woman he'd ever seen.

And because he'd sooner chop off his right hand than allow himself to touch her again, he'd be hurling himself into the depths of a temptation so strong he had no idea how he would fight it.

Fancie looked out the window of the room she was sharing with Tessa. It would be the last time she ever shared a bed with her sister. Tessa, who'd crawled into Fancie's bed when she was only two years old, claiming there were Indians under her own, and had been there ever since. Tessa, who'd been born when Fancie was eight years old and whom Fancie had mothered and protected every day since then. Tessa, whose chances of getting a marriage proposal back in Chicago were just about nil, thanks to her sister.

Fancie stood at the window, listening. Tessa and Cody were on the porch and Fancie could hear her sister's laughter as it floated up toward the stars, which would soon be winking down at them from the night sky.

Tessa was marrying Cody the next day, and she was clearly happy about that, despite the fact that they hadn't seen each other since they were children. Tessa was one of those infuriating people who always managed to remain happy, no matter what situation she fell into.

Fancie, it seemed, was always striving for something just a little bit better than what she had. She was always sure that the answer to her happiness would be at the end of the road she was traveling, or at the end of the book she was reading, or at the end of the rally for the latest good cause she had embraced.

But no matter how hard she tried, true happiness was always just beyond her grasp. Fancie found herself wishing for nothing more than to simply be able to stop *looking*. She didn't want to search for meaning in her life anymore. She didn't want to keep chasing dreams she could never quite catch up with.

Fancie wanted to be content.

This marriage would *not* provide that.

Through the walls, she heard the low rumbling of Luke's voice as he visited with his mother. She didn't need to make out the words; she knew what he was feeling. The look in his eyes when she'd first seen him had told her all she needed to know.

Luke Winston wanted nothing to do with her.

She turned from the window and lay down on the bed, curling herself into a tight little ball. She'd close her eyes. Maybe when she opened them again, this bad dream would be over.

Chapter Three

"Wake up, Fancie! Wake up!"

Tessa shook her sister's shoulder, and Fancie struggled to pull herself up from the depths of a deep sleep. She opened her eyes and blinked at the sunshine pouring in through the windows.

"What time is it?" she mumbled.

"It's seven-thirty. You'd better hurry. We have to be at the church for twelve, and Luke said it takes nearly an hour to get there."

Tessa's words sped past Fancie's ears so fast that her sleepy brain wasn't able to decipher them all. "What church?"

Tessa laughed. "Come on, sleepyhead. It's our wedding day, and I, for one, do not plan to keep my groom waiting."

Wedding! Fancie sat up in a panic. It was her wedding day.

"What did I . . . when did I fall asleep?"

"Right after dinner." Tessa bent from the waist and pulled a brush through her curls. "Mrs. Winston is having the housekeeper fill tubs for us. Would you braid my hair before you take your bath? It's so much easier to do if it's still wet."

"Of course," Fancie answered automatically, running a hand over her own disheveled topknot.

"How are you wearing your hair?"

"I-I don't know. I hadn't really thought about it."

Tessa stood up and planted her hands on her hips. "Well, you'd better start thinking about it." She hurried to a drawer and removed from it a clean white chemise, a corset, and pantaloons. From a hook on the door she removed a fluffy, lace-edged petticoat. "Do you want roses for your hair?"

Fancie stood up slowly, as if she was afraid her legs wouldn't support her. "I don't care."

"Fancie! What is wrong with you?"

"Nothing."

"Nothing?" Tessa advanced on her sister and pointed a finger at her. "You listen to me. I don't care what happened all those years ago! Get over it! This is the only wedding day you'll ever have. Make the most of it!"

Fancie looked at her sister as though seeing her for the first time. Tessa never lost her temper! "Tessa, what's gotten into you?"

Tessa snatched her underclothes from the bed, where she had lain them, and clutched them to her chest. "*I* am going to get ready for my groom. When you're through feeling sorry for yourself, I suggest you do the same." She spun away and sailed through the door, slamming it behind herself.

Fancie stood staring at the door. Tessa *never* slammed doors! "Well!" she muttered, blinking and trying to come fully awake. She turned to look at herself in the mirror. Her hair was a tangled mess, her dress looked as if she had been wearing it for a week (she had been), and she hadn't had a good bath—a real bath—since leaving Chicago.

She reached up to pull the remaining pins from her hair and struggled to pull a brush through the knots, cursing the fates that had blessed Tessa with perfect blond curls while Fancie had been given stick-straight brown hair.

She had every right to feel sorry for herself, she thought, as she brushed with a vengeance. She'd just had all her dreams ripped from her hands and replaced with a fate she'd been avoiding for most of her life! She wanted to *do* things! She wanted to make some difference in the world. What could she possibly contribute by becoming a rancher's wife? The fact that this particular rancher was Luke Winston did nothing to help the situation.

Fancie walked toward the window, pushed the curtain aside, and looked down on the place that would be her home. It sure was a different view from the alley she saw out of her bedroom window back in Chicago.

Montana *was* pretty, she had to admit. And the Billy D Ranch was about as pretty as it got. The grass surrounding the house was thick and green, punctuated at uneven intervals with rosebushes of every type, size, and color imaginable. They climbed up fence posts and tree trunks, spread over slopes and rocks, and splashed their vibrant color and sweet fragrance everywhere.

Beyond the immediate yard, there were four massive barns, each with its own silo, a number of sheds and lean-tos, and a bunkhouse, which was home to the cowboys the Winstons employed.

From the second floor of the house, Fancie could look out on the fields beyond. The rolling hills stretched out as far as she could see, settled between a softly swelling mountain to the east and a rocky, jutting cliff far to the west. The ranch ranged from river-bottom meadows to high-elevation pastures surrounded by aspen and pine. It was a beautiful place, with hundreds of acres left virtually untouched by man.

The morning sun was everywhere, and Fancie could see spots here and there that positively sparkled in the light. That would be the ponds and creeks that wound their way through the Winston's land.

As Fancie gazed out her window, she remembered the many summers of her childhood that were spent swimming in those ponds and floating makeshift boats down the creeks that swelled in the springtime and, by late summer, virtually dried up. She used to imagine that she was on those boats, traveling to distant places, meeting different people. And in her dreams, Luke was always beside her. Fancie sighed and closed her eyes, thinking back to those long-ago days.

The Parlay land had bordered the Winston's, and the children of both families had known the combined three hundred and twenty acres well. Fancie's father had worked his hundred and sixty acres for the five years mandated by the Homestead Act, which made the land officially his to do with as he wished. Then the winter of '71 had come along, with wind and cold so severe that it wiped out nearly his entire stock. And he'd decided that what he wished to do with his land was to sell it and move back to the city. And that was when Fancie's life had taken a turn she never expected. For the first time in her life, Luke Winston had not been beside her.

From outside, Fancie heard a dog barking, and she looked toward the sound. A rider came into view, his face shaded from the sun by a black Stetson, the long legs that straddled the horse sheathed in blue denim, his feet encased in the pointy-toed boots no one in the city wore.

She recognized everything about him, and she didn't have to see his face to know it was Luke. Something she couldn't put a name on clenched inside her. He stopped and slid from the horse's back, and the dog went wild.

Luke bent over and the beautiful black-and-white Border collie leapt up at him, so excited to see his master that he nearly knocked Luke over. The two played in the grass, Luke tossing sticks and his dog Lucky retrieving them.

Fancie watched him shower the dog with affection, and her heart jumped. She let out a little sound, more like a rushing of air than anything else, and reached out to hold on to the windowsill.

He couldn't possibly have heard her; he was at least fifty yards away. But he snapped his head up and looked straight at her.

Fancie felt as if her feet had been nailed to the floor. She stood there, dressed in the previous day's dress, with her tangled hair hanging over her shoulders, struggling to catch her breath. She reached up and touched her neck with her fingertips. Suddenly, the air that had been trapped there was freed, and she gulped big breaths, as though she had been drowning and was now trying to make up for it.

She stood there, clutching the windowsill and breathing too quickly, and she watched as Luke stood, never taking his eyes off of her. He spread his feet and tilted his head back and stood staring at her. Fancie felt the heat of his gaze as surely as if she could feel the warmth of his breath on her skin.

She closed her eyes, hung her head back, and fought the attraction she was feeling with everything she had. She did *not* want to marry this man. She did *not* want to stay here. She squeezed her eyes shut and repeated that thought over and over. When she opened her eyes, Luke was gone.

Luke stomped into the barn, ripping the bandanna from around his neck as he went. He marched straight through, past the stalls that held some of the best horseflesh in this part of the country, and out the back, so that he was inside the fence that held their stock. There was a pump beside the door, with a big wooden trough placed to catch the water it drew up out of the earth.

His shirt was halfway unbuttoned by the time he reached the pump. He grabbed the handle of the pump and filled the tub with icy-cold water.

He kicked off his boots, peeled off his clothes, and plunged himself into the frigid water. The pump served as a washroom, of sorts, for the hands they employed, and sometimes even for Luke and Cody, when they were too dirty to step foot in the kitchen, where the water would have been warmed.

It served him fine right now. He scrubbed his hide and tried to wash off the desire he was feeling.

She'd *left* him, damn it! Broken his heart and left him. And after so many years, the mere sight of her still had the ability to make him rock hard.

He dunked his head beneath the surface and listened to the muffled sounds that filtered through the insulating water. He stayed under until he thought his lungs would burst; only then did he come up.

He sat in the soapy water, breathing hard. Had he no pride? How could he still want her after all this time?

"Luke?"

He looked up and found his brother watching him. "What?"

"What are you doing?"

"I'm taking a bath. In case you didn't know, I'm getting married today, and I wanted to take a bath," he said sarcastically.

"Out here?"

Luke looked around as though he had only just realized that he was sitting in a water trough in the middle of an open field. He reached up and rubbed a wet hand across his forehead. "Hell, I don't know." He sighed. "It seemed like a good idea at the time."

Cody nodded and leaned back against the building. "You know you stormed right past me in the barn."

"I didn't even see you."

"No kidding."

Luke ran his hands through his wet hair. "Ah, Cody, what am I gonna do?"

"You're gonna marry Francine Parlay."

"Yeah, I'm gonna marry Francine Parlay, and then I'll know what hell feels like because I'll be living it for the rest of my life."

Cody shook his head. "I don't know why you're fighting it."

"Fighting what?"

When Cody just raised his eyebrows, Luke looked away. Then Cody said, "That girl gets you all fired up, and there's no sense denying it."

"I don't deny it," Luke said quietly. "But I will fight it. I'll fight it till my dying day."

"Why? Why can't you just give in to it? In a few hours you're going to take her as your wife, Luke. You're going to promise to love her. Why are you so eager to break that promise?"

"I'll tell you why. When her papa decided to move back to the city, Fancie and I were this close"—he held up his thumb and index finger a scant half inch apart—"we were this close to . . ." He let his hand flop back down into the water. "I begged her to stay here with me. Offered her everything I had. And she turned me down."

He looked up at Cody, and he was glad his hair was dripping water on his face because he knew his eyes were wet with tears. "I loved her, Cody. And if I hadn't hardened my heart against it, it would have killed me. I can't do it again."

"But she's marrying you, Luke. She's not going anywhere this time," Cody argued.

"You don't know that! Fancie's every bit as hardheaded

as our mother, and if she decides she's going to do something, by damn, she'll do it. And if it means ripping my heart out again, I don't think she'd care."

"Luke, you can't mean that," Cody said, shaking his head. "She didn't leave because she wanted to hurt you— you *know* that. And besides, she came back, didn't she?"

"Sorry, kid. I can't take that chance." He splashed a handful of water over his face. "I'll marry her, but she'll stay on her side of the bed, and I'll stay on mine."

Cody just shook his head and looked down at the ground. "You're a stronger man than I could ever be. The thought of lyin' next to Tessa and not being able to touch her . . . Well, I couldn't do it." He looked up with a guilty grin on his face. "I can't wait till tonight."

Luke grunted and smiled. "Randy kid."

"Yeah, well, it's about time, wouldn't you say?"

Luke just shook his head. It was clear that his baby brother was in love with his intended. "Do me a favor?"

"Sure, anything." Cody looked at him as if he was expecting to hear something profound.

"Go up to the house and get me some clothes." Luke lifted his hands out of the water as though to demonstrate his point. "Forgot about clothes."

Cody laughed. "Oh, yeah," he said, shaking his head and opening the door to the barn, "you'll be staying on your side of the bed, all right." The door closed behind him, but Luke could still hear him talking. "Man hasn't got enough sense to keep from walkin' round naked. Own side of the bed . . ."

God help him, the kid was right. Damned woman had him worked up into a frenzy. He couldn't even think straight. He cupped a handful of icy water and rubbed it on his face.

His head might be spinning, but one thing was perfectly clear in his mind: Until he figured out some way to guarantee that Miss Francine Parlay wouldn't take off the first chance she got, he had to keep his distance.

His sanity depended on it.

"Gentlemen," the minister said, closing the small book he'd been reading from, "you may kiss your brides."

The words were barely out of his mouth before Cody and Tessa reached for each other. Beside Luke and Fancie they kissed, and everyone in the room knew that it wasn't the first time they'd done it.

Fancie whipped her head around, uncomfortable with the idea of witnessing even a little bit of the passion that was brewing between her sister and her young husband. Unfortunately, avoiding that scene left her face-to-face with Luke, who was looking at the minister as though he'd like to choke him.

"Go on," the nervous, little man said quietly. "Kiss your bride! It's not official without a kiss." He smiled at Luke as though the two of them were in on some big secret. "Go on."

Luke hadn't so much as touched Fancie since her arrival yesterday. In fact, except for those few minutes on the stage platform, and the brief encounter from across the yard that morning, he hadn't even looked her way. Fancie knew the last thing he wanted to do was kiss her.

Still, the minister was waiting. Watching and waiting. And in what was possibly the world's fastest kiss, Luke leaned forward and pressed his lips against hers. Fancie barely had time to close her eyes before it was over.

"There you go!" the minister said. "Congratulations Mr. and Mrs. Winston," he said, turning toward Cody and Tessa, who managed, briefly, to separate themselves from each other. "And congratulations also to you, Mr. and Mrs. Winston," he said, turning back to face Luke and Fancie. "I wish you all a long life of happiness."

Fancie watched as the minister turned and walked into a small room off to the side of the front of the small chapel, leaving the four of them alone. She looked up at Luke, who, with an expression of disgust on his face, was watching the minister leave. It was clear that he didn't want to be left alone with his new wife.

"Well, what do you say, Luke?" Cody asked, his arm wrapped protectively around Tessa's shoulders. "How does it feel?"

Luke turned toward his brother slowly. "No different that I can tell. Let's get a move on. I have work to do." He turned and walked out of the church, leaving Fancie behind with Cody and Tessa.

Fancie closed her eyes, close to tears and mortified that anyone else would know it. She had just as many reservations about their marriage as Luke had, but ever since she was a little girl, she'd thought about what her wedding day would be like. She'd never imagined anything like this.

"Don't worry, Fancie," Cody said, squeezing her shoulder reassuringly. "He'll come around."

She opened her eyes and nodded quickly, afraid that her voice would fail her if she tried to speak. Cody put one arm around each of them and led them out of the chapel. It was sweet of him. Fancie appreciated his efforts to make her feel better, but he needn't have bothered.

She was married to Luke Winston, a man who obviously despised her. Fancie feared she'd never feel better again.

Chapter Four

He couldn't possibly eat another bite.

Luke leaned back in his chair and stared at what remained of the wedding dinner his mother had had the housekeeper prepare. Marjorie had gone all out, and the big kitchen looked as festive as Luke ever remembered seeing it. She'd had so many roses cut that the entire house was filled with their fragrance. They were poked in vases and bottles and glasses and set on every conceivable surface, from the tabletops to the mantel to the windowsills. She'd also draped white ribbons and big, fluffy bows around each doorway into the room. Where she'd found white ribbon way out here, Luke couldn't imagine.

It was as pretty a room as he had ever been in, and even a hard-hearted, solitary rancher like himself knew that it was meant to inspire romance.

But Luke wasn't buying into it. Marjorie Winston would have to be a miracle worker to inspire romance in her son's heart. Right now, the only thing he was feeling was dread.

It was already after eight, and everyone had finished eating long ago. Everyone except Luke. He'd eaten as if he hadn't seen food in a week, and every time it seemed he was finally finished, he'd reach for something else. The longer he sat at this table, he reasoned, the less time he'd have to spend alone with Fancie.

And though his words to his brother had sounded determined enough, Luke was beginning to have second thoughts about his ability to keep his hands to himself when he and his new wife retired for the night.

At twenty-four, Fancie was infinitely more tempting than she'd been at sixteen. She'd only been a girl before. Now she was a woman. And while she had outgrown the youthful innocence he remembered, it had been replaced with a worldliness that made Luke's body respond in ways his mind kept trying to subdue.

How could he stay detached when that beautiful woman was sitting beside him, so close that he could smell the sweet scent of her, even over the roses? How could he lie beside her and not touch the body he had known almost as well as his own all those years ago?

There had to be a way. And Luke didn't care if it killed him, which, at this point, he was reasonably sure it would. He would *not* touch Fancie.

Not that night.

Not any other night.

Fancie pulled the bed covers up to her chin. The room was pitch-black, and though she couldn't see a thing, she lay with her eyes wide open.

Her husband had offered to let her prepare for bed in privacy, a gesture she deeply appreciated. This night was going to be awkward enough. She wasn't sure she could have endured Luke's angry eyes watching her while she undressed.

Not that he'd never seen her naked before. He had. But so many years had passed since then, and so much had changed between them, that Fancie couldn't have been more nervous if she was waiting for a complete stranger.

Cody and Tessa had gone up to bed together, the hunger they had for each other so clear in their eyes that everyone in the room had been able to see it. Even the housekeeper, who smiled shyly as she offered them wrapped pieces of wedding cake and said, "In case you get hungry later."

But Luke had gone outside, ostensibly to give her privacy, though Fancie suspected his gesture had nothing to do with chivalry—and everything to do with disgust.

He hated her. Her husband hated her.

How had they come to this? There had been a time when she'd loved Luke so much, she'd thought she would die. There'd been a time when they'd explored each other's bodies with hands and mouths that were driven by a passion so strong she'd thought it would drown them both. She remembered those days and wondered how they had ever been able to find the strength to keep themselves from . . .

There was no point in thinking about the past. The fact of the matter was, she was Luke's wife. And as his wife, she'd be expected to perform certain duties. Luke would take what he had denied himself all those years ago. Fancie would just have to accept that, for her husband, this act would never be inspired by love.

Her leaving had killed that long ago.

The house had been dark for well over an hour, and still, Luke sat outside by the barn, waiting. Drinking. He raised the bottle of whiskey to his lips and swallowed again. He didn't drink much anymore, hadn't since he'd taken those first tentative steps toward manhood. But that night was different. That night he had to numb his body and his mind as quickly as possible. That night, he drank with the intention of getting good and drunk. So drunk that he passed out the second he hit the bed.

It was the only thing he could think of that might work.

Fancie had looked beautiful in her wedding dress. Her hair was twisted up into a loose knot at the top of her head that left long strands free to fall around her face. She'd worked roses into it, the same apricot-colored roses that she'd carried.

Luke knew what she looked like beneath that dress. He remembered how the curve of her breasts had filled his hands. He knew that the hollow at the base of her throat was ticklish, the skin on her belly, sensitive. He'd never forgotten the sight of her lying beneath him with her hair all loose and wild around her. Maybe if he hadn't forced himself to stop the last time he'd seen her like that, he wouldn't be going through this torment now. Maybe he'd have gotten her pregnant, and she would have had to stay and marry him.

He lifted the bottle and drank deeply, ignoring the searing burn that shot down his throat to his stomach.

When would he ever stop feeling the burn of wanting Francine Parlay? Would there ever come a day in this sorry marriage when he could touch her and feel nothing and know he'd had enough of her?

He drank again, and this time, the bottle came back down empty. There was no delaying it any longer.

He stood up and felt himself weave until he caught his balance. *Go to bed, Luke. Go to bed and leave your wife alone.*

Stepping up onto the porch, he reached up and removed his hat, just as his mama had taught him to do as a child. A man never wore a hat indoors, she'd always said. He walked through the dark house, trying not to knock into anything, trying to be quiet. Maybe Fancie would be asleep already. He climbed the steps and staggered down the hall, brushing his shoulder along the wall as he went. He couldn't seem to stand straight up on his own. He needed the wall.

At his door, Luke stood staring down at the spot where he knew the doorknob was. *Stay on your own side of the bed, Luke. Stay on your own side.*

He opened the door and stepped into the room. It was black as pitch; he stood blinking his eyes and trying to get his bearings. He was a little dizzy, and when he closed the door, he leaned against it for a few seconds, hoping to steady himself. It didn't work. He pushed himself away from the door and walked to the bed. He'd almost sat down to remove his boots before he realized that he didn't know which side she was sleeping on. He hadn't been in there to let her know which side he preferred. She would have had no way of knowing.

Luke took a deep breath and reached out to touch the bed, on the side where he always slept.

It was empty.

He let out his breath and carefully lowered himself to the mattress. He pulled off his boots, stripped out of his clothing, and crawled beneath the covers, rather quietly, he thought, for a man as drunk as he was. He settled back onto his pillow and lay staring up at the ceiling. He couldn't even hear her breathing.

Was she even there?

The thought came as a surprise, and he lay still, trying to determine, without reaching over to touch her, whether Fancie was in the bed with him.

Stop thinking about it, Luke. Just go to sleep. What difference does it make whether she's beside you or not?

He yawned. Sleep would come quickly. The whiskey would guarantee that. He was almost asleep when she spoke.

"Luke?"

He jumped. She *was* in his bed! "What?"

She hesitated. "Aren't we going to—"

"No, Fancie, we're not."

A long pause this time. "When?"

The exhaustion Luke had been praying for was seeping through his body, numbing his mind. He didn't want to think about this. He didn't want to have this conversation. He rolled over onto his side and yanked the covers up over his shoulder. "Never," he said, knowing, even as he said the word, how cruel he sounded. He didn't care.

And with that thought, he passed out.

Chapter Five

The next morning, when Luke opened the door and stepped into the kitchen, four sets of eyes turned toward him, and it seemed as though time had stopped. Everyone went stone still, even the housekeeper Mattie.

" 'Mornin', everyone," he said, moving toward the table.

"You're up early today," his mother said.

"No earlier than usual," he said, reaching for a sausage link and wrapping it in a piece of bread. "I get a lot done before breakfast." He sat down at the table and looked around. "Where's Fancie?"

"Didn't feel up to breakfast with the family this morning," Marjorie said. She didn't blink. Luke felt as if he was five years old again and had gotten caught doing something he knew he shouldn't have done.

"Oh, that's too bad," he said without the slightest trace of sympathy. "Cody, I want you to take a ride up to the north pasture today. Get a rough count. Should be two hundred and ten." Luke reached for the pan of hashed browned potatoes and spooned a pile onto his plate.

"Sure, Luke, if that's—"

"Cody can't go today," Marjorie interrupted. "Get one of the hired hands to do it."

"Mama, it's Sunday."

"I don't care if it's judgment day!" she shouted. "Cody and his bride deserve at least one day together before he gets back to work. Get someone else to do it!"

"Mama, I don't mind—" Cody began.

"Well, I do!" She pushed away from the table and struggled to stand. "Luke, I want to talk to you." She turned and walked toward the steps with the aid of a cane. At the bottom of the steps, she turned and pierced her son with her gaze. "Now." She began the arduous job of climbing the stairs. Her breathing was labored, but she was mad— and determined.

Luke stopped chewing and watched as his mother made her way upstairs. He glanced at Cody, who had a grim expression on his face. Tessa hadn't looked up from her plate. "Now what?" he asked.

"You'd better get up there," Cody said quietly, "before she—"

"Luke!"

Both men looked up at the ceiling. Sick or not, their mother was not a patient woman.

Luke scraped his chair back and stood, then walked past the housekeeper. He winked at her and said, "Pray for me, Mattie."

She swatted at him with the dishtowel she held. "Go on. Git up there 'fore she yells again! Move it!"

When had the women in his life gotten so bossy? Luke sauntered past her and climbed the steps to his mother's bedroom. She was looking out the window and struggling to catch her breath.

She turned around and fixed him with that glare again. "Close the door." She spoke quietly, although it was clear that she did so with great difficulty.

Luke closed the door, and she pointed to a chair with the end of her cane. "Sit."

"Mama, I don't—"

"Sit!"

Luke sighed. It wasn't good for her to get so worked up. It would take days for her to recover from the strain of the episode. He sat.

"What did you do to that poor girl?"

"Who?"

"Your wife, that's who!" Marjorie's eyes were blazing.

"Nothing. I don't know what you're talking about. She was still asleep when I got up this morning."

"She was *not* asleep. From the looks of her, I'd say she'd been up and crying for several hours."

"Crying?" Luke snapped to attention. "What was she crying about?"

"You tell me."

"How the hell would I know?" he asked, jumping to his feet. "I've barely spoken to her since she got here. Maybe she doesn't like the idea of being married to me any more now than she did eight years ago. Do you think that could be it, Mother?" he asked. "Do you think, maybe, she didn't *like* being forced to marry me? Do you think that could have made her cry? I told you this would not work!" he said, jabbing his finger in the air toward his mother. "*You* wanted this marriage. I didn't. Obviously, Fancie didn't either."

He whipped the door open and stormed out, his boots stomping noisily down the stairs. He stormed past Cody, Tessa, and Mattie, all of whom stared at him as if they were afraid he was unstable. Damn it, he didn't care what they thought!

He grabbed his hat off the rack by the door and marched outside, calling to Lucky as he went. He mounted his horse and took off at a gallop, not even giving the dog a chance to catch up.

He hadn't asked for such misery! In fact, he'd fought against it as hard as he could. But short of refusing what his mother had dramatically taken to calling her "last dying wish," there was nothing Luke could have done to avoid it.

Marjorie had gotten them into this mess. He'd let her figure out a way to get them all out of it.

"Fancie, dear, may I come in?"

Fancie sat up and dabbed at her eyes with a wet handkerchief. "Just a minute." She ran her hands over her hair, trying to hide the damage lying in bed had caused. She looked in the mirror.

What use was it? She'd been crying for hours, and she looked it. There was nothing she'd be able to do to fix her hair before Luke's mother saw. She opened the door. "Come in."

Marjorie took one look at her and said, "Oh, Fancie, honey, what happened?"

And that was the end of Fancie's resolve. She burst into tears. Again.

"Oh, come here, come here," Marjorie said, holding out her arms.

Fancie went into them gratefully. "Oh, Mrs. Winston, this was a mistake! I knew it was! He hates me. Luke hates me." She sobbed into her mother-in-law's hair.

"Hates you? Nonsense! That boy loves you, Francine."

"He does not! I don't know how you can say that. He doesn't." She turned and flopped down onto the edge of the bed. "This was a big mistake," she said again.

"Tell me what happened."

Fancie shook her head. "I can't." How she wished for her own mother! But she didn't have that. All she had was

Luke's mother, and it didn't feel right to be talking about this with her. "I just can't."

Marjorie waited for a few seconds, then said, "All right then. You stay up here as long as you like. I'll have Mattie bring your lunch up to you—and your dinner too if you want."

Fancie nodded. "Thank you."

The older woman turned as if to go, but paused, facing the door. "My son is stubborn. No doubt he gets that from me. But he doesn't hate you, Fancie. Even if he says he does, and I can't imagine that he would be so cruel. Marriage takes some getting used to. Some growing into. You and Luke might just need to work at it a little bit, that's all." She opened the door and went out. Fancie could hear her close the door to her own room on the other side of the wall.

Work at it? How could she work at it when her husband despised her so much that he wouldn't even touch her?

Fancie had not wanted this marriage. But here they were, married, just the same, and it hadn't taken much more than that look across the yard the day before to show Fancie that Luke could still command her body to respond to him, even without a touch, without a word. If he had reached out for her the previous night, Fancie knew that her body would have ignited.

But he hadn't touched her. And she had lain beside him all night aching inside. Hungering for the feel of his hands on her body. Craving the release she had waited for all these years.

She'd never have that release, she thought, as the tears came again. Luke had control like no one she'd ever met. If he told himself never, then never it would be.

She rolled onto the pillow, not caring what it did to her hair. She cried hard, not caring if anyone heard her.

She let go of her dreams, not caring if it killed her.

* * *

Luke sat in the shade of a scrubby tree, Lucky by his side. Lazily, he scratched the dog's head. Lucky closed his eyes and promptly fell asleep.

He'd made Fancie cry. That was what he'd wanted, wasn't it? Hadn't he wanted to give her a taste of the pain she'd caused him?

He'd told himself that he had, but faced with actual tears, it didn't seem like such a good idea anymore. In fact, it seemed like an awful idea. The pain in his heart that he'd learned to ignore years ago was back full force. He'd made Fancie cry, and that thought hurt like hell.

He looked out at the cattle Lucky had rounded up for him. Two hundred and eight, as best as he could count. The animals had another two months to fatten up before they got shipped off to the slaughterhouse.

Luke watched as the herd began to spread out, none of them needing to go very far to find a supply of sweet green grass. What a simple life they led. They were born, they ate, they grew, they died.

Luke wished his own life was that simple. But no such luck. *He* had to be saddled with a conscience that berated him for his treatment of Fancie. After all, she had been pushed into this every bit as much as he had.

Fancie had broken his heart, and now his stubborn pride wouldn't let him forgive her. So what did he do with this marriage of his? He'd be married to her till the day he died. How long would it take him to learn forgiveness? A year? Five years? Forever?

Lucky picked his head up at the sound of approaching hooves. Luke followed the sound and saw Cody riding toward him. He had his arms wrapped around Tessa, who was squeezed into the saddle with him.

They stopped when they reached Luke, and Cody slid down. "Hey, Luke."

"Hey."

"Come on," Cody said to his new bride. "I'll catch you." He held up his arms. Tessa looked down as though to judge the distance to the ground; then she leaned over and fell into her husband's arms.

It only took witnessing that one small act for Luke to see what was missing between him and Fancie. Trust. Simple trust.

"You get 'em all counted?" Cody asked.

"Yep. Two hundred and eight."

"Close enough, for now."

"Yep."

Cody and Tessa stood looking down at Luke, who gazed out into the distance. "I thought I'd take Tessa for a ride and show her the place. See if she remembered any of it."

"Do you?" Luke asked.

"I'm not sure," Tessa said. "Some things look familiar, but I'm not sure if I'm remembering being here or at our old place."

Luke nodded. "You were little when you left."

"Only eight."

He nodded again, but kept his eyes on the horizon.

"Oh, look," Tessa said, pointing to a patch of cream-colored wildflowers. "Wild tulips. I'm going to go pick some."

"Just be careful," Cody said. "Don't go too far."

"I won't," she said, turning away to give the brothers some privacy.

Lucky stood up and barked at her. He looked at Luke and whined.

"Go on. Go with her, boy," Luke said, and the dog took off after Tessa, barking as though to say, "Wait for me!"

The brothers watched as Tessa spun around, her blond hair flying out around her while she clapped and called to Lucky.

"God, she is beautiful," Cody said reverently.

Luke saw such love on Cody's face he couldn't help envying his brother. "I'm glad you're happy."

Cody tore his eyes away from Tessa with great difficulty. "I am," he said, sitting down beside Luke. "It feels so right."

Luke nodded and looked away. He didn't want to dull his brother's joy. He pulled a fistful of grass out of the ground, then opened his hand and let the blades float down.

"What happened with Fancie?" Cody asked quietly.

Luke sighed and closed his eyes. "This is a mess."

"Luke, things have changed."

Suddenly, the sound of Tessa's screams filled the air. Luke and Cody jumped to their feet, both of them reaching for the guns they wore strapped around their hips. Lucky was barking like wild, and Cody was yelling, "What is it? What is it?"

But Tessa was too terrified to answer him, and as they came to her side, they both skidded to a halt.

"Whoa," Luke said, reaching out to stop Cody. "Move slow."

"Tessa, don't move!" Cody said. "Don't move!"

Lucky kept up his barking, which kept the coiled rattlesnake momentarily distracted.

"Oh, God, Cody," Tessa said, tears streaming down her face. "I stepped right next to it!"

"Close your eyes, Tessa," Luke said. He fired one shot. The snake jumped from the force of it, then lay still.

"Oh, my God," Tessa said, covering her face with her hands. "I could have died."

"Don't say that!" Cody shouted, pulling his shaking wife into his arms. He buried his fingers in her hair and set her head against his chest. His other hand, wrapped around her back, still held his gun.

"Your gun, Cody," Luke said. They'd been taught safety from a young age.

Cody shook his head, his eyes still clenched shut. "I know," he said, dropping his arm from around Tessa long enough to secure the weapon in the holster at his side.

"Take me back to the house, Cody." She had stopped crying, but was still pale and shaken.

Cody nodded. "Okay. We'll look around another day." He put his hand on her shoulder and turned her to go. "We'll see you back at the house," he called over his shoulder.

Luke watched as Cody climbed up on the horse, then showed Tessa where to put her foot. After she did as he instructed, she held up her arms. Cody lifted her up onto the saddle and settled her comfortably in front of him. He leaned forward and whispered something into her ear, and she rested her head back against his chest for a second before they headed home.

Cody and Tessa were in love. Their marriage would make it. Luke was sure of it.

He couldn't say the same for his own.

Chapter Six

It was Sunday evening. Fancie had spent the whole day locked in her room, and the confinement was beginning to get to her. She paced around the bed like a caged animal.

There must be *something* she could do. Back in Chicago, she'd volunteered for so many charities and good causes that every minute of her day was filled. Looking back now, she realized that she'd kept herself busy for a reason. With all of her energies focused on other people, she'd never had to face her own problems.

She'd never had to think about Luke.

She took a deep breath and pushed the troublesome thought away. "There must be something. There must be something," she muttered, thinking back to her activities in Chicago. She'd gotten quite a reputation as a woman who could get things done, and requests for her help were frequent. It was just such a request that had forced her back to Montana.

Back to Luke.

She stopped in front of the windows, crossed her arms in front of her, and looked down on the property below. What kind of good works were there to be done on a cattle ranch? There must be someone who needed her. Someone who would benefit from—

"That's it!" she said quietly. She looked out at the bunkhouse. The windows were glowing a soft yellow from the lamps inside. "Perfect," she whispered. "Absolutely perfect."

Fancie felt that familiar sense of expectancy flood through her. She wasn't about to waste another day mourning this hopeless marriage to Luke! She knelt on the floor and felt under the bed. When her fingers found what they were looking for, she laughed, just because of the sheer joy of the realization that all was not lost. She didn't have to give up all of herself. She'd found a way to preserve one little bit of the woman she had become.

Fancie was back on track.

They were lingering over coffee when she walked into the room. All conversation stopped, but Fancie marched right past her husband and the rest of the family without giving them so much as a glance. She closed the door quietly, as though by doing so the interruption would go unnoticed.

"What the hell is she up to now?" Luke muttered, scraping back his chair and walking to the window. His wife was walking through the yard toward the bunkhouse.

"Where's she going?" Cody asked.

"Damned if I know." Luke watched as Fancie stopped at the bunkhouse door and knocked. It was opened a few seconds later, though Luke couldn't tell by whom, and after a brief conversation, Fancie stepped into the building, closing the door firmly behind herself.

"Damn pain in the ass," Luke said, striding toward the door.

"Luke! Watch your mouth," his mother said.

He spun around. "Your daughter-in-law just closed herself up in a building with fifteen cowboys! How else am I supposed to react?"

Marjorie, for once, didn't put up a fight. "Go get her," she said quietly.

Luke stormed out of the house. He was so angry he couldn't think straight. His heart was pounding, his fists clenched. With Luke in such a fury, only God could help any cowpoke who so much as looked sideways at Fancie!

Luke whipped open the door to the bunkhouse so fast it nearly came off its hinges. Fifteen surprised men and one very ornery woman looked up at him. Fancie was seated on a chair in the middle of the room, the men crowded all around her. In front of her, she had spread out a bunch of books.

"What the *hell* do you think you're doing?" Luke asked. He grabbed her hand and yanked her to her feet.

"What do *I* think . . . The question is, what do *you* think you're doing?" She pulled at her arm and wrenched it from his grasp.

"So help me, Fancie," he said advancing on her. She ducked into the protective custody of her group of admirers.

"Leave me alone, Luke! You've found it easy enough to do before."

Luke didn't think it was possible for his anger to build any higher, but he was wrong. "Your choice, Fancie!" he thundered, jabbing his finger in her direction. "*I* didn't leave *you!*" He pushed four men out of the way and lifted his wife over his shoulder.

"Put me down!" she screamed, flailing her fists against the back of his legs. "How dare you—"

"Put the lady down, Luke," one of the cowboys said, stepping forward. "She doesn't want to go with you."

"Yeah, put her down," said another, then another. Before Luke knew what had happened, he was facing fifteen riled cowboys, who were willing to fight for Fancie's honor.

"Hold on," Luke said, holding up one palm toward the men. "This little hellcat"—he gestured at the woman tossed over his shoulder—"is my wife. When I say it's time to go, it's time to go."

"Your wife?"

"You got married?"

"She doesn't seem to like you none."

Luke stood still while the cowboys digested his news. "No, she doesn't seem to like me. Still, she is my wife."

"Put me down this instant, you brute!" Fancie kicked her legs and fought like heck, but Luke held her firmly over his shoulder, his arm wrapped around her legs.

He looked over his shoulder at her, then turned back to the men he employed. "She is my wife," he continued as though Fancie's interruption had never happened. "Keep your hands off her."

Luke turned and pushed open the door. All the way across the yard, Fancie kicked and screamed, calling him every name in the book. And his mother had been worried about *his* language?

He slammed into the house, storming past his family as if they weren't even there.

"Put me down! Tessa, Marjorie, make him stop! Cody, I—"

"That's enough!" Luke yelled, reaching up to give her a swat on the behind.

"Oh! Did you see what he did? Did all of you see . . . ?" Fancie's voice faded away as Luke pounded up the steps.

He went straight to their bedroom, where he unceremoniously dumped her on the bed. She scrambled to get up, straightening her dress as she did. Her hair had come loose, and her face was red. Whether it was from anger or from being held upside down so long, Luke couldn't be sure.

"How dare you treat me this way!" she said, advancing on him.

"What in God's name were you thinking to go into the bunkhouse like that?"

"I didn't do anything wrong! You act as if—"

"Wrong? Your behavior couldn't be more wrong! You're a woman, Fancie! You don't belong—"

"Aha! I am a woman, and therefore, not entitled to make any decisions."

"Not if they're stupid decisions, no! You're not entitled!"

She put her hands on her hips. "Well, tell me, dear husband," she said softly, "exactly what am I entitled to?" She let her eyes drift over him. "You don't want me. You've made that very clear. What difference does it make to you what I do?"

"The difference is, I am your husband! You should have gotten permission from me."

"Permission?" Fancie shouted. She clamped her mouth shut, then spun away from Luke so fast he just stood there blinking when she walked out of the room and slammed the door.

Luke's temper flared again. He opened the door and followed her. She was already down the stairs and out of the house. Luke glanced at his brother, who was sitting with his wife as though the entire scene had been staged for their entertainment. No one had lifted a finger to stop her!

"Fancie! Get back here right now!" he shouted. She ignored him and ran straight for . . . the bunkhouse! She wouldn't!

She did.

She didn't even knock this time. She just opened the door and barged right in. Luke was right behind her. He flopped Fancie over his shoulder, then looked at the men, who were standing around in various degrees of undress. He glared at them, and when he turned to go, none of them said a word to stop him.

Back to the house, through the kitchen, past the family, and all the way to their bedroom, Fancie cursed a blue streak. And every step he took brought Luke closer to the precipice of the rage he was feeling. Once again, he dropped her onto their bed. She didn't waste a second getting to her feet.

"Don't you dare," Luke threatened.

"You have no right to tell me what to do!"

"I have every right."

"No, you don't. You have *no* right! This isn't even a real marriage! It hasn't been consummated, and everyone knows that when a marriage hasn't been—"

Luke's anger had reached the boiling point. He'd never in his life felt fury such as he was feeling that moment. He grabbed Fancie's shoulders and backed her against the wall. He pressed his aroused body into her. "Is that what you want?" he whispered.

Fancie's eyes widened. "No!" She pushed against his chest to no avail. Luke grabbed one tiny wrist in each of his hands and held them over her head, against the wall.

Luke thought he had the situation under control. He thought he had *himself* under control. All it took was having his body pressed up against Fancie for him to know that any control he'd had had vanished. He looked down at her, and as if he had no ability to stop himself, he kissed her.

The kiss was long, hard, and deep. Luke leaned into her and ravaged her mouth, and Fancie let him. In his grasp, her arms, which had been straining to get free, grew limp. He let go of them and slid his hands down her body. When his fingers brushed against the sides of her breasts, she gasped.

Their kisses became fevered, their hands hungered for the touch of bare skin. Without taking his mouth from hers, Luke backed her down onto the bed. It happened so fast that he didn't even realize what he'd done until he opened his eyes and saw Fancie lying beneath him.

She opened her eyes, but lay silently, and Luke knew in that instant that she would not stop him. It was his call. Around them, time seemed to stand still, waiting for his decision. Would he stand a safe distance from the cliff or jump headlong over the edge? Guard his heart or offer it?

Luke swallowed hard and pushed himself off the bed. Long seconds passed while he stood looking down at her.

Fancie was the most beautiful, sexy woman he had ever seen. She was the woman who had broken his heart.

He turned and left the room, closing the door firmly behind himself.

It was almost dark. Cody, Tessa and Marjorie sat on the porch, where the squeak from the porch swing hooks provided a much needed distraction from the fighting upstairs.

"You're going back to work tomorrow?" Marjorie asked Cody. She knew that he was.

"Yup. Vacation's over." He squeezed Tessa's shoulder and smiled down at her.

"It's a beautiful night," Marjorie said, looking out at the sky.

"It is," Cody answered unnecessarily. Luke and Fancie's room was right above the porch, and with weather so warm, the windows were open. He didn't want to overhear any more of their argument than he already had, and he struggled to find something to say. "What are you two going to do tomorrow?"

"Oh," Marjorie said, perking up with the thought of a lively conversation. "I want to show Tessa and Fancie how we handle the bookkeeping for the ranch. It's a lot to learn, and I won't be able to do it much longer."

"Bookkeeping?" Tessa asked, lifting her head from her husband's shoulder. "I'm not very good at math."

"That's all right. You don't need to be. You can add and subtract, can't you?"

"Of course I can."

"Well, then, you know enough math to do the job. The most important thing is to stay organized."

"I suppose I can do that."

"I'm sure of it. Do you know—"

Suddenly, the front door flew open, and Luke stomped past them. He was off the porch and headed across the yard so quickly he didn't even seen them.

"Where's he going?" Cody asked, turning to look over his shoulder at his brother.

"The bunkhouse!" Marjorie said. "Oh, Cody, go after him. Don't let him start a fight."

Cody looked at his mother and raised his eyebrows.

"Well, at least, if he does get in a fight, be on his side," she amended. They both knew that, if Luke felt justified in fighting, no one was going to talk him out of it.

"You stay here," Cody said to Tessa, as he stood and followed his brother across the yard. Luke had already disappeared inside the bunkhouse, and as Cody approached it, he could hear Luke's voice.

"Did she bring these books?"

"She said she thought we might like to read 'em," a cowboy said. "Thought we might be lonely when we're working, and the books might be company for us."

"Why in the world would she think a thing like that?"

Luke asked. "Did you tell her you're busy when you're working?"

"No, sir. We told her there ain't but three of us here that know how to read any."

A pause. "You don't know how to read?"

"No, sir."

Another pause. "What did she say to that?"

"She said she'd teach us by readin' to us if we wanted to. Said we could work on our letters. Ain't much else to do round here, so we said okay. We was just gettin' set to pick out a book to start with when you came bustin' in."

Outside the window, Cody smiled. His brother was jealous.

Luke cleared his throat. "Um ... I'm not sure yet whether Mrs. Winston will be following through with the offer to teach you all to read. But if she does, I expect all of you to treat her like a lady. She is used to city life. She isn't used to being around men who haven't seen a woman for weeks on end."

"Yes, sir," the spokesman said. "We'll treat her respectfully. Ain't that right, boys?"

From outside, Cody could hear the rest of the group's emphatic agreement. He turned away from the bunkhouse and walked back toward the porch.

"Well," Marjorie said. "What was she doing in there?"

"Mother," Cody said, as he draped his arm around his wife, "you just might have the most literate bunch of cowboys in the entire territory."

"What do you mean?" Marjorie knit her brows together in confusion.

"She's teaching them to read."

Tessa grunted. "Leave it to my sister to find a good cause to support smack-dab in the middle of a cattle ranch."

Marjorie began to laugh. Before long, all three of them were hysterical. Luke stepped onto the porch a minute later, which only made them laugh harder. He went into the house, shaking his head and mumbling to himself. He obviously didn't see the humor in the situation.

Luke Winston was falling in love with his wife.

Chapter Seven

Fancie walked down the steps and found Luke already seated at the breakfast table. He looked up at her as she walked into the room. Apparently, eight hours of lying in bed beside her hadn't done anything to improve his mood. He glared at her as she approached the table.

The only empty seat was beside him. Determined not to make a scene, Fancie slid into it without blinking. "Good morning, everyone. Sleep well?"

"Like a rock," Cody said.

"It's a beautiful day," Fancie said, reaching for a slice of bread. "I can hardly wait to get outside." She spread strawberry jam on her bread and took a bite. "Mmm. This jam is delicious. Did you make it, Mrs. Winston?"

"Mattie did. Thank God, we have her. You wouldn't live long on my cooking."

"Oh, it can't be that bad!" Fancie said.

Cody looked at his new sister-in-law. "It's that bad."

Fancie laughed at his seriousness. "Cody! What a thing to say about your mother."

"I love my mother dearly," he said, flashing an exaggerated grin at Marjorie. "But she can't cook to save her life."

Marjorie sighed. "It's true. I admit it. I hate cooking and always have. Don't suppose that's going to change now."

"We all have our weaknesses," Fancie said, glancing at her husband, who had not uttered a single word since she'd walked into the room. What was Luke's weakness?

After those kisses yesterday, she didn't have to wonder what her own weakness might be. Eight years later and mad as hell, Luke still had the ability to rob her of all rational thought. She'd skipped weak and gone straight to helpless under the spell of his kiss.

Fancie shook her head to clear away the troublesome thought. She'd determined, the previous night, what she thought was the most effective way of achieving her goal. She wanted to teach the cowboys to read. Luke refused to allow it. It didn't take a genius to see that Marjorie Winston still had a lot of control over her sons. After all, she been able to convince them to marry women they hadn't seen in years. She'd probably also be able to convince them that what Fancie proposed was perfectly acceptable.

"Mrs. Winston, I've been thinking," Fancie said, as she poured herself a cup of coffee. "You know that I did a lot of volunteer work while I was in Chicago. I also held a full-time job."

"Your mother mentioned that to me," Marjorie said. "A lending library, was it?"

"Yes," Fancie said. "I was there for three years. I loved it."

"You must miss it," Marjorie said, not knowing how much she was helping Fancie reach her objective.

"I do miss it. Very much. It has come to my attention," Fancie said, watching Luke out of the corner of her eye, "that the majority of the men you employ do not know how to read."

"I found that out last night."

"It's a most unfortunate situation, especially since it's so easily corrected. I was wondering if you would have any objections to my teaching them—during their time off, of course. They've expressed the desire to learn."

"Fancie," Luke said slowly, "I don't think that's a good idea."

She turned to look at him. He sat beside her as still as ever. But his eyes were blazing. "I was speaking to your mother," Fancie said, reaching past him for the sugar bowl.

"I don't like the idea," Luke said.

"I already know that. I want to see what everybody else thinks." She turned toward her mother-in-law. "Mrs. Winston?"

Marjorie raised her eyebrows and shrugged. "I hadn't really thought about it. They really want to learn?"

"They seem to. I—"

"We aren't running a grade school here!" Luke said, putting his fork down.

Fancie turned toward him slowly. "I know that. Still, education benefits everyone, and that's a fact. I'm here, and I'm willing to do it. So why shouldn't I?"

Luke jumped up. "Because I don't want you to!"

Fancie raised her eyebrows. "That's a little dictatorial, isn't it?" she asked calmly. She turned toward her brother-in-law. "Cody, what do you think?"

"Uh . . ." He looked from his brother to Fancie and back again. "I think I'd rather not get involved."

"Oh, come on," Fancie urged, as she stirred a spoonful of sugar into her coffee. "I'm just asking for your opinion. Surely, Luke doesn't dictate that too, does he?" She wasn't playing fair, and she knew it, but darn it, this was important to her!

"Watch it, Fancie," Luke muttered.

"What? I'm just saying it seems as though you're the

only one opposed to the idea, and I can't help wondering why."

"Because I don't want my wife hanging around a bunch of love-starved cowboys—that's why!"

"They behaved like perfect gentlemen," she said, moving in for the kill. "It's not like any of them tossed me over their shoulder and carried me away against my will."

"Fancie!"

"And certainly, none of them took advantage of my admittedly fragile state of mind to press unwelcome advances—"

"That's enough!" Luke shouted

Fancie didn't even acknowledge that he'd spoken. "I'm quite sure that none of them would use their considerable strength against me."

"I said, that's enough!"

"In fact, they even came to my aid when— Oh!" Fancie stopped speaking in midsentence when Luke grabbed her arm and hauled her out of her seat. He walked purposefully toward the parlor while she scampered along behind him, still holding the sugar spoon in her right hand. "Let go of me!"

He didn't. He held her wrist and pulled her into the room, closing the heavy double doors and sealing them in privacy. "I didn't do anything to you that you didn't want me to do," Luke said softly.

"You behaved like an ape, Luke." She planted her hands on her hips. "I've *never* had a man treat me like that in my entire life. Never!"

"Really?" he said, advancing a step toward her. "I'd wondered about that." He took another step forward, looking into her eyes all the while.

Fancie was so mad that it took a minute for his thinly veiled insult to penetrate her anger. She opened her mouth and drew a deep breath. "I can't believe you just said that."

Luke shrugged. "I'm only being honest."

"No, you're not," she said, shaking her head and backing up a step. "You're being rude, insulting, and downright nasty."

"Nasty?" Luke said, raising his eyebrows and moving a step toward her. "That's pretty harsh, don't you think?"

"No, I don't think it's harsh at all," she said, turning away from him. "We're stuck in this together, Luke. The least you could do is try to be civil to me."

She turned away before he could see the tears in her eyes. She didn't want to cry, darn it! She wanted to stand here, hold her ground, and hash the situation out until they settled it. Her nerves were rubbed raw from all the tension between them. She felt like everything that was bottled up inside of her was demanding to be *let out*, and she couldn't hold it in anymore.

Luke spoke quietly. "I probably should be more civil," he said. "Maybe even . . . friendly."

"If you can manage it," she muttered, looking down at the spoon she held in her hands. She rubbed the stem of the spoon between her thumb and forefinger until the silver felt warm from her touch. She stood that way, staring at the spoon and waiting for him to say something, but the seconds ticked by and not another word was spoken. She crossed her arms, closed her eyes, and wondered why she had even bothered trying.

That was when she felt it.

Luke's breath on her neck.

She snapped her eyes open and tried to stand very still. What was he doing? Why was he standing so close to—

"You're right, Fancie," Luke whispered, setting his hands on her shoulders. His mouth was at her ear, his body was pressed up against her backside, his breath was warm on her skin. Fancie's heart began to beat faster. Without even realizing that she had done it, she tilted her head, and his lips brushed against her neck. Luke's hands slid down her arms; then he meshed his fingers with hers, coaxing her head backward with warm, soft kisses on the curve of her ear. The spoon fell to the floor.

"We shouldn't be fighting all the time," he said, his voice all rough and raspy.

She closed her eyes and let her head rest against Luke's chest. "What are you doing to me?" she whispered.

He didn't have to answer. Fancie knew exactly what he was doing. Wonderful things—nibbling, teasing things that made her feel warm all over. Feelings that she hadn't felt in ... too long a time. She reached up and buried her hand in Luke's hair as his mouth nudged its way down her neck.

"Oh, Luke," she muttered, getting lost in the magical, tingling sensations racing through her, from the places he touched with his mouth to a place she'd almost forgotten deep down inside her.

"We'd be good together, Fancie. You know we would be." He kissed her neck, from behind her ear to the edge of her dress, and Fancie felt her resolve slipping away. In the space of a minute, Luke had awakened feelings that had lain dormant for eight long years. Feelings that were hammering at her insides, begging to be set free.

He loosened his hold on her, just enough that their bodies separated a fraction of an inch, and he turned her around, looking deep into her eyes. He reached for her face and took it in both hands, kissing her like a man who'd been without a woman for a long time. In his eyes, she saw the heat of desire, and she couldn't deny the thrill she felt to know that she held that power over him. She gave in to the kiss.

Fancie reached up and threaded the fingers of one hand through the thick, wavy hair at the back of his neck. She held him against her mouth, while the feelings she'd been suppressing for so long fought their way to the surface.

He must have felt her acquiescence because he groaned

and pulled her bottom against him once more. Fancie forgot all about why she should be telling him to stop. She forgot all about the fight they'd been having. She forgot all about everything but the delicious warmth that was slowly seeping through her body.

This was Luke, the man who had taught her all about these feelings long ago. Luke, the only man who had ever been able to make her body respond this way.

"Tell me what you want, Fancie," Luke said, running his hands over her breasts.

She felt a thrill shoot through her at his touch, and she arched her back and offered herself to him.

He rubbed his thumbs over the peaks that were straining to feel his touch. He worked his fingers over them until Fancie thought she would die from wanting him.

"Oh, Luke, please—"

The words were barely out of her mouth when Luke's kiss came crashing down on her. He pressed his hips against her, and Fancie let one hand drift from his belt down over rough denim. She brushed her hand against the hardness she found, and Luke groaned. She did it again, and he stopped kissing her. He rested his chin on the top of her head and breathed heavily while Fancie explored his body through his clothing.

"Fancie, you'd better stop that," he whispered, holding onto her tightly.

"I don't want to stop."

He hesitated just a second before he looked down at her. "Tell me."

Fancie could barely speak. Her heart was hammering, and her hands were shaking. "I want you to make love to me, Luke."

She was looking into his eyes, and for the briefest moment, she saw something flash through them. Luke was looking down at her, and she had the feeling that now was one of those times when he was carefully calculating his next move.

Slowly, he dropped his arms from her shoulders and moved back a step. That something in his eyes was back, and Fancie got a sick feeling in her stomach.

"You knew that I loved you, didn't you?"

It took a moment for Fancie to realize that this wasn't about what was happening that day. It was about something that had happened years before. She felt her heart plummet, and she lowered her eyes to the floor, stunned by his abrupt withdrawal.

"You knew that I loved you, and you went anyway. Did it mean anything at all to you, Fancie? What we had together—did it mean anything?"

"Luke, you know it did."

"Apparently not enough." He backed another step away from her. "Did you find what you were looking for in Chicago? Did you find whatever it was that was so important you had to tear apart what we had to get it?"

"I wanted you to come with me!" she shouted. "You know I did!"

"I've always wondered what you did with all the desire there was between us. Did you unleash it on someone else? Did you find someone in the city to torment with your sweet body the way you used to torment me?"

"I never—"

"Do city boys put up with that kind of thing? Do they?"

She couldn't fight him anymore. It was too draining. She looked up at him and said, "Luke, I married you. I'm not going anywhere."

"You've got that right," he said harshly.

Fancie blinked her eyes, confused by the sound of his voice. "What . . . what—"

"You're my wife, Francine. Now it's my turn to call the shots."

"What do you mean?" She'd given in! She'd assured

him that she meant to keep her wedding vows. What more did he want?

"What I mean is this." He moved toward her until he was so close she had to hold her breath to keep from touching him. "Until I am absolutely sure about what you want," he said, setting his hand at her waist and spreading his fingers, "I'm not willing to risk it." He rubbed his thumb against the swell of her breast.

Fancie drew in her breath and slapped his hand away. "Don't you dare touch me like that!"

Luke backed up a step and flashed just a hint of a cocky smile. "Funny. I didn't hear you complaining before."

Fancie was growing angrier by the second. "I don't know who you think you are! You can't just—"

"I'm your husband, Fancie." He looked at her with eyes as cold as ice. "And, I *can* just. I'm entitled to it, and you know that." He shoved the fingers of one hand into his pocket and stood looking at her as though he was trying to solve a difficult puzzle.

"The trouble is," he said, his gaze roaming freely over her, "I'm not convinced it's genuine this time. I'll need to see some pretty darn good performances before I'm convinced enough to ease the ache that's burnin' inside of you."

"Performances!" she shouted. She'd *never* been so insulted in all her life!

"As I recall, you're good at putting on a show."

She didn't even let him finish. She hauled back and slapped him with all her might. How *dared* he toy with her this way!

He didn't even flinch. It was as though he had *expected* her to lose control that way.

And then he had the nerve to smile at her. Smile! "Very good, Fancie. Uncontrollable passion." He reached up and touched his cheek where her hand had left a red welt. "Now, *that* was real." He let his gaze drift over her, and

Fancie felt as if she was naked. "The rest I'm not so sure about."

He turned and walked out of the room, closing the door silently behind himself. Fancie stood there fuming. She dropped her gaze to the floor. Seizing the first thing her eyes settled on, she picked up the spoon and stormed out after him. He was halfway across the room when she flung it at him. It whacked him in the shoulder, then skidded to a stop on the kitchen floor. He slowly turned around to face her, a smirk on his handsome face, as though he approved of this *performance* as well.

"It'll be a cold day in hell, Luke Winston!" She turned and marched back into the parlor, slamming the door behind her.

Luke backed himself down to the ground, the leafy cottonwood providing ample shade from the scorching sun. He leaned against the trunk, stretched his legs out, and crossed his feet at the ankles.

"It's a hot one, Lucky, isn't it?" he said, rubbing the dog's ears. Lucky flopped down on the ground and stretched out, exhausted from his morning work.

Billy, Luke's father, had started the ranch with one hundred and sixty acres of virgin grasslands. Through the years, thanks to various government acts, he'd acquired well over two thousand acres, most of it well supplied with water from small creeks and streams. In addition, he bought up land from homesteaders who had failed. All in all, at the time of his death, he'd owned nearly three thousand acres—not including the free range, still owned by the government, that the cattlemen used for grazing as if it was their own.

It was a hell of a big job to keep the place going, and Luke had been doing it, and doing it well, for almost five years now. Fancie's father wasn't the only one who'd decided that the cattle industry was too unstable for his liking. Established ranches folded and new ones cropped up with alarming frequency. But the Billy D, from the beginning, had kept its sights on the long-term rewards, and it had paid off nicely. The Winstons were still a far cry off from the big boys, but they were stable and steady in an industry that was anything but. A lot of that was thanks to Luke.

The work could be exhausting at times. As manager of the Billy D, Luke needed skill in business affairs, animal husbandry, and the management of men, as well as a knowledge of markets and supply sources. He worried about the rapid turnover of the cowboys they employed, the seemingly unpredictable expansion and contraction of the market, and as always, the weather. Every now and then, he needed a breather.

Luke closed his eyes, and his thoughts instantly turned to Fancie. How the hell was he going to survive their marriage?

It was no secret he wanted her. A man couldn't hide a thing like that, especially not pressed up against a woman's body the way he'd been pressed up against his wife that morning. He couldn't keep on like this. He and Fancie had their problems, but desire for each other wasn't one of them. He'd even cornered her into saying it out loud. In spite of all his seemingly unbreakable self-control, Luke knew it wouldn't be long before he gave in to the overwhelming urges she brought out in him.

He hadn't slept in two days. How could he sleep when she was lying beside him? How could he be sure he wouldn't reach for her in the middle of the night?

His sleepless nights were beginning to take a toll. He was miserable to be around, and he knew it. He'd lost his temper with Fancie that morning, which was the reason he'd ended up kissing her. If he'd been able to stay calm at breakfast, he would never have been alone with her in the parlor. He'd never have touched her. He'd never have been driven to be so cruel.

God, that woman brought out the worst in him! Even now, hours later, Luke could feel his ire rising as he thought about Fancie's plan to turn his bunkhouse into a schoolroom. Why couldn't she just be reasonable? A bunkhouse was no place for a woman, and that was that!

He got to his feet, too agitated to rest any longer. He set his hat back on his head and walked toward the creek, which was winding its way through this field. Untying the bandanna from around his neck, he bent down and plunged his hands into the cool water. He cupped them together and scooped out enough to rinse his face. He drank deeply, and the water refreshed him.

After wringing out the bandanna, he tied it loosely around his neck. The water would keep him cool until it evaporated.

He whistled, and Lucky jumped up, revived by his brief nap. Luke climbed back on his horse and began riding along the fence, checking every post to make sure the barbed wire was secure.

Fencing in the cattle was a relatively new idea, and the barbed wire, which had only been around for a few years, had cost a small fortune. Still, Luke thought the expenditure was well worth it. It enabled him to provide better care and protection for his herds. It eliminated straying, and it made improvements in the breeds possible. Now, less than a year after the fence had been erected, Luke was even more sure of his decision. With free range disappearing the way it was, fencing was the way of the future. He rode the fence, and his thoughts turned back to Fancie.

What the hell had he been thinking to kiss her that way?

No man in his right mind could walk away unaffected after having touched Fancie. He'd thought to teach her a lesson, and he had, instead, learned something about himself. The control on which he'd always prided himself didn't stand a chance against Francine Parlay.

Luke slid from his horse and bent to examine a different stretch of fencing. "Francine Winston," he muttered to himself. "She's your wife, Luke." His hands stilled, and he stopped breathing. He had a wife.

A wife.

"Oh, my God." He crouched against the post and stared into the grass. How was it that he'd suddenly wound up responsible for yet another person? In addition to his family, who counted on him to keep the place turning a profit, he also had a bunkhouse full of cowboys who looked to him, come payday. And now there was Tessa and Fancie, not to mention any babies that might come along.

Babies!

"Oh, my God," he said again as he dragged his hat off his head and tossed it to the ground. He plunged his fingers into his damp hair while he considered the possibility, which, amazingly, he had only just realized.

There'd soon be babies at the Billy D Ranch. His, as well as Cody's, if the state his brother had himself worked into earlier was any indication. "Oh, good Lord, what do I know about babies?" he asked himself. Beyond how to make them, not a damn thing.

Panic began to tighten his chest as he thought about having to help Fancie deliver a child. *His* child. Cows, horses, yes—those births he could handle. But it was different for a woman. It was harder for them, and Luke realized that he had no idea what to do to help.

Please, God, let my mother live long enough to show me what to do!

The prayer shot through Luke's consciousness so quickly that it was over before he even realized that he needed to pray. His mother. That was it. Marjorie would be there to help. Luke began breathing again. Marjorie and Mattie.

They knew what to do. Confidence began to creep back in.

He pushed to his feet and stood with his hands on his hips looking out at the field before him. It stretched out as far as he could see, and he admired it for long minutes. The land was his. His whole life had been poured into making sure the place not only survived, but thrived. Someday, it would be passed down to his children, just as it had been passed down to him. He drew in a deep breath and bent down to pick up his hat and set it back on his head. Of course he wanted children. Of course he did.

Luke mounted his horse and began moving slowly along the fence. He followed it for miles, and not once in all that time did thoughts of Fancie leave his head.

If he'd been able to be honest about it, he'd have admitted that it was not an altogether unpleasant way to spend the day.

But being a man, and a stubborn one to boot, he'd sooner eat dirt than face that admission.

He turned his horse and headed for home.

"You're not eating, Mama," Cody said.

Marjorie blinked her eyes and looked toward him. "I'm not very hungry," she muttered, looking back toward Fancie, who was sitting beside Luke, as she had since her arrival. But the effort she was expending in order to be sure that her sleeve did not touch his arm seemed disproportionate to the trouble a mere touch would cause.

That was good. That was very good, Marjorie thought.

"Are you feeling all right?" Luke asked.

Marjorie blinked again and tried to pay attention to the conversation. "I'm fine. Just a little tired is all."

"Tired?" Cody put his fork down and stood up immediately. "Let me help you up to bed."

"Cody, I'm just a little tired. I'm not ready for bed."

"But, Mama, the doctor said you shouldn't exert yourself. You know that. Maybe there's been too much excitement around here the past few days."

"Nonsense!" Marjorie straightened herself in her chair. No one watching would ever guess the amount of effort it took. Her heart grew weaker by the day, though she fought to hide it the best she could. "We've needed excitement around here for years."

"Are you sure you feel up to staying through dinner?" Luke asked.

"Of course."

"If you'd like," Fancie said, "I'll come upstairs and visit with you when we're through eating."

Luke turned his head and looked down at Fancie, but she kept her eyes focused on Marjorie, refusing to even acknowledge his presence.

What on earth was going on between those two? "That would be lovely, Fancie," Marjorie said with a smile. "We haven't had much time to catch up since you've arrived, and I have a million and one questions to ask you about Chicago."

"I'd be more than happy to fill you in," Fancie said with a smile.

Luke turned his attention back to his meal, though Marjorie noticed that he glanced in Fancie's direction several times. For her part, Fancie might as well have been sitting next to a wall. She gave absolutely no indication whatsoever that she knew Luke was beside her. Which was exactly how Marjorie knew that his presence was a major distraction.

"Mama, did you get through all the bookkeeping today?" Cody asked.

"Most of it. Tessa is a very quick study." Marjorie looked at her younger daughter-in-law, who smiled at her. "When she said she wasn't very good at math, I admit, I was a little worried."

"Tessa?" Fancie asked. "Not good at math?"

Tessa's smile faded, and she squirmed under her sister's scrutiny. "Well, I-I never liked math is what I meant to say."

"Tessa!" Fancie looked across the table as though she had never been so disgusted in her life. All conversation stopped as everyone looked expectantly from one sister to the next.

They stared at each other, one begging the other to keep the silence, one demanding that it be broken. "Oh, all right!" Tessa finally said. "I was best in my class in math."

"Best in your class?" Fancie asked with her eyebrows raised.

"All right, Fancie! All right. I was best in the Chicago school system! I knew more than the teachers! I knew more than everyone! There!" she shouted, glaring at Fancie. "Are you satisfied?"

Fancie smiled. "Yes, I believe I am."

"Best in the entire city?" Cody asked.

Tessa nodded miserably.

"Well, why didn't you tell us?" Marjorie asked. "Why did you pretend?"

Tessa sighed and closed her eyes, her shoulders slumped. "Because men don't like it when women are smarter than they are," she said quietly.

"What?" Marjorie exclaimed. "I have news for you, honey. Women are almost always smarter than men."

"I beg your pardon!" Luke said.

Marjorie looked at him and lifted one eyebrow. "It's true, Luke. And I'll tell you something else: The smart men—the really, really smart men—know it."

"That's ridiculous, Mama. Intelligence has absolutely nothing to do with gender. If it was possible to measure, it'd probably be an even split. Women are simply more conniving than men."

"Wait just one minute!" Fancie shouted, looking at her

husband for the first time all evening. "I take great offense at that statement."

Luke shrugged. "If the shoe fits . . ."

Fancie drew in a shocked breath. "How *dare* you accuse me of conniving! You! You who—" She stopped speaking suddenly and closed her eyes, as though the mere sight of Luke infuriated her. She sat with her eyes clamped shut and her head turned away from her husband. It was clear she was struggling not to explode.

Marjorie smiled. A few more weeks—maybe even a few more days, if things continued on the way they had been— and she'd be able to look her son in the eye and say, "I told you so."

Oh! The victory would be sweet!

Luke lay flat on his back, his arms pinned to his sides. Normally, he slept with his hands beneath his head, but the times were not normal. His wife was beside him, and he didn't want to risk touching so much as a single strand of her hair.

Fancie had climbed into bed and promptly presented him with her back. They'd been lying stone still for an hour before he felt her relax and, finally, fall asleep. Her breathing was deep and steady. Luke longed to reach out and wrap his arm around her. If he could, he would have pulled her backside firmly against himself. If it were at all possible, he'd rest his head against her hair and breathe in the sweet smell of her.

Of course, he couldn't do any of those things.

Why was he doing it? Why was he refusing to take what was rightfully his? Fancie was his wife, and a wife had certain duties to fulfill. Even she knew that.

Why had she come? How had her mother been able to convince her to come back to Montana and, especially, back to him?

Fancie mumbled in her sleep, and Luke lifted his head off the pillow. He waited, but she was silent. No midnight confessions, no dark secrets. His wife was probably dreaming of wringing his neck with her bare hands. His head fell back onto the pillow.

He'd been lying with his eyes shut for well over an hour when he heard a sound in the hallway. It was Cody, whispering, "Shhh," to his giggling bride. The two made their way down the stairs and out the kitchen door.

Cody and Tessa couldn't get enough of each other. Even an imbecile could see how much in love they were.

Luke had always wanted that.

After Fancie had gone, he'd waited, hoping she would come back. But time passed, turning the heartbroken, but hopeful, sixteen year old into a hard-hearted, cynical man.

So many times he'd wondered what his life would have been like if Fancie had accepted his proposal. As the years went by, he'd thought about it less and less. And then he'd seen her coming off the stagecoach, and those feelings had rushed back over him, leaving his heart as battered and raw as it had been eight years before. And that was when he knew that the hold she had over him had never gone away.

That was when he'd decided to guard his heart very carefully. He wasn't the same trusting kid she'd left behind. He'd learned a lot about the ways of the world, and he wasn't about to be played for a fool again. Fancie was going to have to prove her intentions before Luke invested even one single rushed breath in their relationship. So far, she hadn't proven anything—except that if he pushed her into it, he could still make her heart beat faster.

That wasn't enough, Luke thought, as he pulled the sheet up over his shoulder. It wasn't nearly enough.

Chapter Eight

Luke reached for another bale of hay and tossed it into the loft. Each bale weighed about seventy-five pounds, and he'd been throwing them pretty near nonstop since morning.

"That's it, Harley," he said, wiping his sleeve across his forehead. The hand pulled the cart away, and it was replaced with another, which had been waiting right outside the door. Luke was up on the back of it before the driver had even had the chance to position the thing properly. He began heaving bales over the side.

"Wait, Luke," Cody said as he walked into the barn. "Let me help you with those." He'd been supervising the first baling at the upper two barns. Luke was supposed to have been doing the same.

"I've got it covered," Luke muttered. His arms felt as if they were on fire. His shoulders had never ached so badly in all his life.

"Why isn't Harley doing this?" Harley was by far the strongest of all the men they employed, and he reveled in such work. But instead of being able to show off his strength, he'd been relegated to shuttling a cart from the field to the barns and back again. Cody began stacking the bales Luke had unloaded.

"He's driving."

"I know that. Why is he driving?"

Luke stopped working long enough to yank his gloves back into place. His lungs burned with the effort of breathing the dust-filled air. "He's driving because I told him to."

Cody looked up at Luke, who had his hands planted on his hips. His posture dared anyone to say anything to question his judgment. But Cody was too smart to do that. The day was already creeping toward evening, and he knew that a fight with Luke wouldn't do anything to hurry it along. He turned away and began working again.

Outside, another cart pulled to the door. "This is the last one," the driver called.

"Leave it," Luke shouted back.

"That's okay. I'll wait."

"Leave it!" Luke yelled. "I'll take care of it!"

The hand looked at Cody, who only shrugged. "Go on, Jim," he said. "Luke and I will clean up."

"You sure?"

"Yeah, go on," Cody said. "See you in the mornin'."

The cowboy glanced up at Luke before turning away. It wasn't like any of the Winstons to yell at their help. But everyone on the Billy D knew about Luke and his reluctant bride, and they'd all been doing their best to stay out of his way. Unlike Cody, Luke had been known to fight when he felt the occasion called for it. And with frustration adding to his considerable brawn, no one wanted to be on the receiving end of Luke's wrath.

The brothers worked side by side until both carts had been unloaded, the hay had been stacked, and the equipment and horses had been properly put away. It was only as they walked toward the house that Cody spoke.

"Did it work?"

"Did what work?" Luke asked, staring straight ahead.

"Did you manage to get your wife out from under your skin?"

Luke stopped walking and turned to look toward Cody. "What the hell is that supposed to mean?"

Cody shrugged. "You still have feelings for her."

"She's my wife. I'm supposed to have feelings for her."

"Then why don't you let yourself?" Cody looked toward the house, then back at his brother. "This is tough for her too. Did you ever stop thinking about getting your revenge long enough to wonder why she's here? She wasn't crazy about this marriage either, but she came all the way out here and married you anyway. Have you stopped punishing her long enough to ask her why she did that? Maybe she's been regretting that she left you all those years ago. Maybe she's been loving you all this time."

"I seriously doubt that."

"Luke, will you cut it out!" Cody shouted. "If you put half as much effort into trying to make this marriage work as you've put into making Fancie pay for something she did eight years ago, things would be different."

"What would be different, Cody?" Luke shouted back. "It would still be me begging for whatever scraps she was willing to toss my way! I'm not gonna put myself out there again!"

Cody stared for a long minute. "All right, Luke. You do whatever you think needs to be done. See if it makes you any happier." He turned away and walked to the house, leaving Luke to stare after him.

* * *

"Here they come," Fancie said as she stood looking down on the ranch from Marjorie's bedroom window. "They worked late tonight. It's nearly dark."

"Once that hay is cut and baled, you want to get it in the barns as quickly as possible," Marjorie said. "It isn't likely at this time of year, but if rain came and the bales got wet, they'd be ruined. Damp hay in a barn can start a fire."

Fancie nodded, her gaze glued to the two figures walking toward the house. She sighed and turned away.

"I was right," Marjorie said.

Fancie looked up. "Right about what?"

"You still love him."

Fancie raised her eyebrows and opened her mouth as though she was going to speak, but when her eyes filled with tears, she looked away without saying a word.

"It's nothing to be ashamed of," Marjorie said. "Luke is a fine man."

Fancie sniffed. "A fine man who happens to despise me."

"That's not true. That's not at all true," Marjorie said, shaking her head.

"It is," Fancie whispered, as the tears finally spilled and ran over her cheeks. "You don't know the things he's said. He doesn't want to be married to me."

"Oh, yes, he does. And I don't care what he's said." Marjorie boosted herself up in the bed. "He's been wanting you to come back all this time. You can't imagine what it was like around here when you left."

"I've tried to apologize for that, but he won't listen! I was sixteen years old! I hadn't ever been in any city, let alone a place as big as Chicago. I wanted to see what else was out there in the world. Was that so wrong?" She wiped at her eyes with her fingers.

"No, honey, it wasn't wrong. You and Luke wanted different things. A marriage between you then would have made you miserable. Luke just can't see beyond his wounded pride long enough to realize that."

"I've tried to tell him."

"He won't listen. He went through hell when you left, Fancie."

Fancie was crying in earnest now. "I didn't mean to hurt him. I wanted him to come with us. I wrote him letters begging him to come to Chicago. When I left, I truly thought that he'd follow."

"He couldn't do that. Luke isn't an adventurer the way you are."

They sat in silence for a few minutes, and Marjorie watched her daughter-in-law carefully. There was something she had been wondering about all this time. "Fancie," she finally said, "I want to ask you something." Fancie sniffed, then looked up at her. "Why did you come back?"

"You and my mother planned it all. I wasn't given any choice."

Marjorie nodded. "True. But you said you held a job for the last three years. Surely, if you were that opposed to the idea, you could have simply refused."

Fancie stared at the floor. The tears had stopped, but they'd been replaced with a quiet panic. Fancie was hiding something. Of that, Marjorie was sure.

"It didn't seem right for a single woman to establish her own household. It wouldn't have looked right."

Marjorie didn't answer. Finally, when Fancie looked up at her, she said, "Do you really expect me to believe that you came back here, to a place you hated, and agreed to marry a man whose heart you had broken—a man who hadn't answered a single one of your letters—just because the neighbors might frown on your living alone?"

"Well, I . . . yes. Yes, that's what happened. Mother insisted, and I finally had to give in." Fancie couldn't seem to find any place to rest her gaze. She began nervously tapping her foot on the floor. Marjorie looked down at the boot, and the tapping stopped.

"I don't believe you."

"Why?" Fancie cried, jumping up. "It's a perfectly reasonable explanation!"

"For someone else maybe, but not for you."

"I told you, my mother insisted, and I had no choice but to give in." Fancie recited the words as though she had practiced saying them a thousand times.

"Fancie, look at me." Marjorie waited until Fancie finally worked up the courage to look her in the eye. "There is nothing you could have done that will make Luke send you back."

"What makes you think it was something that I did? I told you, my mother insisted, and I—"

"Had no choice but to give in," Marjorie interrupted. "I know. I've heard it before. And I don't believe it now any more than I did the first time I heard it."

Fancie snapped her head up. "Why? Why do you have to know about this?" she whispered, close to tears again.

"Because this whole thing was my idea. I'd been after your mother for years to send you back. She wouldn't do it . . . wouldn't even suggest it to you, for fear that she'd be talking you into making the wrong decision. I'd brought it up several times, and her answer was always the same." Marjorie looked her daughter-in-law in the eye. "And then, one day I get a letter saying that she's reconsidered. Not only does she want to send you, but she wants to send Tessa as well." Marjorie paused again, giving Fancie time to see where their talk was going. "I couldn't understand her sudden change of heart. It doesn't seem to make sense, does it, Fancie?"

Fancie had gone completely still. She didn't even seem to be breathing.

Marjorie watched her carefully. "I know your mother

didn't change her mind. Something changed it for her. I'd like to know what it was."

Fancie took a deep breath and let it out slowly. She knew that she'd been caught. She sat down on the chair beside the bed. "I never wanted any of you to find out about this," she said quietly.

"It won't change anything. I still believe that you are the perfect wife for my son."

Fancie chuckled. "Not for long, you won't."

"Spit it out, Fancie."

Fancie took a deep breath. Then another. She nodded her head and quietly began to speak.

Luke tugged his boots off and left them beside the kitchen door. Damn, it was hot. He wiped his sleeve across his forehead as he stepped into the kitchen.

"Hey, Mattie," he said to the bustling housekeeper.

"Got your supper in the oven to stay warm," she said over her shoulder as she went about straightening the kitchen.

"Thanks. I'll be back in a minute. I'm gonna clean up before I eat," he said, heading for the stairs.

"Your mama's restin', so be quiet," she warned.

"Will do." Luke climbed the stairs and stepped into the bedroom he shared with Fancie. The late evening sun was streaming through the window washing the entire room in a soft yellow glow. He reached for the top drawer of the heavy oak bureau and slid it out carefully, hoping it wouldn't squeak the way it usually did. That was when he heard the murmur of voices coming from his mother's room on the other side of the wall. So she wasn't sleeping after all, he thought, grabbing a clean set of clothes from the drawer. He was just about to push the thing shut when his mother spoke.

"Prostitution! Oh, Fancie!"

Luke jerked his head up and looked toward the wall, as though he'd be able to see what was going on behind it.

His mother was talking to Fancie about prostitution? What the hell was going on? He stepped closer to the wall and cocked his head, listening carefully, but Fancie spoke quietly, and he couldn't quite make out all of her words.

"Now, I've got a prison record."

"Prison! They put you in prison?"

"Only for five days. A light sentence, actually."

Luke's heart was pounding, and his stomach felt as though it had dropped to the floor. Fancie had been in prison for prostitution? He felt as if he was going to throw up, and he took a deep breath and closed his eyes, trying to wipe out the image of some nameless man paying for Fancie.

Marjorie said something, but the both of them were speaking so quietly that he couldn't make out her words. His stomach lurched at the thought of Fancie working in some squalid whorehouse. How many men had she been with? The thought was sickening, and he clenched a fist across his stomach, thankful that he hadn't eaten in almost twelve hours.

How? How could she have done this? He'd worshiped her body! He'd never done anything to—

"I was involved with several different causes. Just . . . everything. I volunteered for everything."

Their voices were a bit louder, and Luke moved closer to the wall.

"Most people appreciated the work I did. Others thought I was nothing but a troublemaker."

"What did the woman want?"

What woman? Luke had missed something in the conversation. What woman were they talking about?

"Her daughter had run away. She was young."

"Oh, the poor thing!"

"He befriended her. She didn't know that her new friend was actually the owner and operator of a brothel."

"She didn't go, did she?"

"Of course she went. She was fourteen years old. She didn't even know that such places existed."

"They . . . *sold* that . . . that child?"

"That's exactly what they did."

"Couldn't she run away? Couldn't she—"

"What could she do? They frightened her half to death."

Fancie was talking about someone else. Luke let out the breath he had been holding. They were talking about someone else, and Luke had never felt such relief.

"I pleaded with her mother to send someone. She sent me."

"You? How could you be expected—"

"It was simple playacting. I dressed the part. I went there one evening, claiming I was looking for work."

"Fancie! How could you?"

"I couldn't think of any other way . . ."

Luke's mind was racing, trying to fill in the details that he had missed.

"She was out a window, and I was on my way out when the police burst into the room. The judge found me guilty."

"And the girl? What became of her?"

"I heard they went back east."

"And that's why you came," his mother said.

Luke stepped out of the room and hurried down the stairs, his mind spinning from what he'd overheard.

"Where you been?" Mattie demanded, her hands on her hips. "I put your dinner out already. It'll be cold!"

Luke was so distracted that he barely registered what she'd said. "I'm sorry," he muttered. "I'll be right back." He walked out the door, stopping to pick up his boots. He walked across the yard in his bare feet, holding all his clothes against his chest.

Fancie had come here to escape a scandal. She hadn't

come back because she'd been loving him all those years, as he'd secretly been hoping. She hadn't come back because his mother, or her mother, had forced her to. She'd come back because she'd had no choice.

Luke walked through the barn and stood next to the pump undressing. He was learning more about Fancie with each passing day. She was so much different from the way she had been before she left for Chicago.

The water from the pump was icy cold, though Luke barely noticed it. He stood beneath the stream of water, letting it run over his tired, abused body. He rubbed the soap between his hands and thought about how miserably he'd been treating Fancie. It was no small wonder that she avoided him whenever possible.

His feelings were all jumbled up. He didn't want to forgive her for leaving him all those years ago! He didn't want to admit that it was getting harder and harder to pretend indifference toward her.

Still, he couldn't deny the truth. He was falling for her all over again.

Luke stepped beneath the water and rinsed the soap off himself. He reached for the towel draped over the corner of the trough and dried himself, thinking all the while that he wanted to know more about this woman who was his wife.

He stepped into his jeans and pushed his arms through the sleeves of his shirt. Was desperation her only reason for coming here? Did she care about him even a little?

His warring emotions did battle, and as it did every time he thought about Fancie, pride came out on top.

He could be every bit as secretive as she was, damn it! Why couldn't she trust him and tell him some of the things she was thinking . . . some of what she was feeling?

Because you've been a miserable bastard.

Luke sighed and hung his head. He buttoned his shirt and walked back through the barn, steeling himself against the tenderness he was beginning to feel toward her. She'd deceived him! He had no business getting all softhearted over her now. So she'd put herself at a little bit of risk to help someone she barely knew? A lot of people put themselves at risk every day! It meant nothing—less than nothing!

"It means nothing," he muttered to himself as he stepped up onto the porch. "Nothing at all."

Maybe, if he said it enough times, he'd start to believe it.

"I won't tell him," Marjorie said.

Fancie heaved a sigh of relief. She reached out and rested a hand on Marjorie's shoulder. "Thank you. Thank you so much."

"But my silence comes at a price."

Fancie paled. "What price?"

Marjorie was eyeing her like she was trying to make a decision. "Answer me honestly. Do you still love Luke?"

Fancie stopped breathing. She looked toward the floor. The seconds ticked by, and finally, she nodded. "When we moved back to Chicago, I thought he'd come after me. I really did. Eventually, I convinced myself that he didn't love me enough to come after me," she said. "That hurt never went away." Fancie looked up at her mother-in-law. "I guess the love I had for him never really went away either."

"So you really want to stay here? You really want to be Luke's wife?"

Fancie hesitated, then nodded again. "*If* I can get him to be the least bit reasonable. It's been difficult leaving my life behind to come here. My days were spent differently in the city. That's why I wanted to teach the cowboys to read. I thought that at least I could hold on to that one small part of my life."

"Do you still want to do it?" Marjorie asked.

"Of course I do!"

"Then do it. You have my blessings."

"But Luke—"

"I'll take care of Luke. In fact, I want you to go out to the bunkhouse right now. Tell them you'll be starting tomorrow."

"Now?" Fancie looked at the small clock on the bedside table. "But it's nearly nine o'clock!"

"Then you'd better hurry. If the lamp has already been turned out, don't knock."

"Are you sure?" Fancie asked.

"I am. Are you?"

Fancie knew what Marjorie was asking. She smiled and nodded her head. "I am."

"Then go. Hurry. We'll talk again tomorrow after breakfast." As Fancie stood with her hand on the doorknob, Marjorie added, "We have a lot of work to do."

Chapter Nine

June was Luke's favorite time of the year. The rains were well over, and though it was already hot, everything was still green. In another month or so, as summer drew to a close and the water began to dry up, the fields would turn brown and dusty. Always, there was dust.

Luke had spent the morning in the barn with the horses. He'd wanted to watch some of the saddle breaking. At the Billy D, they were fortunate to employ Dan Russell, who was known as the best hand with a horse for miles around. He used a combination of loud voices, gentle handling, and firm retribution to break his horses. It worked. Dan was responsible for some of the best ranch horses ever put out, and watching him at work was the closest thing to a spiritual encounter Luke had ever seen.

It was eight o'clock, a little late for breakfast, but if he was lucky, there'd still be something left on the side of the stove. Luke walked down the hill from the barn and into the yard. He was in a hurry to get back, and he was moving along at a pretty good clip when he saw her. He stopped walking and stood stone still.

Fancie was cutting roses. She was wearing a pretty green dress with big puffy sleeves that left her arms bare from the elbow down. She had her hair slicked back into a tight braid, which hung down her back, ending at the point where her skirt flared out from her tiny waist. She turned slightly, giving Luke a perfect view of her profile.

Lord, she was a pretty woman. She was taller than most women Luke knew, but she moved with such grace that she appeared fragile. He watched her hands move among the flowers, examining and then choosing only the blooms that met with her satisfaction. She cut them with shears and dropped them into a basket at her feet. She bent to lift the basket, and Luke ducked behind a stand of flowering chokecherries. He wanted to watch a little while longer.

She looped the basket over her arm and lifted her skirts to move to another bunch of bushes, and that was when Luke saw it.

Her feet were bare.

The breath caught in his chest as he watched her bare feet moving through the cool green blades of grass. She moved so close that he could hear her humming to herself. It was the sound of a woman at peace with herself. The sound of a woman content with her life. Could she be?

Apparently satisfied that she had enough flowers, she turned back toward the house. He watched her the whole way, as she held her skirts up to keep them from brushing against the grass, which was still wet with dew. On the porch, she sat down on one of the swings and set the basket on the floor beside her. She reached out and snatched something off the other swing, then leaned forward and peered up and down the front yard, as though making certain that she was alone.

Like a man mesmerized, Luke watched as she hiked her skirts up well over her knees and quickly skimmed her stockings up over her legs. He was breathing hard. Her legs were long and as pale as anything he'd ever seen.

His view was abruptly cut off when she fluffed her dress over her legs and bent to lace up her boots. He blinked, trying to wipe the vision from his mind. How could he lie beside her in bed later that night without running his hands over those legs? From her ankles, over calves, behind knees, between—

"Hey."

Luke jumped nearly a foot off the ground. "Jesus, Cody!" he said, backing away a step. "Are you trying to kill me?"

"No." Cody eyed him warily. "I'm just gettin' down for breakfast, and I happened to notice you hiding behind these here bushes."

"I was not hiding!" Luke stalked off toward the house.

"Sure looked like it to me." Cody looked toward the house just as Fancie closed the door behind her. "I think you were spying on your wife," he said with a grin.

Luke glared him with a look meant to warn him. Instead, Cody burst out laughing. "You were! I saw it!" he said, pointing at his brother as he began to walk toward the house.

"I was not!"

"Were too," Cody said, arguing like they had as children. They stepped up onto the porch with Cody still laughing.

When he opened the door, Luke growled, "Cut it out!"

Marjorie looked up from where she was trimming foliage off of rose stems. "What's going on with you two?"

"I caught—"

Luke whacked Cody with his hat before he turned to hang it on a peg. "Nothing. Eat your breakfast, Cody."

Cody made his way to the table, still chuckling, stopping along the way to kiss his mother, his wife, his sister-in-law, and even Mattie on the cheek.

"Someone's happy," Fancie said.

"You know what, Fancie?" Cody said, lifting the lid off the plate Mattie set in front of him. He leaned toward her and whispered, "I have the feeling my happiness just might be contagious."

"Here he comes! Here he comes!" Tessa whispered as she hurried away from the window. She hurried over to the stove and picked up a bowl of mashed potatoes, whipping them as though her life depended on whether or not she served them free of lumps.

Fancie's hands flew to her hair, which had been washed and curled for the occasion. "Do I look all right?"

From across the room, Marjorie said, " You look perfect. Now stop fussin' and finish setting the table."

Fancie sat down in Luke's chair and went back to folding napkins. "Your pork chops smell delicious, Mattie."

"Thank you, honey." The little housekeeper was more like a member of the family than an employee, and she had been in on the plan to soften up Luke from the beginning. Just as the kitchen door opened, she said, "They're Luke's favorite."

"Really?" Fancie said. Of course they were his favorite. Pork chops and every other item on the carefully planned menu.

"What's my favorite?" Luke asked, removing his hat. "No, don't tell me ..." He sniffed. "Pork chops. Ah, Mattie, you're a woman after my heart."

"Nope," she said, thickening the gravy in a heavy cast-iron pan, "just happened to get ahold of some pork chops is all."

"You like them?" Fancie asked, innocently.

He glanced toward her and said, "I love—"

It seemed as if time was standing still. Luke was looking at her as if he'd never seen her before and was wondering what she was doing sitting in his kitchen. Fancie looked back, waiting patiently for him to finish his answer, acting as if she had no idea what had caused him to stumble over his words.

Luke cleared his throat and looked away. "Mattie knows me well. They're my favorite."

"Well, then," Fancie said, looking at him from beneath her eyelashes, "tonight's your lucky night."

Again, everyone stood still, waiting for Luke's response. When he only stared, Tessa finally said, "Come on, everybody. Have a seat." She moved to her place next to Cody, and he pulled her chair out for her, as he had been doing for every meal since she'd arrived.

Fancie looked up at Luke and said, "I'm in your place." She scooted over onto her own chair, hoping that, when he sat down, he'd feel the warmth her body had left behind.

He moved behind to help her adjust her chair—something that he'd not done a single time in all these days.

"Thank you," she said, smiling at him over her shoulder.

"You're welcome," Luke muttered. It was obvious that he was shaken by her appearance, which was gratifying, considering the amount of time Fancie had spent preparing.

As soon as Cody and Luke had left the house after breakfast, Marjorie had started scheming. She thought that if Fancie really poured on the charm, Luke just might start to come around.

With Tessa's help, she'd curled her hair and put on the prettiest dress she owned. It was cream colored, covered with lace, and trimmed with pink ribbon roses. Even Fancie had to admit she looked pretty darn good. Now if only she could get Luke to admit it.

She settled herself in her chair, fluffing her dress out around her so that her elbow brushed against Luke's arm several times. He cleared his throat, and when Fancie finally sneaked a glance at him, she found him staring at his plate as if the carefully prepared food was going to offer up the meaning of life.

He looked good. His freshly combed hair was damp. With the weather being so hot, and the work they were doing being so hard, Luke and Cody bathed out back every night before supper. Beside her, Luke smelled of soap. It made Fancie want to bury her face in his shoulder and just breathe in the scent of him.

It was funny how a person could still smell the same after so many years. It took Fancie back in time, back to when she and Luke had escaped to savor each other at every opportunity. Back to the hundreds of times they'd kissed. Back to the times they'd lain in the shade of a tree so tempted by each other that she still couldn't believe that they hadn't given in to the desire.

"Fancie?"

She blinked and looked up at her sister. "Hmm?"

Tessa was looking at her strangely. "I asked you if you and Luke would like to take a walk out to the spring with Cody and me after dinner. It's really pretty out there, and the air feels so much cooler beside the water."

"Oh, I . . . uh," Fancie said, stumbling over the carefully rehearsed conversation. She'd known that Tessa was going to invite her and Luke along. Why couldn't she remember what she was supposed to say?

"I'm willing if you are," Luke said with a quick look in her direction and a split-second flash of a smile.

He'd smiled at her! "Oh." She took a sip of water. "That would be nice."

"Good," Tessa said as she finished up the food on her plate. " 'Cause after that gingerbread, I don't think I'll be able to breathe unless I walk some of this meal off."

Luke snapped his head up. "Gingerbread?" He looked at Mattie. "You made gingerbread too?"

"Not me," Mattie said, never looking up from her plate.

"Fancie made it with a recipe she brought from back home. I hate to say it, but it smelled even better than mine."

Luke looked down at Fancie. "I love gingerbread."

Fancie smiled. "I told you it was your lucky night." She looked into his eyes and forgot that anyone else was in the room. Why had she been so silly? She belonged with that man. It didn't matter where they lived. It didn't matter what had happened in the past. Why had she fought against it so hard?

Luke stared down at her, and around them, the conversation began again. Fancie blinked and turned away. She could feel the warmth creeping into her cheeks, and she didn't want to let Luke know that just looking at him could make her blush.

So far, so good. He seemed to be in an agreeable mood. He loved his dinner, as she had known he would. And best of all, he'd agreed to walk with her out to the spring.

Maybe, just maybe, this would work.

"The sunsets out here are so pretty," Fancie said as they walked up the hill and away from the house.

"Mmm-hmm." Luke walked slowly, letting Cody and Tessa get a good distance ahead. It had taken a while, but Luke had finally realized what was going on.

He'd been set up.

His wife, his sister-in-law, his mother, and Mattie had planned every detail of the evening. Hell, Cody was probably even in on it, he thought, as he watched his brother chase his pretty bride. Tessa screamed and ran, and the two of them put even more space between themselves and Luke and Fancie.

He'd been set up but good.

"In Chicago, you can't even see the whole sky," Fancie mused.

Her voice sounded strange, and he looked down and saw a wistful expression on her face. "Do you miss it?"

She took a deep breath and said, "Not as much as I thought I would. Of course, I haven't been away that long."

"No, I guess you haven't." He wanted to know so much. He wanted to hear all about every minute of the time she'd spent away from him. What was it like? Who were her friends? Where had she lived? But the thought of her loving the life she was living without him, while he had merely existed day to day, was too painful. He stayed silent.

"You know what I missed most about Montana?" she asked dreamily.

Me. Please say that you missed me. Luke swallowed the lump in his throat. "What?"

They walked a while before she answered. "I missed having someone to confide in."

Close enough. Relief washed over him, and Luke tried not to grin like an idiot. "But you had friends there," he said.

"I did. But . . . it's not the same as the friends you bring from childhood into adulthood. The friends I had there . . . Well, we shared the present, but we didn't share a past. And I moved there at a tough age. A lot of the girls I met that were my age were getting married. I felt as if I had to keep starting over, and I never did find anyone who was as perfectly matched to me as—"

She stopped short of saying the words Luke was dying to hear. She'd missed him, and she hadn't found anyone who could replace what they'd shared. She didn't have to say the words for him to know that was what she'd meant.

They'd reached the spring, and by now, Cody and Tessa were nowhere in sight. Luke looked into the water, then down at the rock that was just big enough for two people to share if they sat very close together, and he took a leap of faith. "Do you think we can still fit?" he asked.

She knew exactly what he was talking about, and he

realized, as she looked at the rock, what she'd been saying earlier. He and Fancie had shared the rock hundreds of times. How many times had they sat side by side and dangled their feet in the ice-cold water? Enough times that they'd each had their fair share of dunkings, accidental and otherwise. Enough times that, years later, she still knew exactly what he was asking.

"I haven't grown that much," she said. She looked up at him, and he could have sworn he saw tears in her eyes. But maybe it was just the light of the sun. "I think if we hold on to each other, we can keep ourselves from falling over the edge."

Luke felt as if he'd gotten a swift blow to the gut. The time for playing games had passed. It was time for some honesty. "Fancie, I don't ever want to go through that again. I fell over the edge once, and it nearly killed me. It hurt so bad that I hoped it would kill me."

She turned toward him and reached for his hands. "Luke, I never meant for that to happen. I wanted you to come with me. I *begged* you to come with me."

"And I begged you to stay."

"I couldn't stay," she said, tears running over her cheeks.

Luke smiled a sad smile that failed to hide the pain he was feeling. "And I couldn't go."

Fancie nodded her head in understanding. Luke reached out and brushed her tears away. "I'm so sorry, Luke."

He nodded. "So am I."

They stood so close. She was crying, and he was hurting. Before he knew what had happened, he was holding her in his arms. He held her tight against his body, soaking up all that he had missed for so many years. Fancie was the only woman he'd ever loved, and he knew that love had never died.

She wrapped her arms around his waist and rubbed her

hands against his back, and Luke thought he could have stood in that spot forever. "Fancie," he whispered, "I have to be sure this time."

She nodded her head against his chest. "I know, Luke. I know."

He closed his eyes and rubbed his fingers in the hair at the back of her neck. Lord, she smelled so good. She felt so good. Everything about this night was telling his body that it was time to take what he'd been denying himself. He loosened his hold, and she tilted her head back, knowing without any words what he wanted. He leaned forward and kissed her. She reached up and wrapped her hands around the back of his neck. When she worked her fingers through his hair, Luke's heart began to beat faster.

They clung together, drinking greedily from each other. Luke stopped thinking and just went with the feeling. He ran his hands down her back and up her sides, rubbing his thumbs over her breasts. She pressed against him, and he filled his hands with her, squeezing and shaping, touching and teasing with his fingertips.

Fancie let her head drop back, and Luke backed himself into the trunk of a tree, settling her firmly between his legs. She was the most beautiful thing he had ever seen. He leaned forward and kissed her neck, lingering in the places he still remembered that she liked best.

"Oh, Luke," she muttered, holding his head with her hands. "It's better," she whispered. "How can it possibly be better than it used to be? But it is."

He kissed her mouth, delving into her sweetness. He rested his hands on her hips and pulled her tighter against himself. She fit perfectly.

"Do I have to say it again?" she asked breathlessly. "Do I?"

He shook his head. "No, I'll say it." He pressed himself against her, and her eyes widened as she felt his desire for her. "I want to make love to you, Fancie. I want to finally know what you feel like around me. I need to know."

She reached down and ran her fingers over his jeans. "Oh, Luke. That's what I want."

"Shhh," he said, holding her arms still. The sound of Cody and Tessa's voices floated toward them. Luke let out a puff of air and closed his eyes. This interruption had happened for a reason. He tried to regain his composure; then he stepped away from Fancie.

"Luke, what are you doing?"

He opened his eyes and shook his head. "Not yet, Fancie. The time isn't right."

"Isn't right?" she asked, the frustration she was feeling making her voice come out like a squeak. "What isn't right? They'll walk right past us! They'll never even notice us here."

"It isn't right," Luke said. He pulled Fancie into his arms and held her tight. "I've waited for this for a long time. I intend to make it perfect." He could feel Fancie's chest rising and falling as she fought to slow her breathing.

"All right, Luke," she said quietly. "We'll wait."

"Good," he said, rubbing her back and standing perfectly still while his brother and Tessa walked right past them, just as Fancie had said they would.

She sighed and pulled out of his embrace slowly, almost as if she hated to do it. "I have to get back anyway."

"Why?" he asked, smiling at her. "Have a hot date?"

She smiled, but Luke could see that it was strained. "Not exactly. But I do have . . . an appointment, of sorts."

"An appointment? What kind of appointment could you—" He stopped talking as it dawned on him. "You're still going to do it?" he asked as he put his hands on his hips.

"Of course I am," she said as though there had never

been any question about it. "Last night we chose our first book, and I promised to go back tonight and read the first chapter."

"Fancie, I told you—"

"I know what you told me, Luke," she said, and that defiant tone was back in her voice. "And I believe I told you that your mother said—"

"Stop hiding behind my mother!" he shouted. "You're doing this because *you* want to, not because she wants you to!"

"All right, I'll admit it. Yes, I do want to teach your cowboys how to read!" She held up her hands at her sides. "What is so wrong about that?"

"What's wrong is that I told you I don't want you to do it!" Luke shook his head. "I can't believe we're back at this same problem again."

"We never left it! Listen to me," Fancie said. "I am not going to do anything wrong. Why don't you trust me?"

"It's not a matter of trusting you. I'm not sure that I trust them. Fancie, I work with those men every day! They don't see a woman from one month's pay to the next. Tomorrow is payday, and do you know where they'll be headed?" He paused until she shook her head. "Into Roxy's, every one of them! They'll drink, they'll fight, and they'll buy the services of whatever woman is available. It's the way they live, Fancie, and I don't want you alone with them. Why is that so hard to understand?"

Fancie stood still for a few moments. "What if I arrange it so that there's always someone else with me?"

"Who, Fancie? Who's going to have time to tag along with you every night? *I* don't have time and neither does Cody. That exhausts your list of available men to accompany you."

Fancie thought a while longer. "Suppose I hold our sessions on the front porch of the house. That way, we'd be in open view of everyone. Certainly, that should ease your mind.''

Luke stood still, steaming inside. Why did she have to be so stubborn about this? Why couldn't she just drop it? Wasn't it enough that her husband just did not want her to do it? Still, her suggestion was a good one, and if he refused it, he'd look like the unreasonable one.

"All right, Fancie. On the porch. We'll see how that works out.''

She smiled at him "Thank you, Luke.''

He glared at her. "You're welcome,'' he muttered. He still wasn't happy.

"Come on. Let's go back so I'm not late.'' She turned and started walking in the direction of the house.

She was ten steps ahead of Luke by the time he finally moved. Lord, that woman drove him insane! Was he going to have to argue with her constantly for the rest of his life? Maybe it was a good thing that Cody and Tessa had come along when they had. If they hadn't, Luke wasn't sure he'd have been able to stop himself from laying Fancie down in the grass and making love to her right out in the wide open. If he'd have done that, and she'd have picked herself up afterward to rush to her "appointment,'' he'd have been furious.

It was better that he waited until he was completely sure. He'd slept with other women, of course, but none that he cared about as much as he cared about Fancie. It was true what he'd said back by the rock: He wasn't willing to jump over the edge unless he was certain Fancie would be there to catch him.

He watched her hurrying toward the house without a backward glance. She was so intent on her mission that she'd left him far behind.

He wasn't certain. He wasn't anywhere near certain.

* * *

It was exhilarating! Reading to those men had been just the thing Fancie needed. They listened to every word she had said, and at the end of the chapter, she'd gone over the first few letters of the alphabet. They were eager to learn, and she was more than happy to teach them.

Luke had sat in the kitchen glaring at them the entire time, and by the time the lesson was over and the men had gone back to the bunkhouse, he'd been wound tight. It was clear that he was against the whole thing, but it was more than that, Fancie knew. It was what had happened between them out by the spring. It had left her frustrated, and she knew that Luke was feeling the same thing.

Despite their disagreement, the night hadn't been a total loss. Finally, Luke had opened up a little. She knew now that he was afraid of being hurt again, and she couldn't blame him for that.

She was already beneath the covers when Luke came into the room, and she decided to go ahead and move to the next level. She lay perfectly still on her side of the bed, waiting for the moment when she felt the bed shift with the weight of him. Finally, he settled in beside her.

Fancie waited a few minutes before she whispered, "Good night, Luke." They hadn't ever spoken to each other in bed before.

The wait was interminable. It seemed like hours passed before he answered. "Good night, Fancie."

In the dark, she smiled. Could she really do the next thing? She rolled to her edge of the bed and concentrated on breathing slowly. Was this how she breathed when she was asleep?

A good fifteen minutes passed. *It's now or never.* Fancie flopped over toward Luke and tossed one leg over him. She mumbled some nonsense and snuggled into his shoulder.

Her husband could have been made of rock. He did not move. Fancie wasn't even sure that he was breathing.

Minutes passed, and she kept up the slow steady breathing. She was beginning to get sleepy for real. Just before she dozed off, Luke shifted his shoulder and wrapped his arms around her.

Smiling, Fancie slept.

Chapter Ten

It was still pitch-black when Luke untangled himself from his wife's limbs and sneaked out of their bed. He hadn't slept all night, and if he lay beside Fancie for one minute longer, he was sure that he would go out of his mind. He stepped into his jeans, shoved his arms through his shirtsleeves and grabbed his boots before slipping silently out the door.

In the kitchen, the embers from the previous day's fire cast a soft glow through the grates of the stove. He sat down and pulled his boots on. He had no idea what time it was.

Outside, the air was chilly, though once the sun rose, the day's temperature would steadily creep into the nineties. Luke looked up at the faintly brightening sky. It was somewhere near morning, he guessed.

Holding Fancie in his arms all night had been like heaven and hell all rolled up into one. He needed to think about things, and he couldn't do that with his hands on her skin. He walked up to the barn and saddled up his favorite horse. He climbed up into the saddle, and as he rode out of the barn, he whistled. Lucky came running from wherever he'd been sleeping.

Luke rode up to the north pasture, to the farthest reaches of the land they owned. It was approaching full daylight; along the way, he checked fence posts, studied the condition of the grass, and looked into the eyes and ears of grazing cattle. Everyday, mindless activities. The kinds of things he could do while still thinking about the way it felt to have Fancie's body pressed up against him all night.

She felt the same way he remembered. A little rounder, a little softer maybe, but still the same woman he'd held on to when the clutches of adolescence had had their hooks into him. He wondered if having given in to those desires would have changed anything. Would Fancie have felt compelled to stay?

He'd waited for her to come back for nearly a year. And as the anniversary of the day she'd gone approached, he'd grown angrier than he ever remembered being. And so, despite his father's warnings, he'd gone into town with the cowboys the next payday. He drank his first whiskey, got into his first barroom brawl, and slept with his first woman. It was easy: Hand over a little gold dust and take your pick. And it didn't matter which one of them he chose, he realized after several trips into town; the girl always made him feel as if he was the best thing that had ever come her way.

There weren't many women in Montana Territory. Fancie wouldn't be easily replaced. But there were a lot of men, and every town had its fair share of whorehouses. The girls that worked the places had a captive audience, and they knew it. Still, they put on a good show, and Luke became a regular. Every weekend, payday or not, he'd head into town and fall into whatever bed wasn't already occupied.

It wasn't much, but it was something, and Luke kept going until he could finally get through the act without thinking of Fancie. At that point, the girls lost some of their allure, and his trips into town grew farther and farther apart.

He no longer did it for fun. He only went to Roxy's when the frustration of his solitary life got to be too much. He only went when he was a little bit angry about the situation in which he found himself. He only went when memories of Fancie came back to haunt him.

Now, Fancie herself had come back to haunt him. Now, he was more frustrated than ever. Now, he was very angry about the plight in which he found himself.

All in all, the entire situation had gotten to be too much.

And Luke made a decision.

"Where on earth have you been?" Fancie demanded when Luke waltzed into the kitchen at six-thirty that night.

He looked at her blankly. "I was working."

"Working? Luke, we haven't seen you all day! No one heard you leave the house this morning. No one had any idea where you'd gone and we were all worried!"

Shrugging nonchalantly, he said, "Sorry." He turned away from her and began climbing the steps.

"Where are you going?" Fancie was more than a little worried. She'd been growing more panicky with every passing minute.

"Out."

"Out? Out where? You haven't—"

Halfway up the stairs, he turned and glared at her. "Get off my back, Fancie," he warned in a low voice.

She stopped talking and stood completely still as he turned and continued up the steps. She heard their bedroom door slam closed. She felt Luke's determined separation in her heart, and her eyes filled with tears.

"Fancie?"

She turned and found Cody standing just inside the kitchen door. Anticipating the fight that was bound to flare up, everyone had scattered as Luke approached the house.

Fancie looked at her brother-in-law and said, "Who is that man, Cody? He isn't the Luke I knew. I don't even recognize him."

Cody came to her and held her in his arms. She rested her head against his shoulder and let the tears come. "I don't even recognize him," she said again.

Cody held her tightly. "Unfortunately, I do."

She pulled away. "What do you mean?"

Cody shook his head. "It doesn't matter."

"Yes, it does matter."

"Fancie, listen to me. What did he say? I could hear your voice, but I didn't hear anything Luke said."

"He didn't say much. When I asked him where he'd been all day, he said he'd been working. Then he stormed up the steps, and when I asked him where he was going, he said, 'Out.' "

Cody's eyes widened. "He said he was going out?" When Fancie nodded, he muttered, "Shit," and turned toward the stairs.

"Where are you going?" she asked.

"To talk some sense into my pigheaded brother before he does something stupid!" he said, taking the stairs two at a time.

Fancie took a deep breath and let it out in a big rush. "Good luck," she whispered.

Cody burst into the room while Luke was pulling on a fresh pair of jeans. "What the hell do you think you're doing?" he asked, slamming the door behind himself.

Luke stared for a few seconds, then yanked his pants up

over his hips. "Putting on my pants. Do you have some problem with that?" he asked calmly.

"Luke, don't even *think* about going into that place!" Cody said advancing a step toward his brother. "You can't—"

"Don't tell me what I can and cannot do, Cody!" Luke thundered. "You don't know a thing about it!"

"But that's what you're doing, aren't you? You're going to Roxy's. Aren't you?"

Luke slid his belt through the loops on his jeans, ignoring Cody's questions. It was easy enough for him to judge! Cody had no idea of the hell Fancie had put him through. And he could see that if he didn't get rid of some of his sexual frustration, she'd have him right back in the same place all over again. She'd kiss him and touch him and probably let him do whatever he wanted to her, just as long as she got her way in the end.

That she wanted to teach a bunch of cowboys how to read didn't even matter anymore. The point was, Fancie wasn't above using her feminine wiles to get to him. Luke had finally figured it out. *That* was why she was being so nice to him. *That* was why she was acting all lovey-dovey. She didn't *love* him. She just wanted him to give in.

The only way to avoid doing so was to shore up his resistance to her. And the only way to do that was to work off a little steam.

"Luke, what the hell is wrong with you?" Cody asked, shoving Luke back a step when he would have walked away. "You have a beautiful woman downstairs who loves you!" he shouted, pointing toward the floor.

Luke shook his head. "No, she doesn't." He tried to push past Cody. Then all hell broke loose.

Cody made a dive for Luke and knocked him flat on his back. Luke would never have thought that the kid was so strong. Luke was the fighter in the family, not Cody.

"When are you gonna quit feeling sorry for yourself?"

Cody said, grabbing the front of Luke's shirt. "Stop acting like such an—"

"Cody, get off of me," Luke growled. He had never hit Cody. Never. But he was asking for it, and Luke's patience was at the breaking point.

"Make me," Cody taunted. "You think you're so strong, Luke. You're so strong and so tough and so damned *stupid* that you can't even see—"

That did it. Luke reached up and grabbed his brother by the shirt, dragging him off balance enough to roll out from under him. The two of them knocked into the nightstand, sending the kerosene lamp crashing to the floor. The glass shattered and skittered across the polished hardwood, but the two grown men fighting on the floor never even noticed it.

Luke had just about pinned Cody, who was giving him a run for his money. Luke balled up his fist and was a split second away from pounding it into his brother's face when the door flew open.

"Luke!" Fancie shouted.

He snapped his head around and saw his wife standing in the doorway. Within seconds, she was joined by Tessa, Marjorie, and Mattie.

"What in God's name is going on in here?" Marjorie asked.

Luke's heart was pounding, and he was breathing heavily. He stared at the women in the doorway, giving his brain a chance to catch up with his body. He dropped his arm and closed his eyes.

"Get off," Cody snarled.

Luke looked down at his brother, who was mad enough to kill him. Maybe it was a good thing they hadn't yet come to blows. Cody looked every bit as eager to damage to Luke as Luke had been ready to damage him. He climbed off and got to his feet. "It was just a—"

Cody jumped up and lunged at him, dragging him back to the floor.

"Cody!" Tessa screamed, trying to get in the doorway. Marjorie and Fancie held her back.

"Tessa!" Fancie cried, pulling her away from the doorway. "Stay out of it! Stay out of it!"

Tessa's shout had distracted Luke, and Cody grabbed him by the front of his shirt, lifting him a few inches off the floor, then slamming him back against it.

"You stupid son of a bitch!" he said as the back of Luke's head hit the floor. "Go ahead and do it, Luke! Go ahead and do it and see if it makes you feel any better." He slammed his fist into Luke's midsection hard enough to knock the breath out of him; then he got up off the floor and pushed past his mother and Mattie. Tessa broke free of Fancie's grasp and ran to his side. Cody wrapped his arm around her shoulders.

Luke dragged himself to his feet, ignoring the stares from Marjorie and Fancie. He was struggling just to breathe, but he'd never let them know it. He stomped out of the room. "I should have hit you while I had the chance, Cody!" he shouted.

Cody stepped away from Tessa and held his arms out to his sides. "Feel free, Luke," he said, tauntingly.

The fury in Luke had reached the boiling point. "Don't turn your back, little brother," he threatened. He pounded down the stairs and out of the kitchen, heading for his horse and the fight he knew he'd find in town.

"Where could he have gone?" Fancie said, for what must have been the hundredth time. "It's nearly midnight!"

Luke had been spoiling for a fight, and the thought of him lying somewhere, broken and bloody, was driving her insane. She'd pushed him too far. Why couldn't she have just let the whole cowboy thing drop? Why couldn't she have found some other way to occupy herself when her husband had made it so perfectly clear that he was against the idea?

"He'll be home soon," Marjorie said. The two of them sat in the darkened kitchen in their nightclothes.

"Oh, my God," Fancie said. "He didn't take his gun with him, did he?"

"He probably did."

"He could get shot! He could die, and it's all my fault!" She began to cry over the hopelessness of the situation.

"No, Fancie, it's my fault," Marjorie said.

"You? What have you done? I've been rebelling against everything he said since the day I got back! It's my fault he's so worked up."

"But it's my fault you're here to begin with."

Fancie looked up at her mother-in-law and shook her head. "No, your suggestion that Tessa and I come out here got me out of a whole lot of trouble. You know that."

"Seems to me that you jumped out of the frying pan and into the fire."

Fancie shook her head again. "Coming here was the best thing that could have happened. I would have lived my whole life stubbornly refusing to admit how much Luke still means to me. I would have missed out on the love of a lifetime." Fancie closed her eyes and dropped her face into her hands. "Things would be different if I just learned to give in a little. *Why* do I have to be so stubborn?"

"Give in? On something you feel strongly about?" Marjorie shook her head. "Girl, you're never gonna learn to do that. You wouldn't be the Fancie we all know and love if you did."

Fancie looked up, and her eyes filled with tears. "If something happens to him, I'll never forgive myself."

Marjorie reached out for her hands. "Luke is a big boy. He knows how to take care of himself. Nothing is going to happen to him. This isn't the first time Luke's gone into town looking for a fight. He'll be fine. Okay?"

Fancie hesitated, then nodded her head.

"Okay. Let's get some sleep."

Fancie followed her mother-in-law up the steps. It was slow going for Marjorie, who began to struggle for air the farther up they went. Fancie barely noticed. She was in no hurry to get to her empty room. "Good night, dear," Marjorie said at the top of the stairs.

Fancie didn't answer. It was not a good night. It was the most awful night of her life.

Luke heard his name, and he turned his head to see who had called him.

"Luke, honey," the girl said, leaning over to run her hands down his back. "Come on. It's your turn, sugar."

He nodded and pushed himself to his feet. He'd swallowed so much whiskey he wasn't sure he'd be able to walk, but the girl wrapped his arm around her shoulder and guided him toward the stairs that led to the rooms where they worked. His fingers dangled against her breast, and she giggled, teasing him in that way that they all had.

"Looks like someone had a little bit too much to drink," she said. "You sure you're ready for this?"

"Yup," he said, staggering down the hallway. "Gotta do it."

"Don't worry, honey. Tina will take your mind off whatever it is that's troubling you." She led him into a room barely big enough to contain the bare bed it held. Thoughts of Fancie sneaking into a place like this to rescue a girl she didn't even know flooded his mind. What had she thought when she'd seen the stripped down conditions in which these women worked night after night? He pushed the disturbing images away.

Tina turned toward him and began unbuttoning his

shirt. "You're my favorite, Luke. Do you know that?" she whispered. "I love it when I get you."

Luke closed his eyes and tried not to think about what he was doing. He tried not to think about Fancie, at home, asleep in their bed.

Tina pushed his shirt over his shoulders and rubbed her breasts against his bare chest. "Do you want to undress me, Luke?"

He opened his eyes and struggled to focus. Tina took his hands and ran them up over her breasts. She was wearing a black lace-edged corset. He looked down and saw his hands on her skin, and he yanked them away from her as though he'd been burned. He looked away.

"What's the matter, honey?" Tina said, wrapping her arms around his neck. "The clock's aticklin'," she said, nodding toward the hourglass that doled out ten minutes to each customer.

Luke looked at the sand slowly flowing through the narrow opening. The pile in the bottom of the glass grew. How many men would Tina service before the night was over? The thought disgusted him, though he'd never even considered it before. How many times had he lain with this woman? Quite a few, as he remembered. And that wasn't even counting the times he'd stumbled into the place so drunk that he wouldn't have even remembered being there, if not for the lack of gold dust in his pouch the next morning.

Tina reached down and caressed him through his jeans. "Come on, Luke," she purred. "It's always so good with you." She stood on her toes and pulled him forward to nibble on his ear. "I'm already wet just thinking about it."

Somehow, Luke knew that she said those same words to every single man that walked through her door.

She reached for his belt and began unbuckling it. He clamped his hands over her wrists, and Tina looked up at him in surprise. "What's the matter, Luke?"

What *was* the matter? He wanted to do this. He *had* to do this, he reminded himself.

"Listen," Tina said, her patience obviously wearing thin. "Do you want to do this or not? Because we don't have much time."

"Not," Luke said.

"What?" Tina was still standing with Luke holding her wrists. "What do you mean?"

"I do *not* want to do this," he said, releasing the hold he had on her. He reached down and refastened his belt buckle.

"What do you mean? You already paid! You—"

"I love my wife," he mumbled. He looked at Tina and smiled. "I love my wife, and I do not want to do this." He was so stupid! *How* had he ever thought this would help?

"You got married? But, Luke—"

"Thanks, Tina," he said, in a hurry to leave since he knew what he should do. "Listen, have a nice life ... a real nice life, and take care of yourself." He stood in the hallway and looked up and down. Which way had he come?

"A nice life?" Tina repeated. Those were so-long-forever words. She put her hands on his back and turned him toward the stairs. " 'Bye, Luke. It was real nice knowin' you. Go on home to your wife." She smiled wistfully as she watched him stumble down the stairs with a goofy grin on his face. She knew he wouldn't be back.

The new Mrs. Winston was one very lucky woman.

Luke put his horse away and started unbuttoning his shirt. He couldn't wait to get himself in the water and wash the film of that place off of himself. He would *not* go to his wife after one of those women had had her hands on his body. He stripped out of his clothes and jumped into the icy water. The ride home had sobered him up some; the cold water finished the job.

Cody had been right. Luke *was* stupid. Did he really want to go back to the life he'd had before Fancie had come back? The women at Roxy's only liked him because he was clean, he never roughed any of them up, and he always had a pouch full of gold dust. But Fancie was different. Fancie loved him. He was sure of it. His wife loved him, and it had taken coming face-to-face with a woman who would say or do anything for the right price to make him realize it.

He'd been trying to get Fancie to bend to his way of thinking, and she never would. She was her own person, and she'd never turn her back on something she believed in. He wondered why he ever thought that she should. Of course, he still didn't want her alone with a bunch of cowboys, but she'd been reasonable about that. And in all fairness, none of his men had shown the slightest bit of disrespect toward her. She was right there too. He'd been more of a threat to her than any of them ever had been.

Luke got out of the water, thoroughly scrubbed and eager to get to Fancie. He shrugged back into his clothes, but left the shirt unbuttoned and the pants unzipped. He picked up his boots and walked to the house.

Luke moved carefully through the kitchen and up the steps to their room. He opened the door slowly, hoping that it wouldn't squeak. It didn't, and he smiled as he closed it behind himself.

The moon was full, and it cast a glow over the tiny form lying curled up in the bed. Luke's heart ached for her. He'd caused this woman a lot of pain, and the healing was going to be difficult for both of them. It had been many years since they'd been completely honest with each other. Luke knew that if this marriage had any chance of surviving, they'd have to learn about honesty all over again.

He set his boots in the corner and shucked off his wet clothes. He looked down at the bed and swallowed. He'd never been so nervous in all his life. Slowly, he sat on the bed and slid between the sheets. Fancie didn't move.

He rolled onto his side and boosted himself up on one elbow. Reaching out to touch her, he whispered, "Fancie, wake up. Wake up, Fancie."

She sighed, stretched, and rolled toward him. Her eyes fluttered open, then slid closed.

Luke smiled. Lord, she was a beautiful woman. "Fancie, come on. Wake up," he said, shaking her shoulder.

She opened her eyes and, realizing who he was, said, "Luke!" She sat up and threw her arms around him. "Are you okay? Are you hurt? You didn't get shot, did you?" she asked, looking at him as though she was searching for some hidden injury.

He chuckled. "I'm fine. Really I am."

"Are you sure?" she asked, resting her hands on his shoulders and running them down the length of his arms. "Are you—" She drew in her breath. "Luke, you're ... you're ..."

"Naked. I know."

She scrambled to sit up all the way, pulling the sheets up to cover herself. "Oh, Lord. Are you drunk?" she asked, backing to the edge of the bed.

"I was," he said, swallowing hard. "Listen, Fancie, I have to tell you some things, okay? It's really important that you know."

She scooted a little closer to the edge of the bed. "What kind of things?"

Luke pushed himself up being careful to be sure his lower half was covered. Fancie's eye's widened, and she whispered, "Oh, my."

Luke smiled and reached for her hands. "Don't be afraid. You know I'd never hurt you." She stared at him with a look so stricken that Luke asked, "You do know that, don't you?"

She nodded her head a little too quickly, as though

she was eager to agree with him to keep him from doing anything crazy.

"Let me hold your hand," Luke said, laying his hand palm up on his knee. After a brief hesitation, Fancie placed her hand in his. He smiled and squeezed it gently. "I'm sorry I've been so hard to live with. I'm sorry I've been so stubborn. You were right. If those men want to learn how to read and you're willing to teach them, there's no reason why you shouldn't do it."

Fancie raised her eyebrows. Long seconds passed before she spoke. "Who are you and what have you done with my husband?" she asked.

Luke laughed. "Oh, Fancie," he said, pulling on her hand until she slid a little closer to him. "Everyone was telling me how right we were for each other. My mother, Cody—they all knew before I did. Cody tried to beat some sense into me and even that didn't work. But as soon as I got alone with Tina, I knew it was—"

"Who's Tina?"

Luke stopped talking. Oh, God! Oh, good God in heaven. He hadn't meant to say anything about Tina! Nothing had happened, and so—

"Luke, who's Tina?" Fancie asked a little more forcefully this time.

Luke sighed and looked down into his lap. "She's just this girl I know. It doesn't—"

"A *girl* you know?" Fancie asked, pulling her hands out of his grasp. "And how exactly would you happen to know this girl way out here in the middle of nowhere? Who is she? Or maybe I should ask, *what* is she?" Fancie got out of the bed and stood with her hands folded across her breasts.

Luke made a move to follow her; then he remembered that he was naked. "Fancie, listen to me," he said, holding out his hand to her. "Come back on the bed."

"I will not. Answer my question, Luke."

"I will—if you can promise to stay calm and let me explain."

Fancie shook her head. "I'm sorry but I cannot promise to stay calm."

"But let me explain? Scream if you have to, but let me explain."

She waited a few seconds, then said, "All right, go ahead. But remember this: You've never been able to lie to me, Luke."

"I've never been able to lie to anyone. Except myself. That, I'm pretty good at."

"What do you mean?"

Luke patted the bed. "Fancie, please sit down. Please?"

She hesitated, then finally sat, being careful not to let her knees touch his. Luke decided that her slight concession was as good as he was going to get. "When you left," he began, "I nearly went crazy from missing you."

"What does that have to do with Tina?" she asked.

Luke held up his hands. "I'm getting to her—just wait." He reached up and ran a hand through his still wet hair. "I was in a bad state, Fancie. Really bad." He paused, thinking back to that time in his life. It still hurt to think about it. "After a while, I worked up a lot of anger toward you."

"I wanted you to come with me!"

"I know, I know," he said, nodding his head. "But that didn't make me feel any better. My ego was shattered. You didn't love me enough to stay, and my pride was severely damaged."

"But I—"

"Let me get this out, Fancie," Luke said, holding up his hands to stop her. "Just let me get it out." He took a deep breath and blew it out. She was not going to like the next part. "About a year after you left, I started going into town. I'd drink a lot. Then I'd go to a place where they always made me feel welcome. Always made me feel . . .

like I was something special. 'Course they charged me for the privilege." He watched her carefully, and he knew the exact second when she understood.

"A bordello?" she whispered.

He nodded. "It worked for a while. I was able to stop thinking about you, at least for a little while."

"But, Luke," she said sadly. "Do you know how many men—"

"I know," he interrupted. "I know." The thought was sickening to him. Why had he never thought about it before? "Eventually, I stopped going. It didn't help me to forget you, so I figured why bother?"

"Then how did you wind up there tonight?" she asked.

He shrugged. "I don't know. I thought you were teasing me. I thought you were only letting me kiss you and touch you so that I'd finally give in about your teaching the men."

"Oh, Luke. How could you think such a thing about me? I would never do that! I would never—" She stopped talking when the tears came.

"I know that now. I know, and I'm so sorry. It only took a minute for me to realize that Tina was getting ready to give a performance. But the times that I kissed you—well . . . you were nothing like that. With you it was real. You weren't just teasing. It was real. I don't know what else to say."

"Say that you'll never ever go back to that place."

"I won't," Luke said, shaking his head. "I won't ever go back."

"So you were . . . you were . . . with this woman tonight? This Tina—"

"No, Fancie, I couldn't. I was going to. . . . I thought that if I . . . I thought that, maybe, if I—hell, I don't know what I thought," he said, looking away from her. "But the second I got in that room alone with her, I knew it wasn't going to work. I practically ran out of the place. Nothing happened, Fancie. Nothing at all. And I won't ever go back. Ever. Because . . . because I love my wife." Luke held his breath while the seconds ticked by.

Fancie looked up at him with a tear-streaked face. "What did you say?"

Luke swallowed the lump in his throat. "I love my wife. I love you, Fancie. I haven't ever stopped loving you." He reached for her hands. "Please forgive me for being so stupid. Just give me another chance, and I promise you won't be sorry. Please. I just . . . I just . . . don't know what else to say." He squeezed her hands. "Nothing happened. I know I haven't exactly been a loving husband, but . . . Nothing happened, I swear. I wouldn't have come to you if I had been . . ." He let his words trail off, knowing that saying any more wasn't going to make what he'd done sound any better.

Fancie stared at him for so long that he started to worry. Maybe she wasn't as forgiving as he had hoped she would be. Maybe his latest stupid stunt had pushed her just a little too far. He was asking her to believe that he'd gone to a whorehouse, but done nothing. Jesus! How could he think that she'd forgive him for—

"I'll give you another chance if you'll give me another chance," Fancie whispered.

"What?" He blinked, trying to focus.

"You aren't the only one who was stupid." She spoke slowly, as though she was making a difficult confession. "You were punishing me for leaving, and I was punishing you for not coming along. I was so determined to be right that I lost sight of what it was that I really wanted." She looked down at her lap and whispered, "What I wanted, what I finally realized that I've always wanted, is you."

Luke felt his heart jump. He wanted so much to believe her. "Are you sure, Fancie? Are you absolutely sure you want to stay here and be married to me? Because—"

"I'm sure."

Luke looked at her in the moonlight. God, she was

beautiful. He took a chance and pulled her toward him and wrapped his arms around her. She hesitated, then put her arms around his neck. "Your hair is wet."

"I took a bath."

"Oh." She pulled away. "Luke, I want to ask you something." She chewed on her lower lip, and Luke knew that, whatever it was she was going to ask him, it wasn't something that she was too eager to hear the answer to. "When was the last time you were . . . with . . . any of those—"

"Nothing happened, Fancie. I swear to you, nothing happened."

"I believe you. Really . . . I do." She fingered the edge of her nightgown, flattening it between her thumb and index finger. "But before tonight. When was the last time that—well, that anything *did* happen?"

Luke hated to even say it. Admitting that he'd paid for the services of a prostitute when Fancie had left him all those years ago was one thing. That was something altogether different. Still, she deserved the truth. He summoned his courage and said, "A few weeks ago. Right after I found out that you were coming back."

"Oh." She looked down at her lap. He had been so against her coming that he'd sought refuge in the arms of another woman. He watched her grapple with the truth, knowing that her feminine pride had taken a deadly blow.

He had to say something. He had to explain his actions to her somehow. But how, when he didn't even understand it himself? He could see now that none of those women had ever satisfied the desire he felt for Fancie.

She was still staring down at her lap. "Will you look at me?" he said, reaching out to tilt her chin upward. "I have never in my life made love to a woman. I've done all sorts of things with all sorts of women, but I've never loved a single one of them. I don't know how to show you or to tell you . . ." He took a deep breath and let it out in one great puff. "Am I making any sense? Do you understand what I'm trying to say?"

She squeezed her lips tightly together and nodded. "I think I do. You're saying that you're scared too but you want to make love to your wife."

"More than anything in the world, Fancie. More than anything."

He could see her swallow. Her eyes were wide, and he knew that she was scared. "I want to stop all this, Luke. I want to stop the fighting and the hurting. I want to move forward from where we are right now," she whispered. "I'm going to believe what you told me. I don't believe that you could lie with someone else and then come to me."

"I couldn't, Fancie. I couldn't."

She nodded. "And since the last time was before our wedding—well, I suppose I have nothing to say about that."

He watched her making a decision that would change the rest of her life. It wasn't something she was willing to do recklessly, and he let her take her time coming to grips with it.

She nodded again, as though she was agreeing with herself, as though she was reassuring herself that she had made the right decision. "I want to put the past firmly in the past. This is—well, this is our wedding night. I've never really felt married to you, and I know that I won't until we ..."

He knew that she wouldn't be able to say it, and he jumped in and rescued her. "I love you, Fancie, and I want to show you how much." He waited until she nodded. "Lie back on the pillow," he said. She did, lying so still that he was sure she had stopped breathing. He stretched out next to her. She was so scared, and he wanted their lovemaking to be so good for her. He looked down at her and smiled.

She looked up at him with eyes that were wide at the

thought of the unknown. Luke felt an overwhelming urge to protect her, to cherish the woman in his bed for the rest of his life.

Forcing himself to move slowly, he reached out for her hand. When their meshed fingers lay across her belly, he said, "I've wanted to do this for so long." He rubbed his thumb across her wrist, where her pulse drummed like crazy.

"Luke?"

"Hmm?"

She lay next to him, staring up at the ceiling and blinking fast. "I can't begin to tell you how terrified I am."

"Don't be," he whispered, gathering her up in his arms. "Don't be afraid." One touch from her and Luke would explode—he was that close. But he knew that if he had any chance of convincing Fancie of his love, he had to move slowly. He leaned forward and kissed her cheek, moving toward her ear, rubbing his lips along its delicate curve and then trailing kisses from her jaw down along her neck and across her shoulder. He stayed where he was until he felt her soften beneath his touch.

"Have you ever wondered what would have happened if we hadn't stopped ourselves that day?" she whispered, hesitantly tilting her head to let him kiss her neck. "Do you remember?"

"Of course I remember. We were next to the stream, under those willows. I've thought about it a million times."

"Me too. I thought I'd never feel those feelings again."

"You will, Fancie."

"Mmm. I think you may be right."

"Fancie?"

"Hmm?" she muttered as he kissed her neck.

"Stop talking."

She did. And he did. And the dance began.

She felt so warm and smooth under his hands. He

couldn't get enough of it, and he ran his fingers over every inch of her. Arms, legs, shoulders . . .

"Take this off," he said, fumbling with her nightgown. He wanted to touch her so badly his hands were shaking.

They'd done this before. This part was not new to them. Fancie sat up and peeled the thin white wrapper over her head. Luke had seen her naked before, and he knew that, even though many years had passed, the memory of that day in the shelter of the willows was strong enough to take away any misgivings Fancie might have had about the moment when her husband would view her unadorned body again. She tossed the nightgown on the floor and lay back against the pillows once more.

Luke's breath was caught in his chest. She was so beautiful. So soft and so inviting. He leaned forward and scooped her against himself. She wrapped her arms around his back and buried her face against his shoulder.

"Oh, Luke, this feels so right," she whispered.

He nodded, bumping his chin against the top of her head. "It is right. It's perfect." He ran his hands down her back, lifting and fitting. It was the most perfect thing.

Fancie clung to him, and in his arms, she felt so small. How could he do this to her? How could he do what he was going to do and not hurt her? She was so fragile. . . .

"Luke, I'm scared," she said. "I've never . . . I didn't . . ." She sighed, and he felt her shrink away from him. She reached up, held his face in her hands, and looked into his eyes. "You know that, all the years I was away from you, there was never anyone else."

Relief washed over him. He was human; he had wondered. He threaded his fingers through her hair and cradled her in his arms. "Don't be scared. I won't do anything until you want me to. I promise."

She nodded her head. "Okay, Luke."

He looked down at her. "Now lie back," he said, pressing lightly against her chest, "and let me see if anything has changed." He grinned lasciviously at her, and she chuckled.

"Let's see," he teased, running his fingertips over her shoulders and down her arms. "Everything seems to be in order. Two arms." He twined his fingers with hers. "Ten fingers." He leaned forward and kissed her, gently at first, then more deeply as she found her footing. He braced himself on one elbow and used his free hand to continue his explorations.

"Ahh," he said, cupping the fullness of her breast in his hand. "Now, here's something that's a little different from the way I remember. A little rounder. Yes?"

"Yes," she whispered, nodding her head, but keeping her eyes closed.

"I thought so. I think this deserves a closer look," he said, settling himself between her legs so that his mouth was only inches above her. He moved closer, letting his breath caress her delicate skin. His thumbs rubbed against the fullness at her sides. Fancie kept her eyes closed. She was breathing quickly, fear and nearly overwhelming curiosity blending to create that unnamed sensation they both remembered so well. Luke welcomed it. He'd never before felt a need to prove himself, and he was experiencing his own fair share of nervousness.

His fingers traced circles on her breasts. Lightly, lightly, he stroked, moving ever nearer the pink buds that rose to urge him on.

Luke waited until he could wait no more before he leaned forward and drew one hardened nipple into his mouth.

"Oh, yes," Fancie said, holding his head in her hands. She pressed her fingers against his scalp, insistent in her desire. Luke drew the tight nub deeper, sucking and stroking it with his tongue. Fancie's back arched away from the bed.

Luke gathered her breasts in his hands, pressing them

together until he was able to turn his head mere inches and still lavish his attentions on both. She tasted so sweet. He teased. He tormented until Fancie moaned and he felt her tilt her bottom the slightest bit, so as to press more firmly against him.

Was she ready? Luke lifted his head to look up at her, and when his absence registered in her head, she opened her eyes.

"You're beautiful," he whispered. His words came out sounding like a prayer.

She smiled and let her head fall back against the pillow. Her fingers touched him everywhere she could reach. His hair, his shoulders, his ears . . .

Luke rolled away from her and rested on his elbow once again. This part would be new for them. He ran his hands over her hips and down her legs to the back of her knees and back up again. She shivered beneath his touch, and he smiled. How would she react when he touched her for the first time? He ran his hand down her leg, and that time, he drew it up between her legs, letting his fingers brush lightly against her most private parts.

She sucked in her breath and seemed to freeze for the space of three seconds. Then she released it, wrapped around a contented sigh.

Luke smiled and did it again, and she did the same thing. She moved her legs apart, and Luke knew that her body was preparing for something that Fancie didn't yet understand. Instinctively, she was opening herself up to him. It was an exhilarating thought, and as Luke thought about loving her completely, a rush of desire so strong it was almost painful swept through him.

He held his breath and tried to slow his blood. He rested his hand on her hip and crept slowly toward what was waiting for him. His fingers touched dampness, and Fancie said, "Oh!"

Quickly, he settled himself against her, reaching to pull

her into a deep kiss. She grasped at his back and wriggled her legs until they rested on either side of Luke's body. "Luke, I don't know. It's—"

"Shh," he said, rising above her. She was ready. He lifted himself and looked into Fancie's eyes as he pushed into her body.

"Oh, Luke!" she cried out, arching against him.

He held her and whispered into her ear, "It's okay, Fancie. It's okay." He kissed her and held her and waited until she had adjusted to the feel of him.

"Are you all right?"

She nodded, and he said, "God, Fancie, you feel so good. I can't . . ." He swallowed and tried again. "I can't believe how good you feel."

Beneath him, Fancie relaxed, and Luke struggled to stay still until she urged him to move. He pushed himself up and kissed her, and she wrapped her arms around him. They clung together. She felt things she did not understand, and he fought to deny his body the release it so desperately wanted.

He braced himself and reached for her breasts again, brushing his fingers over her nipples until he felt her shift beneath him. He watched her carefully, taking his cue from the small signs she was giving.

His touch made her gasp, and with each breath she took, she lifted herself against him. Luke watched her, and it was all he could do to wait for her. She was moving against him in rhythm now, and Luke withdrew a little, matching her movements.

She muttered a wordless sound and moved harder against him.

He withdrew farther each time, until he was thrusting himself into her with a restrained force that was driving him out of his mind. Did she have any idea what she was doing to him? Did she know how hard he was fighting to retain his control?

No, she didn't. If she did, she wouldn't be molding herself to him as though she wanted to meld their bodies together. She wouldn't be arching herself toward him, tempting him with the softness of her breasts, the delicate curve of her neck. She wouldn't be moaning and whimpering and sighing the way she was.

"Luke!" she cried, stiffening against him, and he kept up the rhythm while she seemed to stop breathing. She was on the edge, and he knew it. He watched her and waited until he saw her begin to tumble.

Suddenly, it seemed she could not get enough air, and she could not move against him forcefully enough, and she could not stop herself from crying out his name over and over again.

Luke watched, and he waited, and he knew that he was loved. When she went limp, he closed his eyes and let his body have the release it had been seeking since he'd turned from a boy into a man, since he'd first looked at Fancie and seen her in a different way, since that day beneath the willows so many years ago.

And for him, it was the first time.

He fell forward and held his wife against himself. She was small, soft, and sweet. He was hard, rough, and so much larger. Together, they were perfect.

"Luke?"

"Hmm?"

She was silent for so long that he finally opened his eyes. She was gazing up at him with a look he remembered well. It was the way she used to gaze at him before she went away.

Finally, she smiled and said, "I belong here."

He knew that she was telling him that she'd never leave him again. And he was filled with a wave of emotion that threatened to drown him. He crushed her against his chest, not trusting that his voice would work if he called upon it.

"Chicago wasn't my home," she said, tracing patterns on his chest. "And Montana Territory isn't my home either." She looked up at him. *"You,* Luke Winston—you are my home."

He kissed her forehead. "You can be so sweet when you're not shooting off your mouth," he teased.

"Shooting off my mouth?" she asked, pressing a hand to her heart. "Me?"

"Yes, you."

"Maybe I wouldn't be so mouthy if you weren't so unreasonable," she teased back.

"Unreasonable?" Luke said, settling her against his side. He breathed in the smell of her hair and smiled. "How else can you expect a man to act, married to a little hellcat like you?"

"Hellcat?" she echoed. "Not me. Why, I'm as meek as a kitten."

"Kitten, my—"

"Luke!" she chuckled, swatting at him. He dodged her swing and caught her fingers in his hand, and they nuzzled each other, finding the perfect fit.

They were almost asleep when Luke said, "Hey, kitten?"

"Hmm?" she purred. She arched against him, just like a feline stretching in the sun.

He smiled. "Welcome home."